BLOOD COVENANT

THE GOTHIC
SHADOWS SERIES
BOOK 1

NORA
NIGHTINGALE

Fair warning: There's steam, angst, and morally gray characters doing morally gray things. If you like your romance dark and your scenes explicit, welcome home.

1

I was lost.

The corridor stretched ahead of me, stone walls pressing close on both sides. Candles burned in iron brackets, casting shadows that danced with each flicker. I couldn't remember how I'd gotten here, but I knew I couldn't stop walking.

I kept one hand on the wall as I walked, the stone cold under my palm. Empty doorways lined the corridor. Between them, alcoves with carvings I couldn't make out in the dim light.

The air was thick and stale. It smelled like old paper and something else, blood. The scent should have repelled me, but instead I found myself breathing it in more deeply, my pulse quickening. My body was responding in ways I didn't want to confront.

Somewhere ahead, water dripped onto stone.

"Sera."

The voice came from the darkness ahead. Rich and low, with an accent I couldn't place. I'd been hearing it for weeks in dreams that left me waking breathless, my body humming with a need I couldn't explain.

My feet moved without my permission. Around the bend, the corridor opened into a circular chamber. Dozens of candles, wax *pooling on the stone floor. A figure stood in the center, tall and still.*

Shadow clung to him like a second skin. I could make out broad shoulders and the elegant line of his silhouette, but his face remained hidden in darkness. Yet I could feel his attention on me like heat, like hands trailing across bare skin.

I wanted to run to him. I wanted to drop to my knees. The contradiction should have terrified me.

Instead, I stepped closer, my breath coming faster. Candlelight flickered across his sharp cheekbones, but his eyes remained hidden in shadow. I needed to see them. I had to understand why looking at him felt like déjà vu mixed with dread.

"You came." His voice dripped with satisfaction, rolling over me like velvet. The sound alone made heat pool low in my belly.

Another step brought me to the edge of the candlelight, but he remained wreathed in shadow. The space between us thrummed with something that made my skin feel too tight and my breath come in short gasps.

"I don't know why I'm here," I whispered, my voice trembling.

"But you came anyway," he said, and I could hear the pleasure in his voice.

He lifted one hand, visible against the shadows, stained with something dark that should have terrified me but instead made my pulse race faster. The gesture was an invitation and a command, and my entire being ached to obey. My nipples tightened against the thin fabric of my shirt, and I could feel my arousal building just from his voice, from the promise of his touch.

I reached toward him, trembling with want that I didn't understand. Every inch I closed made my skin burn hotter. I could sense the power emanating from him, something that made the air itself crackle with electricity. My fingertips ached to touch him, to feel whatever forbidden thing he was offering—

The train lurched violently to a stop, throwing me forward in my seat.

I gasped awake, my heart slamming against my ribs. That commanding voice, the power radiating from his shadowed form, the desperate ache to reach him, it had felt so real. My skin was fever-hot and slick with sweat, my body still humming with unfulfilled desire.

The harsh fluorescent lights of the train car and the conductor's voice crackling over the intercom brought me back to reality: "Praha hlavní nádraží. Final stop."

For a moment, I couldn't move, caught between two worlds. The man in the shadows felt more real than the plastic seat beneath me, more solid than the other passengers gathering their luggage. That commanding voice and the glimpses of his angular features haunted me more than any nightmare should.

These dreams had been stealing my sleep for three weeks now. I'd started drinking coffee at all hours just to avoid closing my eyes, but exhaustion always won in the end. And then there he was again, that magnetic pull I couldn't resist, no matter how hard I fought it.

I'd tried everything—different sleep schedules, meditation apps, even sleeping pills that left me groggy but still dreaming. Nothing worked. If anything, the dreams were getting more intense, more real. Sometimes I woke up with the taste of copper in my mouth, or the phantom sensation of cold stone under my palms, reminding me of what awaited me in the darkness.

The exhaustion was becoming impossible to hide. My advisor back at Columbia had noticed my distraction during our last video call. "You look exhausted, Sera. Maybe postpone the Prague research for a semester?" But I couldn't explain that running away to Prague felt less like a choice and more like an inevitability.

I pressed my palms against my thighs, grounding myself in the worn fabric of my jeans. Just a dream. The same dream, growing more vivid and disturbing each time. Stone corridors and a voice that called to me like I was the answer to some desperate, terrible question.

But this time had been different. This time, he'd almost touched me.

My hands trembled as I reached for my coffee. Cold now, bitter on my tongue like disappointment. These dreams left me waking with my heart racing and made me question my sanity.

The logical part of my mind insisted this was just anxiety about my research project. Six months studying medieval manuscripts was a career-making opportunity for a PhD candidate in Medieval Studies. Of course I was nervous.

But logic couldn't explain why the dreams felt so familiar, or why Prague itself seemed to be calling to me from thousands of miles away.

Through the rain-streaked window, Prague emerged from the gray afternoon. Gothic spires pierced through low clouds, dark stone slick with rain. Medieval buildings lined both sides of the Vltava River.

I looked up at Prague Castle on Hradčany Hill, and my breath caught. For a moment, the whole city felt like home. Like somewhere I belonged. The feeling was so intense that it left me dizzy.

The train car lurched again as passengers pushed past me toward the exit. I shook my head and gathered my bags, trying to dismiss the lingering heat from the dream. The voice had sounded so real, so urgent, like someone had been calling my name across centuries of darkness.

I tried to dismiss the strange pull. Just nerves about a new city, new research. Nothing more.

Prague's central station was a study in Art Nouveau architecture, featuring sweeping curves and elegant ironwork that had welcomed travelers for decades. As I made my way through the bustling, I caught glimpses of the city's beauty, but my mind was elsewhere as I searched for a taxi.

Once inside, the ride through Prague's winding streets was quiet, the driver unusually subdued as the rain made the city look as if it were weeping. We passed baroque facades and Gothic churches, everything slightly blurred by the persistent drizzle as cobblestones clicked beneath the wheels.

My hotel was tucked away in a narrow street in Lesser Town, housed in a converted 18th-century mansion. The lobby smelled of old wood and something overly sweet, like flowers past their prime.

My room was on the third floor, up a narrow staircase that creaked with every step. The key got stuck in the lock, grinding against rust or disuse before finally turning. I stepped inside and paused; ornate crown molding and crystal fixtures spoke of past elegance, but dust had settled on every surface.

The room had high ceilings and tall windows that overlooked the city. Heavy wooden furniture filled the corners, and an enormous mirror covered most of one wall, its surface clouded with age.

I set my bags down and moved to the window. Through the rain-streaked glass, Prague Castle loomed on the hill, partially hidden by mist but still grand. Even from afar, I could see the Gothic spires of St. Vitus Cathedral piercing the sky, and the sprawling wings of the Old Royal Palace spreading across the hilltop.

Tomorrow, I would finally access the Schwarzenberg Collection—manuscripts that had been locked away for centuries, some rumored to contain accounts of supernatural encounters that the Church had tried to suppress. My dissertation on medieval folklore and the persecution of supposed supernatural beings could make my career. If I could prove these texts were authentic rather than elaborate hoaxes.

Professor Martinez had warned me: "These manuscripts have driven other researchers to some very dark conclusions, Sera. Promise me you'll remember they're historical curiosities, not instruction manuals."

But something deep inside me whispered that these weren't just historical curiosities. Something insisted I was meant to find them, meant to understand what they really contained. The rational part of my mind called it research intuition. The part that dreamed of shadowed corridors and commanding voices wasn't so sure.

I stepped back from the window, rubbing my arms against a sudden chill.

It would just be six months in one of the most beautiful cities in the world. And according to every local I'd met, it was one of the most haunted.

2

The morning fog clung to Prague like a shroud, muffling my footsteps as I climbed the cobblestone path. Even in daylight, the sprawling complex felt imposing. Gothic spires and baroque facades rising from the mist like something from a dark fairy tale.

I shook off the thought and focused on the practical: finding the monastery library, meeting the head librarian, getting my research credentials sorted. Normal, academic things that had nothing to do with fairy tales.

The path to Strahov Monastery wound along the castle walls, leading me past medieval towers and through narrow passages that tourists rarely found. I followed the brass plaques marking the way.

I found the library entrance tucked beneath a Gothic archway, marked only by a small sign in Czech and English. The heavy wooden door was older than my entire country, its surface scarred by centuries of monastic use. When I pushed it open, the hinges creaked loudly in the morning quiet.

Inside, the library was breathtaking. I stood in the Theological Hall, one of two baroque chambers that made up

Strahov's famous collection. The vaulted ceiling arched high above me, painted with elaborate frescoes depicting scenes of knowledge and wisdom. Gilded stucco work caught the morning light streaming through tall windows.

Floor-to-ceiling wooden shelves lined the walls, filled with leather-bound volumes that had withstood the test of time. The shelves themselves were works of art, carved walnut adorned with intricate baroque details. Antique globes and brass instruments sat on ornate reading tables, and the air was thick with the scent of old parchment and beeswax.

The Philosophical Hall stretched beyond, visible through an archway. Even from here, I could see its soaring ceiling painted with a massive fresco titled "The Struggle of Mankind to Know Real Wisdom." Ladders on rails allowed access to the highest shelves, creating dramatic vertical lines in the golden morning light.

But something was wrong.

Books lay scattered across the floor. Reading tables were overturned, their contents scattered across the polished wooden floor. Manuscript cases stood open and empty. It looked like someone had ransacked the place.

"Dr. Sterling?"

I turned to find a woman emerging from behind an over-turned bookshelf. Silver hair escaped from a loose bun, and her blouse was wrinkled. Dark circles shadowed her eyes as she stepped around scattered papers.

"I'm Helena Dvorak, head librarian." She extended a hand that trembled slightly. "I apologize for the disorder. We had an incident last night."

I shook her hand, noting how cold her fingers were. "What kind of incident? Was there a break-in?"

Helena's laugh was bitter. "Something like that." She gestured at the destruction around us. "Nothing was stolen, as far as we can tell. But someone, or something, was definitely looking for something."

The way she said 'something' raised goosebumps on my arms.

"Should I come back another day? I don't want to interfere with your investigation."

Helena's response was immediate. "No, please. Your work is important. Perhaps more important than you realize." She studied my face with an intensity that made me step back. "Besides, whoever did this is long gone. They only come at night."

Without waiting for a response, Helena was already moving, stepping around the scattered books and overturned furniture. "Come, let me show you to your workspace. We've prepared a special collection for your research."

I followed her deeper into the library, weaving between towering shelves that stretched toward the vaulted ceiling. The destruction seemed selective, whole sections left pristine while others had been ransacked with what looked like desperate fury.

"Ms. Dvorak," I said as we walked, "what exactly were they looking for?"

She stopped so abruptly that I almost walked into her. When she turned, her eyes looked haunted.

"A collection that's been lost for centuries, Dr. Sterling." Her voice dropped to barely above a whisper. "Something many have searched for, but no one has ever found."

A chill ran down my spine. "What kind of collection could be worth all this destruction?"

Helena pressed her lips together, then shook her head. "Perhaps I've said too much. Come, your manuscripts are this way."

She led me through the maze of overturned shelves to a

reading area near the back of the library. Here, the destruction was more focused. Specific manuscript cases had been opened, their contents pulled out and examined before being discarded on the floor.

"Your specialty is medieval folklore, correct?" Helena knelt beside a pile of scattered parchments, her fingers hovering over them without quite touching.

"Yes. I'm particularly interested in illuminated manuscripts, the artistic techniques used in—" I trailed off as Helena knelt there in silence, her eyes moving over the scattered manuscripts.

I crouched down beside her, examining the scattered pages. Beautiful hand-lettered texts with intricate illustrations, some depicting common folk tales, others showing more unusual subjects. But they'd been handled roughly, pages bent and creased.

"This is vandalism," I said, lifting one of the damaged pages. "Have you called the police?"

Helena's expression tightened. "The police filed a report. But they're treating it as a simple break-in, even though nothing was stolen."

I examined the manuscripts more closely. Someone had gone through them page by page, but not randomly. Certain texts showed more wear than others, as if the intruder had spent time studying specific pages. I noticed they'd focused particularly on texts dealing with regional legends and local superstitions.

"What do you think they were looking for?"

Helena was quiet for a moment. "Information about old Prague families. Local histories that don't appear in standard textbooks." She picked up a damaged manuscript, its pages depicting various heraldic symbols and family crests. "Someone is very interested in genealogies."

"Genealogies? That seems like an odd thing to break into a library for. Most of that information is publicly available."

"Not all of it." Helena picked up a torn page and examined it closely. "Some family histories were deliberately hidden."

I frowned, looking at the scattered papers again. "Hidden, why?"

"Old feuds. Political reasons. Some families preferred their past activities remain private."

The way she said 'activities' made me pause, but before I could ask what she meant, Helena was already gathering the manuscripts.

"I'll have these properly sorted by this afternoon," she said, standing and brushing dust from her skirt. "In the meantime, you're welcome to examine our general collection. I recommend that you finish your work before evening. This place can be unsettling after dark."

"Unsettling how?"

Helena paused in her organizing. "Old buildings make strange noises. Shadows play tricks. It's easy to let your imagination run away with you." Her smile didn't reach her eyes. "Better to work during daylight hours."

I wanted to ask more questions, but Helena was already moving away, her arms full of damaged manuscripts. As she disappeared between the towering shelves, I found myself staring at the scattered papers, wondering what could have driven someone to search so desperately through centuries-old texts.

———

THE HOURS PASSED SLOWLY. I examined manuscript after manuscript from Helena's general collection, but found myself constantly glancing toward the restricted area where she'd taken the damaged texts. The library grew quieter as the afternoon wore on, with other researchers finishing their work and heading out into Prague's late October evening.

By six o'clock, the library had emptied of its handful of daily researchers. Helena had left an hour earlier, but not before stopping by my reading table one final time.

"Remember what I said about leaving before dark," she'd murmured, glancing toward the tall windows where shadows were already gathering.

I had nodded absentmindedly, too absorbed in the manuscripts she'd provided to notice her warnings. Now, as the last of the daylight faded from the Gothic windows, I found myself alone with stacks of medieval texts and a growing sense that I was missing something important.

The manuscripts Helena had given me were fascinating, illuminated folklore collections from the 14th and 15th centuries. But as I worked through them, I began to notice oddities. Certain pages had annotations in the margins, written in different hands and appearing to be from different times. Some were in Latin, others in languages I couldn't identify.

The illustrations themselves were even stranger. While most depicted common folk tale subjects like dragons, witches, and forest spirits, several showed scenes that seemed oddly specific, too detailed to be purely imaginative. Figures in medieval dress chasing colorless, elongated creatures through dark woods. Symbols carved into stone that resembled instructions more than decoration.

I took pictures of several pages with my phone, planning to study the annotations later. The marginalia was especially fascinating, with notes that appeared to reference real places and dates rather than mythological events.

As I worked, the library grew darker around me.

Motion-sensor lights flickered on as I moved between shelves, casting long shadows that shifted and wavered. The building settled around me with creaks and sighs that seemed louder in the emptiness.

I should have left when Helena suggested. The rational part of my mind knew that. But I was too engaged in the mystery these manuscripts presented. Someone had clearly used these texts for more than just entertainment; the extensive notes indicated years of serious study.

By seven-thirty, full darkness had fallen outside. The library's automatic lighting system had activated, but it was designed more for security than reading. My table lamp created a small pool of warm light in the shadows.

I was examining a particularly intriguing page, one that featured detailed drawings of weapons or tools alongside Latin text, when I heard it in the silence.

Footsteps.

I looked up from the manuscript, listening. The sound came again, heavy footsteps echoing from somewhere in the stacks. Security, probably. Or maybe Helena had returned to check on me.

"Hello?" I called out. "Is someone there?"

The footsteps stopped.

I waited, but heard nothing else. Just the ambient sounds of an old building: distant settling, air moving through old vents. After a moment, I returned to my work, but found it difficult to concentrate. I couldn't shake the feeling that I was no longer alone.

When the footsteps resumed, they were closer.

I stood up from my chair, straining to see into the darkened stacks. The motion sensors should have triggered the overhead lights if someone was moving through the library, but the areas beyond my reading table remained in shadow.

"Helena? Is that you?"

No response. I strained to listen, but heard only the thundering of my own heartbeat.

I reached for my phone, thinking I should call security, when the lights went out.

Not just my reading lamp—everything. The emergency lights, security floodlights, and even the exit signs. The library descended into total darkness. I couldn't make out anything, not even the faint outline of the windows.

I fumbled for my phone's flashlight, my hands shaking. The small beam cut through the darkness, illuminating the scattered manuscripts on my table, but beyond that circle of light, everything disappeared into shadow.

"Hello?" My voice came out smaller than I'd intended. "The power's gone out. If someone's there, we should—"

Something like a chuckle came from the darkness, raising the hair on my arms.

A man stepped into the circle of light from my phone. At least, I thought it was a man. Every instinct told me to run. When the light illuminated his face, his skin looked unnatural, perfect, and his eyes caught the light like an animal's, reflecting it back with an unnatural green glow that made my stomach drop.

"How convenient that you stayed late." His accent was refined, almost elegant.

I backed away from the table, clutching my phone. "Who are you? What do you want?"

"I want what you don't even realize you have," He said, taking a step closer. "But no matter. You'll serve my purposes well enough."

"I don't understand—"

"Of course you don't." Another step. He was between me and the exit now, moving unnaturally. "Ignorance is so common among your kind. But ignorance won't save you."

My back hit one of the bookcases. Somewhere in my

rational mind, I was trying to make sense of what I was seeing. This couldn't be real. People didn't move like that, didn't look like that.

"What are you?" I whispered.

"Something that shouldn't exist, according to your precious academic texts." He was close enough now that I could see his skin had an odd luminescence, as if lit from within. "But here I am nonetheless."

I fumbled behind me, trying to find something, anything I could use as a weapon. My fingers closed around a heavy bookend.

"Please," I said, "I don't know what you want from me."

"You smell..." He tilted his head, studying me with those reflecting eyes. "Special. Much more special than you should be."

The way he said 'smell' made my skin crawl.

I swung the bookend as hard as I could.

He caught my wrist without even looking, fingers wrapping around my bones like a steel trap. The bookend clattered to the floor as pain shot up my arm.

"Pointless," he murmured, applying pressure until I gasped.

With his other hand, he grabbed my throat. The cold touch of his fingers made me choke, and I realized with dawning horror that this wasn't just some deranged person.

He lifted me off my feet by my throat, my vision starting to darken at the edges. My phone had fallen and spun away, its light creating wild shadows on the ceiling. I clawed at his hands, but it was like trying to bend iron.

"You're coming with me." His grip tightened just enough to make the threat clear.

I tried to speak, but only a croak came out. He seemed to find this amusing.

"Don't bother trying to scream. No one will hear you."

He began moving toward the exit, carrying me like I weighed nothing.

An unseen power crackled in the air, creating a tension that felt thick and oppressive.

Then a commanding voice cut through the darkness. "Let her go."

3

The man holding me by the throat went rigid, his grip loosening just enough for me to drag in a desperate breath.

"Matthias." The man hissed the name like a curse, his eyes darting toward the shadows beyond the light of my fallen phone. "This doesn't concern you."

"You have ten seconds to release her and leave." The response echoed off the stone walls. "After that, things will become unpleasant."

"This isn't your territory."

"Everything in this city is my territory." The voice moved closer, though I still couldn't see him. "You have five seconds left."

The creature's grip on my throat tightened in what felt like panic. "She's just one human—"

"Three seconds."

Then he stepped into the circle of light from my fallen phone, and I forgot how to breathe for an entirely different reason.

He was tall, easily six-foot-three, with dark hair that fell across his forehead and sharp features that looked carved from shadow. High cheekbones cast deep hollows beneath them, and his mouth was full but held a cruel curve that made my pulse skip. But it was his eyes that I couldn't look away from, emerald green and burning with an intensity that seemed to see straight through me.

The way he moved made my stomach drop and flutter at the same time. Each step was calculated, deadly precise, and that should have terrified me.

"Time's up," he said, his voice carrying the finality of a death sentence.

My attacker dropped me. I hit the floor hard, gasping and coughing, my throat burning. Through my watering eyes, I saw the second figure moving through the shadows— tall, graceful, and somehow even more dangerous than the thing that had been killing me.

What happened next was so fast my mind could barely process it.

My attacker hissed and lunged in a blur of motion; fingers extended like claws. Matthias sidestepped with ease, grabbing his wrist and using his own momentum to send him crashing through a reading table.

Wood splintered. Papers scattered. My attacker rolled to his feet, but Matthias was already there, delivering a punch to his chest that sent him flying backward into the stacks.

Books cascaded to the floor as my attacker recovered, snarling. "You have no claim here."

"I have a claim everywhere," Matthias replied, his voice calm, almost bored, as my attacker circled him like a predator seeking an opening.

My attacker faked left, then struck right with blinding speed. He caught his fist in one hand, twisted, and I heard bones crack. The scream echoed through the library as Matthias drove his knee into his ribs with enough force to lift him off his feet.

I scrambled backward on my hands and knees, trying to get away from the violence, my throat still burning. The rational part of my mind was screaming that none of this was possible.

My attacker hit the floor hard but rolled away before Matthias could follow up. He grabbed the heavy brass bookend and hurled it with force. Matthias tilted his head slightly, and the projectile whistled past his ear to embed itself in the stone wall behind him.

"Surely you can do better than that." He said, sounding almost disappointed.

My attacker's eyes burned with rage. He lunged forward in a frantic tackle, but Matthias grabbed him around the throat mid-leap. For a moment, they hung suspended in the air, his feet kicking uselessly, before he slammed him down onto the floor with enough force to crack the hardwood.

"You always were weak, Viktor," he said, his voice casual despite holding the other man down. "Still feeding on innocents instead of finding worthy prey."

Viktor clawed at the hand around his throat, drawing blood that looked black in the dim light. "You have no right," he snarled.

"I have every right." Matthias's voice dropped to barely above a whisper, yet it carried through the darkness with an unsettling authority.

With one swift motion, he tightened his grip, holding Viktor in place as he drew a knife from his belt. In one fluid motion, Matthias plunged the knife into Viktor's heart. The force of the strike sent a shockwave through the air, and Viktor's body went limp, crumbling to ash before it even hit the ground.

For a moment, silence filled the library. Matthias straightened and turned toward me.

I couldn't look away.

He was handsome in a dangerous way, the kind that made wise women do stupid things. And God help me, even after watching him destroy someone with a flick of his wrist, every traitorous cell in my body wanted to move closer to him.

"Are you hurt?"

I tried to speak, but my throat was too sore. I only managed a shake of my head no, not trusting myself to get closer to him.

He stepped over the ashes of Viktor's without a glance, moving toward me with a confidence that radiated danger. Every instinct I had was at war; half of me wanted to run, the other half wanted to move closer to all that power.

I stayed exactly where I was, frozen in place.

He crouched a few feet away, close enough that I could see the way the light caught the sharp planes of his face, close enough to notice how smooth his skin was, almost glowing in the dim light. Close enough that his scent reached me, a mix of leather and smoke, which made my mouth water.

"Let me see." He nodded toward my throat, his voice dropping to that intimate whisper.

I shook my head, wrapping my arms around myself defensively. I didn't trust what might happen if those hands touched my skin. Not when I was already fighting reactions that made no logical sense.

Something flickered across his expression. "I will not harm you."

"You just killed someone," I croaked out.

"I destroyed someone who intended to drag you to a place you would never have returned from."

I believed him, which should have terrified me.

"What are you?" The words came out as barely a whisper.

His dark green eyes never left my face. His slow smile sent warmth spiraling through me.

"Someone who's been searching for you," he said, rising to his feet in one smooth motion. His gaze traveled over me with possessive hunger that made my skin burn.

I struggled to my feet, my legs shaky but functional. Standing put me closer to his eye level, though he still towered over me. "I'm just a graduate student, here for six months."

"Are you?" He tilted his head, studying me. "Then why do you smell so interesting?"

"That doesn't make any sense." Even as I said it, I remembered how Viktor had mentioned my scent, how this man spoke as if my smell told him things about me.

"Doesn't it?" He took a step closer, and I should have backed away. Every rational thought in my head screamed at me to put distance between us. Instead, I didn't move.

He was close enough now that I could see the faint lines around his eyes, close enough to notice that his skin had the same perfection as Viktor's had, but somehow warmer. Close enough that when I breathed, I caught more of that intoxicating scent.

"You have no idea what you are, do you?" His voice had dropped to barely above a whisper.

"I'm just here to work on manuscripts." But my voice shook with uncertainty because, standing this close to him and feeling the dark energy radiating from his skin, I felt anything but ordinary.

He reached up slowly, giving me time to pull away. When I didn't, his fingers brushed against my throat where Viktor's grip had left marks. His touch was gentle, almost reverent, but it sent electricity shooting through my entire nervous system.

"Such delicate skin," he murmured, his thumb tracing along my pulse point. "Such warmth."

I wanted to pull away. Wanted to run. Wanted to demand answers that made sense. Instead, I found myself leaning into his touch, my body betraying every sensible thought in my head.

"I don't understand any of this."

"Our paths were always meant to converge, Sera Sterling. The timing was never in question." The way he said my name made it sound like a prayer, like something sacred.

"That's impossible. We've never met."

"Haven't we?" His eyes searched mine, and for a moment, I felt that strange sense of recognition again, the feeling of déjà vu that made my breath catch and my heart race. "Perhaps you'll remember, in time."

Then he was stepping back, his hand falling away from my throat. The absence of his touch left me feeling cold and strangely bereft.

"Wait," I said, reaching for him instinctively. "You can't just leave. I have questions."

"I'm sure you do." He was already moving toward the shadows, the fluidity of his movements making him seem more like a dream than reality. "But this isn't the time or place for answers."

"When will it be?"

He paused at the edge of the light, turning back to look at me one last time. In the dimness, his eyes seemed to glow with an inner fire of their own.

"Soon. Very soon."

And then he was gone, vanishing into the shadows as if he'd never been there at all. I was left alone with Viktor's ashes, a destroyed library, and the lingering scent of leather and smoke that made me want to follow him into the darkness.

3.5

MATTHIAS

I should have killed Viktor slower.

The thought haunted me as I wandered through the shadowy streets of Prague, putting distance between myself and the library. Between myself and her.

Viktor had been a pitiful excuse for a vampire, feeding on innocents and leaving bodies scattered like breadcrumbs for hunters to follow. But touching her, threatening her, putting his filthy hands around her delicate throat.

For that, he deserved to suffer.

My hands kept trembling. After centuries of living, I couldn't recall the last time I had felt such fury. Such a desperate, overwhelming urge to protect.

She was exactly as I'd dreamed. More beautiful, more vital than my sleeping mind had ever conjured. The cascade of dark brown hair framed a face with a delicate scattering of freckles across the bridge of her nose that somehow made her even more striking. Those warm brown eyes, framed by impossibly long lashes, had looked up at me with wonder instead of fear. Her full lips had parted slightly in surprise when our gazes met. Even in terror, she moved with a natural elegance that captivated me. But it was her scent that had nearly undone me—sweet and complex, with undertones that sang to something primal in my blood.

Sera Sterling.

Even now, blocks away from her, her name lingered on my lips.

I found myself in Wenceslas Square without consciously choosing the destination; my feet carried me there through muscle memory, while my mind replayed every second of our encounter.

The moment I'd touched her throat, felt the rapid flutter of her pulse beneath my fingertips, the chronic ache that had been my constant companion for four centuries had just stopped. For those precious seconds, the curse's grip had loosened, leaving me feeling more alive than I had in decades.

It was her. After all these years of dreams, of visions that had grown more vivid, I'd finally found her.

"Our paths were always meant to converge." The words had spilled from my lips without conscious thought, driven by a certainty that went bone-deep. I'd been dreaming of her face before she was even born, had seen those expressive brown eyes in visions that stretched back years. The dreams had grown more frequent lately, more urgent, as if time itself was running short.

Which it was.

I pressed my back against the cold stone of a building, closing my eyes and trying to regain some semblance of control. But her scent clung to my clothes, my skin, my memory. Sweet and innocent, but with an underlying complexity that made my fangs ache to emerge.

Sterling blood. I'd known what she was the moment I'd scented her, had felt the familiar pull that her bloodline always triggered. But this was different. This wasn't just the call of Sterling blood—this was something more profound, more primal.

Mine.

The possessive thought came unbidden, followed by a wave of want so intense it nearly brought me to my knees. I wanted to claim her, mark her, make it clear to every supernatural creature in Prague that she was under my protection. The way she'd leaned into my touch, the way her pulse had quickened when I'd whispered her name...

She'd felt it too. The connection. The recognition.

Even if she didn't understand what it meant yet.

I should walk away. Should disappear back into the shadows. She was innocent, human, untouched by the darkness that had consumed my existence for centuries.

She deserved better than to be pulled into my world.

But even as I told myself all the logical reasons to stay away, I knew it was already too late. The curse was tightening its grip again, the familiar ache returning as the distance between us grew. And there were others in Prague now—I could sense them moving through the shadows, drawn by whispers of Sterling blood.

Viktor wouldn't be the last to come hunting.

"Such delicate skin. Such warmth."

I'd spoken without thinking, letting my hunger show, and I'd seen the way her breath had caught, the way her pupils had dilated. She should have been terrified. Should have run screaming into the night.

Others would come. Viktor's death would spread through the supernatural underground like wildfire.

Unacceptable.

I changed direction, heading toward the old quarter where the city's supernatural elite maintained their shadowy court. If word was going to spread, let it be the right word. Let every vampire, every creature that hunted in darkness, understand exactly whose protection she was under.

By dawn, every supernatural entity in Prague would know: the Sterling woman belonged to me. Anyone who touched her would answer with their existence.

It wasn't enough. Not nearly enough.

But it would have to do until I could figure out how to tell her the truth. How to explain that I'd been waiting for her for longer than she'd been alive. How to make her understand that the dreams, the connection, the recognition—it was all real.

How to convince her to trust me with her life, when doing so might cost her everything she'd ever known about herself.

The entrance to Isadora's court lay hidden beneath Hradčany Castle, accessible only to those who knew which stone to press in the foundation. The heavy door swung open at my approach, and even her guards recognized my right to enter unannounced.

The throne room was a masterpiece of Gothic excess: soaring stone arches and tapestries that had witnessed centuries of supernatural politics. At the heart of the room sat Isadora Valdris, the vampire queen of Prague for the past six hundred years.

She was beautiful in the way all vampires were: skin that seemed to absorb and reflect candlelight, with dark curly hair that fell to her waist and eyes the color of amber. Tonight she wore crimson silk that pooled around the base of her throne, and rubies that looked like drops of blood.

"Matthias." Her voice carried the faint accent of medieval courts. "How unexpected. And yet..."

"You've already heard."

A smile played at her lips. "Viktor's death? Of course. Though I confess, I'm curious about the circumstances."

I stopped at the base of the dais, skipping the usual courtly politeness. We'd known each other too long for that kind of pretense. "He threatened what's mine."

"Ah." Isadora leaned forward, genuine interest flickering in her eyes. "And what, pray tell, could be worth breaking your centuries of neutrality?"

"The Sterling woman is under my protection."

A hush fell over the room. Even the ever-present whispers of her courtiers ceased. Isadora studied me for a long moment, her expression unreadable.

"A Sterling." She tasted the word like fine wine. "How fascinating. After all these years of refusing to claim territory, to take a seat on any council, to involve yourself in our politics. Now you decide to stake a claim."

"She's not politics."

"Everything is politics, darling." Isadora rose from her throne with grace, descending the steps until we were nearly eye level. "You could have ruled any city in Europe. Could have had a throne beside mine, if you'd chosen. Instead, you've played the ghost for eight centuries. And now, suddenly, you appear in my court making territorial declarations over a mortal girl."

"She's not just any mortal."

"No," Isadora agreed, circling me like a predator. "Sterling blood is quite special. Tell me, does she know what she is yet?"

I remained perfectly still, letting her circle. "That's not your concern."

"Oh, but it is." She stopped in front of me, her smile sharp. "Sterling blood in Prague attracts attention. The kind of attention that threatens the balance I've spent centuries maintaining."

"Then help me maintain it. Spread the word through

your networks, she's mine. Anyone who touches her answers to me."

Isadora's smile turned calculating. "Of course, you know we could use her for—"

"No." The word came out as a growl, and I saw several of her courtiers take an involuntary step back. "Whatever you think you need from her, the answer is no."

"Matthias, be reasonable. Sterling blood during the—"

"I said no." I stepped closer to her, and Isadora's expression changed from amusement to caution. "Let me be absolutely clear, Your Majesty. Just know that if anyone, any creature, comes even close to her with the intent of using her for anything, I will tear them apart. Slowly. And I'll make sure you watch."

The silence that followed was deafening. When Isadora finally spoke, her voice was neutral.

"And if I refuse?"

The atmosphere thickened with ominous energy. "Then you'll discover why I never needed a crown to be feared."

For a heartbeat, I thought she might challenge me. Isadora had ruled Prague through wit, politics, and the art of fear. But she was also old enough to remember what I'd been like before the curse, before I'd withdrawn from the world of supernatural politics.

Then she laughed, a sound like silver bells in the wind.

"There he is. The Matthias I remember." She returned to her throne, settling into the ornate chair. "Very well. Consider your claim acknowledged. But I want something in return."

"Name it."

"When this affair inevitably attracts hunters, enemies, or other complications to my city, you handle it. All of it. I won't allow Prague to become a battlefield just because you've finally decided to feel something."

"Agreed."

She nodded once, regal as any monarch. "Then let it be known throughout Prague and beyond: the Sterling woman belongs to Matthias Cross. Any who threaten her do so at their own peril."

As I turned to leave, her voice followed me.

"Matthias? Do try not to let this one break your heart. You're far too dangerous when wounded."

I paused at the threshold but didn't turn back. "She won't."

"How can you be so certain?"

For the first time in hours, I felt something close to peace settle in my chest. "Because she's going to save me instead."

As I walked through the empty streets toward her hotel, the memory of her pulse beneath my fingertips lingered. The way she'd leaned into my touch instead of pulling away.

Tomorrow night, I would watch her from the shadows again. Make sure she was safe.

And try to convince myself that was enough.

For now.

4

I was back in the stone corridors, but this time everything was sharper, more vivid. The candles burning in their iron brackets cast dancing shadows that seemed to reach for me as I passed. My bare feet made no sound on the cold stone floor.

I knew the way now. Past the empty doorways, around the bend where the corridor opened into that circular chamber. I could feel him waiting for me there, that magnetic pull drawing me forward with each step.

"Sera."

His voice wrapped around me like silk, sending heat spiraling through my body. Rich and low, with that accent that made my name sound like a prayer. I quickened my pace, my heart racing with anticipation.

The chamber looked just as it had before, with dozens of candles casting pools of golden light and wax pooling on the old stone. But this time, he moved forward into the light.

God, he was beautiful.

Tall and lean, with sharp cheekbones and a mouth that seemed both dangerous and inviting. Dark hair brushed across his forehead, and those eyes, deep green and blazing with an intensity that took my breath away. He was dressed simply in dark clothes that appeared to soak up the candlelight, making him look like he was carved from shadow itself.

"You came back to me." His voice was pure velvet, satisfaction rolling through every word.

"I couldn't stay away," I whispered, surprised by my own honesty.

He smiled then, slow and predatory, and my knees nearly buckled. "I know."

I nodded, unable to speak. Every cell in my body was humming with awareness, with need. The space between us crackled with electricity, making my skin feel too tight.

"Come here, Sera."

It wasn't a request. It was a command, spoken in that voice that made liquid fire course through my veins. My body obeyed before my mind could protest, carrying me across the stone floor until I stood just inches from him.

This close, I could see the way the candlelight caught the sharp planes of his face, could smell that intoxicating scent of leather and smoke that seemed to wrap around him. My hands ached to touch him, to trace those elegant cheekbones, to tangle in that dark hair.

"Such sweet innocence," he murmured, reaching up to cup my face in his hands. His skin was cool against my fevered cheeks, but his touch sent electricity shooting through my entire nervous system. "Do you know what you do to me?"

His thumb traced across my lower lip, the gentle pressure making me gasp. The touch sent heat cascading through my body, and I found myself leaning into it despite every rational thought screaming at me to pull away. When he pressed just slightly, my lips parted instinctively.

He stepped closer, close enough that I could feel the coolness coming from his skin, a sharp contrast to the warm candlelit air of the chamber. Close enough that his scent wrapped around me like an embrace.

His hand slowly lifted, giving me a moment to pull away. When I didn't move, his fingers barely brushed along my jawline, so gentle it was almost nonexistent. Yet even that delicate touch sent shivers through me, making my skin hypersensitive to every motion of his fingertips.

His thumb brushed across my cheekbone, then traced down to the corner of my mouth, lingering there as I fought the urge to turn my head and press my lips to his palm. His other hand came up to frame my face, cool fingers slipping into my hair, holding me as if I were something precious, something fragile.

The way he looked at me made my knees weak, like I was the only thing that mattered in the world, as if he'd been searching for me his entire life. His eyes held a hunger that made my breath catch, a need so intense it made my pulse race and my skin flush with heat.

His hands trembled slightly against my face, and I realized he was struggling for control. That whatever he was feeling was just as overwhelming for him as it was for me.

He leaned in closer, his forehead nearly pressing against mine, his cool breath brushing against my lips. I could see the flecks of gold in his green eyes and feel the tension in his body as he held himself back.

My heart pounded against my ribs as he traced my features with his fingers—the curve of my cheek, the line of my jaw, and the sensitive skin just below my ear that made me shiver and arch into his touch when his fingers grazed it.

His thumb returned to my lower lip, tracing its fullness with agonizing slowness. When I let out a soft sigh, my breath warm against his skin, his eyes darkened with something that made heat pool low in my belly.

I wanted him to close that final distance between us. Wanted it so desperately I could barely breathe. My lips parted in invita-

tion, my body swaying toward his, every nerve ending alive with need—

The harsh buzz of my phone alarm shattered the dream.

I jerked awake, gasping, heat coursing through my veins. I fumbled to snooze the alarm, desperate to hold onto the fading images of candlelight and his touch.

My heart was racing, my skin slick with perspiration despite the cool morning air. I could still feel the phantom touch of his fingers on my lips, could still feel the places where his hands had framed my face. My body ached with a need so intense it was almost painful.

"Damn it," I whispered, pressing my palms against my flushed cheeks.

The dream had felt so real. I could still smell his scent lingering on my skin, and I could still hear the echo of his voice whispering my name. My lips felt as if his thumb had actually traced across them.

This was insane. It was just a dream, a very vivid and erotic dream, but still just a product of my subconscious mind.

So why did my body feel like it had actually been touched? Why could I still feel the ghost of his fingers tracing along my jaw?

The thought of him waiting for me in those stone corridors should have terrified me. Instead, it sent another wave of heat spiraling through my body, my thighs clenching together involuntarily as I imagined what might have happened if that alarm hadn't gone off, what it would have felt like if he'd finally closed that last inch between us.

My hand trailed down my body as I tried to recapture the feeling of his touch. My skin was sensitive, every nerve ending alive with need. I closed my eyes, letting my fingers trace the path he had taken: along my jaw, across my lips...

The alarm buzzed again, jarring and insistent.

"No," I groaned, my entire body vibrating with frustration as I reached over to silence it for good this time.

I sat up in bed, pushing my hair back from my face with trembling hands. I stumbled to the bathroom, splashing cold water on my face to clear my head. But when I looked in the mirror, my reflection showed lips that looked like they'd been touched, skin flushed with arousal, pupils dilated with want as if the dream had somehow been real.

As if somewhere in those stone corridors, a man with green eyes was waiting for me to come back to him.

———

BY THE TIME I arrived at the library, I had convinced myself that caffeine and routine would fix everything. Just focus on the manuscripts, get lost in medieval folklore, and pretend that my dreams weren't growing more vivid and disturbing each night.

The first thing I noticed when Helena let me in was that the library looked the same as it had before the attack. Every book was back in its place, every reading table upright and polished. The scattered papers had been collected and sorted; the overturned furniture had been restored. Even the crack in the hardwood floor where Viktor had been slammed down was gone, with the wood smooth and unblemished.

It was as if the violence had never happened at all.

For a moment, I wondered if I had imagined everything. Maybe I'd had some kind of breakdown, hallucinated the attack, the rescue, everything. Maybe the stress of being in a new country, the pressure of my research, the strange dreams... all of it might have combined to create an elaborate delusion.

But no. My throat still ached where Viktor had grabbed me. I could still smell leather and smoke on my skin from the dream. And somewhere deep down, I knew what I'd witnessed had been terrifyingly real.

"Good morning, Dr. Sterling," Helena said, her voice gentle as she watched me take in the pristine state of the library. "I hope you slept well."

I nodded, not trusting my voice.

"The manuscripts you were reviewing are on the same table from yesterday," Helena continued, gesturing toward the back of the library. "I've also pulled a few additional texts that might interest you."

I made my way to the reading area, hyperaware of every shadow, every corner where someone might be lurking. The morning light streaming through the tall windows should have been comforting, but instead it created patterns on the walls that made me jump every time they shifted.

I settled into my chair and opened the first manuscript, determined to make progress. Focus on work. Focus on something normal. academic, and safe.

But the illuminated letters seemed to blur before my eyes. Despite my paranoia, despite the fear still coursing through my system, my treacherous mind kept drifting back to the dream. To the memory of cool fingers tracing my jawline. The way his thumb had pressed against my lower lip. The hunger in those green eyes that had made my entire body ache with need even now, in broad daylight, surrounded by centuries-old books.

I shifted in my chair, pressing my thighs together as desire coiled tight inside me. This was ridiculous. I was sitting in a centuries-old library trying to work on my dissertation, and I couldn't stop thinking about a man who existed only in my dreams.

Except he didn't just exist in my dreams, did he? He'd been real enough to save my life. Real enough to kill Viktor's without breaking a sweat.

The memory of that violence should have terrified me. Instead, all I could think about was the way he'd looked at me afterward, the gentleness in his voice when he'd asked if I was hurt.

I refocused my attention on the manuscript, a 14th-century collection of regional folklore. The text described various supernatural creatures that supposedly haunted the Bohemian countryside, including vampires, werewolves, and spirits of the dead. Stories that had once been dismissed as peasant superstition.

But after what I'd witnessed, I found myself reading with new attention. These weren't just stories, were they? They were documentation—historical records of encounters with things that shouldn't exist.

A shadow moved across my peripheral vision, and I jerked my head up, heart racing. But it was only Helena, moving quietly between the stacks with an armload of books.

I took a shaky breath and returned to my reading, but I couldn't concentrate. Every creak of the old building made me tense. Every shifting shadow made me check the exits. My hands trembled slightly as I turned the pages, and I found myself reading the same paragraph over and over without absorbing a single word.

"Dr. Sterling?" Helena's voice made me jump so violently that I knocked over my coffee cup. The liquid spread across the table, soaking into my notes.

"Oh God, I'm sorry," I gasped, grabbing for napkins as Helena hurried over with a towel.

"It's quite all right," she said gently, helping me blot the spilled coffee. But her light eyes studied my face with concern. "You seem on edge today. Perhaps you should take a break? Get some fresh air?"

I wanted to laugh hysterically. Fresh air wouldn't help when the problem was supernatural creatures trying to kill me and erotic dreams that left me aching with need. But I couldn't exactly explain that to Helena.

"I'm fine," I said, though my voice came out an octave higher than usual. "Just tired. New city, new schedule, you know."

Helena nodded, but she didn't look convinced. "Of course. But perhaps, if you're feeling unsettled, it might be wise to leave before evening. Old buildings can play tricks on the mind when one is already feeling anxious."

The way she said it made me wonder exactly how much Helena knew about what had happened here last night.

"I'll keep that in mind," I said.

Helena squeezed my shoulder gently. "Good. And Dr. Sterling? If you ever need to talk about anything. I'm here."

She walked away, leaving me alone with damp notes and racing thoughts.

I tried to refocus on the manuscripts, but it was a hopeless effort. My mind kept drifting between the dream and the attack, between the memory of gentle touches and violent death. Every time I closed my eyes, I saw green eyes burning with hunger. Every time I opened them, I half-expected to see Viktor's unnatural face emerging from the shadows.

By noon, I'd managed to transcribe exactly three sentences. At this rate, my dissertation would take decades to complete.

I pushed back from the table, frustrated with myself. I was a scholar, trained to focus and analyze. I should be able to compartmentalize, to separate my research from whatever psychological trauma I was experiencing.

But I couldn't stop thinking about him. About how he moved with deadly grace, how his voice wrapped around my name like a caress. About how safe I felt the moment he appeared, even after witnessing him kill someone with his bare hands.

About how desperately I wanted to see him again, even though I knew I should be running as far from Prague as possible.

I glanced at the clock. I'd been here for hours and accomplished nothing. At this rate, Helena's suggestion about leaving early was starting to sound like the most sensible thing I'd heard all day.

My phone buzzed against the reading table, making me jump so hard I nearly knocked over my replacement coffee. Uncle David's name appeared on the screen, our weekly check-in call, right on schedule.

For a moment, I thought about letting it go to voicemail. I wasn't ready to pretend everything was normal or make small talk about my research and the weather. But David would only worry more if I didn't answer, and he had an annoying habit of showing up unannounced when he was concerned.

I swiped to answer. "Hi, David."

"Sera." His familiar voice was warm with affection, and I felt a pang of homesickness that caught me off guard. "How's Prague treating you? Getting settled in okay?"

"It's..." I paused, staring at the manuscript in front of me without really seeing it. How could I possibly explain what the last few days had been like? "It's beautiful here. Really amazing architecture."

"That's not what I asked." David's tone shifted, becoming more focused. He'd always been able to read me too well. "You sound shaken, sweetheart. What's wrong?"

"Nothing's wrong," I said too quickly. "Just tired. New schedule, different time zone, you know how it is."

Silence hung between us. I could practically hear him analyzing my voice, just like he used to when I was a teenager hiding a bad grade or a broken curfew.

"Sera." His voice was gentle but firm. "I've known you your entire life. You don't sound tired. You sound scared."

My throat tightened. God, I wanted to tell him everything. About the attack, about the impossible rescue, about dreams that felt more real than waking life. David had always been my anchor, the steady presence in my life after my parents died. If anyone would believe me, it would be him.

But how could I explain any of this without sounding completely insane?

"I'm fine, really," I managed. "Maybe just a little overwhelmed. The research is more intensive than I expected."

"What kind of overwhelmed?" He wasn't going to let this go. "Academic pressure or something else?"

I closed my eyes, pressing my fingers to my temple where a headache was building. Around me, the library felt too quiet, too full of shadows despite the bright afternoon light.

"Just Prague is different from what I expected. More intense. The history here is so layered and complex. Sometimes it feels like the past is still alive, you know?"

David was quiet for a moment. "Are you sure that's all? You don't sound like yourself."

"I'm adjusting," I said, hating how defensive I sounded. "It's only been a few days. Give me some time to find my footing."

Another pause. I could hear the television in the background of his apartment, some news program—normal, everyday sounds from a world that suddenly felt very far away.

"Alright," he said finally, though I could hear the reluctance in his voice. "But Sera? If anything happens, you call me immediately. I don't care what time it is or how small it seems. Promise me."

The concern in his voice made my chest tighten with guilt. He knew something was wrong, could sense it across thousands of miles, and I was lying to him.

"I promise," I whispered.

"Good. And take care of yourself, okay? Eat regularly, get enough sleep. Don't get so wrapped up in your research that you forget to live a little."

"I will."

"I love you, kiddo."

"Love you too, David."

I hung up and immediately wanted to call him back, to spill everything and let him help me figure out what to do. David was practical and levelheaded.

But I couldn't drag him into this. Whatever was happening to me in Prague, whatever I was caught in the middle of, I wouldn't risk his safety, too.

I set the phone aside and stared at the manuscript in front of me, but the medieval text might as well have been written in hieroglyphics. All I could think about was the worry in David's voice, the way he'd immediately known something was wrong.

The guilt weighed heavy on me. David had raised me, was my guardian, my friend, and the closest thing to a father I'd ever known. I'd never lied to him about anything important.

But how could I tell him that I'd been attacked by something that shouldn't exist and rescued by someone even more impossible? How could I explain that nothing in

Prague was what it seemed, that I was caught in the middle of something I didn't understand?

I couldn't. So I would carry this alone, at least until I understood what was happening to me.

The phone buzzed with a text message: *Call if you need anything. I mean it. – D*

I typed back: *I will. Thank you.*

The lie came so easily now.

5

By four o'clock, I'd given up any pretense of productivity. The guilt from lying to David, combined with my inability to concentrate on anything for more than thirty seconds, had left me feeling restless and on edge. I needed to get out of the library, away from the shadows and the memories of violence, away from Helena's knowing looks.

I packed up my things and headed for the exit, ignoring Helena's raised eyebrow when I told her I was leaving early.

"See you tomorrow," she called after me, and something in her tone made it sound more like a question than a statement.

The streets of Lesser Town bustled with afternoon pedestrians; tourists taking photos of baroque facades, locals heading home from work, street musicians earning coins. I envied their oblivious normalcy.

I found a small wine bar tucked into a narrow side street, the kind of place that mainly served locals rather than travelers. The interior was warm and dimly lit, with exposed brick walls and heavy wooden tables that seemed like they'd been there for decades. Perfect for hiding out and pretending my life hadn't completely spiraled out of control.

I claimed a corner table with a clear view of both the entrance and the back exit, a precaution that would have seemed paranoid just a week ago but now felt like a basic survival instinct. The bartender, a middle-aged man with kind eyes and graying hair, approached with a menu in hand.

"First time here?" he asked in accented English, clearly pegging me as a foreigner.

"Yes. I need something strong," I said, then caught myself. "I mean, something good. A nice red wine."

He smiled sympathetically. "Bad day?"

If only he knew. "Something like that."

"I have just the thing. A local Moravian red, it will help with whatever troubles you."

I nodded gratefully as he disappeared behind the bar. While I waited, I scanned the other patrons. A couple in their sixties sharing a bottle and speaking quietly in Czech. Two young women laughing over white wine and plates of cheese. An older man was reading a newspaper by himself near the window.

All perfectly normal. No immaculate skin, no predatory movements, no eyes that reflected light like an animal's. Just regular people living regular lives.

The bartender returned with a generous pour of dark red wine. I took a sip and felt some of the tension in my shoulders ease. It was rich and full-bodied, with hints of cherry and spice that warmed me from the inside out.

"Better?" the bartender asked.

"Much. Thank you."

He lingered for a moment, wiping down glasses behind the bar while keeping an eye on me. " You have the look of someone carrying heavy thoughts."

I nearly choked on my wine. "Excuse me?"

"Prague can be overwhelming for newcomers. So much history, so many stories. Sometimes the city shows you things you are not expecting."

The way he said it made my skin prickle. Was everyone in this city speaking in riddles?

"I'm just here for research," I said. "Medieval manuscripts."

"Ah." He nodded knowingly. "The old stories. Yes, those can be very interesting."

Before I could ask what he meant, he moved away to serve another customer, leaving me alone with my wine and increasingly paranoid thoughts.

I grabbed my phone and tried to focus on something normal: checking email, scrolling through social media, anything that connected me to the world I knew before Prague.

The wine helped, though. With each sip, the knot of anxiety in my chest loosened a bit. My rational mind began reasserting itself. Maybe I was overreacting. Maybe the stress of being in a new city, the pressure of my research, the jet lag... maybe it had all combined to make me see things that weren't really there.

Except Viktor's hands around my throat felt incredibly real. And the way Matthias moved, with impossible speed and strength, that wasn't my imagination.

The facts were undeniable:

One, I'd been attacked by someone who shouldn't have existed.

Two, I'd been rescued by someone even more impossible.

Three, I was having increasingly vivid dreams about my rescuer.

Four, Everyone in Prague seemed to know more about what was happening to me than I did.

I was so lost in thought that I didn't notice the man approaching my table until he was already standing next to me.

"Excuse me," he said in perfect English with just a hint of an accent. "Are you alright? You look troubled."

I looked up to find a tall, lean man with dark hair and concerned brown eyes.

Handsome in a conventional way, with the kind of smile that probably charmed tourists all over the city.

"I'm fine," I said automatically, my hand tightening around my wine glass. "Just thinking."

"About?"

The question was innocent enough, but something about his persistence made me uncomfortable. "Nothing important. I should probably get going."

I started to stand, but he held up a hand. "Please, I didn't mean to intrude. I'm Nicholas, by the way. I work at the hotel down the street. I've seen you around the neighborhood. American, right?"

Hotel employee. That explained the polished English and the practiced charm. Still, after the past few days, I wasn't taking any chances with strange men approaching me.

"I really should go," I said, reaching for my purse.

"Of course. But if you ever need anything, recommendations for restaurants or help navigating the city, I'm usually around." He pulled out a business card and laid it on the table. "Prague can be a lonely place for newcomers."

I nodded politely but didn't pick up the card. He seemed harmless enough, but my trust in harmless-seeming men had taken a serious hit recently.

After he walked away, I finished my wine in two large gulps and left money on the table. The alcohol had helped calm my nerves, but not enough to make me comfortable sitting alone in public places where strangers could approach me.

As I gathered my things, I caught the bartender watching me with that same knowing expression I'd seen on Helena's face. Like he understood something about my situation that I didn't.

The thought followed me out into the early evening light, where the shadows were already growing long and Prague's Gothic architecture looked more ominous than beautiful. Night was coming, and with it, the possibility of another encounter with the supernatural.

The wine buzz faded quickly in the cool evening air. I'd only made it two blocks when that feeling hit me. That prickle of awareness that told me I wasn't alone.

Someone was following me.

I stopped at a shop window, using the reflection to check behind me: tourists, locals, nothing unusual. But the feeling didn't go away.

I turned down a side street, my footsteps echoing off the narrow stone walls. The feeling persisted. Not actual footsteps, just a presence. Something moving in the shadows, keeping pace.

My pulse quickened.

I ducked into a doorway and waited, counting to ten before looking out again. The street was empty except for an older man walking his dog in the opposite direction.

But as I stepped back onto the sidewalk, I saw it—a tall figure at the far end of the street, just at the edge of the lamplight: dark clothing, familiar silhouette.

My breath caught. "Matthias?"

The figure stepped back into the shadow and vanished.

I stood there for a long moment, heart hammering. Had

I imagined it? Was my desperate brain conjuring him from wishful thinking?

But as I started walking again, something shifted. The anxiety that had been clawing at me all day began to ease. Whatever was out there, it didn't feel threatening.

It felt protective.

By the time I reached my hotel, I was certain. He was watching over me, staying just out of sight, making sure I got home safely.

Any sane woman would have been terrified.

Instead, I found myself hoping he'd follow me into my dreams again.

6

The afternoon light was fading behind the tall windows of the Strahov Monastery Library, casting long shadows across the stone floor. I'd been standing there for the better part of an hour, watching Prague's red rooftops and spires blur into twilight instead of focusing on my research.

All I could think about was the shadow I'd glimpsed last night. The protective presence that had followed me home.

Behind me, the library was quieter now as the day wound down. Most of the tourists had left, and only a few dedicated researchers remained bent over their manuscripts. Helena moved silently between the shelves, preparing for the evening closing.

I stood there, remembering the phantom touch of fingers tracing my jaw. Even now, with darkness approaching and the monastery taking on its more mysterious evening atmosphere, I could still feel the echo of those dreams. The memory of green eyes burning with hunger that matched my own.

"Dr. Sterling?" Helena's voice came from behind me.

I turned to find her approaching with a concerned expression.

"There's someone here to see you," she said, glancing toward the library entrance. "He says he's family."

I followed her gaze to see a familiar tall figure striding through the monastery doors, his steel-gray eyes scanning the library with the intensity of a man expecting trouble.

Uncle David.

"What are you doing here?" The words came out sharper than I intended as I crossed the library floor to meet him.

My uncle's weathered face was etched with concern and a wariness that I'd never seen before. He was dressed in his usual dark jeans and leather jacket, but there was tension in his shoulders that spoke of sleepless nights and urgent travel. A black duffel bag hung from his shoulder, the kind he used for weekend trips.

"I took the first flight I could get after our call yesterday." His hands gripped my shoulders as he studied my face with those observant eyes that had always been able to see through my lies. "I knew you were lying to me, Sera."

My chest tightened with guilt. Around us, other library patrons had started to notice our reunion; their quiet conversations paused as they watched the intense American man who had just walked into their peaceful scholarly sanctuary.

"Can we not do this here?" I glanced around at the curious faces. "There's a reading room we can use."

David nodded, his gaze still scanning the library's baroque architecture and shadowed alcoves. "Lead the way."

I led him into a small private reading room off the main hall, shutting the heavy wooden door behind us. The space was cozy, with a single table, two chairs, and windows overlooking the monastery's old courtyard. David placed his duffel bag on the table with a solid thud.

"Sit down, sweetheart." His voice was gentler now. "We need to talk."

"You flew halfway around the world because I sounded tired on the phone?" I remained standing, my arms crossed.

"You didn't sound tired. You sounded terrified." He pulled out one of the chairs and gestured for me to sit. When I still didn't move, he continued, "I've known you your entire life, Sera. I know the difference between academic stress and real fear."

The accuracy of his observation felt like a gut punch. Of course he'd known. David had been reading my moods since I was seven years old, had been my anchor through every crisis, every loss. How had I thought I could hide something this big from him?

"I don't know what you want me to say," I whispered, finally sinking into the chair.

"The truth." He sat across from me. "What's happened?"

I looked into those familiar steel-gray eyes, the same ones that had comforted me through nightmares and celebrated my successes, and I felt the weight of everything I had been carrying alone.

"You wouldn't believe me if I told you," I said finally.

"Try me."

I opened my mouth, then closed it again. How could I explain Viktor's attack? The impossible speed and strength of both men? The way Matthias had made a man turn into ash and then vanished into shadow?

"I..." I struggled for words. "There was an incident at the library. Someone... someone attacked me."

David's entire body went rigid. "What kind of attack?"

"A man. He was waiting for me after hours. He grabbed me, threatened me." I touched my throat unconsciously, remembering the bruising pressure of Viktor's fingers. "But someone else showed up. Someone who stopped him."

"Are you hurt? Did he—"

"No." I shook my head. "But it all happened so fast and felt unreal."

"What did this attacker look like?"

"Perfect skin, completely flawless, almost translucent. And strong, impossibly strong. He moved too fast, like—" I stopped, realizing how insane it sounded.

"Like what, Sera?"

"Like he wasn't human."

David was quiet for a long moment, his hands clasped tightly on the table. When he finally spoke, his voice was tight with restraint.

"What about the man who helped you? What did he look like?"

I felt heat rise to my cheeks. "Tall. Dark hair. Green eyes. He was..." I trailed off, not sure how to explain the magnetic pull I'd felt, the way my body had responded to his presence.

"Beautiful," David finished quietly. "Supernaturally beautiful."

I jerked back before I could stop myself. "How did you—"

"Because I know what you encountered, Sera." David didn't look at me. "I've been hoping for twenty-eight years that this day wouldn't come."

"What day? David, you're not making sense."

He stared at me for a long moment. "The day I'd have to tell you what we really are."

A knot tightened in my stomach. "What we really are?"

Instead of answering, he reached for his duffel bag with hands that trembled slightly. The zipper opened to reveal contents that made my blood run cold. Weathered-looking silver stakes. A crossbow that gleamed with silver inlay. And beneath it all, thick leather-bound books, worn at the edges.

"What is this?" I whispered, my voice barely audible.

David pulled out one of the books.

"This is our family history, Sera. The real history." He ran a hand over the book's faded cover. "The Sterling family has been hunting vampires for over four hundred years."

I actually recoiled in my chair, gripping the armrests so tightly my knuckles turned white.

"That's impossible. That's—vampires don't exist. They're myths, stories—"

"You just met two of them." David's steel-gray eyes held mine. "And they know exactly what you are."

"What I am?" The words came out as a whisper. "David, I'm a graduate student. I don't understand—"

He carefully opened one of the books, and I saw page after page of handwritten entries, sketches, and dates going back centuries. The ink was faded but still recognizable; these were records of some kind. Records of death.

"This is our family history, Sera. The real history."

I stared at the pages, my mind struggling to process what I was seeing. Names. Dates. Locations. And beside each entry, numbers that made my stomach turn.

"What is this?" I whispered.

"Our legacy." David's voice was hollow. "What we've always been, what we've always done. What your parents died doing."

My grip tightened on the chair. "My parents died in a car accident."

"No, sweetheart." David reached for my hand, but I pulled away. "They died protecting people. Just like their parents before them, and their parents before them."

"Protecting people from what?"

David met my eyes, and I saw the pain there. "From things that shouldn't exist."

"Vampires?"

"Among other things." He closed the book gently. "The

Sterling family has been fighting this war for centuries, Sera. And now it's found you."

I stood abruptly, my chair scraping against the floor. "This is insane. You're talking about monsters, about some kind of supernatural war—"

"Look at me." David's voice was firm. "Look at me and tell me you don't believe what you saw. Tell me the man who attacked you felt human to you."

I bit my cheek and looked away.

"Does Thomas know about all this?" I asked, thinking of my younger brother back home.

"No, your brother doesn't know." David's expression softened slightly. "I've kept him out of it, just like I tried to keep you out of it."

A moment of silence hung between us as I processed his words.

"The man who saved you," David continued. "Did he feel human?"

Heat flooded my cheeks as I remembered Matthias's touch, the electric connection, the way he'd appeared and disappeared like shadow itself.

"He protected me," I said weakly.

"Did he?" David's eyes were sad. "Or did he protect something he needs?"

Before I could ask what he meant, the reading room door burst open with a crash that sent splinters of wood flying across the floor.

Matthias stood in the doorway, his tall frame silhouetted against the dim light of the monastery. But he looked different than he had two nights ago, weaker. There were shadows under his green eyes that spoke of exhaustion, and when he moved into the room, it was with more stiffness that hadn't been there before.

"Step away from her," David said, his voice deadly calm as his hand moved toward the weapons bag.

"I'm not here to fight you, hunter." Matthias's voice was still rich and compelling, but there was a weariness to it that made my chest tighten with unexpected concern. His eyes found mine across the room. "Though I can see you've been busy poisoning her mind against me."

"Poisoning her mind?" David's laugh was sharp and bitter. "I'm telling her the truth about what you are."

"And what am I?" Matthias stepped further into the room, and I noticed the way he favored his left side slightly, as if movement caused him pain. "What terrible things have you told her about me, David Sterling?"

The fact that he knew David's name sent a shiver down my spine. This wasn't a chance encounter; these two had history.

"That you're a predator," David said, his hand now resting on what looked like a silver blade. "That you're using her for whatever dark purpose brought you to Prague."

"Dark purpose." Matthias's green eyes never left mine, and I felt that familiar electric pull even after what David had just told me. "Is that what you call survival?"

"I call it what it is: manipulation of an innocent woman for your own needs."

"Innocent?" Matthias took another step closer, and I found myself unable to look away from his face. "She's a Sterling, David. There's nothing innocent about her bloodline."

"She didn't choose this life."

"Neither did I." For the first time, something raw and vulnerable flickered across Matthias's features. "But here we are, all of us caught in a web that was spun centuries before any of us were born."

David's grip tightened on his weapon. "Stay back."

"I'm not here to hurt her." Matthias's voice was quiet but firm. "I'm here to warn her. Both of you."

"Warn us about what?" I found my voice, stepping slightly forward despite David's protective stance.

"Others are coming," Matthias said, his eyes never leaving mine. "Viktor was just the beginning. Sterling blood in Prague attracts attention. The kind that threatens the balance."

"Because you led them to her," David accused.

"Because they've been hunting her." Matthias's tone was firm. "The moment she arrived in Prague, they knew a Sterling was here. Word is already spreading through supernatural networks."

He paused, and I saw him sway slightly on his feet. "I secured protection for her, but I'm..." His voice dropped. "I'm not strong enough to face the ones that might challenge that."

"What's wrong with you?" The question left my lips before I could stop it.

Something shifted in Matthias's expression. "Nothing that concerns you, Sera."

"It does concern me," I said firmly. "You saved my life. You've been watching over me. I deserve to know why."

"Sera—" David warned.

"No." I turned to face my uncle. "I deserve answers. Real answers. Not just warnings about predators and dark purposes."

Matthias was quiet for a long moment, studying my face. When he finally spoke, his voice was guarded.

"I told you before. You need to understand what you're caught in the middle of."

"That's not an answer."

"It's the only answer I can give you right now." His green

eyes held mine with an intensity that made my breath catch. "There are things you're not ready to know."

David's weapon was now fully drawn, its silver gleaming in the dim light. "How convenient. The vampire who claims to be protecting her won't tell her why."

"I'm protecting her from more than just physical threats," Matthias said, his voice tight with something like pain. "Some knowledge is dangerous, David. You should know that better than anyone."

"What I know is that you're using her," David replied coldly. "Whatever you want from her, whatever brought you to Prague—"

"Is between Sera and me." Matthias's tone was final, but when he looked at me, I saw something vulnerable flicker across his features. "There will come a time when I will reveal everything to you."

The promise in his words sent a wave of heat through me in spite of everything.

Matthias stepped backward toward the window. In one fluid motion, he was gone, vanishing into the gathering dusk, leaving only the faint scent of leather and smoke in the air.

7

The reading room fell silent after Matthias vanished through the window, leaving only his warning about others coming. I stood frozen, staring at the empty window frame, my mind reeling from everything that had just happened.

"Sera." David was already shoving weapons back into his duffel bag. "We're leaving. Now."

"I—what?" I turned to face him, still trying to process the surreal conversation I'd just witnessed. "David, what just happened?"

"Pack your things. We can be at the airport in an hour."

"Wait." I stepped between him and the door. "You know him. That vampire, Matthias, you know him."

David paused, his hands still gripping the bag's zipper. "I know what he is."

"That's not what I meant and you know it." My voice came out sharper than intended. "The way you looked at each other, the things he said. You have history."

"Sera—"

"Stop." I held up a hand. "Just stop. I'm twenty-eight years old, David. I'm not the seven-year-old who needed you to check under her bed for monsters anymore."

David's expression softened slightly. "Sometimes I forget."

Something had shifted inside me during that confrontation. The fear was still there, but underneath it was something stronger. A quiet certainty that hiding wasn't an option anymore.

"Well, remember. Because I'm not running away from something I don't understand." I gestured toward the window where Matthias had disappeared. "He saved my life. And you just had a conversation with him, like you've been expecting him."

"It's complicated."

"Then uncomplicate it." I crossed my arms. "You told me our family hunts vampires, that my parents were murdered, that I have some kind of supernatural sensing ability. But there's more, isn't there? Something about him specifically."

David was quiet for a long moment, studying my face. "You really want to know?"

"I really want to know."

He sank into one of the reading chairs, suddenly looking every one of his fifty-three years. "Matthias Cross isn't like other vampires, Sera. He's older. More dangerous."

"Dangerous how?"

"He's been around for centuries. And he's been in Prague before. Multiple times." David's voice was grim. "Your father thought he was hunting something. Or waiting for something."

"Waiting for what?"

"We never found out." David stood, reaching for his bag again. "Your parents died before they could discover what he was really after. Which is why we're leaving."

"No."

"Sera—"

"I said no." I moved to block his path again. "You just told me my entire life has been a lie. And your solution is to run away?"

"My solution is to keep you alive."

"By hiding? By pretending none of this is real?" I shook my head. "It's too late for that, David. Whatever's happening here, whatever brought me to Prague... it found me. Running won't change that."

"You don't understand the danger—"

"Then help me understand it." I stepped closer, meeting his eyes. "Teach me what I need to know. Show me how to protect myself. But I'm not running."

David stared at me for a long moment, then took a step back.

"You're just like your mother," he said quietly. "Stubborn as hell and twice as brave for your own good."

"Is that why she died?"

"She died because she wouldn't abandon your father when he needed her most." David's voice cracked slightly. "They were partners in everything. Including the hunt."

"Then teach me to be worthy of that legacy."

David was quiet for a long time, his weathered hands gripping the duffel bag. Outside, Prague's cathedral bells tolled the hour, and somewhere in the gathering darkness, I could feel someone watching.

"All right," he said finally. "But not here. Too exposed. We'll go back to your hotel, and I'll tell you what you need to know."

"Everything?"

"Everything I can." David shouldered his bag. "But Sera, once you know the truth about what our family is, what we do. There's no going back to the life you had before."

I looked around the reading room where my academic

career had been turned upside down, where I'd witnessed supernatural violence, where I'd met a vampire who made my pulse race with dangerous possibilities.

"I don't think I can go back anyway," I said quietly.

David nodded grimly. "Then God help us both."

8

My hotel room felt smaller with David's presence filling it, his duffel bag of weapons sitting on the desk beside my laptop. He was pulling out various silver implements: knives, stakes, what looked like bullets, and arranging them on the bed in neat rows.

"Sit," he said, not looking up from his work. "If you're insisting on staying in Prague, you need to know how to keep yourself alive."

I perched on the edge of the bed, careful not to disturb his weapon display. "I thought you said I could sense them."

"Sensing them and surviving them are two different things." David picked up a silver knife, testing its edge. "The feeling you get, that prickle when a vampire's near, that's your early warning system. But it won't help you if you don't know what to do with it."

"So teach me."

David finally looked at me, his steel-gray eyes serious. "Vampires are fast. Faster than anything you can imagine. They're strong enough to snap your neck with one hand, and they heal from most injuries within minutes."

A chill ran down my spine. "Most injuries?"

"Silver slows their healing. A silver blade through the heart kills them permanently." David held up a silver knife. "This blade is your best friend. Aim for the heart or throat - make every strike count."

I swallowed hard. "What about holy water? Crosses?"

"Folklore. Might make you feel better, but it won't save your life." David set the knife aside and picked up a wooden stake. "Old vampires like Matthias, eight centuries or more, they're in a different league entirely. Smarter, faster, stronger. They don't make the mistakes younger ones do."

"Eight centuries?" The number stopped me cold. "He's really that old?"

"At least." David pulled out one of the family journals, flipping to a page near the middle. "Look."

The page showed a sketch of Matthias, dated *Prague, 1647*. Below it, a brief entry: *"The Cross vampire appeared again during the cathedral incident. Observed but did not engage. Purpose unknown."*

"He's been in Prague before," I said quietly.

"Multiple times. Always during supernatural crises." David closed the journal. "But that's not what you need to focus on right now. What you need to focus on is staying alive long enough to understand what he wants."

David stood and moved to his duffel bag, pulling out what looked like a small crossbow. "Your sensing ability will give you maybe thirty seconds' warning before a vampire gets close. That's assuming you pay attention to it and don't dismiss it as anxiety."

"How do I know the difference?"

"Practice. The vampire feeling is distinct—cold dread, as if something predatory is watching you. Your instincts will scream at you to run." David met my eyes. "Listen to them."

"What if I can't run?"

"Then you fight dirty. Vampires are arrogant; they've

been apex predators for so long, they don't expect real resistance from humans." David picked up the silver knife again.

I took the knife when he handed it to me, surprised by its weight. The blade gleamed in the hotel room's lamplight, and something about holding it felt right. Natural.

"You're a Sterling," David said, watching my grip on the weapon. "Fighting supernatural creatures is in your blood. Trust your instincts."

"My instincts told me Viktor was dangerous, but I still almost died."

"Because you froze. Next time, you move." David pulled out a leather sheath. "Keep this on you at all times. Hidden, but accessible. And Sera, if you meet another vampire, don't try to talk to it. Don't hesitate. Strike first and ask questions later."

I clipped the sheath to my belt, covering it with my jacket. "Even Matthias?"

David's expression darkened. "Especially Matthias. Eight-hundred-year-old vampires don't save random humans out of kindness. He wants something from you."

"Maybe he's different—"

"He's not." David's voice was sharp. "I know you felt something when he touched you, when he spoke to you. Vampires like him, they're master manipulators. They make you want to trust them."

Heat flooded my cheeks. "It wasn't like that."

"Wasn't it?" David stepped closer. "Tell me honestly, when he looks at you, how does it make you feel?"

I thought about Matthias's green eyes burning into mine, the way my pulse had raced when he'd checked me for injuries. The electric shock that had run through me at his touch.

"Confused," I said finally.

"That's what he wants. Confusion makes you vulnerable." David ran a hand through his graying hair. "Look, I need to get supplies, call in some backup. The weapons I brought aren't enough if we're dealing with something this old." He glanced at the small arsenal on the bed. "But I don't want to leave you alone."

"I'll be fine. You taught me what to look for."

"There's a hunter safe house across town." David grabbed his jacket. "You stay here. Door locked, silver knife close. Don't let anyone in."

The thought of being trapped in this small room made my chest tighten. "What about food? I haven't eaten since this morning."

David paused, glancing at his watch. "Shit, you're right. Can you order room service?"

"I could go," I offered, trying to keep my voice casual. "The hotel lobby has a café, and I saw some shops nearby. I need some air to process all this."

David's eyes narrowed. "Sera—"

"Public places only. Well-lit areas. I'll be back in an hour." I touched the knife at my hip. "You just spent twenty minutes teaching me how to defend myself."

David was quiet for a long moment, rubbing his jaw. Finally, he sighed.

"One hour. Hotel lobby, nearby shops only. And if anything feels wrong—"

"Silver knife to the throat, ask questions later. I got it."

"I'm serious, Sera. Trust your instincts. If something feels off, even slightly, you run."

After David left, I sat on the bed for a few minutes, looking at the weapons he'd left behind. The weight of the silver knife was oddly comforting, a reminder that I wasn't completely helpless.

9

The October air was crisp against my face as I stepped out of the hotel lobby, a sharp contrast to the stifling atmosphere of revelations and weapons that had filled my room. I pulled my jacket tighter, feeling the reassuring weight of the silver knife at my hip.

Just one hour. Get some food, clear my head, and process everything David had told me.

The hotel café was too bright, too full of normal people living normal lives: tourists planning sightseeing routes, business travelers checking emails. I couldn't sit among them pretending everything was fine when nothing made sense anymore.

I bought a sandwich I didn't want and headed back outside.

The narrow streets beckoned, cobblestones gleaming under the streetlights. I told myself I'd just walk to the corner, maybe find a quiet bench to sit and think. But once I started moving, I couldn't seem to stop.

What we've always been, what we've always done. What your parents died doing.

David's words echoed in my head as my feet carried me

down winding streets. I grappled with all those years of believing a lie. For as long as I could remember, I had thought I was just an ordinary grad student with a boring family history.

The Sterling name is known among vampires.

A family of hunters. Centuries of tracking and killing supernatural creatures, and I'd known nothing about it. How many times had David watched me struggle with some academic problem or relationship drama, knowing that my real legacy was violence and blood?

I turned down a narrow side street, drawn by the Gothic architecture and the way shadows pooled between the old buildings. Prague felt different now that I knew what lurked in those shadows. Every darkened doorway could hide something inhuman. Every footstep behind me could belong to predatory creatures with too-sharp teeth.

Trust your instincts. If something feels wrong, you run.

But what if my instincts were telling me to stay? What if the pull I felt toward this city, toward its dark corners and hidden mysteries, was exactly what I was supposed to follow?

I thought about Matthias's green eyes, how they had burned into mine with recognition and something deeper. The jolt of electricity when he'd touched my throat, checking for injuries with hands that were too cold and too gentle for something that could snap a man's neck.

Eight-hundred-year-old vampires don't save random humans out of kindness.

Maybe David was right. Maybe Matthias did want something from me. But when he'd looked at me, it hadn't felt predatory. It felt familiar.

The realization should have filled me with dread. Instead, it made me walk faster, as if my feet knew where they wanted to go even if my mind didn't.

The streets grew narrower, older. Fewer streetlights, fewer people. I passed under stone archways that had stood for centuries, past buildings that predated my country. The weight of history pressed down around me, and I found myself thinking about all the Sterlings who had walked these same streets over the generations.

Had they felt this pull too? This sense of being called toward something dangerous and inevitable?

I turned another corner and realized I had no idea where I was. The familiar landmarks of the hotel district had disappeared, replaced by a maze of streets that all looked the same in the darkness. I pulled out my phone to check the time, forty-five minutes since I'd left. I needed to head back.

But as I turned to retrace my steps, that feeling hit me.

Cold dread, like something predatory watching from the shadows. Every hair on my arms stood up, and my hand instinctively moved to the knife at my hip.

I started walking faster, my heels clicking against the cobblestones. The feeling followed me, that sense of being hunted. I turned down another street, then another, but couldn't shake the sensation that something was tracking my every move.

The streets were empty now, too quiet for a city center. No tourists, no locals, no normal people living normal lives. Just me and whatever was following in the darkness behind me.

I ducked into an alley, pressing my back against the stone wall, the dampness seeping through my clothes as I tried to control my breathing. Maybe I was being paranoid. Maybe the stress of everything I'd learned was making me imagine threats that weren't there.

Then I heard footsteps.

Not walking. Stalking. My heart hammered against my ribs as the footsteps came closer, echoing off the walls.

I drew the silver knife, feeling the motion come instinctively. The blade gleamed in the dim light filtering down from the street, filling me with a sense of confidence as I held it.

The footsteps stopped.

For a moment, silence filled the alley. Then a voice drifted out of the darkness.

"Well, well. What do we have here?"

Two figures stepped into the mouth of the alley, and I knew immediately what they were. The crawling sensation made me stagger, that predatory coldness that screamed danger. But these weren't like Viktor, rough and desperate. These vampires moved with confidence, dressed in expensive clothes that belonged in corporate boardrooms, not dark alleys.

"A Sterling," the second one said, inhaling deeply. "How delightful. It's been a while since I've smelled your delicious blood."

They started walking toward me slowly, and I realized I was cornered. The alley ended with a wall behind me, no way to escape or hide.

"A Sterling, wandering the streets alone," the first vampire said conversationally. "How careless. Don't they teach you anything about self-preservation?"

I raised the knife, trying to remember everything David had taught me. Go for the throat. Make them bleed faster than they can heal.

"Now, now," the second vampire said, noticing my weapon. "Let's not make this unpleasant. We're not here to kill you, little Sterling. Quite the opposite."

"We have plans for you," the first one added, his smile

revealing fangs that gleamed white in the darkness. "Plans that require you to be very much alive."

They were close enough now that I could see their faces clearly, handsome in that inhuman way, with skin too perfect and eyes that were too bright in the darkness.

Close enough to strike.

I lunged forward with the knife, aiming for the nearest vampire's throat just like David had taught me. But he moved quickly, catching my wrist before the blade could connect.

"So eager to fight," he said, his grip like iron around my bones. "How refreshing."

The second vampire circled behind me while the first held my knife hand immobilized. I tried to pull free, but it was like trying to bend steel.

"Don't struggle," the one behind me said, his cold breath against my neck. "This will be so much easier if you simply—"

The vampire behind me suddenly screamed.

I spun around to see him flying through the air, crashing into the stone wall hard enough to crack mortar. Matthias stood where the vampire had been, as if he'd materialized from nothing.

"Release her," he said, his voice carrying quiet menace.

The vampire holding my wrist smiled, but I could see uncertainty flickering in his eyes. "Matthias. We wondered when you'd appear."

"Not soon enough." Matthias stepped over the groaning form of the first vampire. "Release her. Now."

"I think not." The vampire's grip tightened on my wrist until I gasped. "She's exactly what we came for."

Matthias's green eyes blazed with cold fire. "Her safety is of interest to me."

"Your interest?" The vampire laughed. "How touching. But I'm afraid that changes nothing."

Matthias moved, and suddenly the vampire holding me was flying through the air to crash into the opposite wall. My knife clattered to the cobblestones as I stumbled backward.

Both vampires recovered quickly, moving to flank Matthias. But something was wrong; Matthias moved more slowly than before, still favoring his left side. Whatever was weakening him was getting worse.

"Kill him," one of them snarled. "Take the girl."

They attacked simultaneously, but Matthias was ready. He ducked the first vampire's lunge and drove his elbow into the second one's ribs with enough force to shatter bone. But the first vampire's claws raked across his shoulder, and I saw dark blood stain his shirt.

I scrambled for the knife, my fingers closing around the silver handle just as one of the vampires broke away from the fight and lunged toward me.

This time, I didn't hesitate.

The blade sliced across his throat in a spray of black blood, and he stumbled backward with a scream that echoed off the alley walls. He clutched at the wound, but I could see it wasn't healing as quickly as it should have.

"Silver," he hissed.

Matthias moved quickly, drawing a blade that found the wounded vampire's heart first. The body burst into ash before it could hit the ground.

The second vampire tried to flee, but Matthias caught him by the throat. I heard the sharp crack of breaking bone, then sudden silence.

When I looked up, Matthias was driving his knife into the vampire's heart, reducing him to ash in an instant. The ground was littered with the remnants of those two creatures. Matthias stood there, breathing hard, dark blood seeping through his shirt.

"How are you?" he asked, his eyes scanning me for injuries.

"I'm Fine." Still gripping the bloody knife. "You're bleeding."

"I'll heal." He stepped closer, and I caught his intoxicating scent despite the metallic smell of vampire blood in the air. "You shouldn't have come out alone."

"David went to get supplies. I just needed—"

"Space to think?" Matthias's jaw tightened. "I could sense you were in trouble."

"How did you—"

"You called to me. Perhaps not consciously, but your blood smells different when threatened." His gaze dropped to the blood on my knife. "You fought well."

"I didn't kill him."

"No, but you drew blood. Silver in the throat, that was well done." His eyes glinted with something like approval. "Most humans freeze when they see fangs."

Matthias held out his hand. "Come. We need to get off the streets before more of them arrive."

I stared at his outstretched hand, remembering the electric shock from before. Every rational thought in my head screamed that I should find David, should stay in well-lit public areas, should not go anywhere with an eight-hundred-year-old vampire.

But those same vampires had said I was exactly what they'd come for. Had spoken of plans that required me to be alive.

And Matthias had saved me. Again.

I took his hand.

The shock was immediate and overwhelming, electricity

racing up my arm and straight to my core. But this time, I didn't pull away.

"Where are we going?" I asked.

"Somewhere safe. Somewhere we can talk without interruption." His fingers tightened around mine, and the electric current between us made it impossible to think clearly about anything else.

"The catacombs beneath the cathedral. Where no one will think to look for us."

10

Matthias led me through unfamiliar streets, his hand firm against mine. I should pull away. Every instinct screamed that letting him touch me like this was dangerous, but his palm against mine drowned out reason, made it impossible to think past the next step.

We approached the cathedral from a different angle than I'd ever seen, moving through shadows that seemed to hide us. An iron gate stood slightly ajar in what looked like a solid stone wall, hidden behind overgrown ivy.

"How did you—"

"These passages are older than the cathedral itself," Matthias said, pulling the gate wider. "Built when Prague was nothing more than a collection of settlements on the river."

The space beyond was pitch black. He moved forward while I stumbled over uneven stones, grateful for his steadying grip.

"I can't see anything."

Without a word, he stopped and turned toward me. His free hand cupped my face, with his thumb gently brushing my cheekbone.

"Close your eyes," he murmured, his voice low and intimate in the darkness. "Trust me."

I should have refused. Instead, I let my eyes drift shut, surrendering to the unknown.

"Now," His breath cool against my ear. "Feel the path instead of seeing it."

With my eyes closed, I could sense the stone walls pressing in on either side and feel the passage gently sloping downward. My other senses grew sharper: the sound of our footsteps echoing off stone, and the steady rhythm of his breathing beside me.

"Better?"

I nodded, not trusting my voice. The intimacy of moving blind through darkness with only his hand to guide me felt more dangerous than the vampire attack. More dangerous and infinitely more tempting.

The passage opened into a larger space, and I could sense the change in the air; it felt cooler. Matthias finally let go of my hand, and I immediately missed the connection.

"You can open your eyes now."

Candles flickered in iron brackets along stone walls, casting shadows across what appeared to be a medieval chamber. The ceiling arched high above us, supported by pillars carved with symbols I recognized from the manuscripts I'd been studying. This was the place from my dreams, the stone corridors that had been calling to me since before I arrived in Prague.

"How is this possible?" I breathed.

"You recognize this place." Matthias moved silently to light more candles, and the additional illumination revealed the true scope of the space. It was beautiful, stone carved with symbols that seemed to writhe in the flickering light, alcoves that disappeared into shadow, and at the far end, a raised platform that looked disturbingly like an altar.

"The catacombs," I whispered.

"Among other things." Matthias turned to face me, and in the candlelight, his features looked sharper, more inhuman. "You've been dreaming of this place."

It wasn't a question. I wrapped my arms around myself, suddenly feeling exposed despite being fully clothed. "How do you know that?"

"Because you've been calling to me in those dreams." He stepped closer, and I caught that intoxicating scent of leather and smoke that made my head spin. "The connection between us grows stronger each night."

"What connection?" I whispered.

Something flickered across his expression, hunger and longing that made my breath catch. But instead of answering, he moved to the stone platform, his movements slower than usual. I noticed him briefly steady himself against the stone.

"You're hurt," I said, noticing the way he winced as he moved his shoulder.

"I'm fine."

But he wasn't. In the candlelight, I could see the exhaustion pulling at his features, the rigid way he held himself. He looked diminished somehow. Less vital than he had been even hours ago.

"You're not fine. What's wrong?"

"Nothing that concerns you." His voice was sharp, but when he saw my expression, it softened. "I'm sorry. I don't mean to be short with you. I'm just tired."

I let out a resigned sigh, knowing he wouldn't give me a straight answer. "The vampires tonight," I said, my voice barely above a whisper. "They said they had plans for me. That they needed me alive."

Matthias went very still. "What exactly did they say?"

"That I was 'the one they'd been searching for.' That I

would 'serve their purpose perfectly.'" I took a step back, needing distance to think clearly. "What purpose, Matthias? What do they want from me?"

He was quiet for a long moment, his green eyes reflecting the candlelight. When he finally spoke, his voice was quiet. "Sterling blood isn't like other human blood, Sera. Your family's bloodline carries properties that vampires want."

"What kind of properties?"

"It makes us stronger. Faster. It heals injuries that would otherwise take days to mend." His voice dropped to that intimate murmur that sent a shiver down my spine. "One taste of Sterling blood can sustain a vampire far longer than ordinary feeding."

My mouth went dry. "So I'm food to you. Enhanced food."

"No." The word came out sharp, almost angry. "You're not food. You're not prey. You're something I never expected to find."

"Which is?"

"Something I can't explain yet." He ran a hand through his dark hair, his eyes never leaving mine. "Not until you're ready for what that means. For what I want it to mean."

A chill ran through me. "The vampires hunting me—they're not just hungry, are they?"

"They're organized. Coordinated." His jaw tightened. "I've heard whispers in the supernatural community. Something about an old ritual, something that requires specific bloodlines. But the details..." He shook his head. "I don't know enough yet."

"But you saved me. Why?"

Something flickered across his expression, longing so intense it made my breath catch. "Because the moment I saw you, I recognized what had always been inevitable."

"You're not making sense."

"I know." He reached toward me, then stopped, his hand hovering inches from my face. "There's so much you need to know, Sera." His voice dropped lower, rougher. "But if I tell you everything now, you'll run from me. And I can't—" He swallowed hard. "I can't lose you. Not when I've finally found you."

The raw honesty in his voice made my chest ache. "Found me for what?"

"For everything I've been missing for longer than you can imagine." His eyes darkened. "But first, I need to keep you alive long enough to understand."

"What do you want from me then?" I whispered.

His hand finally made contact, fingers tracing along my jawline with agonizing gentleness. "Everything." The dark promise in his words sent heat spiraling through me, pooling low in my belly. "Your trust. Your choice. Your surrender. Your body beneath mine."

The last words were barely a whisper, but they made my heart stutter in my chest, a rush of warmth and trepidation flooding me.

"Everything?" I whispered, my voice barely above a breath.

"I can hear your heart racing," he murmured, his voice dropping to that predatory purr that made my knees weak. "I can smell how much you want me. How much your body is responding to mine."

His thumb traced my lower lip, and I couldn't suppress the small sound that escaped me.

My face flushed with heat, but I couldn't deny any of it. "Matthias, I—"

"Tell me you don't feel it," he said, stepping closer until there was no space between us. "Tell me you don't want this."

I tried to form the words, to be sensible and rational, recalling everything David had taught me about not trusting vampires. But all I could think about was how Matthias looked at me like I was both precious and dangerous, how his presence made every nerve ending in my body come alive.

"I can't," I whispered.

"Can't what?"

"Can't tell you that I don't want this." The words came out in a rush, like I'd been holding my breath. "Even though I should. Even though I'm supposed to fear you."

Something blazed in his eyes: triumph and over-whelming hunger.

"So honest," he murmured. "Do you have any idea what that does to me? What you do to me?"

His other hand found my waist, pulling me closer until I could feel the energy radiating from his body.

I felt myself sway toward him, my eyes fluttering closed, lips parting as every nerve ending in my body came alive. The space between us felt electric, charged with possibility. He was going to kiss me. Finally, after all the tension and loaded glances and the way he looked at me like he wanted to devour me, he was going to—

He pulled back.

My eyes snapped open to find him watching me with an expression of such raw want that it made me dizzy. His breathing was ragged, his hands clenched at his sides like it was taking all his control not to reach for me, not to take what I was so clearly offering.

"Not yet," he said, his voice rough with restraint. "Not like this. Not when you don't understand what you're choosing."

"And if I'm not ready for that?"

"Then I'll wait." He moved to blow out several of the candles, throwing the chamber back into intimate shadow.

But I noticed the way his hand shook slightly as he reached for them. "I've waited centuries for someone like you."

Something about the way he said it made me study his face more closely. The exhaustion I'd noticed earlier was more pronounced now, and there was something fragile about him that hadn't been there before.

"Please tell me what's wrong with you," I said quietly.

His hand stilled on the candle. "What makes you think anything's wrong?"

"You're moving differently. Slower. And you keep fading somehow." I stepped closer, concern overriding caution.

For a moment, something desperate flickered across his expression before his usual control reasserted itself. "There is something," he admitted. "But once you know, everything changes. And I won't trap you with knowledge you're not ready for. Please, just trust me on this."

"Trust you." I laughed, but there was no humor in it. "Everyone keeps asking me to trust them without telling me anything. My uncle, you, even Helena at the library."

"Helena knows more about your family's history in Prague than she's admitted." Matthias's expression grew serious. "Tomorrow, you should ask her about the real reason those manuscripts were scattered. And about why certain pages were specifically torn out."

"She'll tell me the truth?"

"She'll tell you what she thinks you need to know." He moved toward the passage we'd entered through. "But Sera, be careful who you trust completely. Even allies can have their own agendas."

"Including you?"

He paused, his back to me. "Especially me."

The honesty in his admission should have frightened me. Instead, it made me want to comfort him, to ease whatever burden he was carrying.

"Matthias—"

"Close your eyes," he said softly.

I blinked, and suddenly I was standing on the sidewalk outside my hotel, the cool night air shocking against my flushed skin. The cobblestones beneath my feet, the familiar glow of the hotel's lobby lights, the distant sounds of Prague's nightlife: all of it felt surreal after the candlelit intimacy of the catacombs.

I spun around, but Matthias was nowhere to be seen.

10.5

MATTHIAS

They'd tried to take her again.

The scent of vampire ash still clung to my clothes as I descended through the hidden passages beneath Hradčany Castle. This time, I had faced two of them, organized and prepared in ways others hadn't been.

Someone had given them information.

The rage building in my chest had everything to do with betrayal. I'd made myself clear, Sera Sterling was under my protection. The claim had been acknowledged, witnessed, and spread throughout Prague's supernatural community.

Yet somehow, vampires continued to hunt her as if my words meant nothing.

I bypassed the throne room completely, moving through passages that even some of Isadora's guards weren't aware of. Her personal chambers were deep beneath the castle's foundation, guarded by wards that had been decades in the making.

They recognized me. They always had.

The door to her private sanctuary swung open as I approached, a heavy oak adorned with intricate carvings and an aged brass handle. I entered without warning, my anger leading the way.

Isadora's chambers were a study in luxury: silk tapestries from long-dead empires, furniture carved from woods that no longer existed, and books that predated the printing press. At the room's heart sat a massive four-poster bed draped in midnight velvet, and before it, Isadora herself.

She was seated at an ornate vanity, brushing her hair with a comb made from dragon bone. In the candlelight, her skin seemed to glow with its own inner fire, and she was dressed in nothing but a silk robe the color of fresh blood.

"Oh, hello Matthias," she said to my reflection in her mirror, a slow smile playing at her lips. "How unexpected. Have you come to my chambers for something more pleasant than business?" Her eyes met mine in the glass with an amused look. "You do seem rather worked up."

"I told you she was under my protection." My voice carried through the intimate space with enough menace to make the candles flicker. "Why are vampires still hunting her?"

She set down the comb slowly and turned to face me. "I'm sure I don't know what you mean."

I was across the room before she could blink, my hand slamming against the mirror beside her head hard enough to crack the glass. The crack spread outward like a spiderweb.

"Two vampires attacked her tonight. Two vampires who came prepared, who knew exactly what they were hunting." I leaned close enough that she had to meet my eyes. "That kind of coordination doesn't happen by accident."

"Matthias—"

"Someone told them. Someone with access to information about her movements, her routines." The energy in the room shifted as my control began to slip. "I want to know who."

The sound of the shattering mirror had brought her guards running. I could hear them gathering in the corridor outside, unsure whether to enter their queen's private chambers uninvited.

For a moment, Isadora stared at me. Then she sighed.

"Stand down," she commanded toward the door. "Leave us."

The corridor outside fell silent as her guards retreated. When we were alone, I noticed a flicker of uncertainty in her gaze.

"You really don't know, do you?" She rose from her vanity, moving to a side table where crystal decanters held blood. "The vampires hunting your Sterling girl aren't mine, Matthias. They're not even from Prague."

"Then who—"

"They're part of something much larger. Much more dangerous than random feeding." She poured herself a measure of the dark liquid, her movements betraying the first real tension I'd seen from her. "There's a faction of vampires who believe it's time for our kind to stop hiding in shadows."

My jaw clenched. "A faction?"

"They've been gathering forces across Europe, recruiting from the oldest bloodlines. Prague was supposed to remain neutral territory, but then your Sterling woman arrived and..." Isadora shrugged elegantly. "Suddenly, everyone became very interested in my city."

"You should have told me."

"And what would you have done? Declared war on half the vampire nobility in Europe?" Her laugh was bitter. "Even you have limits, darling."

I thought about Sera, probably still trying to process

everything I'd told her, still trusting that I could protect her from threats I barely understood myself. She had no idea she was at the center of something that could reshape the supernatural world.

"How many?" I asked.

"Dozens. Maybe more. They're not exactly sending me detailed reports." Isadora set down her glass. "Matthias, these aren't hungry fledglings or desperate outcasts. These are vampires with armies, with resources, with centuries of planning behind them."

"Planning what exactly?"

"That's what I'm trying to determine." Isadora moved closer, her expression serious. "But whatever they want her for, it's not just about Sterling blood's healing properties. This is something bigger."

"How much bigger?"

"The kind that makes old vampires abandon their territories and converge on one city." Her voice dropped. "The kind that has them willing to defy your protection claim and risk your wrath."

My hands clenched into fists. If vampires were willing to face me directly, whatever they were planning was worth the risk of my retaliation.

"How long do we have?"

"I don't know. But new vampires have been arriving every night. Old ones, powerful ones." Isadora studied my face. "This isn't just about territory anymore, is it? This isn't even about Sterling blood or its properties. This is personal."

I didn't answer. Didn't need to. She'd ruled for six centuries by reading the motivations of dangerous creatures, and whatever she saw in my face was apparently answer enough.

"Very well. I can see this means more to you than territorial politics." She moved back toward her vanity, settling into the ornate chair with renewed authority. "If it comes down to it, I will deploy my guards to protect her."

"That won't be enough."

"No," she agreed. "It won't. Which is why you're going to have to decide how much you're willing to sacrifice to keep her safe."

"Which is?"

"Stop playing games with her family. Stop letting David Sterling dictate the terms of engagement." Isadora's smile was knowing. "Either claim her properly, or lose her to whatever these vampires are planning."

The suggestion sent heat racing through my veins, but I forced myself to remain still. "She's not ready for that kind of truth."

"Then you'd better hope you can keep her alive long enough to become ready," Isadora said softly. "Because something tells me we don't have as much time as you think."

I turned and walked toward the door, my mind already racing with possibilities. Behind me, Isadora's voice followed.

"Matthias? Whatever you're planning, do it quickly. Soon, even I won't be able to keep them at bay."

The stone corridors stretched before me as I made my way to the surface. The weakness was spreading faster now, and I could feel my strength ebbing with each passing day.

If I didn't act soon, there would be nothing left of me to save her.

11

I barely slept.

Every time I closed my eyes, I was back in that candlelit chamber with Matthias, feeling his touch and the weight of his words: *Because the moment I saw you, I recognized what had always been inevitable.*

The memory made my skin flush with heat, even as my rational mind screamed warnings. *Eight-hundred-year-old vampires don't save random humans out of kindness.* David's voice echoed in my head, but it was becoming harder to believe when I remembered the way Matthias looked at me.

I was nursing my second cup of coffee when David's key jingled in the lock.

"You're up early," he said, shouldering his duffel bag. Dark circles shadowed his eyes, and his clothes looked like he'd slept in them.

"Couldn't sleep." I gestured to the coffee cup beside me. "How did it go at the safe house?"

David's expression grew focused as he set his bag on the desk. "Better than expected. Got the weapons we need, and the backup I called for is en route to Prague."

"Backup?"

"Elite hunters. The best of the best." David pulled out his phone, showing me a text message. "They'll be here later today."

The message was brief: *Assets in position. Ready for Phase Two on arrival.*

I took a breath, knowing I couldn't keep hiding what Matthias had told me. "David, there's something you need to know about last night."

He looked up, immediately alert. "What happened?"

"The vampires that have been after me... Matthias said they weren't random. That they're part of something organized." I wrapped my hands around my coffee mug for warmth. "Something that requires specific blood."

David went still. "When did you see him? Where?"

"He found me—"

"Found you where, Sera?" All trace of exhaustion was gone from David's voice. "You were supposed to stay near the hotel."

"I was near the hotel. He came to me." The half-truth felt necessary. I wasn't ready to explain the catacombs or how he'd taken me there. "He wanted to make sure I was okay."

"What did he tell you?" His voice was dangerously quiet.

"That Sterling blood has properties that make vampires stronger. That there are whispers about some kind of old ritual." I studied his face, seeing the way his jaw tightened. "You know something, don't you? About why they'd want our family specifically?"

David was quiet for a long moment, then stood and moved to the window. "Sterling family records were deliberately scattered centuries ago. Hidden across Europe to keep them from falling into the wrong hands."

"What kind of records?"

"The kind that detail our bloodline's unique properties." David turned back to me.

The library attack came back to me. Helena's reaction when she heard the Sterling name, the way she'd said "they've been searching for something." And Matthias had told me Helena was an ally, someone who could help me understand what I was facing.

"David," I said slowly, "I think I know where we can get answers."

He looked up. "What do you mean?"

"The library. When I first arrived, it had been ransacked. Helena was nervous about it, said someone had been searching for something." I met his eyes. "And when she heard the Sterling name, she got this look—like she knew exactly who I was and why I mattered."

"What kind of reaction?"

"Like she recognized it. She said something vague about 'them' searching for documents, but when I asked who 'they' were, she got evasive. Like she was hiding something."

"Why didn't you tell me this before?"

"Because I thought it was just a coincidence." I stood, pacing to the window.

David was silent for a long moment, his jaw working. "If vampires have been hunting for those records..."

"They're looking for something specific," I finished. "Something that tells them how to use our blood most effectively."

David's voice was grim. "Or something that tells them how to stop us."

The thought made my stomach drop. "We need to talk to Helena."

"We do." David stood, reaching for his jacket. "And we need to do it before the elite hunters arrive. If there's information about our family that vampires are desperate to get their hands on, I want to know what it is."

"Let's go," I said, checking that the silver knife was secure at my hip.

12

The library felt different when we arrived. The morning light streaming through the tall windows couldn't quite dispel the shadows that seemed to cling to the corners, and the air held that electric tension I was learning to associate with supernatural activity.

Helena looked up from her desk as we entered, and I saw her eyes widen slightly when she took in David's grim expression and the duffel bag slung over his shoulder.

"Dr. Sterling, Mr. Sterling," her voice more formal than usual.

"The break-ins," David said, stepping closer to her desk. "Sera told me someone ransacked this place looking for documents. What documents?"

Helena's eyes darted between us. "It was random vandalism. These old buildings are targets—"

"Don't lie to me." David's voice was sharp. "Sera said you mentioned 'they' were searching for something specific. Who are 'they'?"

Helena stood abruptly, her chair scraping against the floor. "Mr. Sterling, I think you're misunderstanding—"

"Am I?" David pulled out his phone, showing her something on the screen. "Because I just got word that libraries across Europe have been hit. Same pattern. Same kind of damage. All targeting medieval manuscript collections."

Helena's face drained of color as she looked at whatever David was showing her.

"So I'll ask you again," David said, his voice deadly quiet. "What were they looking for?"

Helena stared at the phone for a long moment, her hands trembling slightly. When she looked up, something had changed in her expression.

"You're not just a concerned uncle, are you?" she said quietly.

David slipped his phone back into his pocket. "What gave it away?"

"The way you move. The way you watch corners. The weapons." Helena's voice was steadier now. "You're a hunter."

"And you are not just a librarian."

Helena was quiet for a long moment, then moved to the tall bookshelf behind her desk. "No," she said softly. "I'm not."

She ran her fingers along the spines of old volumes, and I could swear I saw something shimmer in the air where she touched them.

"The break-ins weren't random vandalism," Helena said, not turning around. "They were vampires. And they've been searching for Sterling family documents across Europe for months."

David's hand moved toward his jacket. "How do you know that?"

"Because I've been protecting those documents." Helena pulled a leather-bound book from the shelf, and as she did, something shifted in the air around us. The shadows in the corners seemed to deepen, and the temperature dropped several degrees. "My family has been protecting them for generations."

She turned to face us, the book cradled in her arms, and I saw something in her eyes that hadn't been there before. Power.

"I've been waiting for a Sterling to return to Prague for twenty years," she said. "My grandmother helped your great-grandfather, Mr. Sterling. When he came to Prague in 1943, hunting a vampire coven that had been terrorizing the city."

David's hand was still on his weapon, but I could see uncertainty flickering in his eyes. "Why should I believe you?"

"Because," Helena said, opening the book, "I have this."

The pages were filled with handwritten notes in multiple languages, maps, sketches of supernatural creatures, and family trees that stretched back centuries. But what made me freeze was the photograph tucked between the pages.

A man who looked remarkably like David stood beside a woman with Helena's sharp features. Both were covered in blood, silver weapons in their hands, standing over the bodies of what were clearly vampires.

"Prague, 1943," Helena said softly. "Your great-grandfather, Thomas Sterling, and my grandmother, Marta Dvorak. They saved this city from a vampire uprising."

David took the photograph with shaking hands. "This is impossible. The family records never mentioned—"

"The family records were scattered for a reason," Helena interrupted. "Hidden, protected, kept from falling into the wrong hands. My family has been one of the guardians of that knowledge."

She moved to another section of the bookshelf, and this

time when her fingers brushed the books, I saw sparks of actual light dance between them. The shelf swung inward, revealing a hidden room beyond.

"The question is," Helena said, "are you ready to know what they contain?"

13

The hidden room was unlike anything I'd ever seen. Books lined the walls, their leather bindings cracked with age. Maps covered every available surface, marked with symbols that seemed to shift and move in the candlelight. And everywhere, scattered across tables and hanging from the ceiling, were protective charms that glowed with soft, silver light.

"Welcome," Helena said, "to the real Strahov library. The one that matters."

David stepped into the room, his weapon finally lowered. "How long have you been—"

"Guarding this knowledge? Since I was sixteen." Helena raised her hand, and with a gesture, dozens of candles throughout the room flickered to life simultaneously, filling the space with warm, golden light. "Since the night I discovered I had the power to fight back."

She moved to the largest map of Prague, pointing to symbols that pulsed with faint light. "In 1943, vampires discovered something beneath this city. Sacred ritual sites, chambers carved into the bedrock where old magic still runs strong."

"What kind of ritual sites?" David asked.

"The kind that can amplify supernatural ceremonies beyond normal limitations." Helena's expression was grim. "Your great-grandfather came here because they were planning to use these sites to create a vampire leader nearly impossible to kill—one powerful enough to command others and build an army that could reshape Europe."

"And they're trying again," I said quietly.

"Yes. But this time, they have what they lacked before." Helena's eyes met mine. "A female Sterling from the direct bloodline whose blood carries the exact magical signature the ritual requires."

"How do you know that?" I asked.

"Because I can sense the magical currents building. Dark magic, old magic." Helena gestured to the maps and charts around us. "The same magic that was used for the last attempt."

David stepped forward. "How much time do we have?"

"The blood moon is in three weeks," Helena said quietly. "And I can feel them gathering. Old vampires, powerful ones, all converging on Prague."

"That's why they wanted the manuscripts," David said, understanding dawning in his voice. "The ritual instructions."

"The location of the ritual sites, the specific require-ments, the timing." Helena nodded. "Everything they need to succeed."

I felt sick. "And they need me alive for it to work."

"Yes," Helena said softly.

"I need to tell the other hunters about this," David said, pulling out his phone.

Suddenly, the protective charms hanging throughout Helena's hidden room began to glow brighter, pulsing with urgent silver light. The candles flickered as if touched by an unseen wind.

Helena's head snapped up; her expression immediately alert. "Someone's in the library," she said quietly. "Someone with weapons."

David's hand moved instinctively to his jacket. "How many?"

"One. But powerful." Helena was already moving toward the hidden entrance, her fingers weaving dismissal patterns over the concealing wards. "We should go see who—"

"David?" A familiar voice called from the main library. "I know you're here somewhere."

14

Helena's wards shimmered and faded, revealing the entrance to the main library. We stepped through to find Elena Sterling, my cousin, standing among the towering bookshelves, her dark hair pulled back in a tight bun, and her hazel eyes scanning the baroque interior.

But the woman walking toward us bore little resemblance to the laughing teenager I remembered from childhood visits. This woman looked capable of snapping someone's neck without blinking, dressed in dark tactical gear that revealed the arsenal of silver tools strapped to her body.

Elena's gaze found us immediately, then swept past us to take in the still-glowing entrance to Helena's hidden room. Her expression turned to disgust.

"A witch?" Elena's voice dripped with contempt. "You're trusting a witch?"

"Elena," David said, his voice carrying a warning. "Helena has information we need."

"Information that conveniently supports whatever agenda she's pushing." Elena's hand moved to rest on a silver blade at her hip. "How long has she been manipulating you?"

"She hasn't been manipulating anyone," I said, finding my voice. "She's been protecting our family's history."

Elena's attention snapped to me. "Our family's history? Sera, you've been in Prague for less than a week. You don't know what our history really is."

"Then maybe you should tell me," I said, surprising myself with my defiance.

"Our history is four centuries of hunting vampires alone. Of staying pure, staying focused, staying alive by trusting only family." Elena's voice was cold. "Magic corrupts everything it touches. Including allies."

Helena stepped forward, her chin lifted with quiet dignity. "Your great-grandfather didn't think so when my grandmother saved his life."

"I've heard enough," Elena said, her hand tightening on her weapon's hilt.

Helena's hands glowed faintly with light, preparing to defend herself. "Miss Sterling, I understand your distrust, but—"

David stepped between them, hands raised. "Enough. Both of you." He turned to Elena. "What's the situation with the other hunters?"

Elena relaxed her grip, but her stance remained ready for violence. "They're in position. Twelve elite hunters, the best the Council could spare." Her eyes flicked to me. "Everything's ready."

David nodded grimly. "Good. The sooner we move, the better."

"And we do it clean," Elena said, her eyes flicking back to Helena. "No magical interference."

"This isn't interference," Helena said steadily. "This is an offer of help from someone who's been fighting vampires longer than you've been alive."

Elena's laugh was bitter. "Help that comes with strings attached. Magic always does." She turned to David. "Tell me you're not seriously considering this."

David was quiet for a long moment, his steel-gray eyes moving between Helena and Elena. "I'm considering using every advantage we have," he said finally.

"Hunters work alone, David. It's what keeps us alive." Elena's voice carried finality. "Even allies can become liabilities."

"And what if you're wrong?" I asked, my voice stronger than I expected. "What if Helena's right about how dangerous these vampires are? What if your plan isn't enough?"

Elena's attention focused on me with laser intensity. "Then we adapt. We fight. We die if necessary." Her voice softened slightly. "But we do it as Sterlings. As hunters. Not as pawns in some witch's game."

The finality in her tone made it clear that no amount of arguing would change her mind. Elena had made her decision about Helena long before she'd walked into this room.

"Fine," David said, his voice heavy with resignation. "We do this your way, Elena. Sterling methods only."

Helena's expression was sad but unsurprised. "If that's your choice, I won't interfere."

Elena's face filled with satisfaction. "Good." She turned to David. "We need to move. The safe house is ready, and the others are waiting for a briefing."

"Give us a few minutes," David said. "I want to gather some of those manuscripts Helena showed us. Intelligence we can use."

Elena nodded curtly. "Five minutes. Then we leave." She

moved toward the main library, clearly wanting distance from Helena's magical sanctuary.

As Elena disappeared through the entrance, the tension in the room felt heavier, weighted with missed opportunities and the growing certainty that we were heading into something far more dangerous than Elena's confidence indicated.

David moved to examine the old maps Helena had shown us, his weathered fingers tracing the supernatural energy lines that crisscrossed beneath Prague. The candlelight cast deep shadows across his face, making him look older, more tired than I'd ever seen him.

Helena approached me quietly, her eyes filled with concern. When she spoke, her voice was barely above a whisper.

"You've been with him," she said.

I felt heat rise in my cheeks. "I don't know what you mean."

Helena's light eyes studied my face with unsettling intensity. "The old one. The vampire who's been watching you." She tilted her head slightly, as if listening to something I couldn't hear. "His scent is all over you."

My pulse quickened. "How do you know about him?"

"I can sense supernatural encounters. Old magic leaves traces." Helena moved to a shelf lined with small glass vials and silver trinkets. "He's powerful. And he's been protecting you."

"He saved my life," I said quietly.

"More than once, I'd guess." Helena's fingers moved over her collection. "And each time, the bond between you grows stronger."

I thought about the electric shock every time Matthias touched me, the way my dreams had grown more vivid since arriving in Prague, the pull I felt toward him that defied all logic.

"Is that bad?" I asked quietly.

Helena was quiet for a moment, selecting a small silver pendant from her collection. "That depends on what you choose to do about it."

She held up the pendant, carved with intricate symbols that seemed to shift and move. As she whispered words in a language I didn't recognize, the pendant began to glow with soft, warm light.

"Your family doesn't understand the true scope of what they're facing," Helena said, fastening the pendant around my neck. The metal was warm against my skin, and I felt a subtle shift in the air around me, as if I'd been wrapped in an invisible shield. "The vampires planning this ritual aren't just any vampires. They're old, powerful. Desperate."

"What do you mean?"

"Female Sterling blood from the direct bloodline carries ancient magic." Helena's eyes met mine. "The ritual requires something very specific: your heritage, your gender, your connection to the original Sterling power. That's why they've been searching so desperately for you."

"The pendant will help," Helena continued. "It will hide your scent from weaker vampires, make you harder to track. But it won't work against him, your connection is too strong for simple magic to mask."

Helena pressed something else into my hand—a small piece of parchment covered in symbols. "If you need me," she said quietly, "burn this. I'll know."

I nodded, touching the pendant through my shirt. Its warmth pulsed against my palm.

"I've seen glimpses of possible futures," Helena said softly, "and in most of them, the choices you make in the coming days determine whether Prague falls to darkness or finds a new kind of balance."

"Balance?"

"Between the supernatural world and the human one. Between hunters and their prey." Helena's expression was grave. "Some choices can't be undone, Sera. And some bonds, once acknowledged, can never be broken."

Before I could ask what she meant, David's voice interrupted us. "Sera, we need to go. Elena's getting impatient."

I turned to see David approaching, several of Helena's manuscripts tucked under his arm. His steel-gray eyes took in the pendant at my throat, but he didn't comment.

"Ready?" he asked.

I looked back at Helena. "Thank you."

"Don't thank me yet," she said softly. "Save your gratitude for when you're still alive to give it."

As we left Helena's sanctuary and stepped back into the main library, I could feel the protective magic settling around me like a second skin. It was comforting, but it also served as a reminder of how much danger I was really in.

Elena was waiting for us near the library entrance, her eyes immediately fixing on my new pendant.

"What's that?" she demanded.

"A gift," I said, meeting her gaze steadily.

Elena's expression darkened. "We don't accept gifts from witches."

"Well," I said, lifting my chin, "maybe it's time we started making some exceptions."

Elena's eyes narrowed, but David stepped between us before she could speak.

"Enough," he said firmly. "We have work to do."

15

The hunter safe house was nothing like I'd expected. Located in a converted warehouse in Prague's industrial district, it looked abandoned from the outside. Broken windows covered with plywood, graffiti scrawled across brick walls. But the moment Elena led us through the reinforced steel door, I stepped into what could only be described as a military operation.

Silver weapons lined the walls in neat, deadly arrays. Maps of Prague covered every surface, marked with red pins. Computer screens displayed what looked like surveillance footage from across the city. And in the center of it all, twelve figures dressed in black tactical gear turned to assess me with cold, calculating eyes.

"Everyone," Elena announced, her voice carrying authority. "Meet our primary asset."

Asset. Not person, not family member. Asset.

The hunters moved to form a loose circle around me, and I felt like a specimen under examination. Men and women of various ages and builds, but they all shared the same predatory stillness that reminded me of the vampires

I'd encountered. The only difference was that these predators hunted the supernatural rather than humans.

"Sterling bloodline confirmed?" asked a tall man with graying temples and scars that traced white lines across his throat.

"Female direct bloodline confirmed," David said quietly. "And we now know why that matters specifically."

The way he said it made my stomach churn, as if my worth as a person had been decided by some supernatural genetic lottery and my complete ignorance of my own heritage.

"Excellent." The scarred man's smile widened. "I'm Commander Hayes. These are my specialists, the best vampire hunters the Council has produced in three generations."

Hayes gestured to the others, rattling off specialties. Demolitions. Tracking. Weapons. Torture and interrogation. Each introduction made me feel smaller, more like a tool in their war than a person with agency.

"David briefed us on the intelligence you gathered," Hayes continued, moving to the largest map of Prague. "Vampires converging on the city for a ritual that requires her specifically. Our strategy is straightforward: we use their desperation against them."

"The scope is larger than we initially assessed," Elena added, pointing to marked locations on the map. "This isn't just a local threat. Intelligence indicates vampires from across Europe are involved."

"And they're all here for the blood moon deadline," Hayes said grimly. "When supernatural energy peaks and their ceremony becomes possible."

I thought about Helena's warnings, about the magical currents she could sense building. "And you think your plan can stop them?"

"It's our best chance," Hayes said grimly. "Maybe our only chance."

The room fell silent except for the hum of electronic equipment. I looked around at the faces surrounding me— focused, determined, completely committed to a plan that required me to walk into mortal danger.

"How?" David asked, his voice tight.

Hayes's smile made my skin crawl. "We let them take her."

"Absolutely not." David was on his feet instantly, his hand moving toward his weapon. "I won't let you use her as bait."

"She's not bait," Elena said calmly. "She's the key to ending this threat permanently. We let them take her, track them to their ritual site, and eliminate the entire vampire leadership in one coordinated strike."

"And if something goes wrong?" I found my voice, surprised by how steady it sounded. "If your timing is off, or they change locations, or—"

"Then we kill you ourselves," Hayes said flatly. "Better you die than they create a vampire king with female Sterling blood. If we lose you, at least the ritual becomes impossible forever."

The casual way he spoke about my death sent a cold chill down my spine. These people didn't see me as family or even as human. I was a tool to be used and discarded if necessary.

"There has to be another way," David insisted.

"There is no other way," Elena replied. "We've been hunting vampires for four centuries, David. This is how it works. Sacrifice for the greater good."

"Easy to say when it's not your life on the line," I said quietly.

Elena's hazel eyes fixed on me with something like

disappointment. "It has been my life on the line. Multiple times. I've taken wounds that should have killed me, lost partners, watched good hunters die because we couldn't get close enough to vampire leadership to make a real difference."

She stepped closer. "This is our chance to end it. To make their deaths mean something."

"And if I refuse?"

"You don't get to refuse," Hayes said. "You're irreplaceable to them, which makes you irreplaceable to us."

The casual cruelty of it left me speechless. I looked at David, hoping for support, for someone to tell Hayes he was wrong. But my uncle's face was filled with resignation.

"There might be other options," David said weakly. "If we had more time to plan—"

"We don't have time," Elena interrupted. "Every day we wait, more vampires arrive in Prague. More civilians die. The longer we delay, the stronger they become."

She pulled out a tablet, showing surveillance footage of Prague's streets. Dark figures moving too fast for the cameras to capture clearly. Bodies found drained of blood in alleyways. Missing persons reports that police couldn't explain.

"They're not waiting for the blood moon to start killing," Elena said. "Every night brings more death. How many lives are you willing to sacrifice to protect one?"

The footage made me sick, but something about Elena's argument felt rehearsed. Too convenient.

"The blood moon gives us three weeks to position our people," Elena added. "Time to prepare for the largest vampire hunting operation in Prague's history."

I thought about Matthias, about the way he'd looked at me in the candlelit chamber. *I can't lose you. Not when I've finally found you.* If the hunters were right, if every vampire in Prague was hunting me, then he was just another predator. Another monster using me for his own purposes.

But when he'd touched my throat, checking for injuries, it hadn't felt predatory. It had felt protective.

"What if you're wrong?" I said quietly. "What if there are vampires who don't want me dead? What if some of them are trying to help?"

The reaction was immediate and visceral. Several hunters reached for weapons. Hayes's expression turned thunderous.

"There are no good vampires," Elena said flatly. "They're parasites, Sera. Killers who feed on human blood and death. Any vampire who seems helpful is just a more sophisticated predator."

"But—"

"No." David stood, his voice carrying an authority I rarely heard from him. "Elena's right. I know you want to believe there might be exceptions, but there aren't. Vampires lie, manipulate, and seduce. It's what they do."

The conviction in his voice hurt more than Hayes's casual cruelty. David knew me, loved me, and he was telling me that any vampire who seemed to care was just playing a game.

"The plan is sound," Hayes continued, moving back to the maps. "We have three weeks to prepare. Sera will continue her normal routine: the library, her research, visible and accessible. When they come for her, we'll be ready."

"What's my part in this?" David asked.

"Stay close but not too close," Elena replied. "We need her to look vulnerable, not protected. And David?" She met his eyes. "When the time comes, you let her go. No heroic rescue attempts. No deviation from the plan."

David's jaw worked silently, but he nodded.

"Any questions?" Hayes asked.

I had a thousand questions, but looking around the room at the faces of trained killers, I realized none of them would matter. These people had already decided my fate. I was a weapon in their war, nothing more.

"When do we start?" I asked.

"You already have," Elena said with satisfaction. "Every time you leave your hotel, every time you go to the library or walk Prague's streets, you're fulfilling your part of the plan."

As the hunters began discussing logistics and positioning, I found myself thinking about Helena's hidden sanctuary, about the pendant warming against my skin, about the way Matthias had looked at me in those candlelit chambers when he'd said I was everything to him.

The hunters saw me as a sacrifice for the greater good. But maybe there were other choices. Maybe there were people, or things, in Prague who saw me as more than just a weapon.

I touched the pendant beneath my shirt, feeling its subtle pulse. Three weeks until the blood moon. Twenty-one days to decide whether I trusted my family's certainty or my own growing instincts.

The countdown had begun.

16

The hotel room felt like a cage.

I'd been pacing for most of two hours, wearing a path between the tall windows and the antique desk where my laptop sat closed and untouched. Every attempt to focus on something normal: checking email, reviewing my research notes, even mindless social media scrolling, lasted maybe five minutes before my thoughts circled back to the safe house briefing.

Then we kill you ourselves.

Hayes's words echoed in my head. My own family, people who claimed to love me, had contingency plans for my murder. Not if I was turned into a vampire, not if I became a threat, but simply if their tactical plan went wrong. I was acceptable collateral damage in their war.

I stopped at the window, my forehead resting against the cool glass. Outside, Prague's red rooftops stretched toward the castle on the hill, the same view that had enchanted me just days ago. Now it looked different. Every shadow could hide something hunting me, and every person who claimed to protect me saw me as expendable.

Helena's pendant pulsed warmly against my skin,

keeping a steady rhythm that seemed to mirror my emotional state. When I first put it on, the warmth had been gentle, barely noticeable. But as the afternoon went on and my agitation increased, it became more noticeable. Now it felt almost alive against my throat, like a second heartbeat.

I pulled the small piece of parchment from my pocket, the one Helena had pressed into my hand before we left the library. The symbols covering its surface seemed to shift in the lamplight, not quite moving but not quite still either. *If you need me, burn this. I'll know.*

Magic. Real magic, from someone who'd offered to help without treating me like a weapon or a sacrifice. The contrast with my family's approach was stark.

My phone buzzed against the desk. A text from David: *Staying at safe house tonight. Coordination meetings. Door locked?*

I typed back: *Yes. Fine here.*

Another lie. I wasn't fine. I was trapped in a hotel room, waiting to be used as bait by people who would kill me if their plan failed. Meanwhile, somewhere in Prague's underground passages, an eight-hundred-year-old vampire had looked at me with possessive hunger and promised things I didn't understand but desperately wanted to.

The memory of him sent heat spiraling through my body despite everything I'd been told. Matthias had saved my life twice, had shown me gentleness even after displaying lethal violence. When he touched me, it didn't feel like manipulation or predation. It felt like recognition.

But David's voice echoed alongside the memory: *Vampires lie, manipulate, and seduce. It's what they do.*

I sank into the antique chair by the window, rubbing my temples where a headache was building. How was I supposed to know who to trust? My family, who'd lied to me my entire life and now saw me as expendable? Helena, who offered magical protection but remained mysterious about her true nature? Or Matthias, who made me feel things I'd never experienced but whose very existence challenged everything I'd been taught about right and wrong?

The pendant pulsed again, stronger this time, and I found myself thinking about those candlelit chambers beneath the cathedral. The way shadows had danced across the stone, the electric tension in the air when Matthias had stepped close enough for me to catch his scent

Soon. Very soon.

That had been his promise. But when was soon? And what exactly was I supposed to understand before he'd tell me the truth?

I pulled out my laptop, thinking academic work might distract me from my thoughts. But when I opened my research files, all I could see were the annotations in those scattered manuscripts, the marginalia that suggested centuries of supernatural encounters. Evidence that the folklore I'd been studying wasn't folklore at all, but historical documentation of a hidden world.

A world I was now part of, whether I wanted to be or not.

The cursor blinked in the empty document, mocking my inability to focus. I had a dissertation to write, academic deadlines to meet, and a career to build. Normal concerns from a life that felt increasingly distant and irrelevant.

Outside, the afternoon light was beginning to fade. Soon it would be evening, then night. And at night, Prague's supernatural residents emerged from whatever hiding places they used during the day.

At night, I might see him again.

I should have been afraid. According to my family, according to centuries of Sterling tradition, vampires were monsters who used and discarded humans without conscience. I should be afraid of Matthias, should want nothing more than to stay locked in this hotel room until the hunters could eliminate the threat he represented.

Instead, I found myself reflecting on the way he'd pulled back when I leaned into his touch. The restraint in his voice when he said *Not yet.* If he had been a manipulative predator, wouldn't he have taken advantage of my obvious attraction? Wouldn't he have pushed for more instead of stepping away?

Not until you understand what you're choosing.

What was I choosing? And when would I understand enough to make that choice?

The pendant pulsed again, and I wondered if it was responding to something more than just my emotional state. Helena had said it would hide my scent from weaker vampires, but that it wouldn't work against him. That our connection was too strong for simple magic to mask.

Our connection.

Even Helena, a witch who'd been fighting vampires since she was sixteen, acknowledged that there was something between Matthias and me. Something that transcended the usual predator-prey dynamic.

I stood up, abandoning any pretense of working. The hotel room felt smaller with each passing minute, the walls closing in like a prison. I needed air, space, movement. I needed to think somewhere other than this suffocating box where my family's expectations and fears pressed in from all sides.

The hunters wanted me to continue my normal routine. Go to the library, walk Prague's streets, be visible and accessible. They saw it as fulfilling my role in their plan, making myself available as bait.

But what if I used that freedom differently? What if,

instead of passively waiting to be captured, I took control of the situation?

I grabbed my jacket, checking that the silver knife was secure at my hip. Helena's pendant pulsed warm against my throat, and the parchment with her communication spell crinkled softly in my pocket.

Twenty-one days of being treated like an object by my own family, waiting for a plan that ended with my potential murder.

Or I could make my own choice. Seek my own answers.

Find out what *soon* meant.

The door clicked shut behind me as I stepped into the hotel corridor. I felt like I could breathe again. Somewhere in this city, a vampire was waiting.

17

I had no conscious plan when I left the hotel, but my feet seemed to know where they were going.

Through the winding cobblestone streets, past the baroque facades and Gothic spires that had become familiar landmarks. The evening air carried the scent of autumn and old stone, and shadows gathered in doorways. But for the first time since arriving in Prague, I wasn't afraid of what might be hiding in those shadows.

The pull I felt was different tonight. Not the vague sense of being called that had haunted my dreams, but something more immediate. More urgent. Like a compass needle finding true north, every step felt inevitable.

St. Vitus Cathedral rose before me as I climbed the hill toward Prague Castle, its Gothic spires piercing the darkening sky. During the day, it was a tourist destination filled with visitors and tour guides. But now, with evening settling over the city, it felt timeless and mysterious, a monument to secrets older than the stones that built it.

I circled the cathedral's exterior, running my fingers along the weathered stone walls. Somewhere beneath this ground were the chambers I'd seen in my dreams, the passages Matthias had led me through just two nights ago. But how was I supposed to find them on my own?

Feel the path instead of seeing it.

His words echoed in my memory as I closed my eyes, letting my other senses guide me. The wind carried hints of leather and smoke, so faint I might have imagined them. But Helena's pendant grew warm against my throat, confirming what my instincts already knew.

He was here. Somewhere below.

I found the iron gate hidden behind overgrown ivy almost by accident, my searching fingers brushing against cold metal where there should have been only stone. It stood slightly ajar, just as it had before, waiting for me.

The passage beyond was pitch black, but I didn't hesitate. I'd done this before, guided by his hand and his voice. Now I would do it alone.

The descent felt longer without his steadying presence beside me. My phone's flashlight created a small circle of illumination, but beyond its reach, darkness pressed in from all sides. The stone walls were damp with moisture, carved with symbols that seemed to shift in the moving light.

When the passage finally opened into the familiar chamber, I almost cried with relief.

Dozens of candles flickered in their iron brackets, casting dancing shadows across the walls. The space looked exactly as I remembered. It was beautiful and somehow alive with power that made the air itself electric.

But Matthias was nowhere to be seen.

"Hello?" My voice echoed off the vaulted ceiling, smaller than I'd intended. "I know you're here."

Silence answered me, broken only by the soft drip of water somewhere in the darkness beyond the candlelight. I moved deeper into the chamber, my footsteps loud on the stone floor.

"I came to find you," I called out, feeling slightly foolish. "I need answers."

"Do you?"

His voice came from behind me, rich and low with that accent that sent shivers down my spine. I spun around to find him emerging from an alcove I hadn't noticed, moving with that control that made my pulse race.

But something was wrong.

He looked different from how he did two nights ago. He looked drained, with shadows under his green eyes that suggested exhaustion or pain. When he moved into the candlelight, I could see the sharp planes of his face more clearly, and his usual poise seemed diminished, as if his strength was fading.

"You look terrible," I said before I could stop myself.

A ghost of a smile crossed his lips. "Such flattery. No wonder I'm enamored."

"I'm serious." I stepped closer, noting the way he held himself with forced stillness, as if movement cost him effort. "What's wrong with you?"

"Nothing that concerns—" He started to give me the same dismissive answer as before, then stopped, studying my face in the flickering light. "You came to me. Alone. By choice."

"Yes."

Something shifted in his expression. "Why?

I thought about the safe house briefing, about being treated like an asset and threatened with execution if their plan failed. About my family's casual willingness to sacrifice me for the greater good.

"Because everyone else in this city sees me as a tool," I said quietly. "Something to be used and discarded when convenient. But you told me I was everything to you." I paused, searching his face. "What does that actually mean?"

His eyes darkened. "It means I'd burn this entire city to keep you safe."

His quiet, intense words sent a surge of heat through me.

"What's happening to you?" I stepped closer, noting the way he held himself. "You're weaker than you were two nights ago."

He was quiet for a long moment, seeming to weigh his words. "Time is running out."

"What do you mean?"

"For choices to be made." His fingers brushed against my cheek. "For you to decide what you want."

I searched his face, looking for more answers, but found nothing. "You're being evasive."

"I'm being careful." His thumb traced along my jawline. "Some knowledge comes with a price."

"Is it more dangerous than being hunted by old vampires who want to use my blood?" I moved closer, close enough that there was no space between us. "More dangerous than my own family planning to kill me if their rescue plan fails?"

His entire body went rigid. "They what?"

"You heard me. If the hunters can't extract me before the ritual is completed, they'll kill me themselves rather than let my blood be used." I reached up, my fingers tracing the sharp line of his jaw. "So don't talk to me about danger, Matthias. I'm already living on borrowed time."

Something blazed in his eyes, a fury and possession so intense it should have terrified me. Instead, it made heat pool low in my belly.

"They wouldn't dare—" He stopped, visibly struggling for control. "You're under my protection."

"What right do you have?" I challenged. "You keep saying I'm yours, but you won't tell me what that means." My voice dropped to barely above a whisper. "You won't even kiss me."

My words lingered, a challenge and a confession rolled

into one. His eyes darkened, and I could see the control he'd been maintaining start to crack.

"Sera," he said, my name a warning.

"What?" I closed the distance between us, my body barely brushing against his. "Are you afraid of what I might choose if you actually told me the truth?"

"I'm afraid," he said, his voice rough with something deeper than restraint, "that you'd choose me for the wrong reasons."

"What if I choose you anyway?"

The question hung between us as he stared at me for a long moment, something raw and hungry flickering across his features.

"Beg me," he said, his voice dropping to that commanding whisper that made liquid heat pool between my thighs.

"What?"

His hands slid down to my hips, fingers gripping with possessiveness. "If you want this, then beg me to kiss you."

He leaned closer, his lips barely grazing the shell of my ear. "And say please," he murmured, his breath cool against my heated skin.

I shivered as he traced a path down the side of my neck with his nose, just breathing me in. One hand released my hip to slide into my hair, tilting my head back to expose my throat.

"I can hear your heartbeat," he whispered against my pulse point, his lips so close I could feel them brushing against my skin. "Racing. For me." His voice dropped even lower. "I can smell how much you want this."

The power dynamic shifted between us. He was giving me control while taking it away at the same time, making me acknowledge exactly what I wanted while torturing me with almost-touches that left me aching for more.

I should have been offended. Should have turned around and walked away. Instead, I felt myself melting under the heat of his gaze.

"Please," I whispered, my voice barely audible in the candlelit chamber.

His smile was slow and predatory, full of dark promise. "Please what?"

"Please kiss me."

He reached up, his hands framing my face with that gentleness that made my heart race. For a moment, we stood frozen like that, his lips brushing against mine.

"When I finally claim you," he murmured, "you'll surrender everything to me. Your body, your blood, your choice." His eyes searched mine. "Are you ready for that?"

"I—" I started to answer.

"You hesitate," he said, though I could see the strain of that restraint in every line of his body. "That tells me everything I need to know."

Frustration and desire warred in my chest, leaving me breathless and aching. "There's just so much I don't know. So much happening."

"I know," he said, moving toward the shadows at the edge of the chamber. "Soon."

"That's not an answer," I called after him.

He paused at the edge of the candlelight, turning back to look at me one last time. In the flickering shadows, his eyes seemed to glow with an inner fire.

"You won't have to wait much longer," he said softly.

And then he was gone, vanishing into the darkness as if he'd never been there at all. I was left alone in the candlelit chamber, desire still coiling tight in my chest and my mind reeling with questions he'd refused to answer.

18

The streets felt different as I made my way back through town. The narrow alleys were quieter now, most of the late-night crowds having moved toward the busier squares. Streetlamps cast pools of amber light every fifty feet, leaving deep shadows between the baroque facades.

Please kiss me.

The memory of my own voice, breathless and pleading in that candlelit chamber, made heat flood my cheeks again. The way he'd looked at me when I'd begged, like he wanted to devour me whole. The promise in his words about claiming me, owning me completely.

And then he'd walked away. Again.

I pulled my jacket tighter, my footsteps echoing off the stones. Matthias kept pushing me to the edge, making me want things I'd never wanted before, then pulling back just when I thought he might finally—

A shadow moved in my peripheral vision.

I stopped, skin prickling with sudden awareness. I looked into the alley between two buildings, but nothing stirred in its depths. Just the gleam of wet cobblestones and the distant drip of water from a downspout. The protection pendant Helena had given me remained cool against my throat.

Maybe I was being paranoid. After everything that had happened tonight—the intensity of being alone with Matthias, the way he'd made my body respond to his every word and touch—it was natural to feel unsettled.

But as I continued walking, the sensation of being watched settled between my shoulder blades like a target. The street felt too quiet now, too empty. Even the distant sounds of Prague's nightlife seemed muffled.

The road curved ahead, leading toward the main square where late-night cafes still glowed with warm light. Safety lay in that direction: people, witnesses, the kind of public spaces where supernatural predators rarely struck. I quickened my pace.

Fear shot through me as hands grabbed me from behind, one clamping over my mouth before I could scream. The taste of iron filled my senses as I was lifted off my feet and dragged backward. *No, no, no*— My mind reeled between panic and the desperate need to fight.

My training kicked in through the fear—I bit down hard on the fingers covering my mouth, tasting blood, and drove my elbow back into my captor's ribs with everything I had.

He grunted but didn't release me. His grip was like steel, inhuman in its strength. The realization that I was truly helpless sent terror through me.

"Spirited little thing," a voice said with cold amusement. "I can see why he's taken such an interest."

Two more figures emerged from the shadows ahead of me, moving with that same elegance that meant only one thing. My stomach dropped. Vampires. The way they moved, casual and confident, told me I was completely outmatched.

Helena's pendant suddenly blazed with silver light against my throat, hot enough to sear my skin. My captor cursed in a language I didn't recognize, his grip loosening just enough for me to twist partially free. Adrenaline and desperation gave me strength I didn't know I had. I managed to get one arm loose and reached for the silver knife at my hip.

A hand shot out faster than my eyes could track, wrapping around my wrist and squeezing until I felt bones grinding together. The knife clattered uselessly to the rain-slicked stone.

"Now, now," the vampire said with mock gentleness. His accent carried hints of old Europe, cultured and aristocratic. "We can't have you hurting yourself."

He was tall and lean, with sharp features and dark hair slicked back. When he smiled, showing his fangs, I recoiled.

"Sterling blood," the female vampire murmured, inhaling deeply. Auburn hair framed a striking face. "Even better than the legends suggested."

"The master will be pleased," the one behind me said. "We can finally proceed as planned."

"I won't help you with anything." The words came out fiercer than I felt.

"Oh, but you will." The female vampire smiled, and the certainty in her voice made nausea rise in my throat.

"Matthias won't let you—" I started, grasping for anything that might make them hesitate.

The tall one laughed. "The vampire who's been terrorizing Prague? Oh yes, he's certainly become inconvenient." His grip tightened on my wrist until I bit back a cry of pain. "But we're not some desperate fledglings hunting alone. We're older, patient, and we've been studying his patterns for weeks."

The female vampire pulled out a metal collar, inscribed

with strange symbols. "This will mask your scent completely and sap your strength. Your vampire won't be able to track you."

Dread washed over me as I realized what she meant. The collar would cut me off from any possibility of rescue, make me invisible to whatever supernatural senses Matthias used to find me.

"Please," I whispered, hating how small my voice sounded. "You don't have to do this."

"But we do." The tall vampire's smile was cold. "Sterling blood is too valuable to leave unguarded, and your protector has become too much of a threat to our operations."

The collar snapped around my throat, cold metal burning against my skin. Immediately, I felt something vital drain away—my strength, the sharpened awareness I'd been developing. The world seemed duller, muted.

"Much better," the female vampire said with satisfaction. "Now your scent is completely masked."

They began moving through the alley, half-carrying me between them. I struggled, but whatever the collar was doing had left me weak and disoriented.

"Where are you taking me?" I managed to ask.

"Somewhere safe," the tall vampire replied. "Somewhere your cursed knight will never think to look."

We emerged from the alley onto a side street I didn't recognize. A black sedan waited with its engine running, windows tinted dark enough to hide what was inside.

As they pushed me toward the car, I caught sight of a familiar figure at the far end of the street. Tall, dark-haired, moving with desperate speed through the shadows.

Matthias.

He must have sensed something was wrong, must have followed my path from the cathedral. But even as I opened my mouth to scream for him, I knew it was useless. The collar had severed his ability to track me.

The car door opened, and I was shoved inside. Through the rear window, I watched Matthias reach the mouth of the alley we'd emerged from, his head turning as he searched for some trace of where I'd gone.

He was too late.

19

I'd lost track of time in this windowless room. The collar around my neck made everything feel distant and hazy, muted. Without windows or clocks, I could only guess that it had been two days since they'd shoved me into the car and brought me here.

The room was small, stone-walled, lit by a single bare bulb that cast shadows in the corners. Old stonework, probably part of Prague's underground tunnels. My wrists were shackled to the wall with heavy iron chains, the metal now slick with dried blood from my earlier struggles.

Eight vampires took shifts watching me, rotating in pairs. I'd counted them during the lucid moments when the collar's effects lessened slightly. Always two sets of eyes, always alert. Organized and disciplined.

The first day had been the worst. They'd given me water twice and some kind of stale bread once. Just enough to keep me alive, nothing more. By now, my stomach had stopped cramping with hunger and settled into a hollow ache that the collar's draining effects made feel almost bearable. Almost.

I'd tested the chains early on, pulling until my wrists

were raw. The iron was solid, the bolts secure. All I'd accomplished was making the shackles slippery and adding another layer of discomfort.

The door opened with its familiar creak, and two guards entered: the auburn-haired woman from my capture and a stocky vampire with scarred hands. They settled into chairs across from me.

"Still refusing to cooperate?" the woman asked, pulling out her small notebook. "Lord Casimir grows impatient."

I didn't answer. The collar sapped not just my strength, but my will to fight. Now I focused on staying conscious, on keeping some part of myself intact under the magical suppression.

"The Sterling archives," the scarred vampire said, leaning forward. "The old texts, the ceremonial instructions. We know your family has them hidden somewhere."

When I remained silent, he sighed and stood. "Perhaps you need encouragement."

He produced a knife and dragged it across his palm, letting the wound heal immediately before holding his bloody hand near my face. The scent of vampire blood made my stomach lurch.

"Your blood calls to vampires," he said conversationally. "But vampire blood can have interesting effects on humans with supernatural heritage. A few drops in your water, and you'll be much more talkative."

"No," I managed to whisper.

"Then tell us what we want to know." The woman consulted her notebook. "You came to Prague as a student, but that's quite a coincidence, isn't it? Your family must have sent you here for a reason. Where are the archives?"

I closed my eyes, trying to think through the mental fog. They thought my coming here was part of some family plan, but it wasn't. I'd chosen this university program myself, drawn by my love of medieval history. David had only come after vampires started targeting me.

But I did know about archives. Helena's collection, hidden in her sanctuary. The secret texts, the family histories, the protective spells. Everything Casimir would need. I'd rather die than tell them about Helena.

"I don't know about any texts," I lied.

The scarred vampire studied my face. "Your heart rate increased. You're lying."

"Basic training. How to identify vampires, how to use silver weapons. Nothing about rituals."

He made a note, asked a few more questions I deflected, then they left me alone.

Time became fluid. I dozed fitfully, jolting awake whenever the chains rattled or footsteps echoed outside. The collar made sleep strange. I'd drift off but never felt rested, like floating just below the surface of consciousness while being slowly drained away.

When lucid enough, I tried to keep my mind sharp by cataloging observations. Which guards seemed aggressive versus bored. The sounds from the corridor: footsteps, distant voices, the occasional slam of a door. The irregular intervals when they brought me water, sometimes with crackers or fruit. Never enough to satisfy, but calculated to keep me functional without strength.

The second interrogation brought new players and worse threats.

A tall, elegant vampire I hadn't seen before entered alone, standing over me with complete stillness and cold eyes.

"You're wondering if anyone will come for you," he said in a cultured accent. "Your vampire protector, perhaps?"

I tried not to react, but something must have shown.

"Ah yes, Matthias Cross, your devoted guardian." The

vampire smiled coldly. "He's been quite busy searching for you. Quite touching, really."

My heart jumped, but his next words killed that hope.

"Unfortunately, Lord Casimir has laid traps throughout the city. Your protector's desperation makes him reckless. When he finally tracks you down, he'll walk straight into our hands."

"You're lying."

"Am I? He's already fallen for three false trails." The vampire leaned closer. "Even if he finds this place, what then? Eight of us, one of him, in a stronghold warded against intrusion. He'll die, and you'll watch."

After he left, I slumped against the wall. The collar's effects seemed to pulse stronger, or maybe I was just wearing down. Everything required enormous effort now, even thinking felt like pushing through thick water.

I tried the mental exercises David had taught me. Reciting poetry, working through medieval history time-lines, anything to prove I was still me. But it was getting harder. I caught myself staring at the stone wall for what felt like hours, mind completely blank.

The breakdown came without warning.

All of it crashed down at once: the isolation, the constant threat, the way the collar was slowly erasing pieces of myself. I pulled at the chains until fresh blood ran down my arms, screamed until my throat was raw, sobbed until I had no tears left.

The guards watched with mild interest, like I was an animal having a tantrum.

Afterward, I felt hollow but somehow clearer. The emotional release had given me back some sense of myself, even under the collar's influence. I wasn't going to lie here and wait to die.

I started small. Testing the chains deliberately this time,

looking for any weakness in the walls or the door. The guards noticed my renewed activity but seemed unconcerned.

I tried engaging the auburn-haired woman in conversation during her shifts.

"How long have you worked for Casimir?"

"Long enough to know better than to chat with prisoners."

"Do you enjoy holding innocent people captive?"

"You're hardly innocent. You're a Sterling. Your family has killed hundreds of us over the centuries."

"I never killed anyone."

"Yet." She smiled, showing fangs. "But you would have, given the chance. It's in your blood."

I wanted to argue, but couldn't honestly say what I would have done if I'd grown up knowing what I was, trained from childhood to see vampires as enemies.

The hours crawled by. Sometimes I'd lose entire conversations mid-sentence, my mind drifting away under the collar's influence. I found myself thinking about Matthias more than expected—not just hoping for rescue, but actually missing him. His dry humor, the way he looked at me like I was precious, even the danger surrounding him. I'd been so focused on the threat he represented that I'd barely acknowledged how I felt about the man himself.

Then the lights flickered.

A brief stutter that made me lift my head. The two guards glanced toward the ceiling with mild annoyance.

"Probably the old wiring," the auburn-haired woman said, but uncertainty edged her voice.

The lights flickered again, longer this time, plunging us into brief darkness before buzzing back to life. In that moment of blackness, I heard something—distant breaking glass.

Both vampires were on their feet now, tense. The woman moved to the door, pressing her ear against the wood.

"Do you hear that?" she whispered.

I strained to listen. At first, nothing. Then, faintly, footsteps in the corridor beyond. Multiple sets, moving with purpose.

"Impossible," the other vampire breathed. "The wards would have detected—"

The lights went out completely.

20

In the sudden darkness, I heard the auburn-haired vampire's sharp intake of breath, followed by steel sliding from leather.

"Stay with the girl," the other vampire hissed. "I'll check the perimeter."

The door opened and closed, leaving me alone with her in absolute darkness. Her breathing came quick and shallow. Whatever was happening, she hadn't expected it. Panic thrummed in the silence between us, and I could feel the weight of uncertainty pressing down.

From somewhere far above, a scream pierced the darkness, loud and inhuman, before it was abruptly silenced.

The vampire cursed, her footsteps moving toward the door.

Then the door exploded inward.

Wood splintered and metal shrieked as the heavy door was torn from its hinges. In the doorway stood a figure wreathed in shadow, but I recognized the silhouette immediately—

Matthias.

The auburn-haired vampire raised her blade, but

Matthias was already moving. He crossed the room in a blur, metal shining in his hand. Her own blade clattered to the floor as his struck true, piercing her heart. For a moment, they were frozen. Then she began to crumble, her body disintegrating to ash before it hit the ground, gray dust scattering across the stone.

"Sera?" His voice cut through the darkness, rough with worry.

"Here," I whispered.

Light flared, a torch blazing bright. In its glow, I saw Matthias clearly for the first time in days. His face was a mask of rage, eyes burning with fury, his clothes torn and bloodstained, evidence of the fight he must have endured to reach me.

"What did they do to you?" He knelt beside me, examining the collar.

"Blocks my scent, makes me weak," I managed.

His hands moved to the chains at my wrists. With a display of supernatural strength, he snapped the iron links apart with a sharp crack.

"My lord," a voice called from the doorway. "More coming. We need to move."

I tried to stand but immediately swayed. Matthias swept me up, cradling me against his chest.

"Who are they?" I asked as we moved into the corridor. Bodies littered the stone floor. All Casimir's people, all dead.

"The Queen's guards," he said grimly. "She doesn't approve of kidnapping."

"Six confirmed dead," one reported. "Two fled."

"Let them run," Matthias said coldly. "They can tell Casimir what happens when he touches what's mine."

We reached the stairs leading up. Through narrow windows, I caught glimpses of Prague's spires.

As we emerged into the alley. The night air enveloped me, a refreshing shock after days in that windowless room.

Instead of heading toward the street, Matthias looked up at the Gothic building beside us.

"What are you doing?" I asked.

"Getting you somewhere safe," he said, sweeping me up in his arms again. "Hold tight."

He moved up, scaling the building with astonishing speed, his hands finding purchase on ledges that seemed far too narrow, but he climbed as effortlessly as if he were walking on solid ground.

We reached the roof in moments. Matthias set me down, keeping one arm around me as my legs shook.

"Why here?"

"Because you need the collar removed before we can move again." He was scanning the surrounding buildings, alert for threats.

His fingers traced the inscribed metal at my throat. "This will hurt. The magic is woven deep."

"I don't care. I want it gone."

Power gathered around him, a force both wild and intense, like a storm ready to break just beneath the surface.

"Ready?"

The collar shattered with a sound like breaking bells. A searing pain shot through me as the magic tore free, a jagged force that felt like fire racing through my veins. For a moment, it was overwhelming, like my body was being torn apart from the inside out. But just as quickly, I felt strength surge back into me—awareness flooding my mind, the sharpened senses I'd been developing reawakening with an intensity I hadn't expected.

I could smell Matthias again, leather and smoke wrapping around me. I could hear the city below with perfect clarity, every distant sound vivid.

And for the first time since my capture, I felt like myself.

"Better?" he asked.

I nodded, then stiffened. "They wanted information about the Sterling archives. They know about Helena."

His eyes went cold. "We'll deal with that." He helped me to my feet, testing my balance. "Can you walk?"

"Yes." The word came out stronger than I felt, but I was tired of being carried like a helpless victim.

We were on a rooftop somewhere in the city, surrounded by towering buildings that framed our view. The castle glowed in the distance, while below us, the Vltava River gleamed in the darkness.

"Are we safe here?" I asked, still pressed against his chest.

"For now." His hands remained on my waist, as if he couldn't bear to break the contact.

I reached up to touch his face. "I thought I'd never see you again."

"Never," he said fiercely. "I will always find you."

His mouth crashed against mine with desperate hunger. This wasn't the gentle, restrained touches we'd shared before. This was raw need unleashed, all the tension and desire that had been building between us finally breaking free.

His lips moved against mine with possessive demand, one hand tangling in my hair while the other gripped my waist, pulling me against him. I could taste the danger on his tongue, could feel the simmering power in the way his body pressed against mine.

When he backed me against a chimney stack, the brick solid behind me, I didn't resist. I wanted this, wanted him, with an intensity that should have terrified me.

His mouth trailed down the column of my throat, leaving a blazing path that made me gasp. I could feel the scrape of his teeth against my pulse point, not quite breaking the skin but promising so much more. My hands fisted in his shirt, pulling him closer as heat pooled between my thighs.

"Mine," he growled against my throat, his voice rough with something primal. The vibration of it against my skin sent shivers through my entire body, and I arched into his touch as one of his hands slid down to grip my hip possessively.

His other hand traced along my collarbone, fingers skimming the sensitive skin just above the neckline of my shirt. His touch left fire in its wake. When his thumb brushed across the curve at the base of my throat, I couldn't suppress the soft moan that escaped me.

The few scattered candles in the nearby windows suddenly burst into bright flames, their light flickering across the rooftops. The air itself seemed to crackle with electricity, responding to the connection between us.

His hands were everywhere—framing my face, tracing my collarbone with possessive hunger, sliding down to grip my hips as he pressed me more firmly against the brick behind me. Each touch sent shockwaves through me, and I found myself pressing closer, desperate for more contact, more heat, more of whatever this was between us.

"Sera," he breathed against my lips, and I could hear the desperate need that matched my own.

I reached up to tangle my fingers in his dark hair, the strands soft and cool against my heated palms. When I pulled him in for another kiss, he groaned low in his throat, the sound vibrating against my mouth.

This kiss was even more consuming than the first, all heat and desperate longing. His hand slid from my hip to the small of my back, his palm burning through the thin fabric of my shirt. I could feel the strength in his fingers as they pressed against my spine, pulling me closer until there was no space between us.

But just as I felt his control finally shatter completely, he staggered. His weight pressed against me suddenly, heavily, and when I looked up at his face, those green eyes went unfocused. Dark veins spread beneath his skin.

"Matthias?" Fear cut through the haze of desire. "What's wrong?"

He tried to straighten, tried to step back, but his legs buckled. I caught him as best I could, but he was too heavy. We both sank to the rooftop's stone surface, his head coming to rest against my shoulder.

"Time," he whispered, his voice barely audible. "Running out of time."

His eyes fluttered closed, and I felt his body go limp in my arms.

21

"Matthias!" I shook his shoulders, panic rising in my throat. His skin had gone translucent, and the dark veins beneath had spread like spider webs across his throat and down his arms. "Matthias, wake up!"

His eyes fluttered open, unfocused and glassy. When he tried to speak, only a whisper came out. "Cannot... the cost..."

"Matthias!" I pressed my palm to his forehead, and his skin felt like ice. Not the cool temperature I'd grown used to, but the cold of something dying. "Stay with me!"

His breathing was becoming more labored, each exhale weaker than the last. The dark veins had spread from his throat down to his chest now, pulsing with a sickly rhythm that seemed to be draining the life from him with every beat.

"The rescue... took everything," he managed, his voice barely audible. "Too much... power used."

My stomach dropped. The fight, the supernatural strength he'd displayed breaking my chains, scaling the building—it had all come at a cost.

"How long do we have?"

His eyes drifted closed without answering, and for a

terrifying moment, I thought I'd lost him. Then his chest rose with another shallow breath.

But even as I processed the immediate crisis, something nagged at me. He'd looked weak before the rescue, back in his sanctuary. The exhaustion, the way he'd favored his left side, this wasn't entirely from tonight.

"This isn't just from the rescue," I said quietly, studying the pattern of darkened veins. "Tell me what's going on."

A ghost of his usual smile flickered across his lips, but he didn't answer. Deflecting, even while dying.

I stared at the dark veins spreading beneath his skin, my mind racing. There had to be something. Some way to help him.

Sterling blood isn't like other human blood, Sera. It has properties. His words from the sanctuary came rushing back. *It heals vampires. Strengthens them. Makes them faster, more powerful than they would be otherwise.*

I pressed my hand to his chest, feeling his heartbeat growing weaker beneath my palm. If Sterling blood could strengthen a healthy vampire, enhance their natural abilities...

One feeding from a Sterling can sustain a vampire for months instead of weeks.

My pulse quickened as the pieces fell into place. Not just sustain. It could heal and strengthen. The properties he'd described weren't just about feeding. They were about restoration.

"You need blood," I said, the realization cutting through my panic. "My blood specifically."

His eyes snapped open, suddenly more focused. "Sera, no."

But I was already reaching for the silver knife at Matthias's belt. He was too weak to stop me as I pulled it free. The irony wasn't lost on me, using a vampire's own weapon to save his life.

"You said Sterling blood heals vampires," I continued, testing the blade's edge against my thumb. Sharp enough. "How much do you need?"

"Don't." He tried to sit up but couldn't manage it, collapsing back against me with a pained gasp. "You don't understand what you're offering."

"I understand that you're dying." I pushed up my sleeve, exposing the inside skin of my wrist. "I understand that I can help you."

I could see the war playing out across his features, with desperate need battling protectiveness. "You don't know what you're saying," he whispered, his eyes locked on my exposed wrist. "The connection it creates, you'll be bound to me in ways you can't imagine."

The dark veins pulsed and spread visibly as he spoke. I could see them creeping toward his heart now, and his breathing was becoming more shallow with each passing second. I didn't have time for his warnings.

"Will it save you?" I demanded.

"Yes, but—"

"Then that's all that matters." I drew the silver blade across my wrist in one swift motion. The cut was deeper than I'd intended, and blood immediately began to well up, dark red in the moonlight.

His nostrils flared, and for a split second, his control cracked entirely. I saw the predator beneath the restraint— pupils dilating, fangs emerging slightly. Then he pulled himself back.

"Sera..." His voice was rough with barely controlled hunger.

"Take it," I said, holding my bleeding wrist toward his lips. "Before it's too late."

He stared at the blood streaming down my arm, his breathing labored and weak. The dark veins beneath his skin pulsed faster now, as if the scent of my blood was accelerating whatever poison was killing him. When he tried to lift his hand toward me, it trembled with effort.

"You don't understand what this will cost you," he whispered, his voice barely audible. His eyes met mine, searching my face.

"I don't care."

His control finally shattered. He caught my wrist in both hands, bringing it to his lips with desperate hunger. The moment his mouth touched my skin, the world exploded.

Electric fire shot through my veins, radiating out from where his lips pressed against my wrist. It was pure sensation, raw, overwhelming, and addictive. My back arched involuntarily as waves of pleasure crashed through me, each pull of his mouth sending shockwaves to every nerve ending.

My breath came in short gasps, and I felt my nipples tighten against the thin fabric of my shirt, heat pooling between my thighs in a way that should have embarrassed me but only made me crave more.

I could feel him drinking, sense my blood flowing into him, and somehow I could feel what it was doing. The dark veins beneath his skin started to fade, and color returned to his face. His grip on my wrist became stronger, firmer.

But it wasn't just healing him; something was building between us. With each heartbeat, I felt flashes of sensation that weren't my own. Brief echoes of his relief, glimpses of desperate gratitude, hints of the way my blood was flooding his system with strength and life.

And woven through it all, something possessive that made my toes curl, though I couldn't tell if it was his emotion or mine.

Mine, a voice whispered at the edge of my consciousness, faint but unmistakable.

The sensation was intoxicating. Better than any drug, more consuming than any pleasure I'd ever experienced. I wanted more of it, wanted to lose myself completely in whatever was building between us.

My free hand tangled in his dark hair, pulling him closer, encouraging him to take more. Every cell in my body felt alive, sensitized, aching for more contact. Without thinking, I shifted closer, swinging my leg over to straddle his lap.

The new position brought us impossibly close, and I could feel the strength returning to his body, the way his hands came up to grip my hips with renewed power.

He slightly lifted his head, his green eyes blazing with an inner fire I'd never seen before. The dark veins had almost completely disappeared, and his skin had returned to its usual flawless state. But more than that, he looked powerful again, dangerous, like the predator who had torn through Casimir's guards to reach me.

"Sera," he breathed against my wrist, and I caught a flash of something through our forming connection. His wonder at being able to sense me, however faintly. I could sense him in return. "I can feel you. Your heartbeat, your breath..."

His eyes darkened as they took in my flushed face, the way my chest rose and fell with rapid breaths, the obvious signs of my arousal. "Your desire."

Heat flooded my cheeks, but I didn't pull away. The faint echoes of connection were too intriguing, too precious to break. I could catch glimpses of his hunger. Not just for blood anymore, but for me. All of me.

And I wanted him to have it, wanted to give him everything despite the voice in my head warning me.

He pressed his lips to my wrist again, not to drink but to kiss the healing wound. The gentle pressure sent another faint pulse through whatever was forming between us, and I gasped.

"The connection," he murmured, his voice rough. "Can you feel it? The way it's beginning between us?"

I nodded, though I could only catch hints, fragments of sensation that came and went like whispers. I could sense he felt much more than I did, could access something I was only touching the edges of.

"Good," I whispered, surprising myself with the honesty. "I want to be connected to you."

Something burned in his eyes at my words. Triumph and possession that made my stomach flutter with anticipation. His hands tightened on my hips where I straddled him, and he was leaning closer, his lips moving toward mine, when he suddenly went rigid.

His head snapped up, every muscle in his body coiling with tension. In one fluid motion, he lifted me off his lap and was on his feet, pulling me behind him with gentle but firm hands.

"Someone's coming," he said quietly.

22

The rooftop door burst open with a crash that sent metal fragments skittering across the stone. David emerged first, his crossbow already raised, followed by Elena and four hunters in full tactical gear. Their boots thundered against the rooftop as they spread out in formation, silver weapons gleaming in the moonlight.

But they stopped short when they saw us. I was pressed behind Matthias, his body ready for violence despite the weakness that lingered from his near-death. My clothes were disheveled from our interrupted intimate moment, my blouse partially unbuttoned, and my hair mussed from his hands. The evidence of what we'd been doing was impossible to hide.

David's steel-gray eyes took in my appearance, and I watched his face go white with horror. "No," he breathed, his weapon wavering. "Sera, tell me you weren't—"

"She was." Elena's voice was flat, but I could hear the tremor beneath it. She stepped closer, her hazel eyes taking in every detail: my flushed face, the way I stayed close to Matthias, the protective stance he'd taken. "Look at her, David. She's completely lost."

"Lost?" The words came out sharper than intended. "Is that what you call making my own choices?"

David lowered his weapon slightly, paternal anguish overriding hunter training. "We came to rescue you. We tracked Casimir's people to that building, found it empty, bodies everywhere..." His voice cracked. "We thought you were dead."

"We followed the trail here," Elena added, emotion fracturing her control. "We came to save you, and instead we find you... like this."

Matthias shifted, radiating controlled menace that made the hunters tense. Even injured, he moved like death itself. "Lower your weapons. I have no quarrel with you tonight."

"He saved my life," I said, moving closer to Matthias. "He came for me when no one else could."

"We were searching for days!" David's voice shattered completely. "Do you have any idea what we've been going through, thinking you were dead?"

The pain cut deep, but I couldn't retreat. "I didn't ask you to find me."

"You're our family," David said desperately. "Of course, we were going to find you."

Elena raised her blade. "We love you. But we can't let him destroy who you are."

The hunters closed in, cutting off escape routes. Matthias tensed, ready to fight despite his vulnerability. They had numbers, weapons, and tactical advantage.

"We're not going to hurt her," David said sadly. "Just keep her safe until this passes."

Elena raised her hand, and the hunters lifted their weapons—silver nets designed to restrain supernatural creatures, tranquilizer guns loaded with suppressants.

"We'll have to sedate her," Elena said quietly to David, though her voice carried clearly across the rooftop. "The bond makes her unpredictable. We can't risk her fighting us."

"Sedate me?" My voice cracked with disbelief.

David's expression crumpled with pain. "Just temporarily, sweetheart. Until we can get you somewhere safe, away from his influence. The tranquilizers will help suppress whatever hold he has on you."

"It's not influence!" I said desperately. "This is me choosing—"

"No," Elena interrupted firmly. "This is supernatural compulsion. Vampires can influence humans, make them defend their captors even when they know better. The sedatives will clear your head."

I was trapped. They had the numbers, the weapons, and the tactical advantage. And Matthias, despite his protective instincts, was too weak to fight them all.

The hunters stepped closer, tranquilizer guns trained on me now. David's face was full of regret but unwavering determination.

"I'm sorry, Sera," he said quietly. "But this is for your own good."

Then I drew the blade before anyone could react, pressing it to my throat with steady hands. The edge bit into skin just enough to draw blood.

Everyone froze.

"Stay back," I said quietly, my voice carrying across the rooftop. "All of you."

David's face drained of color, hands trembling. "Sera, what are you doing?"

"Taking control." I pressed deeper, letting the blade bite. Blood welled and trickled down my throat, dark against my skin. "You want to drug me? Force compliance? Make my choices for me?" I smiled without warmth. "Not anymore."

Elena stepped forward, horror twisting her features. "You don't understand—"

"Stop." The command carried more authority than I'd ever used. "One more step and I cut deeper. Another, and I end this permanently."

The hunters lowered their weapons, uncertainty flickering across trained faces. Without me, their plans crumbled. Without my cooperation, they were just a small group facing an enemy they couldn't find.

I held all the power. For the first time since Prague, I was going to use it.

"You want to sedate me so I'll be compliant? Force me to break a bond I chose to make?" I shook my head. "Not anymore."

David dropped the crossbow entirely, desperation replacing strategy. "Please, let's talk. Put the knife down and—"

"No." I cut him off. "I've listened to you, trusted you, let you decide for me my entire life. But I'm done being your weapon."

Behind me, Matthias had gone completely still. Through our bond, I felt his terror—pure, overwhelming fear unlike anything I'd sensed from him. The centuries-old vampire who'd torn through Casimir's guards was genuinely afraid, and it was all for me.

The emotion nearly broke my resolve.

"What do you want?" Elena asked quietly.

"Matthias goes free," I said immediately. "You never hunt him again. Permanently."

"Sera—" David started.

"Non-negotiable." I pressed the blade deeper, another drop joining the stream down my throat.

David and Elena exchanged a look—silent communication passing between them. The other hunters remained frozen, trained killers rendered helpless by the threat I posed to myself.

"Fine," Elena said finally, her voice hollow. "We won't hunt him. But you have to choose." She paused, grief flickering across her face. "Us or him. You can't have both."

The words stole my breath. I'd known this moment was coming, felt it building since my first night here. But hearing it stated so bluntly made it devastatingly real.

"That's not fair," I whispered.

"Fair?" David's voice cracked. "Look around you. You were kidnapped, nearly killed. If you choose him, you choose everything that follows: the danger, the enemies, constant threat of death. Is that really what you want?"

I felt Matthias tense, emotions surging through our connection. Pain, resignation, desperate fear for my safety, and beneath it all, fierce protectiveness that made my chest ache.

"Choose them," he said softly, his voice reaching only me. "Go with your family. They'll keep you safe."

I spun to face him, the knife wavering. "What?"

His green eyes held pain but resolve. "You heard David. I've brought nothing but danger into your life. Death follows me everywhere." He stepped back, creating distance. "You deserve better."

"That's not your choice to make," I said fiercely.

"Isn't it?" His smile was sad, beautiful, devastating. "I've had centuries to make mistakes, accumulate enemies, become the threat they say I am. But you..." He reached up as if to touch my face, then let his hand fall. "You could still have a normal life."

"I don't want normal," I said desperately. "Not if it means losing this."

"I know." His voice was gentle. "But sometimes protecting someone means stepping away."

The knife trembled in my grip. Around us, the hunters waited with patient confidence, sensing victory. My family stood ready to take me home, to keep me safe, to pretend none of this had happened.

And Matthias stood alone, prepared to watch me walk away.

"It's time to choose," David said softly.

I looked between them—the family that had raised and protected me in their complicated way, and the vampire who had saved my life, awakened desires I'd never known, shown me a connection that transcended everything I'd understood about myself.

The blade was steady now, but my heart was breaking.

"I choose..." I began, then stopped. The words wouldn't come. Either choice would destroy me.

"I need time," I whispered finally. "Just give me a moment."

Elena's expression softened slightly. "You have until sunrise. After that, we can't guarantee safety—yours or his. Other hunters are coming, ones who won't be as understanding."

I nodded numbly, lowering the blade. The thin cut stung in cool air, a reminder of how close I'd come to ending everything.

David holstered his weapon and stepped closer, face full of desperate hope. "Come back with us, sweetheart. We'll figure the rest out later."

But I was looking at Matthias, at the resigned acceptance in his eyes, the way he was already pulling away emotionally as well as physically.

Then he was gone.

I stared at empty air where he'd vanished, waiting to feel

something other than the growing numbness spreading through my chest.

Finally, I turned back toward my family with a hollow weight settling in my bones, a pain I couldn't name.

"Okay." My throat felt tight. "Let's go."

22.5

MATTHIAS

The scent of her family's silver filled my nostrils like poison, sharp and burning, but it was nothing compared to the agony of watching Sera's world crumble around her. Through our newly formed connection, I felt every tremor of her heartbreak, every spike of her terror as the people she'd loved her entire life looked at her like she'd become something monstrous.

Because of me. Because I hadn't been strong enough to stay away from her.

Choose them, I'd told her, even as the words felt like swallowing molten silver. *Go with your family, Sera. They'll keep you safe.*

The look of betrayal that flashed across her face nearly brought me to my knees. But what choice did I have? The blood moon would rise, and either she would transform to save my existence, or enemy vampires would drain her blood to create their vampire king. Either way, her human life would end.

At least with her family, she had a chance at normalcy. At the life she'd been meant to have before I'd selfishly dragged her into my nightmare.

Even as the rational part of my mind formed these thoughts, every instinct I possessed screamed in violent protest. She was *mine*. The bond that had snapped into place when she'd first given me her blood was still new, still raw, but it ran deeper than anything I'd experienced in eight centuries of existence. The very idea of letting her walk away made the beast in me claw against my restraint.

But caring for someone—truly caring—required sacrifice. And if keeping Sera safe meant watching her choose a life without me, then I would endure it.

Even if it killed me.

Which, given my state, it very well might.

I could feel the familiar drain already beginning again, that relentless pull that had been sapping my strength for four hundred years. Without Sera's blood to sustain me, without our connection to anchor me to something beyond mere survival, I had perhaps days before the effects of her blood faded.

But her family didn't need to know that. They didn't need to understand that their presence here, their demand that she choose, was essentially signing my death warrant. All they needed to know was that I wouldn't fight them for her.

The silver blade pressed against her throat changed everything.

Terror, unlike anything I'd experienced, crashed through me so intensely I nearly staggered. Not terror for myself. I'd faced death countless times. This was the absolute certainty that she would rather die than be separated from me again, and the knowledge that she might actually do it.

No, I wanted to roar at her. *No, you beautiful, stubborn fool. Live. Choose them. Live.*

But the words died in my throat as I watched her transformation. This wasn't the frightened young woman who'd stumbled into my world weeks ago. This was someone who had found her power and was willing to use it, even if it meant threatening the very life I was desperate to protect.

"Taking control," she said, and the authority in her voice sent an unexpected surge of pride through me. Even as horror followed immediately after.

The Sterling blood called to every vampire within miles when it was spilled. Even this small trickle from the shallow cut was enough to make my fangs ache and my vision sharpen. But more than the scent of her blood, it was her courage that stole my breath.

She was magnificent. Absolutely, terrifyingly magnificent.

And completely out of control.

"Matthias goes free," she demanded, and I felt something crack in my chest. Eight centuries of existence, and no one had ever fought for me the way this fierce, impossible woman was fighting right now. No one had ever looked at a group of armed hunters and said, essentially, *You'll have to go through me.*

The bond thrummed between us, carrying her emotions in overwhelming waves. Determination so fierce it took my breath away. And underneath it all, a depth of commitment that humbled me.

She wasn't just willing to die for me. She was willing to live for me, to choose a life her family couldn't understand, to walk away from everything she'd ever known.

How could I ask that of her? How could I be selfish enough to let her sacrifice everything for a monster who'd brought nothing but death and danger into her perfect life?

But even as my conscience demanded I send her away, my soul—what remained of it after centuries of darkness—cried out in desperate need. She was the only light I'd found in four hundred years of dying. The only hope I had of breaking free from the witch's curse. The only person who'd ever looked at me and seen something worth saving.

When she spun to face me, the knife wavering at her throat, her eyes blazing with fury and hurt, I knew I'd already lost this battle with myself.

"You heard your uncle," I said, each word cutting deeper than any silver blade. "I've brought nothing but danger into your life. Death follows me everywhere I go."

The truth of it was a constant weight on my shoulders. Every person I'd ever cared about had suffered for knowing me. Every village I'd tried to protect had eventually fallen to my enemies. The witch's curse hadn't just been about draining my power—it had been about ensuring that I could never find peace, never build anything lasting, never love without destroying what I loved.

"You deserve better," I continued, forcing myself to take a step back from her. Away from the warmth of her body, the intoxicating scent of her skin, the terrible temptation of her love.

She fought me, of course. She would fight anyone who tried to make choices for her—I'd learned that much about her. But under her confident words, I could feel the seed of doubt her family had planted beginning to grow.

What if they were right? What if she couldn't trust her own feelings?

The doubt cut through our bond like acid, burning away the certainty that had sustained me through the stolen moments and growing intimacy. If she questioned what was between us, questioned whether it was real or simply supernatural manipulation, then I had already lost her.

Better to let her go now, with her life intact, than to fight for her and risk her destruction in the process. Better to face the curse's final victory alone than to drag her down with me.

Even if watching her walk away destroyed what remained of my soul.

The bond stretched between us, protesting the separation with physical pain that doubled me over. Through the connection, I felt her own agony, the way every step away from me felt like tearing away pieces of herself.

But she was strong. Stronger than I'd given her credit for. She would survive this. She would heal from whatever damage knowing me had caused, find someone worthy of her light, and build the life she was meant to have.

The thought should have comforted me.

Instead, it felt like the final death blow to the hope I'd been carrying for four centuries.

As I disappeared into the Prague night, leaving my heart behind with her, I felt our bond stretch and strain with the distance. The curse's hunger rose within me immediately, sensing the severing of our connection, eager to reclaim the ground it had lost while Sera's blood sustained me.

Soon I would need to prepare for the possibility that the witch would finally have her victory, and I would face eternity as the hollow shell she'd always intended me to become.

But if that was the price of Sera's freedom, of her chance at happiness, then I would pay it gladly.

Even if it destroyed me.

The candles flickered around me as I knelt alone in the sanctuary that had become both my salvation and my tomb, feeling the curse's grip tighten with every breath I took.

Time was running out.

And for the first time in four hundred years, I wasn't sure I had the strength to fight it anymore.

23

The illuminated manuscript blurred before my eyes for the third time in ten minutes. I blinked hard, trying to focus on the medieval text describing protective wards against supernatural creatures, but the Latin words might as well have been hieroglyphics for all the sense they made.

I pressed my fingertips to my temples, where a migraine had been building since dawn. Seven days. It had been exactly seven days since that rooftop confrontation, since Matthias had stepped back and told me to choose my family. Since I'd watched him disappear into Prague's shadows, taking part of myself with him.

"Any luck with the ritual references?" Helena's voice made me jump.

I looked up to find her approaching my reading table, her expression concerned as she took in my obvious frustration. She carried a steaming cup of tea that smelled like chamomile.

"Nothing useful," I said, gesturing to the scattered manuscripts around me. "Plenty of general information about blood moon ceremonies, but nothing specific about the ritual they're planning. It's like the most important pages were deliberately removed."

"They probably were." Helena set the tea beside my elbow and settled into the chair across from me. "Information that dangerous has a way of disappearing over the centuries."

I nodded absently, my attention already drifting back to the meaningless text. But instead of reading, I found myself unconsciously rubbing my left wrist. The cut had healed completely, leaving only the faintest line of scar tissue, but I could still feel it. The memory of silver blade against skin, of blood welling up dark in the moonlight.

Of his mouth against my wrist, desperate and grateful and hungry all at once.

"Sera." Helena's voice was gentler now. "When's the last time you slept through the night?"

I forced myself to stop touching my wrist, folding my hands in my lap. "I sleep fine."

"Do you?" She tilted her head, studying my face with those light eyes that seemed to see too much. "Because you look exhausted. Distracted. Like you're carrying a weight that's slowly crushing you."

I picked up the tea, using the motion to avoid her gaze. The liquid was warm and soothing, but it couldn't touch the cold ache that had settled in my bones since that night.

"I'm just frustrated with the research," I said finally. "All these manuscripts, all this history, and none of it tells me what I actually need to know."

"What do you need to know?"

What did I need to know? How to stop thinking about green eyes and leather smoke? How to forget the electric shock of supernatural connection? How to live with half of myself missing?

"How to help my family," I said instead. "How to understand what we're really fighting."

Helena was quiet for a moment, her fingers tracing patterns on the wooden table. "Sometimes the most important knowledge can't be found in books."

"What's that supposed to mean?"

"It means that some understanding only comes through experience. Through connection." Her eyes met mine, and I saw something there that made my pulse quicken. "Through choices that can't be undone."

I set the tea down with hands that trembled slightly. "Helena—"

"I know what you're going through," she said quietly. "The separation pain. The way everything feels muted, like you're experiencing life through thick glass."

I stiffened. "I don't know what you're talking about."

"Don't you?" She leaned forward, her voice dropping to barely above a whisper. "When supernatural beings form connections, breaking them isn't clean. It leaves wounds that don't heal properly. Phantom limbs of the soul."

The words hit too close to home. I pushed back from the table, standing abruptly. "I should get back to the hotel. David is expecting me."

"Sera." Helena rose as well, her expression full of something that looked like sympathy. "Running from it won't make it stop hurting."

"I'm not running from anything," I said, but even I could hear the lie in my voice.

"Aren't you?" She stepped closer, and I caught a whiff of that strange energy that always seemed to surround her. "You've been coming here every day for a week, burying yourself in research that's going nowhere, pretending that academic work can fill the hole he left behind."

"There is no hole," I said firmly, gathering my things. "I made my choice. I chose my family."

"Did you?" Helena's question stopped me. "Or did you just stop fighting when he stepped away?"

I stared at her, my hands frozen on my laptop bag. The truth of her words cut deep, deeper than I wanted to admit. I hadn't chosen my family so much as I'd let Matthias choose for me. Let him decide what I could and couldn't handle, what I did and didn't deserve.

"It doesn't matter now," I said quietly. "It's over."

I backed toward the library entrance, an ache settling in my chest. "I have to go."

"Be careful, Sera," Helena called after me.

The walk back to my hotel passed in a blur of cobble-stone streets and Gothic architecture that no longer seemed beautiful, just oppressive. Everything in this city reminded me of him—the shadows that might hide his presence, the stones that had witnessed our encounters, the very air that still carried hints of leather and smoke if I breathed deeply enough.

By the time I reached the hotel lobby, my hands were shaking and the lingering ache in my wrist had spread to my entire arm. I rubbed at the healed cut, remembering the way his mouth had felt against my skin, the connection that had flowed between us.

Mine, his voice whispered in my memory.

But I wasn't his. I'd chosen otherwise. I'd chosen safety, family, the life I was supposed to want.

So why did every breath feel like suffocation?

I was so lost in my thoughts that I didn't notice David waiting in the lobby until he stood up from one of the ornate chairs, his steel-gray eyes immediately looking me over.

"There you are," he said, relief evident in his voice. "I was starting to worry."

I forced a smile. "Sorry, I lost track of time at the library. You know how I get when I'm researching."

David studied my face with those observant eyes that had always been able to see through my lies. But after a moment, his expression softened with what looked like approval.

"That's good to hear," he said, moving to walk beside me toward the hotel elevator. "Elena was concerned that you might be struggling with the adjustment."

Struggling. Such an inadequate word for the way every breath felt like I was drowning.

"I'm fine," I said, pressing the elevator button. "Actually, I'm grateful. You and Elena saved me from making a terrible mistake."

The lie came easily now, after a week of practice. David's relief was visible, his shoulders relaxing as we stepped into the elevator.

"I'm glad you can see that now," he said quietly. "I know it was hard, sweetheart. But supernatural influence can be powerful. It takes time to shake off the effects."

I nodded, staring at the elevator buttons instead of meeting his eyes. "How much longer do you think it will take? To feel normal again?"

"Everyone's different," David said, his voice gentle. "But the worst should be over. You're thinking more clearly, focusing on your work again. That's all good signs."

If only he knew that my "work" was just a way to keep my hands busy while my mind circled endlessly around those green eyes.

The elevator dinged as we reached my floor. David walked me to my door, his protective instincts clearly still on high alert despite his casual demeanor.

"How about dinner?" he asked as I fumbled for my key card. "There's a nice place down the street. Elena could meet us."

I couldn't face sitting through a meal, pretending to have an appetite while they watched me for signs of "improvement."

"I'm not really hungry," I said, which was true. Food had lost all appeal since that night on the rooftop. "Maybe tomorrow?"

David's expression flickered with concern, but he nodded. "Of course. Rest is probably better anyway."

He paused as I opened my door, his expression becoming more serious. "Sera, I need you to know that if you ever feel drawn to seek him out, or if you start having dreams or visions, you need to tell me immediately. That bond can create lingering effects."

I met his eyes, letting him see what he wanted to see: gratitude, trust, the dutiful niece who'd learned her lesson.

"Good." He squeezed my shoulder gently. "Get some rest. You look tired."

I waited until I heard his footsteps disappear down the hall before closing the door and sagging against it. The performance was exhausting, pretending to be grateful for my own cage, acting like I was healing when every day felt like dying a little more.

My phone buzzed with a text message. Elena's name flashed on the screen: *Status check. Everything normal?*

I typed back: *All good. Tired but fine.*

Another message came immediately: *David says you're doing well. Proud of you for making the right choice.*

The right choice. I stared at the words until they blurred, my throat tight with unshed tears. If this was the right choice, why did it feel like I was being hollowed out from the inside?

I moved to the window, looking out at Prague's darkening streets. Somewhere out there, Matthias was moving through the shadows, probably hunting, probably feeding. Probably not thinking about me at all.

The rational part of my mind insisted that it was for the best. He was dangerous and everything my family had warned me about. I should be relieved that he'd stepped away, grateful that I'd been saved from a fate worse than death.

But as I watched night settle over the city, all I could think about was the way he'd looked at me in those final moments on the rooftop. The resignation in his eyes, the way he'd pulled away even though every line of his body had screamed against it.

Choose them. Go with your family, Sera. They'll keep you safe.

He'd made the choice for me, deciding what I could and couldn't handle. Just like David and Elena were doing now, monitoring my recovery, checking my status, making sure I stayed on the path they'd chosen for me.

My reflection stared back from the window, hollow-eyed and drawn. I looked like a ghost of myself, and maybe that's what I was. The real Sera had died on that rooftop, leaving behind this empty shell that went through the motions of living.

Another text from Elena: *Remember, no going out alone after dark. Prague is still dangerous.*

I almost laughed at the irony. They were so worried about external threats, they couldn't see that the real danger was internal. The way I lay awake every night staring at the ceiling, the way food tasted like ash, the way I caught myself holding my breath as if I could capture some trace of leather and smoke in the air.

A week ago, I'd been connected to someone who could

hear my heartbeat, sense my emotions, and feel my presence across the city. Now I was more alone than I'd ever been in my life.

I turned away from the window, away from the darkening streets where shadows appeared to move. Away from the part of Prague where immortal creatures hunted, loved, and lived with an intensity that made human existence seem dull in comparison.

Tomorrow would be another day of pretending. Another day of meaningless research, forced smiles, and grateful words, slowly dying inside while everyone congratulated me on my recovery.

24

I stared at the digital clock beside my bed, watching the minutes crawl by with agonizing slowness. 3:17. 3:18. 3:19.

Sleep was impossible. It had been impossible for seven straight nights, despite the exhaustion that weighed me down. Every time I closed my eyes, I saw green fire and felt phantom touches that left me aching and alone when I woke.

I threw off the tangled sheets and began pacing again, wearing a path in the carpet between the window and the door. My hotel room felt like a tomb, all heavy furniture and oppressive silence. The walls seemed to be closing in with each circuit I made.

Outside, Prague slept under a blanket of stars, its Gothic spires dark against the night sky. But I knew it wasn't really sleeping. In the shadows between buildings, in the underground passages beneath the castle, in places humans weren't meant to go, there was life. A dangerous, electric, intoxicating life.

And I was trapped in this box, slowly dying of safety.

I caught sight of myself in the ornate mirror across the room and stopped pacing abruptly. The woman staring back at me looked like a stranger. Hollow cheeks, dark circles under eyes that had lost their spark, skin drained of all life. I looked like I was wasting away.

Was Matthias out there thinking about me? Did he miss the connection we'd shared, or had he already moved on to more willing prey?

The thought sent a spike of something that felt suspiciously like jealousy through my chest. The idea of him touching someone else, sharing blood with another woman, whispering possessive endearments in that voice that turned my knees to jelly—

"Stop," I whispered to my reflection. "Just stop."

But I couldn't stop. That was the problem. Every rational thought, every attempt to move forward, every smile I forced for David and Elena, it was all just surface pretense covering the raw wound underneath.

I moved away from the mirror, my hands shaking with frustrated energy. The pendant around my neck felt heavy and cold, a constant reminder of the magical world I'd briefly touched before being dragged back to mundane reality.

My laptop sat closed on the desk, surrounded by research notes that meant nothing. Academic work that had once driven me now felt like trying to color inside the lines while the real picture blazed in brilliant, terrifying color outside the borders.

I grabbed my phone, scrolling through the meaningless notifications. Social media updates from friends back home, email reminders about dissertation deadlines, calendar alerts for a life that felt increasingly unreal.

3:47 AM.

The ache was unbearable. Had been for days now. A constant gnawing hunger that food couldn't touch, a restlessness that exercise couldn't cure, a loneliness that human company only made worse.

David's warnings echoed in my head: *If you ever feel drawn to seek him out. You need to tell me immediately.*

But what if I didn't want to tell him? What if I were tired of being monitored, managed, and protected from my own choices?

What if I were tired of being safe?

I stopped moving, my heart hammering against my ribs as a dangerous thought took shape. Elena had texted me to stay inside after dark, to avoid going out alone. David checked on me constantly, worried about lingering supernatural influence.

They were so focused on protecting me that they didn't realize their containment might cause me to do exactly what they feared most.

My hands moved without conscious thought, pulling on jeans and a simple button-down. shirt. I grabbed my jacket from the chair, checking that the silver knife was still secure at my hip. Helena's pendant felt warm against my skin for the first time in days, as if it sensed what I was planning.

This was insane. Reckless. Exactly the kind of dangerous behavior that proved I was still under supernatural influence.

But as I stood there in my hotel room at four in the morning, staring at my tired reflection, I realized I didn't care.

I was tired of being a good girl. Tired of making the right choices. Tired of slowly suffocating in a life that felt like wearing clothes three sizes too small.

If they thought I was being influenced by supernatural forces, then maybe I should give them something to really worry about.

I slipped out of my room and down the hotel's back

stairs, avoiding the lobby where night staff might see me leave. The service entrance opened onto a narrow alley that smelled of old stone and a faint metallic scent, which made my Sterling senses prickle with awareness.

Prague's streets were different at this hour. Darker, more alive with possibility. The shadows seemed deeper, more welcoming, as if the city itself was inviting me to step off the safe path and into something more dangerous.

More real.

I started walking, my footsteps echoing off cobblestones as I headed away from the tourist areas, away from well-lit squares and patrol routes. Toward the parts of the city where normal people didn't go after midnight.

Where supernatural creatures might be hunting.

Where someone might need rescuing.

My heart raced with equal parts terror and anticipation as I disappeared into Prague's maze of streets. Behind me, the hotel grew smaller and safer with each step.

Ahead lay darkness, danger, and the possibility of seeing green eyes that burned like fire in the night.

I felt truly alive.

The streets twisted and turned, leading me deeper into Prague's medieval heart. I passed under stone archways that had stood for centuries, my footsteps the only sound in the pre-dawn quiet. Each step was taking me further from the numbness that had been consuming me.

And with each step, Helena's pendant grew warmer against my skin.

I wasn't exactly sure what I was searching for. Danger, yes, but what kind? My logical mind argued this was madness and that I was risking myself for nothing. But the rest of me, the part that had been slowly dying in that hotel room, felt more alive with every shadow I passed.

The pendant pulsed against my throat, its warmth now

nearly unbearable. I was close to something. Something supernatural, something dangerous. Everything David and Elena had warned me to stay away from.

I smiled grimly and walked faster.

The alley opened into a small square I didn't recognize, surrounded by buildings that looked like they hadn't been renovated in decades. Broken streetlights cast uneven pools of yellow light, leaving large patches of shadow where anything could be hiding. A fountain sat in the center, its water black and still in the darkness.

Perfect.

I moved to the center of the square, making myself as visible as possible. If there were supernatural creatures hunting tonight, I wanted them to see me. Wanted them to smell my Sterling blood and recognize what I was.

The pendant was almost burning now, and I could feel that familiar prickle of awareness that meant something was watching me. Something that shouldn't exist.

I pulled out my phone, pretending to check messages while scanning the shadows with my peripheral vision. There—movement near the fountain. And there, behind the broken street lamp. At least three figures, moving with that unnatural stillness I was starting to recognize.

My heart hammered against my ribs, but it was excitement as much as fear. After a week of numbness, of going through the motions of living, this felt real. Dangerous and stupid and absolutely real.

"Well, well," a cultured voice drifted from the shadows. "What do we have here?"

Four figures stepped into the dim light, and I knew immediately what they were. The cold dread washed over me, that predatory sensation that screamed danger. But these weren't like the sophisticated vampires who'd captured me before. These moved with barely contained hunger, less controlled, more desperate.

Younger vampires. Hungrier ones.

"There's something..." the apparent leader said, inhaling deeply as he studied me. He was tall and lean, with dark hair that looked like it hadn't been washed in days. His clothes were expensive but rumpled, as if he'd been wearing them for weeks. "Something different about you."

The other three spread out around me, cutting off escape routes. Two men and a woman, all carrying themselves with that tense readiness but lacking the control I'd seen in older vampires.

"Human, but not quite," the woman said, tilting her head as she studied me. Her blonde hair was matted, and her blue eyes held the vacant intensity of someone who'd been feeding exclusively on human blood for too long. "There's magic on you."

"Sterling," one of the men said suddenly, his eyes widening. "She's a Sterling. I can smell it now, underneath the magic."

"The Sterling," the leader corrected, his voice taking on a greedy tone. "The one they're all looking for. The ritual prize."

"Think they'd notice if we took a small taste before turning her in?" the woman asked, licking her lips. "Just enough to sample what all the fuss is about."

"The blood moon isn't for weeks," the fourth vampire added, fangs extending slightly. "Surely we deserve a reward for finding her first."

This was it. This was what I'd been looking for, real danger, the kind that would force Matthias to come for me. The kind that would shatter the containment my family had built around me.

I reached for the silver knife at my hip, drawing it with a

motion that was becoming second nature. The blade gleamed in the dim light, and all four vampires tensed.

"Oh, she wants to fight," the leader said with amusement. "How delightful. Just don't damage her too badly; she needs to be intact for delivery."

"A little blood loss won't hurt the ritual," the woman added, her eyes fixed hungrily on my throat. "Might even make her more compliant."

I raised the knife, trying to remember everything David had taught me. Go for major arteries. Make them bleed faster than they could heal. Don't hesitate.

But as they began to circle me like wolves around wounded prey, I realized I might have made a terrible mistake.

These vampires moved with coordination, and there were four of them. The pendant might provide some protection, but against odds like these...

The leader lunged first, moving faster than my eyes could track. I slashed with the knife, felt it connect with solid flesh, and heard him hiss in pain. Dark blood sprayed across the stone as he staggered back.

"Silver burns," I said grimly, raising the blade again.

A second vampire tried to grab me from behind, but I spun and drove the knife toward his chest. He twisted away, the blade slicing across his ribs instead of finding his heart. Still, he screamed and retreated, a hiss coming from the wound.

"She's actually fighting back," one of them snarled, circling more warily now.

The leader pressed his hand to his bleeding shoulder, eyes filled with new respect. "Sterling blood and a silver blade. No wonder she's drawing blood."

They were more cautious now, but still closing in. I kept

the knife moving between them, trying to watch all four at once.

"Just grab her!" the wounded one snapped.

The third vampire lunged right. This time, when I slashed, the vampire knocked the blade out of my hand.

As I scrambled for the fallen knife, cold fingers wrapped around my wrist. The moment his skin touched mine, Helena's pendant flared with brilliant silver light. The vampire screamed, his grip releasing instantly as he staggered backward, smoke rising from his burned palm.

"What the hell—" he snarled, cradling his injured hand.

"Protective charm," the woman hissed.

But my advantage was short-lived. I'd dropped the knife again when the pendant discharged, and now I was weaponless against four angry vampires who were no longer underestimating me.

"Grab her from behind," the leader ordered, his burned hand already beginning to heal. "Don't touch her skin directly."

The woman circled around me while the other two moved to flank me. I was surrounded, just as stupid as David would have said I was.

But as their fingers reached for me, as I prepared to scream for help that wouldn't come, the air in the square seemed to crackle with energy.

And the streetlights flickered and went out.

25

In the sudden darkness, I heard the first vampire die.

A tearing sound, followed by a gurgle that cut off abruptly. Then the soft whisper of ash scattering across stone.

"What—" one of them started to say.

The second death was quieter. Just a sharp crack like breaking bone, and another pile of ash drifted in the night breeze.

"Run!" the leader screamed.

But it was too late.

The lights flickered on from the surrounding buildings, casting everything in yellow. And there, standing amid swirling ash that had once been two vampires, was Matthias.

He looked magnificent and terrifying at the same time. His dark hair was disheveled, his green eyes blazing with fury that seemed to set the air around him on fire. A wooden stake in his hand, dark blood dripping from its point.

"Matthias," the surviving vampire woman breathed, her voice cracking with terror.

He turned toward her with a slow, relentless purpose,

and I noticed something in his expression that made my blood run cold. This wasn't the controlled violence I'd seen before. This was rage unleashed.

"You touched what belongs to me," he said quietly.

The woman tried to run. She took three steps before Matthias caught her, driving the wooden stake through her back and into her heart. She had just enough time to look shocked before she crumbled to ash.

The leader was backing away, his burned hand pressed against his chest, his eyes wide with terror.

"Please," he whispered. "We didn't know she was yours. We thought—"

"You thought wrong."

Matthias moved. The wooden stake flashed once in the lamplight, finding the vampire's heart. He collapsed into ash before he could even scream.

Silence enveloped the square, broken only by my ragged breathing and the distant hum of the lights. Four piles of ash were scattered around the fountain, and in the middle of it all stood Matthias—beautiful, deadly, and utterly furious.

When he turned toward me, I saw something in his eyes that made me take a step back.

"Sera." His voice was deceptively calm, but I could hear the rage simmering beneath the surface.

"You came," I whispered, relief flooding through me despite his obvious anger.

"Of course I came." He stepped over the ash without glancing down, his eyes never leaving mine. "Did you think I wouldn't sense your terror? Your pain?"

There was something in his tone that made my stomach clench with dread. This wasn't the gentle protector who had rescued me before. This was something much more dangerous.

"Matthias—"

"You deliberately put yourself in danger." Each word was precisely enunciated, controlled fury wrapped in velvet. "You walked into the darkest part of Prague, alone, in the middle of the night, and made yourself bait."

My mouth went dry. "How did you—"

"How did I know?" He laughed, but there was no humor in it. "Because I know you, Sera. I know the way your mind works, the way you feel. And I felt every moment of your plan."

He was close enough now that I could see the gold flecks in his angry eyes, could smell leather and smoke mixed with the copper scent of vampire blood.

"You used our connection to force my hand," he continued, his voice dropping to a dangerous whisper. "Made me watch through our bond as you walked into mortal danger."

"I—" I started, but he cut me off.

"Do you have any idea what that did to me?" His hands clenched into fists at his sides. "Feeling your fear, your pain, knowing you were in danger and that you'd put yourself there deliberately?"

Through our faint connection, I caught echoes of what he'd experienced: terror, rage, desperate need to reach me, fury at being manipulated.

"I couldn't stay away," I whispered. "The separation was killing me."

"So you decided to get yourself killed instead?" His voice rose, control finally cracking. "You think I want to find your drained corpse because you were too stubborn to accept that we're better apart?"

"We're not better apart!" The words burst out of me with more force than I'd intended. "I'm struggling without you, Matthias. Every breath feels like drowning. Every day feels like losing more and more of myself."

Something flickered in his eyes.

"That doesn't give you the right to manipulate our connection," he said, but his voice had lost some of its edge. "To use what exists between us as a weapon."

"What else was I supposed to do?" I stepped closer, noting how his entire body tensed as the distance between us decreased. "You made the choice for me. Decided I couldn't handle the danger, couldn't make my own decisions about what I wanted."

"Because what you want will get you killed!"

"Maybe!" I threw my hands up in frustration. "But that should be my choice to make, not yours!"

We stared at each other, two people caught between fury and desperate longing. The lights casting strange shadows across his face, making him look even more inhuman than usual.

"You knew I'd come," he said finally, his voice quiet. "You knew I'd sense your distress and come running."

It wasn't a question, but I nodded anyway.

"That's manipulation, Sera. You manipulated me."

The accusation felt like a slap. "How dare you," I whispered. "How dare you stand there covered in blood from saving my life and call what I feel manipulation."

"Then what would you call it?"

"Desperation." The word came out broken, raw with emotion.

His expression softened slightly, some of the rage fading from his eyes.

I looked around the square at the ashes of four vampires who had died because they'd threatened me. At the man who had torn through them like they were nothing, who was standing here arguing with me instead of disappearing back into the shadows.

The silence stretched between us, heavy with unspoken

truths and the metallic scent of vampire blood. Matthias stood perfectly still, watching me with those burning green eyes that seemed to see straight through every defense I'd ever built.

"I tried, Matthias," I admitted, the words tumbling out in a rush. "I tried to be grateful for my family's protection, tried to go back to my normal life, tried to pretend that what happened between us didn't matter."

His expression didn't change.

"But it was killing me," I continued, stepping closer despite the danger radiating from him. "The separation, the emptiness, the way everything felt muted and gray. I couldn't eat, couldn't sleep, couldn't concentrate on anything that didn't remind me of you."

"Sera—"

"No, let me finish." I held up a hand, surprised when he actually fell silent. "I needed to see you. I needed to know if what we shared was real or if I'd been living in some kind of supernatural delusion. And the only way I could think to make that happen was to put myself in danger."

His jaw tightened. "So you decided to go on a suicide mission."

"Yes." I lifted my chin defiantly. "I did. Because being safe without you felt like dying anyway."

Something shifted in his expression.

"You incredible, reckless, beautiful fool," he said softly, and I heard the affection beneath the exasperation.

"I'm your fool," I said, the words slipping out before I could stop them.

His eyes blazed at my admission. "Are you?"

"Yes." The certainty in my voice surprised even me. "I'm yours, Matthias. I've been yours since that first night in the library, maybe even before that. Since I started dreaming of stone corridors and voices calling my name."

He moved toward me then, closing the distance between us. "I'm tired of pretending you don't mean everything to me."

"Then don't pretend." I reached up to touch his face, my fingers tracing the sharp line of his jaw. "Don't step away this time. Don't decide what I can and can't handle."

His hand covered mine, pressing my palm against his cheek. "If I don't step away," he said, his voice rough, "I won't be able to stop."

"Good," I whispered. "I don't want you to stop."

The last thread of his control snapped.

His mouth collided with mine with desperate hunger, finally abandoning the restraint and cautious distance of our previous encounters. This kiss was need unleashed, possessive, demanding, and utterly consuming.

I gasped against his lips, and he took advantage, his tongue sliding against mine in a way that made heat pool between my thighs. His hands gripped my waist, lifting me slightly as he backed me against the stone wall of the nearest building.

The cold stone against my back was a sharp contrast to the heat of his body pressed against mine. I could feel every hard line of him, the way his chest rose and fell with heavy breathing, the controlled strength in his hands as they roamed over my body.

"Tell me you need this," he demanded against my mouth, his voice rough with desire and command.

"I need this," I breathed, my hands fisting in his shirt. "I need you."

"Say you're mine." His lips trailed down the column of my throat, and I felt the scrape of his teeth against my pulse point. "Say it, Sera."

"I'm yours," I gasped as he found that sensitive spot just below my ear. "I've always been yours."

His growl of satisfaction vibrated against my throat, and I felt it echo through our connection. He pulled back just enough to look at me, his green eyes blazing with possessive hunger.

"Don't move," he commanded, his hands framing my face. "Let me look at you."

I obeyed instinctively, holding perfectly still as his gaze traveled over my flushed face, my parted lips, the way my chest rose and fell with rapid breathing. The intensity of his attention made me feel exposed and desired in equal measure.

"Beautiful," he murmured, his thumb tracing my lower lip. "So beautiful when you surrender to me."

Before I could respond, his hands grabbed my jacket, pushing it off my shoulders and letting it fall to the cobblestones. The cool night air struck my heated skin, but his touch immediately followed, warming every inch he explored.

My own hands moved to his shirt, fingers fumbling with buttons until his chest was partially exposed. The sight of his smooth skin in the dim light made my mouth water, and I leaned forward to press my lips to the hollow of his throat.

"Sera," he groaned, his head falling back as I tasted him. His skin was cool and smooth, with that faint taste of leather and smoke that was uniquely his.

"Let me taste you," he said, his voice commanding as he gently pulled my head back to expose my throat. "Let me have what I've been craving."

I nodded, unable to form words as he lowered his head to my neck. But instead of biting immediately, he pressed soft kisses to my pulse point, his tongue darting out to taste my skin.

"Tell me what you want," he murmured against my throat.

"You," I breathed. "All of you. Everything you're willing to give me."

He pulled back to meet my eyes, and what I saw in his gaze made my knees weak. Possession, hunger, and something deeper that made my heart race for entirely different reasons.

"Everything?" he asked, his voice soft but loaded with promise.

"Everything," I confirmed.

His smile was slow and predatory as he lowered his head to the nape of my neck. "Then everything is what you'll have."

The moment his lips touched my skin, the world exploded in sensation. But this time was different from our desperate encounter on the rooftop. This was controlled, deliberate, and designed to drive me to the edge of sanity.

He didn't bite immediately. Instead, he kissed and licked and sucked at the sensitive skin, making me writhe against the stone wall. My free hand tangled in his dark hair, holding him to me as pleasure built and built without release.

"Please," I whimpered, and felt his smile against my skin.

"Please what?" he asked, lifting his head just enough to speak.

"Bite me," I begged, past caring how desperate I sounded. "Please, Matthias."

"Good girl," he praised, and the approval in his voice made heat flood through me.

When his teeth finally pierced the skin of my neck, the sensation was indescribable. Electric fire shot through my veins, but this time I could feel our connection flaring to life again, still faint but there.

Through the haze of pleasure, I felt his hands moving over my body with increasing boldness. My blouse had somehow become unbuttoned, and cool air hit my skin just before his palm covered my breast through the thin fabric of my bra.

I arched into his touch with a moan that should have embarrassed me, but only seemed to encourage him further. His thumb brushed across my nipple, and the sensation combined with the blood-sharing nearly undid me completely.

"More," I gasped, pressing closer to him.

"Someone's greedy," he murmured against my collar-bone, but I could hear the satisfaction in his voice. "Tell me exactly what you want, Sera."

"I want..." I struggled for words as his mouth worked at my neck and his hands explored my body. "I want your hands on me. I want to feel you everywhere."

His free hand slid down to my hip, then lower, his fingers tracing patterns over my jeans that made me writhe against the stone. "Like this?"

"Yes," I breathed, my head falling back against the wall.

Just as his hand began to move toward the waistband of my jeans, just as I thought I might die from want, the sound of footsteps echoed through the square.

We froze, still pressed together against the wall. The footsteps were getting closer, multiple sets, moving with the same rhythm I'd learned to associate with hunters on patrol.

Matthias lifted his head from my throat, his expression shifting from passion to alertness in an instant. His tongue swept across the bite marks, and I felt the puncture wounds close, healing without a trace.

"Sera!" A familiar voice called out. "Sera, are you out here?"

Elena. My stomach dropped.

"Four hunters, approaching from the north," Matthias

said calmly, his hands already moving to help me straighten my clothes. "You have perhaps ninety seconds."

His own shirt was refastened in smooth, controlled movements, though his eyes never left the entrance to the square.

"What do I tell them?" I whispered, frantically trying to button my blouse with shaking fingers.

"The truth, with modifications." His voice was steady. "You fought them off yourself. The pendant and the silver knife were enough. I was never here."

"Sera!" Elena's voice was closer now, tinged with anger and worry.

Matthias stepped back, already beginning to fade into the shadows. "Tell them what they want to hear, that you're becoming the hunter they trained you to be."

"When will I see you again?"

His smile was slow, possessive. "Sooner than your family would like." Then he blended into the darkness as if he'd never existed, just as Elena appeared at the mouth of the square.

I barely had time to kick my jacket further away and pick up the silver knife just as Elena burst into the square, followed by three other hunters in tactical gear.

"Sera!" She rushed toward me, her hazel eyes taking in the scene: four dead vampires, me standing in the center holding a bloodied silver blade, looking flushed and disheveled but alive.

"I'm okay," I said quickly, trying to catch my breath. "They... they cornered me, but I managed to fight them off."

Elena's eyes narrowed as she studied my appearance. My hair was messed, my lips were swollen from kissing, and despite my attempts to straighten my clothes, I probably looked exactly like someone who'd been thoroughly made out with.

"You fought off four vampires," she said slowly. "By yourself."

"The pendant helped," I said, touching Helena's charm. "It shocked one of them when he tried to grab me. And the silver knife—David's training worked."

One of the other hunters was examining the ash piles, his expression impressed. "Heart strikes," he called out. "Clean kills, turned them all to dust. Professional work."

I felt heat flood my cheeks, but lifted my chin. "Adrenaline, I guess."

Elena stepped closer, her nose wrinkling slightly. "You smell like..." She paused, her expression growing suspicious. "Like a vampire."

My heart hammered against my ribs. "I was fighting them. Of course, I smell like a vampire."

"No," Elena said slowly, circling me like a predator. "You smell like vampire blood, yes. But also like something else. Something..." Her eyes widened with realization. "Leather. And smoke."

The scent of Matthias's skin, still clinging to me from our embrace. I fought to keep my expression neutral.

"I don't know what you mean," I said. "I've been running through Prague's streets for hours. I probably smell like everything."

Elena's hand moved to the silver blade at her hip. "Sera, I specifically told you not to leave the hotel after dark. What the hell were you thinking?"

There it was, the anger I'd been expecting. I straightened my shoulders, meeting her furious gaze.

"I was thinking that I'm tired of being treated like a prisoner," I said, letting real frustration color my voice. "I'm tired of being monitored and managed and protected from my own choices."

"Your choices almost got you killed!"

"But they didn't." I gestured to the dead vampires around us. "I handled it. I protected myself, just like you and David taught me."

Elena looked at me for a long moment, conflict crossing her face. Pride in my apparent progress clashed with suspicion about my flushed look and the details of my "victory."

"We're going back to the hotel," she said finally. "Now. And tomorrow, we're having a very long conversation about following orders."

I nodded meekly, sheathing the silver knife. But as we left the square, I caught Elena glancing back at the ash piles with a confused expression.

The walk back to the hotel was tense and silent. Elena kept shooting me suspicious looks, while the other hunters flanked us like an honor guard. Or a prison escort.

"How did you end up in that particular square?" Elena asked as we reached the hotel's front entrance.

"I was walking," I said, which was technically true. "Couldn't sleep, needed air. They found me."

"Just happened to find you in the most dangerous part of Prague at four in the morning."

"Luck of the draw, I guess."

Elena's jaw tightened, but she didn't press further. The lobby was empty except for the night clerk, who looked startled to see our small army entering his quiet hotel.

In the elevator, one of the hunters, a tall man with graying temples, spoke up. "The silver work was impressive. Most people panic when faced with multiple attackers."

I shrugged.

"Four vampires, though," another hunter mused. "That's unusually organized for random street predators."

Elena's eyes flicked to me. "Unless they weren't random."

"What do you mean?" I asked, though my stomach clenched with dread.

"I mean, they might have been hunting you specifically. Looking for the Sterling bloodline." Elena's voice was cold. "Which means your little midnight stroll wasn't just reckless —it was exactly what they wanted."

The elevator dinged at my floor, and Elena walked me to my door.

"Get some sleep," she said, her voice still tinged with anger. "And Sera? Next time you decide to ignore my instructions about staying inside, remember that you got lucky tonight. Very lucky."

She waited until I was safely inside before heading back down the hall.

After she left, I sank onto the bed, my hands shaking with delayed reaction. The lie had held, but Elena's suspicions were clearly growing. How long before she put the pieces together?

I moved to the bathroom mirror, studying my reflection. My lips were still swollen from Matthias's kisses, my skin flushed with lingering arousal. I looked exactly like someone who'd been thoroughly ravished.

I tilted my head, checking my neck where he'd bitten me. The skin was unmarked; he'd healed it completely before the hunters arrived. But I could still feel the pull of his mouth there, the memory of his teeth piercing my skin.

I touched my fingers to my lips, remembering the heat of his mouth, the commanding tone when he'd told me to tell him what I wanted. The way our connection had flared to life when he'd fed from me, stronger and more real than anything I'd ever experienced.

Heat flooded through me again at the thought, my body responding as if he were still pressed against me. I gripped the edge of the sink, trying to steady myself.

I needed a cold shower. A very cold shower.

26

I woke to the sound of my phone buzzing insistently on the nightstand, dragging me from dreams that were far more vivid than sleep should allow. For a moment, I lay still, caught between the memory of cool hands on my skin and the harsh reality of morning light streaming through the hotel curtains.

My mind was still reeling from the interrupted passion of the night before. Every nerve ending felt hypersensitive, alive in a way that made the cotton sheets against my skin almost unbearable. I pressed my fingertips to my throat, searching for marks that I knew wouldn't be there, but I could still feel the phantom pull of his mouth, the electric shock of connection when he'd fed from me.

The phone buzzed again. David's name flashed on the screen.

I cleared my throat, trying to sound normal. "Morning, David."

"Sera." His familiar voice was a mix of relief and concern. "How did you sleep?"

Heat flooded my cheeks as memories crashed over me. Matthias pressed against me in that square, his hands roaming over my body with possessive hunger, the way I'd begged him to bite me. The way our connection had flared back to life when he finally did.

"I slept fine," I lied, my voice coming out steadier than I felt. "Just tired from yesterday's excitement."

"That's understandable. Four vampires is no small thing." David paused, and I could practically hear him analyzing my tone. "Elena mentioned you seemed different afterward. More confident. Like you'd found your footing as a hunter."

If only he knew what I'd actually found. Or rather, who had found me, claimed me, marked me in ways that went far deeper than physical.

"I guess surviving something like that changes you," I said, which was true enough. I had been changed by last night, just not in the way my family thought.

"It does. Your parents would be proud." The warmth in David's voice made guilt twist in my stomach. "Are you planning to do any research at the library today? I know you've been making progress on understanding the ritual texts."

"Probably." I sat up in bed, immediately regretting the movement as the sheets slid against my sensitized skin. "I want to keep working while I can focus."

"Good. Just remember what we discussed about staying in public areas." David hesitated. "Sera, you're sure you're feeling alright? You sound a little breathless."

Because I was. Just the act of sitting up had made me aware of how my body felt different this morning—more alive, more aware, like every cell was humming with some new frequency. The ache between my thighs reminded me of exactly how our encounter had ended, how close we'd come before the hunters interrupted.

"Just waking up," I managed. "You know how I am before coffee."

David laughed, the tension in his voice easing. "Right. Well, get some caffeine and breakfast. And Sera? Be careful out there. Even in daylight."

After he hung up, I slumped back against the pillows, pressing my palms to my flushed cheeks. This was insane. I was lying in my hotel bed, aroused beyond reason by memories of a vampire's touch, while my family planned strategies to hunt his kind.

I forced myself to get up, to move through the motions of a normal morning. Shower, coffee, breakfast. But every mundane action felt surreal, like I was wearing a costume of my old life while something fundamental had shifted underneath.

The shower was torture. The hot water cascading over my hypersensitive skin made me think of cool hands and commanding whispers. I found myself leaning against the tile wall, my fingers tracing the spots where his mouth had been, where his hands had explored.

"Tell me what you want, Sera."

His voice echoed in my memory, rich with that accent that made my name sound like a prayer. I could still feel the electric shock when our connection had sparked to life, faint but unmistakable.

My hand started moving lower, following the path his had taken—

I turned the water to cold, gasping as the shock erased both the physical need and thoughts I wasn't ready to face. Whatever was happening between Matthias and me, it was becoming impossible to ignore. The separation from him now felt physical, like missing a limb.

By the time I was dressed and sitting down to eat break-fast in the hotel's dining room, I'd managed to compose myself enough to look normal. But inside, every cell in my body was waiting. Listening. Hoping for some sign that he was thinking about me too.

The elderly couple at the next table was discussing their sightseeing plans, their voices a comfortable murmur in the background. Around me, normal people lived normal lives, completely unaware that their city was home to immortal predators and the descendants of those who hunted them.

Just weeks ago, I'd been one of them. Now I sat here, outwardly calm, while my body burned with memories of supernatural desire and my mind raced with questions I couldn't ask anyone.

My phone buzzed with a text from Elena: *Remember, no going out alone at night. Last night proved Prague is more dangerous than we thought.*

I stared at the message, almost laughing at the irony. They had no idea that the real danger wasn't the vampires hunting in Prague's shadows. It was the way my heart raced every time I thought about green eyes and the promise in a voice that whispered my name like he owned it.

27

The Strahov Monastery Library felt quieter and more intimate, with most of the tourists at other attractions. I claimed my usual table in the back corner, spreading out my research materials with the kind of focused determination that had gotten me through graduate school.

But concentration proved impossible.

Every few minutes, my attention would drift from the illuminated manuscripts to the shadows between the towering bookshelves. My body still hummed with restless energy, and I caught myself touching my throat repeatedly, searching for marks that weren't there.

"You seem more energetic today," Helena observed as she appeared beside my table. Her light eyes scrutinized my face with an intensity that made me uncomfortable.

Heat flooded my cheeks. Could she sense what had happened? Did I look different somehow?

"Just had a lot of coffee this morning," I said, forcing myself to focus on the manuscript in front of me. "Trying to make up for lost research time after yesterday's excitement."

Helena nodded but didn't move away. "The vampire

attack must have been quite traumatic. It's natural for such encounters to leave you feeling altered."

The way she said 'altered' made my skin prickle. I looked up to find her watching me with an expression that suggested she knew far more than she was saying.

"I'm fine," I said firmly. "Actually, I was hoping to look into some genealogical records today. Family history research. Do you have anything like that in the collection?"

"Of course." Helena's expression brightened with genuine interest. "What family line are you researching?"

"Sterling. I realized yesterday that I know very little about my ancestors beyond a few generations."

Something flickered across Helena's face. "Sterling genealogies... yes, I believe we have some records. Scattered and incomplete, but they might provide some insight."

She vanished among the stacks, leaving me alone with my racing thoughts and the lingering ache that wouldn't fade. When she came back twenty minutes later, she carried a leather portfolio that looked centuries old.

"These are fragments," she explained, setting it on my table. "Collected from various sources over the years. The Sterling family records were deliberately dispersed, for reasons that aren't entirely clear."

I opened the portfolio with trembling fingers, expecting to find neat genealogical charts like the ones I'd seen in academic research.

Instead, I found chaos.

The family tree extended across multiple sheets of parchment, some clearly much older than others. Names and dates were written in different handwriting styles and inks, as if the records had been added to and revised over centuries. I instantly understood why Helena had seemed cautious. These weren't just genealogical charts; they were a labyrinth of contradictions and mysteries.

It was the gaps that caught my attention first.

Entire generations were absent. Not just individuals, entire branches of the family tree suddenly vanished, with no reason or clue as to where the bloodlines had gone.

Sterling daughters appeared throughout the records, but many of them lacked death dates. While other family trees might list "died 1847" or "deceased 1623," these entries just stopped. Names that appeared in one generation were absent from the next, with no explanation for where they'd gone.

I traced my finger along the parchment, following bloodlines that seemed to vanish into thin air. It was as if entire branches of my family had simply disappeared from history.

I focused on a particular branch, following it through generations until I reached the most recent entries. The records seemed to stop abruptly in the early 1900s, but next to several of the female names across the centuries, someone had drawn strange symbols in faded ink. They looked almost like brands or marks of some kind.

"Helena," I called softly, not wanting to attract attention from other researchers.

She appeared at my shoulder with that silent movement I was starting to associate with people who knew more about Prague's supernatural community than they let on.

"These symbols," I said, pointing to the marks beside certain names. "Do you know what they mean?"

Helena leaned closer, studying the markings. Her expression grew troubled.

"I'm not certain," she said slowly. "They appear to be classification marks of some kind. Perhaps indicating different branches of the family, or different paths chosen."

"Different paths?" I looked up at her. "What kind of paths?"

Helena's eyes met mine, and I saw something there that made my stomach clench with unease.

"Perhaps that's a question you should ask your family," she said quietly. "They would know the Sterling history far better than I do."

But even as she said it, I could see in her expression that she doubted my family would tell me the truth.

I turned back to the records, my mind racing. The more I studied the family tree, the more questions arose. Why were there so many missing women? Why did some branches just stop? And what did these symbols mean?

I found myself sketching the strange marks in my notebook, copying them along with the names they accompanied. There were at least six different symbols that appeared next to different names over the centuries. Some appeared more often than others, and some seemed to cluster during certain time periods.

One symbol appeared beside my great-great-grandmother's name: Elisara Sterling, 1889-?. No death date.

"What the hell does that mean?" I muttered under my breath.

I studied the tree more closely, trying to trace patterns. The symbols seemed to appear more frequently during certain periods: the 1600s, the 1800s, the early 1900s. Times of historical upheaval, perhaps? Wars, plagues, social changes?

But that didn't explain the consistent thread of missing women, or the cryptic language used to describe their fates.

"Helena," I said slowly, "have you ever heard the phrase 'lost to darkness' in a historical context? Maybe related to Prague's history?"

Her expression grew even more guarded. "There are many ways to interpret such language. Plagues, wars, personal tragedies..."

"But?"

"But sometimes," she said, "old families developed their own terminology for situations that were difficult to explain in conventional terms."

The way she said it made me pause, as if there were family secrets hidden in these records that I wasn't meant to understand.

I spent another hour studying the documents, making notes and sketches, but the more I learned, the more confused I became. My family tree looked like a puzzle with half the pieces missing, and the remaining pieces seemed designed to hide rather than reveal.

By the time I packed up my research, it was beginning to get dark outside. I had pages of notes and sketches, but no real answers—only more questions and a growing certainty that my family had been hiding something big from me, bigger than the hunting history.

As I gathered my things, Helena approached one final time.

"Miss Sterling," she said quietly, "a word of advice. When you ask your family about these records, be prepared for the possibility that some knowledge comes with a price."

"What kind of price?"

Her light eyes held mine for a long moment. "The kind that changes everything you thought you knew about yourself."

I left the library with Helena's warning echoing in my mind, my notebook filled with more mysteries than answers. The afternoon shadows felt longer as I walked back toward the hotel, and I couldn't shake the feeling that I was missing something important.

28

I jolted awake to urgent knocking at my door, my heart hammering as I struggled to orient myself. The morning light filtered through the curtains, and the bedside clock read 6:47 AM.

The knocking came again.

"Sera!" Elena's voice, tight with tension. "Open up. Now."

I stumbled out of bed, grabbing a robe as I made my way to the door. When I opened it, Elena stood in the hallway fully dressed in tactical gear, her hazel eyes sharp and alert.

"Get dressed," she said, pushing past me into the room. "We have a situation."

"What kind of situation?" I asked, still trying to shake off sleep.

Elena was already moving to my window, pulling the curtains wider to scan the street below. "Multiple coordinated attacks across Prague last night. Seven dead, three missing. All drained of blood."

My stomach dropped. "Vampires?"

"Pack behavior. Organized hunting parties." Elena turned from the window, her expression grim. "This level of coordination is unprecedented. Something's got them stirred up."

I felt the blood drain from my face as the realization hit me. Two nights ago, I'd fed Matthias my blood in that square. Made him stronger. And now vampires across the city were hunting in coordinated groups.

"How do you know it was coordinated?" I managed.

"Witnesses reported seeing multiple attackers working together. Same time frame across different districts." Elena pulled out her tablet, showing me a map of Prague dotted with red pins. "These aren't random feeding frenzies. This is organized supernatural warfare."

Each red pin felt like an accusation. Bodies were scattered across the city because I'd strengthened one of their kind. Because I'd let desire override judgment.

"The bodies were found at dawn," Elena continued, swiping through crime scene photos that made me nauseous. "All completely drained. But here's the strange part: they were left in public places. Almost like a message."

"A message saying what?"

Elena's eyes met mine, and I saw something there that made my chest tighten with dread. "That the balance of power in Prague is shifting. And we need to figure out why."

I forced myself to look at the photos, at the drained, lifeless faces of people who had been going about their normal lives just hours before. Young and old, locals and tourists. All dead because vampires had suddenly become more aggressive.

Because Matthias had become stronger.

"There's an emergency meeting at the safe house in an hour," Elena said, closing the tablet. "Command wants all available hunters mobilized."

"Of course." I wrapped my robe tighter around myself, trying to hide the trembling in my hands. "I'll get ready."

Elena stared at my face with that intensity I was beginning to hate. "You look sick. Are you feeling alright?"

"Just tired," I lied. "The attack two nights ago. I guess it's still affecting me."

"Understandable." Elena's expression softened slightly. "But Sera, I need you sharp today. Whatever's happening in Prague, it's escalating fast. We can't afford any more surprises."

After she left, I slumped against the closed door, guilt and fear churning in my chest. I'd known there would be consequences to feeding Matthias. I'd seen how the blood had strengthened him, how it had restored his power.

But I'd done it anyway. Because I couldn't bear to watch him die.

And now people were dead because of that choice.

I moved to the window, staring out at Prague's morning streets. Somewhere out there, families were waking up to discover their loved ones would never come home. Police were trying to explain deaths that defied rational explanation. And my family was preparing for a war that I might have helped trigger.

I wasn't ready for any of this. I wasn't ready to sit in that safe house and plan strategies against creatures I was just starting to understand. I wasn't ready to pretend that I hadn't played a role in escalating the violence.

And I definitely wasn't ready to face the possibility that my feelings for Matthias had made me complicit in murder.

As I got ready to leave, one thought echoed through my mind: I needed to see him again. Not just to satisfy the longing that was eating me alive, but to understand what we'd set in motion.

The emergency briefing had been a blur of tactical discussions and grim statistics that made my stomach churn. Seven victims. Three missing. Coordinated vampire attacks across Prague's most populated districts. And through it all, I'd sat there with guilt consuming me, knowing I might have played a role in triggering the violence.

Now, hours later, I was restless in my hotel room. The sketches from my family tree lay forgotten on the desk, over-shadowed by crime scene photos that refused to leave my mind. Every time I closed my eyes, I saw those drained faces.

29

The clock on my nightstand read 11:47 PM.

I moved to the window for the hundredth time and looked out at Prague's dark streets. Somewhere out there, vampires were hunting in coordinated packs. Somewhere out there, Matthias was—

The air in my room seemed to crackle instantly.

I spun around, my heart pounding against my ribs, to find him standing near my bed. He had appeared silently, without warning, like a shadow. In the dim light from the bedside lamp, his skin seemed to glow, and his green eyes held an intensity that took my breath away.

But something was off. He looked more dangerous than before. More powerful. The weakness I'd sensed nights earlier was gone entirely, replaced by a predatory energy that filled the entire room.

"Matthias," I breathed, relief flooding through me before fear crashed back in.

"Sera." His voice was soft, but I could hear the tension beneath it. "I needed to see you."

"Seven people are dead," I said, the words tumbling out

before I could stop them. "Elena showed me the photos. Seven people drained by vampire packs, and I—" My voice broke. "Did I cause this? By feeding you, did I somehow—

"Stop." He moved toward me, and I saw something flicker across his features. "This isn't your fault."

"Isn't it?" I backed against the window, my hands pressed to the glass behind me. "You're stronger now. I can see it, feel it. The other vampires—Elena said they're more coordinated, more aggressive. They can sense your returning strength, can't they?"

Matthias went very still, and that was answer enough.

"They can," I whispered, horror flooding through me. "Oh God, those people died because—"

"Because vampires are predators," he said firmly, stepping closer. "Because they hunt and kill regardless of what happens between us. Don't take that burden on yourself."

"But you're a leader, aren't you?" I studied his face, seeing the truth in his eyes. "That's why your strength matters. That's why they're all stirred up."

He was quiet for a long moment, his gaze never leaving mine.

"There are hierarchies among my kind. Age, power, territory. They all matter. When an old vampire grows stronger, it shifts the balance."

"And you're old and now stronger because of my blood."
"Yes."

I slumped against the window, feeling the heavy burden of seven deaths on me.

"You saved my life," Matthias interrupted, his voice rough with something that sounded like pain. "Don't you understand, Sera? Without your blood, I would have died. And if I had died, the power vacuum would have triggered something far worse than coordinated hunting."

"What do you mean?"

"I mean that my death would have started a war." His eyes blazed with an inner fire that made my pulse race despite everything. "Every vampire in Eastern Europe would have descended on Prague to claim my territory. The bloodshed you're mourning would be nothing compared to what would have followed."

The words hung in the air between us, heavy with consequences I was only beginning to understand.

"So those seven people died because I saved you, but more would have died if I'd let you die?"

"Yes."

"That's..." I laughed bitterly. "That's a hell of a choice."

"You don't understand," He said quietly. "Your blood is the only thing keeping me alive."

I looked up at him. "What does that mean?"

"It means I'm dying, Sera. Have been for a very long time." His jaw clenched. "Your blood doesn't just heal me, it's the only thing slowing the process."

My chest tightened with something that felt dangerously close to panic. "Dying from what?"

"Something I can't explain without putting you in more danger."

"That's not good enough," I said, standing to face him. "People are dying because of choices I'm making blindly. I deserve to understand what's happening."

His expression shuttered. "You deserve to stay alive. And knowing more would put that at risk."

"So what's the plan? I just keep feeding you my blood forever?"

Something raw and vulnerable flickered across his face. "I'm not sure."

The honesty in those three words cut deeper than any

elaborate explanation could have. He looked lost, desperate, caught between needing me and wanting to protect me.

"Show me," I said quietly.

"Show you what?"

"What happens between us when you feed from me. I can feel something, something I've never felt before." I stepped closer. "I need to understand that much, at least."

His eyes darkened, and I saw his control wavering. "Sera—"

"Please." I reached up, my fingers barely brushing his cheek. "If you can't tell me about why you need my blood, at least help me understand this."

For a moment, we stood frozen, the air between us electric with tension. Then his hands came up to frame my face.

"If I show you," he said quietly, "you'll understand why this is so dangerous. Why I should stay away from you."

"Then let me understand."

Something shifted in his expression, hunger replacing the control he'd been maintaining. His mouth crashed against mine with desperate hunger. Immediately, I felt it— an electric shock, stronger and more real now. When his tongue slid against mine, I tasted something dark and intoxicating that made my knees weak.

But more than that, I could sense something at the edge of my consciousness. Not just his emotions, but his power— dark, overwhelming, predatory in a way that should have sent me running.

For a split second, I glimpsed what he really was beneath the controlled exterior: something that had survived centuries by being the apex predator. I saw flashes of violence and a raw, unfiltered instinct to dominate. The image of a room full of bodies, chaos erupting as he unleashed his full strength, sent a jolt of fear through me.

When he pulled back, we were both breathing hard, the air thick with tension.

"That," he said, his voice rough, "is what makes this dangerous. What makes you dangerous to me."

I stared into his burning green eyes, my body still humming from his touch. "I don't care about the danger."

Something blazed in his expression at my words. "You should."

"Why?" I stepped closer, eliminating the distance he'd tried to create. "Because I might get hurt? Because I might make the wrong choice? Everyone in this city is so concerned with protecting me from myself."

"Because," he said, his voice dropping to that commanding whisper that made heat pool between my thighs, "once I start touching you the way I want to, you'll be mine in ways I can't take back."

"Good," I breathed. "I want to be yours."

He backed me against the wall, his body pressing against mine as his mouth found my throat. This wasn't the gentle, tender feeding from before. This was hunger unbound, and when his teeth grazed my pulse point, I gasped and arched into him.

"Tell me what you want," he commanded against my skin, his voice rough with barely restrained desire.

"You," I managed, my hands fisting in his shirt. "I want you."

His hands moved to the buttons of my shirt, fingers working with control despite the tension radiating from his body. "Look at me when I touch you," he ordered, his green eyes blazing as the fabric parted.

I obeyed instinctively, holding his gaze as he pushed the material off my shoulders. The cool air hit my skin, but his touch immediately followed, warming every inch he explored.

"So perfect when you surrender to me," he murmured, his hands tracing the lace edge of my bra.

The praise made me clench my thighs, and I found myself leaning into his touch, craving more. When his thumbs brushed across my nipples through the thin fabric, I couldn't suppress the soft moan that escaped me.

"That's it," he said, satisfaction clear in his voice. "Let me hear you."

My hands moved to his shirt with more confidence this time, no fumbling as I worked the buttons free. When his chest was exposed, I didn't hesitate—I pressed my palms flat against his skin, marveling at the way he shivered under my touch.

"Sera," he breathed, his head falling back.

"I love the way you say my name," I murmured, my lips finding the pulse point at his throat.

His hands tightened on my waist, lifting me slightly so I was pressed more firmly against the wall. The new position brought us impossibly closer, and I could feel every hard line of his body against mine.

"Tell me what you need," he said, his mouth moving to that sensitive spot just below my ear that made me shiver.

"More," I gasped as his teeth scraped against my skin. "I need more of you."

His hands moved purposefully, removing the rest of my clothes, leaving me breathless. When I stood before him naked in the dim lamplight, his eyes burned with such intensity I felt it like a physical touch.

"Perfect," he breathed, his hands mapping every curve, every sensitive spot that made me arch and gasp. "You're absolutely perfect."

I reached for his remaining clothes, desperate to feel his skin against mine, but he caught my hands gently.

"This is about you," he said, his voice commanding but tender. "Let me worship you."

Before I could object, he lowered his mouth to my neck, following a line along my collarbone and pausing momentarily as if to relish the experience. Then his lips reached my nipple, where he started to suck softly, evoking a feeling that made me press against him.

"Matthias," I gasped, my hands tangling in his dark hair.

"Let go," he commanded against my skin. "Let me take care of you."

His hand traveled slowly downward, each touch igniting a trail of fire across my skin, until it finally settled on that sensitive spot that sent a shiver of electricity through my body. Pressed against the wall, I arched and gasped as his fingers began to expertly rub over my clit, coaxing waves of pleasure that made me writhe with an insatiable yearning.

As his fingers began to explore, he gently tested my boundaries, slipping one inside me with a deliberate, tantalizing slowness. The moment he did, a cry of pleasure tore from my throat, raw and unrestrained.

Instinctively, my hips began to move, seeking more of the intoxicating sensations he was igniting. When a second finger joined the first, the intensity multiplied, a crescendo of bliss that was almost too much to bear.

His touch grew more insistent, each stroke and caress more precise. I could feel myself ascending toward a peak I'd never known, every nerve alive with a thrilling, almost unbearable awareness. My breaths came in ragged gasps, each one a battle against the tidal wave of pleasure that threatened to sweep me away entirely.

"That's it," he urged, his voice a gravelly whisper full of urgency and hunger. "Give yourself to me."

As I teetered on the brink of climax, his lips traveled to

my throat, the coolness of his breath offering a stark contrast to the heat enveloping me. His presence was electric, and his words were a sensual promise murmured against my skin.

"Let me taste you while you fall apart for me," he murmured, his voice a seductive caress against my skin.

His teeth pierced my neck, right as his touch sent me spiraling over the edge. The combined sensations, pleasure, and the electric jolt of our connection surged through me with staggering intensity. I called out his name as my body trembled, waves of ecstasy coursing through me while I felt my blood flowing into him.

Mine, his voice whispered again through the bond.

When he finally lifted his head, I was shaking from both the climax and the loss of that intoxicating connection.

"You taste like everything I've ever wanted," he breathed, his eyes blazing with renewed power and something that looked dangerously like possession.

As my breathing slowly returned to normal, I reached for him with shaking hands, wanting to return the pleasure he'd given me. But he caught my wrists gently, bringing them to his lips to press a soft kiss to each palm.

"Not yet, my darling," he said, his eyes burning with promise. "When I finally let you touch me like that, I want you to understand exactly what it means."

"What does it mean?" I whispered, still floating in the aftermath of what he'd done to me.

His smile was soft but edged with something darker.

Then he lifted me easily and carried me to the bed, laying me down gently among the tangled sheets.

"Get some sleep, Sera," he said quietly.

And then he was gone, leaving me alone with his lingering scent on my skin.

I lay there in the darkness, my body still humming from what we'd shared. Through the faint connection between us, I could sense him moving through Prague's shadows, stronger now because of my blood.

Seven people had died because vampires were stirring. And I'd just made their leader more powerful than ever.

I should have felt guilty. Terrified.

Instead, all I wanted was more.

30

The urgent pounding on my hotel room door jolted me from the deepest, most satisfying sleep I'd had in weeks. For a moment, I lay still in the tangled sheets, warmth still radiating through me from the memory of Matthias's touch, the phantom sensation of his fingers made me shiver with renewed desire.

The knocking came again, more insistent.

"Sera!" David's voice carried through the door, tight with tension. "Open up. Now."

I stumbled out of bed, grabbing the hotel robe as I made my way to the door. My reflection in the hallway mirror stopped. My hair was thoroughly messed, my lips still swollen from his kisses, and my skin held that flushed, satisfied glow that was impossible to hide.

But it was my throat that made my breath catch. Two perfect puncture wounds marked the skin of my neck, dark against my skin like a brand of ownership.

"Sera!" Elena's voice joined David's. "We know you're in there!"

I pulled the robe's collar higher, trying to hide the marks, and opened the door before they could use their key.

David and Elena stood in the hallway, both fully dressed despite the early hour, their faces grim.

"Thank God," David said, relief flooding his voice as he pushed past me into the room. "We need to move you to a safer location immediately. The vampire attacks last night—"

He stopped mid-sentence, his steel-gray eyes taking in my disheveled appearance, the way I clutched the robe closed at my throat. Elena followed his gaze, her hazel eyes sharpening.

"Sera," David said slowly, his voice changing. "What happened to your neck?"

I tried to tighten my robe around my neck even more, but it was too late. Elena was already moving closer, her nostrils flaring slightly as she caught the scent lingering on my skin.

"Leather," she breathed, her face going white with horror. "And smoke."

David stepped closer, and I saw the exact moment he spotted the bite marks despite my attempts to hide them. The color drained from his face completely.

"No," he whispered. "Sera, tell me you didn't—"

"She did." Elena's voice was flat. She circled me like a predator, taking in every detail: my flushed skin, my swollen lips, the obvious signs of an intimate encounter. "Look at her, David. She's practically glowing with it."

I lifted my chin defiantly, even as my heart hammered against my ribs. "Yes, I was with him. Last night."

Elena's expression twisted with disgust. "While people were dying across Prague. While vampire packs were hunting in coordinated groups, draining innocent civilians, you were—" She gestured at my obvious state. "You were feeding yourself to the monster responsible."

"He's not a monster," I said firmly, though the words felt empty given what Elena was describing.

"More people died last night, Sera." David's voice cracked with pain and anger. "After the seven from the other night, there were three more. The vampire attacks are escalating, becoming more organized, more vicious. And you were with one of them while it happened."

The guilt settled heavy in my chest, but I forced myself to stand straighter. "That's not—he wouldn't—"

"Look in the mirror!" Elena grabbed my shoulders, spinning me toward the full-length mirror on the wall. "Look at what you've become!"

I stared at my reflection, at the bite marks stark against my throat, at the satisfied glow in my skin, at the clear evidence of what I shared with Matthias while people died across the city.

"You're compromised," Elena continued. "Completely compromised. The Sera we knew would never have chosen personal pleasure over innocent lives."

"I didn't know—" I started.

"You didn't want to know," David interrupted, his voice thick with disappointment. "Because knowing would have meant choosing between him and doing what's right."

I turned to face them, my hands shaking. I wanted to defend him, to explain that it wasn't that simple, but the words wouldn't come.

David stepped closer, hope flickering in his eyes.

"Then let us help you," he said gently. "Let us figure this out together."

"It may be too late for that," Elena said. "She's already marked. Already his."

"Elena—" David warned.

Elena shook her head grimly. "She's not defending him, David, but she's not condemning him either. Look at those marks. She's bonded to him whether she understands it or not."

I touched my throat unconsciously, and Elena's eyes tracked the movement.

"What happens now?" I asked quietly.

"Now we figure out how to break whatever hold he has on you,' David said gently. "Before it's too late."

"Get dressed," Elena commanded, already moving toward my suitcase. "We're leaving. Now."

"No," I said.

"We'll go somewhere safe," David said, but he wouldn't meet my eyes. "Somewhere we can assess the situation properly."

"I'm not going."

"Please don't make this harder than it needs to be," David said, his eyes pleading.

"I won't let you lock me up."

I backed toward the window, but Elena was already moving.

"I'm sorry, Sera," David said as Elena pulled silver-lined restraints from her bag.

"But we can't trust your judgment anymore."

I tried to run for the door, but David stepped into my path while Elena moved behind me. Between the two of them, I didn't stand a chance.

"I'm sorry," Elena whispered as her arms locked around me, her voice breaking.

The silver restraints clicked around my wrists, and I felt Elena's hands trembling as she secured them.

———

THE DRIVE to the safe house passed in tense silence. I sat in the back seat between David and Elena, my wrists bound.

The metal bit into my skin, a constant reminder that I was no longer family, I was a threat to be contained.

The warehouse looked the same as ever, but this time when we entered, I was greeted by a team of specialists I'd never seen before. Men and women in tactical gear, their eyes cold and calculating as they evaluated me like a specimen. Hayes stood among them, his scarred face impassive as he watched me with the same detachment.

"Subject is heavily compromised," announced a stern woman with graying hair and scars across her throat. "Blood bond markers are visible, and supernatural scent contamination is severe. How long since the last feeding?"

"Last night," Elena replied curtly. "Fresh bite marks, obvious intimate contact."

The woman, apparently some kind of expert in supernatural corruption, circled me slowly. "The bond is deeper than initial reports suggested. She's not just influenced; she's partially claimed."

"What does that mean?" David demanded.

"It means she's too dangerous to leave free," the woman said bluntly. "The blood bond creates a psychic link. She could be feeding him information, calling to him, even unconsciously guiding him to targets."

"That's not true," I protested, but my voice came out weak, uncertain.

Hayes stepped closer. "The blood bond makes you a walking transmitter. Every thought, every plan, every weakness goes straight to the enemy." His voice was flat. "You're not just compromised. You're a security breach."

David's face crumpled with pain and resignation. "What do you recommend?"

"Containment until we can determine the full extent of the corruption," the specialist said. "Silver-lined isolation to prevent supernatural communication. We'll need to assess whether the bond can be severed or if more permanent measures are required."

"Permanent measures?" I asked, though I was afraid to hear the answer.

Hayes's smile was cold. "That depends on how cooperative you are."

They led me to a cell in the back of the safehouse. The silver-lined walls gleamed dully in the harsh fluorescent light, casting a cold glow. The air felt oppressive, like breathing through wet cotton, stifling and heavy in my lungs.

"This is the only way to help you," Elena said, her voice strained as they guided me inside.

A single cot sat bolted to the floor, along with a metal toilet and sink. The door was the same solid steel with no handle on the inside, just a small window reinforced with silver mesh.

"How long?" I asked as they prepared to leave me there again.

Elena paused at the threshold. "We don't know. The blood moon is still weeks away. That gives us time to explore our options."

"What options?"

"First, we find a way to break the bond and restore you to who you were," David said, his voice heavy with false hope. "Second, we use you as bait for the ritual."

"If that fails?" I whispered.

Elena closed her eyes briefly, pain flickering across her face. "We make sure you can never be used as a weapon against innocent people. Whatever that takes."

The door slammed shut, leaving me alone in the silver-lined cell, cut off from everything I knew and felt.

But worst of all, I couldn't feel Matthias anymore. The faint connection that had been growing between us was muffled by the silver, reduced to barely a whisper at the edge of my consciousness.

I felt truly alone.

And I finally understood what my family was capable of when they decided someone was a threat.

31

They came for me the next morning.

I'd spent the night curled on the narrow cot, trying to reach through the silver dampening field to feel some trace of Matthias. But there was nothing, just a hollow ache where the connection had been, like a phantom limb that wouldn't stop hurting.

"Time to go," Hayes announced as the cell door opened. He was flanked by two hunters I didn't recognize, both carrying silver restraints.

Where?" I asked.

"To fix what he did to you," David said quietly from behind them. His face was haggard, as if he hadn't slept either. "To bring you back to us."

They led me deeper into the safe house, down corridors I'd never seen before. The air grew thicker, heavier, charged with something that made my skin crawl. We stopped at a heavy steel door carved with a red cross.

It resembled a medical facility combined with an interrogation room. Sterile white walls with silver mesh accents, bright fluorescent lights that eliminated any shadows. Electronic equipment buzzed along the walls—monitors, unknown machines, all built for a single purpose.

At the center sat a modified dentist's chair, but the restraints built into it were clearly meant for more than routine procedures. Silver-lined straps, electrodes, and IV stands loaded with fluids that glowed with an unnatural light.

"What is this place?" I whispered.

"Purification chamber," said a familiar voice. The same specialist from before stepped forward from where she'd been preparing the equipment, the stern woman with graying hair and scars across her throat. "Time to see if the bond can actually be severed."

They guided me to the chair, and I didn't resist. What was the point? The silver restraints locked around my wrists and ankles.

The pendant," the specialist said, noticing Helena's charm around my neck. "Remove it. Any protective magic will interfere with the process."

David approached reluctantly, his hands gentle as he lifted the pendant from around my neck. I felt the loss immediately—the last barrier between me and whatever they were planning to do was gone.

The specialist began arranging tools on a nearby table. Syringes filled with viscous liquid, vials of substances that emitted a faint glow, and an array of metallic instruments that felt more threatening than reassuring.

"The bond is even deeper than my initial assessment," she said to David and Elena, as if I weren't even there. "The corruption has spread further since yesterday. This will be more difficult than anticipated."

"Will it work?" David asked.

"It will sever the connection permanently," the woman replied. "But there may be side effects."

"What kind of side effects?" I found my voice.

She looked at me for the first time, her eyes conveying something that might have been sympathy. "When supernatural bonds are forcibly severed, there's often psychological trauma. Depression, inability to form emotional connections, a sense of incompleteness that never fully heals."

"You're talking about destroying part of my soul," I whispered.

"We're talking about saving what's left of it," Elena insisted.

The specialist continued her preparations, adjusting the IV stands and checking the syringes. The air felt charged as I realized the weight of what was about to happen.

I looked up at them. "And if I say no?"

"You don't get to say no," Elena replied before David could answer. "You're too dangerous the way you are."

The specialist approached me with a syringe filled with a shimmering liquid. "This will hurt," she said. "The bond won't want to be severed. It will fight back."

She inserted the syringe into the port on the IV line connected to my arm, and the liquid began to flow slowly into my vein. Within seconds, I felt an icy burn spreading through me.

The specialist then made a small cut on my palm with a sterile scalpel, and my blood dripped onto the sterile floor. The moment it hit, the room thrummed with energy, and the monitors around us flickered with static.

Pain tore through me, starting in my chest and radiating outward. It felt like something essential was being ripped away, torn from the very core of my being. I screamed, my back arching against the restraints as the force of the separation threatened to shatter me completely.

Through the agony, I could feel it happening. The thin

thread that connected me to Matthias being wrapped in something cold and suffocating, like chains around a beating heart. The connection was still there, but I couldn't reach it anymore, couldn't touch the warmth that had been growing between us.

"Stop!" I gasped, tears streaming down my face. "Please, stop!"

"Almost there," the specialist murmured, her hands moving deftly as she adjusted the settings on the nearby machines, monitoring my vital signs. "The bond is resisting, but it's weakening. Stay with me. Concentrate on your breathing."

The pain intensified, becoming something beyond physical, beyond anything I'd ever experienced. It was like having a vital part of me locked away and buried so deep I could never reach it again.

And then, with a sensation like a door slamming shut, the connection went silent.

The sudden absence was worse than the pain had been. Where there had been warmth, connection, the faint but precious sense of another soul touching mine, there was now nothing. A void so complete it left me gasping for breath that wouldn't come.

"I can't feel him," I whispered, my voice breaking. "I can't feel him anymore."

"Good," the specialist said. "It worked."

But as I sat there in the aftermath, silver restraints still binding me to the chair, I realized they were wrong. It hadn't worked. It had just traded one kind of imprisonment for another.

I was free of Matthias's influence, but I was also free of everything that had made life worth living.

32

Three days passed in a gray haze.

I lay on the narrow cot in my cell, staring at the silver-lined ceiling, feeling nothing. Not hunger, not thirst, not even the basic human need for movement or conversation. The world had been drained of color, reduced to varying shades of empty.

David visited twice a day, bringing food I couldn't taste and speaking words I couldn't process. His voice seemed to come from very far away, muffled by the cotton that had wrapped itself around my thoughts.

"You'll feel better soon," he said on the morning of the fourth day, setting a tray beside my untouched dinner from the day before. "The influence is gone. You're free now."

Free. The word felt like a joke. I turned my face toward the wall, away from his hopeful expression.

"Sera, please," David continued, his voice tight with worry. "You need to eat something. You need to try."

But what was the point? Food was just fuel for a body I no longer cared about. Words were just noise filling the silence where something infinitely more precious used to be. Even breathing felt like too much effort.

"Talk to me," David pleaded. "Tell me what you're feeling."

Nothing. I was feeling nothing. That was the problem.

The connection to Matthias hadn't just been about him. It had been about being alive, about feeling every sensation with heightened awareness, about existing in full color instead of this muted gray wasteland. Without it, I was a ghost inhabiting my own body.

"She's getting worse," his voice carried through the door. "She won't eat, won't speak. It's like she's fading away."

"The psychological effects are normal," the specialist's voice replied. "Complete withdrawal from supernatural stimulation often causes depression in the first few weeks."

"Depression?" David's voice cracked. "She looks like she's dying."

"She's not dying. She's detoxifying. This is what happens when supernatural addiction is broken. She needs time to remember how to be human again."

But I didn't want to be human again. Not if being human meant this endless, colorless void where nothing mattered and nothing felt real.

I closed my eyes and tried to remember what it had felt like when Matthias touched me, when his presence had made every nerve ending come alive. But the memories were fading, growing dimmer each day, as if the procedure had stolen those too.

The cell door opened again, and I heard footsteps approach my cot.

"We have a problem," Elena said without preamble.

I didn't answer. What was the point?

Elena pulled up the single chair and sat down, her posture tense. "They found the documents."

Something in her tone made me turn my head slightly, the first voluntary movement I'd made in days.

"What documents?" My voice came out as barely a whisper.

"The ritual ones. Instructions for the blood moon cere- mony." Elena's voice was grim. "Now they know exactly what they need to do."

I felt a spike of concern pierce through the numbness.

Elena was quiet for a moment, studying my face. "They have everything they need now, Sera. Everything except you." She stood to leave, pausing at the door. "Which means they'll be coming for you soon."

The door closed softly, leaving me alone with the weight of what was coming.

33

The next two days passed in a blur of gray emptiness. I slept more than I was awake, my body conserving energy it no longer had. The meals David brought went largely untouched, though I forced myself to drink water when the thirst became unbearable.

On the second day, I was drifting in that space between sleep and consciousness when voices in the corridor outside my cell made me freeze.

"—seven days until the blood moon," Hayes was saying, his voice tense. "We need to finalize the positioning."

"I still think this is too dangerous," David replied, and I could hear the strain in his voice. "There are too many variables, too many things that could go wrong."

I quietly slid off the cot and pressed my ear to the door, my heartbeat pounding. They were talking about the mission, and I needed to hear this.

"The plan is solid," Hayes continued. "We move her three days before the blood moon. Make it look like a transport gone wrong, let them take her. They'll think they've won."

"And then?" David's voice was weary.

"Then we let them start the ceremony. The vampire leadership will all be there, focused on the ritual. They'll be vulnerable, distracted." Hayes's footsteps paced back and forth. "That's when we strike. Silver weapons, coordinated assault, eliminate the entire hierarchy in one move."

My breath caught. Let them start the ceremony. They weren't planning to rescue me before the ritual began—they were planning to let the vampires actually start using my blood for their dark magic.

"What if we're too late?" David asked, voicing the question that was screaming in my head. "What if they complete the ritual before we can stop them?"

Hayes's pause was long enough to make my stomach clench with dread.

"Then at least we'll have taken out their leadership," he said finally. "Prague will be safe."

"And Sera?"

"Sometimes soldiers don't come home, David. That doesn't make the mission less necessary," Hayes said.

Their footsteps moved away, leaving me collapsed against the door.

They were willing to let me die. More than that, they were counting on the possibility that I might not survive, as long as they could eliminate the vampire threat.

The days that followed blurred together in a haze of growing weakness and mounting dread. Without the connection to Matthias, I felt myself fading more each day. My body was failing, slowly but steadily, as if the suppressed bond was taking some vital energy with it.

David visited less frequently now, and when he did, he could barely meet my eyes. The guilt was eating him alive, but not enough to change the plan.

Elena came by once, looking tired and stressed. "You're getting weaker," she said. "I wish there was another way to do this."

"Elena," I whispered, my voice barely audible. "What if the timing goes wrong? What if you can't get to me in time?"

Her expression crumpled for a moment before she composed herself. "We're going to do everything we can to get you out in time."

After she left, I lay on my cot staring at the ceiling, counting down the days. Six days. Five days. Four days.

Each day brought me closer to a ritual where powerful vampires would use my blood for dark magic while my family waited in the shadows, hoping I'd live long enough for them to spring their trap.

By the time I heard the guards discussing the final preparations outside my cell, three days remained. Their voices carried through the steel door as they talked about transport schedules and positioning.

"...move her tomorrow night..."

"...fake ambush has to look real..."

"...once they take her, no communication until the strike..."

Tomorrow night. They were moving me tomorrow night.

I sat up on my cot, my heart racing for the first time in days. A desperate energy flooded through me as I realized this might be my last chance to take control of my own fate.

I spent the rest of that day studying every inch of my cell with new eyes. The silver-lined walls that had seemed impenetrable before now became a challenge to overcome. The door lock that had been an insurmountable barrier now seemed possible to defeat.

Without the connection to Matthias, I had no supernatural strength to rely on. But I still had my mind, and right now, that was enough.

The guards changed shifts every eight hours. I'd been counting. The night shift was smaller—only two guards for the entire level, and they spent most of their time in the break room down the hall. I could hear them talking, laughing, and playing cards to pass the time.

During the dinner shift change, I'd noticed something. The guard who brought my meals had a habit of checking his phone while unlocking my door, dividing his attention for those crucial few seconds. If I could time it right...

But even if I got out of the cell, then what? I was weak, disoriented, in the middle of a hunter safe house filled with people who saw me as a threat. I needed help.

I needed Matthias.

Closing my eyes, I pressed my palm to my chest, trying to feel for any trace of the connection that had been buried so deep. The specialists had said the bond structure was severed, but if I could reach it somehow, even for a moment...

Matthias, I thought desperately, pouring every ounce of will I had into the silent call. *If you can hear me at all, I need you. They're moving me tomorrow night. They're going to let the ritual start before they try to save me.*

Nothing. Just the same empty void where warmth used to be.

I tried again, pressing harder, ignoring the way the effort made my head pound. *Please. I know you're out there. I know you can feel me somewhere beneath all this.*

Still nothing. The silver in the walls was too strong, or the suppression too complete, or—

Wait.

There, for just a split second, I could have sworn I felt something. Not the full warmth of our connection, but like hearing someone call your name from very far away. Faint, but there.

Matthias, I tried again, focusing every particle of my being on that tiny spark. *Three days. Blood moon. Ritual site. It's a trap.*

The effort left me gasping, drained, but I thought—maybe—I'd felt an answering pulse. Brief as a heartbeat, but real.

It would have to be enough.

The next day dragged by with agonizing slowness. I forced myself to eat the breakfast David brought, needing whatever strength I could get. He seemed surprised by my sudden appetite.

"You're looking better," he said hopefully. "More like yourself."

If only he knew. I was planning to escape from a silver-lined cell, evade trained hunters, and somehow survive long enough to get to Matthias. I'd never been less like my academic, rule-following self.

"Just trying to stay strong," I said, which was true enough.

Evening came too quickly and not quickly enough. I listened to the dinner shift change, timing the guards' routines one last time. Everything had to be perfect.

When the night guard finally came with my meal, I was ready.

He fumbled with his keys while checking a text message, just like always. The lock clicked open. He stepped inside, setting the tray on the small table while still looking at his phone.

I moved.

Years of self-defense classes that David had insisted on, combined with desperation and adrenaline, gave me just enough edge. I grabbed the metal water pitcher from my sink and brought it down hard on the back of his head. He crumpled without a sound.

My hands shook as I grabbed his keys, flashlight, and radio, then dragged his unconscious form onto my cot. It wouldn't fool anyone for long, but it might buy me precious minutes.

I locked the cell door behind me and ran.

The corridors were darker than I remembered, lit only by emergency lighting. I moved as quietly as I could, following the path they'd brought me down days ago. Up one flight of stairs, then another, my bare feet silent on the concrete.

I could hear voices from the break room—the other guard talking to someone on the phone. Good. He was distracted.

Another flight of stairs, and then I was at ground level. The exit was just ahead, marked by a red emergency light. I could taste freedom, could almost feel the cool night air of Prague on my skin.

The door was alarmed. Of course it was.

The moment I pushed it open, sirens began wailing throughout the building. I ran anyway, bursting out into the industrial district where the safe house was hidden. Behind me, I could hear shouts, the sound of boots on concrete.

I started running as fast as I could.

34

The pull was different this time—not the gentle tugging that had haunted my dreams, but something desperate bleeding through the silver's dampening effect. For days, our connection had been nothing but an ache, a void where warmth used to live. But now, it felt muffled and distant, I could feel something urgent clawing through the barriers they'd placed around my soul.

Something's wrong.

The passage beneath the cathedral was darker than I'd expected. The guard's flashlight barely cut through the black, and every step forward made the walls feel closer. But even through the silver suppressors, even through whatever barriers they'd built around us, I could feel Matthias's distress like a knife in my chest.

I broke into a run.

The passage opened into his sanctuary, and the sight that greeted me drove all breath from my lungs. Dozens of candles still flickered in their iron brackets, shadows across the stone walls, but many had burned down to nothing, leaving pools of cold wax. The air felt stale, wrong, as if the very life had drained from this sacred space.

And there, collapsed on the raised platform at the far end of the chamber, was Matthias.

"No." The word tore from my throat as I rushed toward him. "No, no, no."

He lay motionless on the stone, his usually perfect clothes rumpled and torn. His dark hair was damp with perspiration, and his skin—God, his skin was even more translucent with dark black veins covering every surface. The sharp planes of his face looked gaunt, hollowed, as if he'd aged decades in the week since I'd seen him.

But it was his eyes that nearly broke me. When they fluttered open at the sound of my approach, the emerald green had gone dim and unfocused, glazed with pain.

"Sera?" His voice was barely a whisper. He tried to sit up and failed, his strength so depleted he could barely lift his head. "You came."

"Of course I came." I dropped to my knees beside him, my hands hovering over his chest, afraid to touch him, afraid not to. Even through the dampening effect of the severing, I could feel echoes of his suffering. Something terrible was happening to him that I didn't understand. "I felt you. I felt you slipping away."

A ghost of a smile touched his lips. "The blood moon is in three days." His breath came in shallow gasps, each word seeming to cost him enormous effort. "I thought...I thought you'd chosen them."

"I'm here." The words came out softer than I intended. "I couldn't stay away from you."

I took in his appearance—the way he held himself, the ashen quality of his skin, the deliberate stillness that spoke of conserving what little strength remained.

Horror crashed over me as understanding dawned. He'd told me he was dying, that my blood was the only thing keeping him alive. But seeing him like this, barely clinging to life, made it terrifyingly real. "The thing that's been killing you, the severing made it worse, didn't it?"

"Much worse." His grip tightened on my hand with what little strength he had left. "I told you your blood was the only thing slowing the process. Without our bond, without you..." He closed his eyes, and when he opened them again, I saw resignation there that terrified me more than any threat. "I don't have much time left."

"Don't you dare." The words came out more forcefully than I intended, tinged with panic and fury. "Don't you dare give up on me now."

The sight of him—this powerful, eternal being reduced to little more than a whisper of himself, shattered something inside me. I'd thought the separation was agony for me, but I could see now that it had been torture for him. The curse was feeding on his pain, growing stronger as he grew weaker.

But I could fix this. I could save him.

My hand was already moving to search for something sharp, anything that could break the skin. I found a loose stone from the crumbling stone platform, its edge sharp enough to serve my purpose, and pressed it to my wrist without hesitation.

I met his gaze steadily as the blade bit into my skin, sending a thin line of crimson welling to the surface. "You don't get to die on me, Matthias. Not now."

The scent of my blood hit the air, and I watched his pupils dilate. But even starving, even dying, he tried to turn his head away.

"I won't. I could accidentally drain you right now," he whispered.

"You won't drain me." I moved closer, bringing my bleeding wrist toward his lips. "Take what you need. Take it all if you have to."

"Sera..."

"That's an order."

The slight smile that crossed his face told me he appreciated my attempt at dominance, but we both knew who held the power here. I was offering, and he was too far gone to refuse.

When his lips finally closed over the wound, the effect was instantaneous and overwhelming.

Heat exploded through our connection like liquid lightning, burning away the silver's dampening effect and racing through my veins. For the first time in days, I could feel him fully, not just echoes and whispers, but the complete force of our bond restored. This time, it was different from our previous sharing. This time, I felt his life force drinking deeply from mine, felt his strength returning in waves that crashed over us both and obliterated every barrier they'd tried to place between us.

The euphoria was intoxicating—better than wine, better than any drug. Through our restored connection, I felt his relief, his gratitude, the way my blood sang through his system and pulled him back from the brink of oblivion. His color returned first, the deathly look giving way to the vitality I remembered. Then his breathing deepened, steadied, and finally his eyes brightened from dull glass to brilliant emerald.

When he finally pulled back, we were both gasping for air. The change in him was incredible; just moments earlier, he'd been barely more than a fading shadow, but now he looked almost himself again. Not at full strength, but alive. *Mine.*

"Better?" I asked, though I could feel the answer through our restored connection.

Instead of responding with words, he sat up in one fluid movement and pulled me against him with renewed strength. His arms came around me like steel bands, holding me so tightly I could barely breathe, and I felt the fine tremor that ran through his powerful frame.

"I thought I'd lost you," he whispered against my hair, his voice rough with emotion. "I thought... God, Sera, I can't survive that again."

The way he looked at me, like I was salvation and damnation all at once, wrapped in a fragile human form, ignited something in my chest. Before I could think or doubt, I reached up and pulled his mouth down to mine.

The kiss was full of desperation and passion, born from the fear of almost losing each other. His lips pressed against mine with frantic need, and I could taste the copper of my own blood mixed with something dark and intoxicating that was entirely him.

Something shifted in his expression—relief turning into something more intense. The way he looked at me changed, his emerald eyes burning with an awareness that made heat pool in my stomach.

"You saved me," he said, his voice dropping to that low, intimate register that always made my pulse race. "Again."

I couldn't stop myself from reaching for him, my hands sliding up his chest to frame his face. "Matthias," I whispered, and this time his name came out like a question, like an invitation, like a plea all at once.

"Sera," he warned, but his voice was rough with desire, and his hands were already moving, skimming down my arms to settle at my waist. "If we do this now..."

"If we do what?" I challenged, getting closer until there was no space between us. "If we stop pretending we don't need this? If we stop pretending that separation doesn't feel like dying?"

A low growl rumbled in his chest, and I felt the vibration

against my palms where they rested on his shirt. "You don't know what you're asking for."

"Then show me."

His mouth collided with mine desperately, and this time, there was nothing gentle about it. His lips moved with the possession of someone who'd almost lost everything, and I met his intensity with my own. When his tongue swept against mine, I tasted power and desperation.

His hands fisted in my hair, angling my head exactly where he wanted it, and I gasped at the dominant gesture.

"I need to touch you," he said against my lips, his voice a rough command that sent heat spiraling through me. "I need to feel that you're real, that you're here."

His jacket hit the floor, followed immediately by his shirt, and in the flickering candlelight, I saw him like I never had before — all lean muscle and skin marked with scars that told of centuries of violence. But it was the way he looked at me that stole my breath—like I was something precious, necessary, and entirely his.

"Stay still for me," he commanded softly, his hands moving to the hem of my sweater. "Let me show you what you mean to me."

The quiet authority in his voice made me shiver with antici-pation. I lifted my arms obediently, letting him pull the fabric over my head, leaving me in just my bra and jeans. The cool air of the chamber raised goosebumps on my skin, but his burning gaze was like a physical touch, warming me from the inside out.

"Beautiful," he murmured, his hands skimming over my shoulders, down my arms, mapping every inch of exposed skin with adoring fingers. "I want to memorize every inch of you."

When his thumbs brushed over my pulse points, throat, wrists, and the curve of my collarbone, I felt that awareness flare between us. He could feel my heartbeat, hear the way my breathing quickened under his touch.

"Feel what you do to me," he said, taking my hands and placing them flat against his chest. Beneath my palms, his heart raced with the same desperate rhythm as mine. "Every time you're near me, every time you touch me. This is what you do to me."

His skin was smooth, and I could feel the barely leashed power thrumming beneath the surface. But more than that, I could feel his vulnerability—the way he trembled slightly under my touch, as if my hands on his skin meant everything.

"Say my name," he commanded, his voice dropping to that intimate whisper that made my core tighten. "I need to hear you say it."

"Matthias," I breathed, watching his eyes blaze brighter at the sound, a hungry spark igniting between us.

"Again."

"Matthias." This time it slipped out like a plea, and something savage and satisfied crossed his features.

"Good," he murmured, his hands tracing the line of my collarbone with gentle fingers, igniting a trail of fire across my skin. "I love the way you say my name when you're breathless."

His touch was worship and possession, gentle enough to send me into a haze of longing but firm enough to remind me exactly who was in control. When his mouth followed the path his hands had traced, pressing soft, lingering kisses to my throat, I felt my knees buckle.

"I need you to understand something," he whispered against my skin, his voice rough and thick with emotion. "What happened today, almost losing you, feeling our bond severed. I can't face that again."

His hands cupped my face, forcing me to meet his

burning gaze. In the candlelight, his features looked sharper, more otherworldly, but his eyes held a vulnerability that made my chest tight.

"You're everything to me," he said, the words pouring out like a confession from deep within him. "Not just because your blood keeps me alive, not just because of some supernatural bond. You, Sera. Your brilliant mind, your stubborn courage, and the way you chose to save me, even when everyone told you I was a monster."

My breath hitched. "Matthias—"

"Say you're mine," he demanded, his thumbs brushing over my cheekbones, his gaze deep and intense. "I need to hear you say it. I need to know you understand what you mean to me."

The intensity in his voice shattered the last of my resistance. This wasn't just desire speaking. This was centuries of loneliness, of waiting, of almost losing the one thing that made existence bearable.

"I'm yours," I whispered, my voice trembling with the weight of the promise. I watched something fierce and possessive blaze in his eyes.

"Say it again."

"I'm yours, Matthias." This time, the words came out stronger, more certain, fueled by the heat pooling between us. "I'm yours."

The sound he made was part growl, part relief, entirely male satisfaction that echoed through me. "And I'm yours," he said, pressing his forehead against mine. "Always. Forever. Nothing will change that."

As his lips pressed against mine, I saw need in his eyes, a possessive fire that burned brighter with each passing moment. His hands roamed over my body with an urgency that left me trembling, tracing the curves of my waist and arching my back as if memorizing every inch of me.

"I want you," I breathed against his lips, the admission slipping out before I could stop it. "I want this. I want you."

His eyes blazed at my confession. "Are you sure?" His voice was strained, like he was hanging onto control by a thread.

"Yes." The word came out fierce, absolute. "I'm sure."

As Matthias's expression shifted, the tension in his face melted away, replaced with a primal need. I saw the slight quiver in his jaw, the way his eyes darkened with desire, and the slight curl of his lips as his hands moved towards my bra clasp.

"Perfect," he breathed, his hands skimming over newly exposed skin. "You're absolutely perfect."

As his mouth descended upon my breast, I drew in a sharp breath, my body instinctively arching toward him. My fingers wove themselves into his thick, dark hair, each strand soft and silken under my touch. The sensation was electrifying, a thrilling current that coursed through me, intensified by the otherworldly connection we shared.

I could feel his desire through our bond, could sense the way my response affected him.

"More," I whispered, barely recognizing my own voice. "Please, Matthias, I need more."

He lifted his head to look at me, his eyes burning with possession and something deeper. "Tell me you need me," he commanded, his voice rough with desire. "Tell me you need this as much as I do."

"I need you," I gasped as his hands moved lower, fingers working at the button of my jeans. "I need this. I need you so much it hurts."

"Good," he murmured, his voice a soft, husky whisper that sent shivers down my spine as his mouth found that sensitive spot just below my ear. His breath was warm and tantalizing against my skin, a gentle caress that lingered in the air. His hands slipped beneath the waistband of my jeans, the coolness of his touch contrasting with the heat of my body. His fingers traced the lace of my underwear, making me ache with anticipation. His touch was firm and possessive, his thumbs circling my hipbones before moving to the front, stroking me through the fabric, evoking a wave of sensation that made me arch involuntarily toward him. "Because I need you more than my next breath," he confessed, his voice a primal growl as his hand slipped inside my underwear, fingers stroking my slick folds. "I need to feel you, to taste you, to make you mine."

The remaining barriers between us fell away with desperate urgency. He peeled my jeans down my legs, his mouth following the path of his hands, pressing hot, lingering kisses to my thighs that made me gasp and writhe beneath him. As I reached for his belt, my fingers fumbled with the buckle, but he caught my hands, his grip firm yet possessive.

"Allow me," he murmured, his voice thick with desire, barely contained. In moments, his clothes were discarded, falling onto the stone floor, revealing him in all his glory: sleek muscle, flawless skin, a vision of beauty intertwined with danger, and he was entirely mine.

When he lifted me onto the stone platform, the cool surface against my heated skin sent a shiver of electricity coursing through me. I felt an intense longing to feel every inch of him pressed against me, a fierce desire igniting within. He settled between my thighs, the weight of his bare skin pressing into me, sending waves of sensation spiraling through my body.

"Sera," he murmured, his voice low and intimate, thick with need. His hands, both firm and possessive, cradled my head as he held me captive in his gaze. His body, hot and hard, pressed against mine, sending shivers down my spine. The desperate control in his burning eyes was palpable.

"Are you absolutely certain?" he asked, his voice rough with anticipation.

"I'm certain," I whispered, my voice a blend of anticipation and resolve, as I pulled his mouth down to meet mine.

The last thread of control snapped. His mouth crashed against mine with desperate hunger, his tongue invading, claiming, setting off a wildfire within me. I could feel his hard length pressed against my thigh, the raw, primal need that turned him into something dangerous.

I wrapped my legs around his waist, pulling him closer, grinding against him, feeling him hot and hard against me. We were right there, on the edge, hearts pounding, breaths ragged, my body aching with need. I arched against him, ready to cross that final line, ready to feel all of him.

I felt him begin to press forward, the exquisite pressure building as he started to claim me completely. The sensation was overwhelming, a blend of pleasure and raw need. My body responded instinctively, arching into him, craving more, wanting to feel every inch of him fill me, to lose myself completely in this moment.

The heavy wooden door to the chamber burst open with a crash that sent splinters flying across the stone floor. The sound echoed through the sanctuary like thunder, shattering the intimate cocoon we'd built around ourselves.

35

"**S** ERA!"

David's voice boomed through the chamber, followed immediately by the thunder of boots on stone. I barely had time to register what was happening before Matthias was moving, his body covering mine completely as he shielded me from view.

"Stay behind me," he commanded, his voice calm despite the chaos erupting around us. His hands moved with supernatural speed, grabbing his shirt and pulling it over my head to cover me.

Through the gap between his arm and torso, I caught glimpses of the invasion. David emerged first, his crossbow raised, followed by Elena and six hunters in full tactical gear. Their weapons gleamed silver in the candlelight, all trained on Matthias with deadly focus.

But they stopped short when they saw us, me half-dressed and trembling behind Matthias, him naked from the waist up and positioned protectively over me like a predator guarding his mate.

David's face went white with horror as he took in the scene. "Jesus Christ, Sera. What has he done to you?"

"Nothing I didn't want," I managed to say, my voice shaking with adrenaline and fury at the interruption.

Elena's expression was one of pure disgust. "Look at her, David. She's completely corrupted. We're too late."

"You're not too late for anything," Matthias said, his voice carrying that dangerous edge that meant violence was about to follow. Even partially recovered, even caught at his most vulnerable, he moved with a threatening, smooth motion as he stepped between me and the hunters. "You're simply not welcome."

"Get away from her," David demanded, his weapon never wavering. "Now."

"No." The word came out flat. Matthias's stance shifted subtly, and I could feel the lethal energy coiling in his muscles. "You've taken her from me twice. It won't happen again."

Elena raised her silver blade higher. "She's not yours to take, monster. She never was."

The change in Matthias was instantaneous and terrifying. The man who had just been worshipping my body with gentle touches transformed into the predator he truly was. His eyes blazed with supernatural fire, and when he smiled, I caught a glimpse of fangs.

"Isn't she?" His voice dropped to that soft, conversational tone that meant someone was about to die. "Then why did she risk everything to save me? Why did she choose to come here instead of staying safely locked away?"

"Because you've corrupted her mind," Elena snarled. "Made her your pet."

"Have I?" Matthias tilted his head slightly, and the gesture was so predatory it made my skin crawl. "Sera, tell them whose choice this was."

All eyes turned to me, and I felt the weight of the

moment pressing down on me. I was barely covered by Matthias's shirt, my lips still swollen from his kisses, my heart still racing with unresolved tension. There was no hiding what had been happening, no pretending this was anything other than what it looked like.

"Mine," I said, my voice stronger than I felt. "It was my choice."

David's face crumpled with pain. "Sera, no. You don't understand what you're saying—"

"I understand perfectly." I stepped closer to Matthias, drawing strength from his presence. "I chose to come here. I chose to save him. And I chose this."

Elena's expression turned murderous. "Then you're no longer family. You're a liability that needs to be eliminated."

The words had barely left her lips when Matthias moved.

I'd seen him fight before, but this was different. This wasn't calculated violence or controlled aggression. This was pure, protective wrath unleashed by someone who had been pushed beyond all reasonable limits.

He moved quickly, crossing the distance to Elena before she could even register the threat. Her silver blade swept toward him in a deadly arc, but he caught her wrist mid-strike with a grip that made her bones creak audibly.

"You would threaten her?" His voice was soft, almost gentle, but I could hear the promise of violence underneath. "Your own family?"

"She's not my family anymore," Elena snarled, struggling against his iron grip. "She's yours. And that makes her the enemy."

Matthias smiled, and the expression was terrifying in its cold beauty. "Then let me show you what happens to people who try to harm what's mine."

He caught her wrist and used her own momentum against her, spinning her around and releasing her in a move that sent her flying across the chamber. She hit the far wall hard enough to knock the wind out of her.

David raised his crossbow, but Matthias was already moving again. He flowed across the stone floor like a shadow, and before David could fire, strong fingers wrapped around the crossbow's body. With a casual flex of his wrist, Matthias crushed the weapon to splinters.

"You brought hunters into my sanctuary," he said, his voice lethal, meaning someone was about to die. "You interrupted a private moment. And now you want to take her from me again?"

The backup hunters opened fire with their silver-tipped crossbow bolts, but Matthias moved through them like they were standing still. He caught two bolts mid-flight, snapped them in half, and used the broken shafts to disable two hunters with strikes too fast for my eyes to follow.

The third hunter managed to graze him across the ribs with a silver blade, and Matthias hissed at the contact. But instead of slowing him down, the pain seemed to fuel his rage. He grabbed the hunter by the throat and lifted him off his feet with one hand.

"Silver may burn," he said, as if he wasn't currently strangling a man. "But it doesn't kill me. Would you like to know what does?"

"Matthias, stop!" I called out, terrified by the violence but more terrified of what would happen if he killed my family. "Don't kill them!"

He paused, the hunter still dangling from his grip, and looked back at me. Something in my voice seemed to reach him through the haze of protective violence.

"They would have killed you," he said, his voice trembling with barely controlled rage. "Elena just said she'd eliminate you."

"I know." I stepped closer, careful not to make any sudden movements. "But they're still my family. Please."

For a moment, the chamber was silent except for the sound of ragged breathing and Elena's quiet whimpers. Matthias's eyes burned with inhuman fire as he looked between me and the hunters who had dared to threaten what he treasured most.

Finally, he released his grip. The hunter dropped to the floor, gasping and clutching his throat.

"You have thirty seconds to leave my sanctuary," Matthias said, his voice carrying authority. "If I see any of you again, if you come near her again, I will not be so merciful."

David struggled to his feet, the blood draining from his face in shock and something that might have been fear. "This isn't over, Sera. Whatever hold he has on you—"

"The only hold I have on her," Matthias interrupted, moving to stand beside me, "is the one she's given me freely. Again and again."

He pulled me against his side, and I could feel the fine tremor in his muscles, the barely contained violence still coursing through him. But his touch was gentle as he brushed a strand of hair from my face.

"Tell them, Sera," he said softly. "Tell them what you told me."

I looked at my family, at David's heartbroken expression, at Elena still catching her breath, and at the hunters sprawled across the floor, feeling something final settle in my chest.

"I'm his," I said quietly. "And he's mine."

The words hung in the air like a declaration of war.

David's face went pale. "Sera—"

"No." Matthias's voice cut through any protest like a blade. His arm tightened around me possessively, and when he spoke again, his words carried the weight of unshakeable certainty. "She's made her choice. Respect it."

Elena struggled to her feet; one hand pressed against her ribs where she'd hit the wall. "This isn't over," she spat. "The family will never accept this. Never."

"Then the family will learn to live with disappointment," Matthias replied, his tone deceptively casual despite the threat underneath. "Nothing will stop me from claiming her completely. Nothing will stop me from making her mine in every way that matters. And if you try to interfere again..."

He paused, letting the silence stretch until it became unbearable.

The smile he gave them was lethal and magnificent. "I'll kill every last one of you."

The promise hung in the candlelit air, and I felt a shiver run down my spine that had nothing to do with the cold. This wasn't the gentle man who had just been worshipping my body. This was something primal and certain of what belonged to him.

"Go," he said softly. "Before I change my mind about letting you live."

The hunters didn't need to be told twice. They gathered their wounded and their broken weapons, and within moments, the sanctuary was empty except for the echo of their retreating footsteps.

When the last sound had faded, Matthias turned to me, his expression softening from deadly predator to something infinitely more dangerous—a man looking at the woman he would kill for.

"Are you hurt?" he asked, his hands moving over me with gentle care, checking for injuries.

"No," I whispered, still shaking from the adrenaline. "But Matthias, what you said—"

"I meant every word." His fingers tilted my chin up, forcing me to meet his burning gaze. "Next time, Sera. Next time, nothing will stop me from making you completely mine. Nothing and no one."

36

I sat on the edge of the stone platform where Matthias
had been dying just hours earlier, my hands still trembling slightly as I smoothed down my disheveled clothes.
The sanctuary looked like a battlefield: scattered candles,
overturned furniture, dark stains on the stone where blood
had spilled. The air still held the lingering charge of supernatural energy.

Matthias moved through the space, righting fallen
candlesticks and straightening overturned furniture. But I
could feel his eyes on me constantly, that intense emerald
gaze that seemed to see straight through to my soul.

"Are you okay?" he asked for the third time, setting a
fallen candlestick back in its iron bracket.

"Yes." I touched my throat where my pulse still raced.
"Just processing."

Processing felt like an inadequate word for what had just
happened. An hour ago, I'd been pressed against him,
desperate and wanting, on the verge of crossing a line I
could never uncross. Then my family had burst in with
weapons and threats and a certainty that I was lost to them.

Now here I sat, in the ruins of my old life, with my family's shocked faces burned into my memory.

"Sera." Matthias's voice was soft. He approached slowly, as if I might bolt like a frightened animal. "What you did tonight—"

"I chose you over them." The words sounded flat. I looked down at my hands, which had reached for him instead of my family. "I didn't hesitate. I didn't even think about it."

"You protected what matters to you." He knelt beside the platform, bringing himself to my eye level. "There's nothing wrong with that."

"Isn't there?" I looked up at him, searching his face for some sign that what I'd done was as monumental as it felt. "Normal people don't choose a vampire over the people who raised them."

Something shifted in his expression—a flicker of pain, quickly masked. "Is that what you think you did? Chose a monster over your family?"

"I don't know what I think anymore." I laughed, but there was no humor in it. "Everything I thought I knew about myself, about my life, about what I wanted. It's all gone. I'm sitting in a vampire's lair and the terrifying part is that I don't regret it."

Matthias was quiet for a long moment, his gaze never leaving my face. When he finally spoke, his voice carried a weight I'd never heard before.

"Sera, there are things you need to know. Before we go any further, before you make any more choices you can't take back."

Something in his tone made my stomach clench. "What kind of things?"

"The kind that will change everything." He stood, pacing

to the wall of old books, his shoulders tense. "I've been selec-tive with the truth. Protecting you from information I thought you weren't ready for."

"Like my family did?" The bitterness in my voice surprised me.

"Yes." He turned back to me, and I saw something vulnerable flicker across his features. "Like your family did. And I was wrong to do it."

I studied his face, seeing the internal struggle written in the tight line of his jaw, the way his hands clenched and unclenched at his sides. "What aren't you telling me?"

"Everything." He moved closer, and I caught the scent of leather and smoke that always clung to him. "What I am, what happened to me, why your blood affects me the way it does. Why I came to Prague. Why I can't let you go."

My heart hammered against my ribs. "Matthias—"

"What I'm about to tell you will change everything," he said, his voice soft but unrelenting. "And once you know, you'll have to make a choice I should have let you make long ago."

He moved to the ornate chair across from me, settling into it with the fluidity that marked him as something other than human. But his eyes, his eyes held centuries of pain and a desperate hope that made my chest tight.

"Will you let me tell you?" he asked quietly. "All of it? Even if it means you might choose to walk away from me forever?"

I looked at him, this beautiful, dangerous man who'd saved my life and turned my world upside down. Who'd made me feel more alive in a few weeks than I had in twenty-eight years. Who'd just watched me choose him over my own family and hadn't looked at me with anything but admiration.

"Yes," I whispered. "Tell me everything."

Matthias was quiet for so long I began to wonder if he'd changed his mind about telling me everything. He sat perfectly still in the ornate chair, his hands resting on the carved armrests, but I could see the tension in the line of his shoulders, the way his jaw worked as if he were testing words before speaking them.

"Four hundred years ago," he finally said, his voice barely above a whisper, "I killed a witch."

I felt my breath catch, but I didn't speak. Something in his tone warned me that interrupting would shatter whatever fragile resolve had brought him to this moment.

"She was powerful beyond measure, and she was murdering children in a village under my protection." His emerald eyes found mine, and I saw centuries of pain reflected there. "I thought I was doing the right thing. I thought justice demanded it."

He stood abruptly and walked to the wall of flickering candles. The light cast shifting shadows across his sharp features, making him look more otherworldly than ever.

"I hunted her down and killed her," he continued, his back to me. "But as her life ebbed away from the wounds I'd given her, she looked at me with such hatred..." He turned, and I saw his hands trembling slightly. "And she cursed me with her final breath."

"What kind of curse?" I asked softly.

"The cruelest kind imaginable." A bitter smile twisted his lips. "She cursed me to slowly lose everything that made my immortal life worth living. My power, my strength, my ability to connect with others. All of it draining away, century by century, until I would face eternity as a hollow shell of what I once was."

The magnitude of it hit me completely. "Four hundred years of dying slowly?"

"Yes." He moved closer, his gaze never leaving my face.

"But the witch wasn't finished. She made the curse specific. It could only be broken by my true mate from a particular bloodline. The Sterling bloodline."

My heart stopped. "What?"

"Not just any Sterling," he continued, his voice growing softer, more vulnerable. "My destined mate. The one person in all the world whose soul calls to mine." He knelt beside my chair, bringing himself to my eye level. "You, Sera. It's always been you."

I drew in a sharp breath. "That's why you came to Prague. You sensed me."

"I felt the pull of Sterling blood, yes. But I expected to find another hunter to kill or be killed by." Vulnerability flickered across his features. "I never expected to find this. You."

"And that's why my blood affects you the way it does."

"Your blood can slow the curse, give me temporary relief. But only you, only your willing acceptance of our bond, can break it completely." His hands moved to frame my face, gentle but desperate. "The witch made sure the curse could only be broken by love freely given, never taken by force."

I stared at him, trying to process the enormity of what he was telling me. "What does that mean? How is it broken then?"

"In a couple of days, during the blood moon, we could perform the binding ritual." His thumbs brushed across my cheekbones, and I felt the fine tremor in his touch. "It would break the curse permanently, bind us together forever, and..."

My mouth went dry. "The blood moon. That's when the other vampires want to use me for their ritual too, isn't it?"

His expression darkened. "Yes. They want to perform a different ritual, one that would drain your blood to grant them power over the supernatural world. Only one ritual can succeed during the blood moon, Sera. If they complete theirs first..."

"You die, and they get what they want."

"And if we complete ours first, the blood moon's power is spent. They lose their chance." His hands tightened slightly on my face. "This isn't just about saving me anymore. It's about stopping them from using you for something far worse."

"And what would the binding ritual do?"

"Transform you." The words came out like a confession. "You wouldn't become a vampire, but you wouldn't remain fully human either. Something new. Something between. Longer life, enhanced abilities, a permanent connection to the supernatural world."

My chest felt tight. "You're asking me to give up being human."

"I'm asking you to choose," he said, his voice breaking slightly. "Freely. With full knowledge of what that choice means. If you say no, if you choose to remain human and walk away from this, I'll respect that decision. The curse will continue, and eventually, it will kill me. But..." His expression grew pained. "You need to understand, the other vampires won't just forget about you. They'll keep hunting you, keep trying to use your blood for their own purposes."

I hesitated. "And if I say yes?"

"Then you'll be bound to me for eternity. You'll share my world, with all its dangers and darkness. You'll never age the way humans do, never have a completely normal life. But we'll face that together."

I looked into his eyes, seeing the desperate hope he was trying so hard to hide. Four hundred years of slowly dying, and I was his one chance at salvation, but only if I chose it willingly.

"The ritual," I whispered. "What does it involve?"

"Blood magic. Sacred words. A joining that goes deeper than anything you've ever experienced." His hands moved to take mine, his touch warm and solid and real. "It's not just about breaking my curse, Sera. It's about binding our souls together. Forever means forever."

I felt the full impact of what he was saying. This wasn't just about love or desire or even saving his life. This was about permanently changing what I was, choosing a destiny I'd never imagined possible.

"I need time," I said, my voice barely audible. "To think about this. Really think."

"Of course." He brought my hands to his lips, pressing a soft kiss to my knuckles. "This isn't a decision to make lightly. I've waited four hundred years, Sera. I can wait a little longer for you to be sure."

He released my hands and stepped back, giving me space. Everything Matthias had told me was too much to process. I sat in the chair, staring at my hands, trying to wrap my mind around the enormity of what he was asking.

Four hundred years of suffering. A witch's curse. A ritual that would bind us forever and transform me into something between human and vampire. Enemy vampires who wanted to drain my blood for power. A deadline.

It was too much. Too overwhelming. Too life-altering to process in the span of a single conversation.

I stood on unsteady legs, my mind still reeling. "The hotel. I should go back to my hotel room. Try to think clearly."

"Sera." His voice was soft. "The other vampires—"

"I'll be careful." I met his eyes, seeing the concern there, the hope he was trying so hard to hide. "I just... I need to be alone with this. To figure out who I am and what I want without you here influencing my thoughts."

He flinched slightly, then nodded. "I understand."

He walked me to the hidden entrance, his presence both comforting and overwhelming. At the threshold, he caught my hand gently.

"Whatever you decide," he said quietly, "know that I meant what I said. Your choice has to be freely made. Even if that choice is to walk away from me."

The sincerity in his voice, the absolute lack of manipulation or pressure, made my chest tight. "I know."

"Two days now," he said, and there was something vulnerable in the way he said it. "Until the blood moon."

"Two days," I said.

He released my hand, and I stepped through the hidden doorway into the monastery corridors. Behind me, I heard the soft sound of stone sliding back into place, sealing him away from me.

I walked through the cathedral in a daze, passing the sleeping quarters and moving through the grand halls. The first faint light of dawn was spreading across the sky as I stepped onto Prague's streets, the air cool and crisp with the promise of morning. Around me, the city was caught in that quiet hour between night and day. A few early workers headed to their jobs, the last of the late-night revelers making their way home, streetlights starting to fade against the rising light.

Everything looked exactly the same as it had hours ago. But I felt like a completely different person.

The Sera who had entered that sanctuary tonight had been running on instinct and attraction, making choices in the heat of the moment. The Sera walking through Prague's streets now carried the weight of knowledge—about Matthias, about the supernatural world, about her own destiny.

In two days, I would have to choose between the life I'd always known and a love that would remake me entirely.

The thought should have terrified me. Instead, as I walked through the sleeping city with his revelations echoing in my mind, I felt something that might have been anticipation.

36.5

MATTHIAS

The hidden door sealed shut with the grinding of stone against stone, and I was alone. I stood motionless in the sanctuary, listening to the echo of Sera's footsteps fade away through the corridors above. Each retreating sound felt like another nail being driven into the coffin of my hope.

She's gone.

The thought drove me to my knees on the cold stone floor. Four hundred years I'd waited for this moment. The chance to finally tell her everything, to lay my centuries of suffering at her feet and beg for salvation. And now that I had, she'd walked away.

Not fled. Not run screaming into the night as any sane person would have done upon learning their lover was a cursed monster whose existence depended on a ritual that would steal her humanity. She just walked away. To think. To choose.

The distinction should have been comforting. It meant she was considering it, weighing the impossible decision I'd forced upon her. But as I knelt among the still scattered candles and overturned furniture, the ruins of the moment her family had torn us apart, all I could feel was the crushing certainty that when she finished thinking, she would choose to remain human. Choose to live. Choose to leave me to die slowly, as I'd been dying for four centuries.

A spasm of pain lanced through my chest, sharp enough to double me over. The curse was accelerating again, feeding on my despair. Without Sera's presence to anchor me, without the hope her blood had given me, my supernatural strength was draining away like water through cupped hands.

I forced myself to stand, though my legs shook with the effort. The sanctuary felt vast and empty without her light filling it. The candles she'd knocked over during our desperate reunion still lay scattered across the floor, their flames long since extinguished. Even the air seemed thinner, robbed of that electric charge that always surrounded her.

Two days. Two days until the blood moon. Two days until the other vampires could complete their ritual and drain every drop of Sterling blood from her veins, leaving her a desiccated corpse and me a powerless shadow of what I'd once been. Or two days until she agreed to the binding ritual and saved us both.

Or two days until she somehow found a way to stay human—to save herself without surrendering to either of us.

I laughed, the sound echoing off the walls like the cry of a wounded animal. Who was I kidding? Sera was brilliant, principled, good in a way I'd forgotten was possible after centuries of violence and darkness. What sane woman would choose to bind herself for eternity to a monster who'd already stolen so much from her?

I'd watched her face as I'd explained what the ritual would cost her. Seen the flash of fear when I'd told her she'd be transformed, no longer fully human. She'd hidden it well, but I'd lived long enough to recognize terror when I saw it.

The curse pulsed again, stronger this time, and I collapsed onto the stone platform where she'd sat just hours before. My vision grayed at the edges as the weakness consumed me. Her scent still lingered there—vanilla with hints of jasmine, warmth, and innocence—everything I'd lost when that witch had cursed me with her dying breath.

"You will lose everything that makes your immortal life worth living," the witch had hissed as her blood pooled beneath my feet. *"Your power, your strength, your ability to connect with others—all of it draining away until you face eternity as a hollow shell."*

She'd been as good as her word. Decade by decade, century by century, I'd felt pieces of myself simply vanish. My supernatural abilities had weakened. My capacity for forming meaningful connections had withered. Even physical pleasure had become muted, distant, until I'd begun to wonder if I'd ever truly feel anything again.

Then Sera Sterling had walked into Prague, and suddenly I could feel everything.

The first time I sensed her presence, she'd been working alone among the manuscripts, and it was like something dormant in my chest suddenly burst into life. I had been dreaming of her for years. Initially, just fragments, then clearer visions as the time drew near. A woman with dark hair and warm brown eyes, someone whose soul seemed to call to mine across impossible distances.

But actually feeling her, sensing the pull of her presence just a floor above me, was so intense I almost materialized right there in the reading room. She'd been hunched over a manuscript, dark hair falling like a curtain around her face, fully absorbed in her work. The sight of her—brilliant, passionate, alive—had stolen what little breath I still drew.

Even without seeing her face, even hidden in the shadows watching her work with such focused dedication, I'd felt an emotion I'd thought was dead forever. *Recognition.* Not just the call of Sterling blood, though the pull of her heritage had been undeniable. Recognition of the woman from my dreams, the face I'd been seeing in visions for years before she was even born.

My destined mate.

For the first time in four hundred years, I'd wanted something more than mere survival.

I'd told myself I was protecting her by staying in the shadows that first night, by watching from a distance as she worked. But the truth was simpler: I'd been afraid. When Viktor had arrived that same night, when I'd had no choice but to reveal myself to save her life, I'd expected revulsion.

Instead, she'd looked at me with wonder. Those warm brown eyes were wide with amazement rather than terror. Even now, even knowing what I'd told her tonight, I could still see that expression on her face. The way her eyes had widened when she'd first seen me fully materialized in the library. The way she'd leaned into my touch instead of pulling away. The way she'd kissed me back with a hunger that matched my own.

"Yes. Tell me everything."

Those had been her words when I'd offered her the choice to learn the truth. No hesitation. No fear. Just that consistent courage that had drawn me to her from the beginning.

But courage in the heat of the moment was different from acceptance after consideration. Now that she had time to think, to truly understand what binding herself to me would mean...

In the growing darkness of the sanctuary, I could almost see the witch's face as she'd died, her features twisted with malicious satisfaction.

"Only your true mate from the Sterling bloodline can break it," she'd whispered with her final breath. *"But the choice must be freely given, never taken by force. Love earned, not compelled."*

Even in death, the witch had been cruelly precise. She'd given me hope, the possibility of salvation, but made it conditional on the one thing I'd never been able to inspire in another being.

Genuine love.

Oh, I'd had admirers over the centuries. Humans drawn to my supernatural charisma, vampires seeking alliance with my power, mortals fascinated by the danger I represented. But none of them had ever seen past the monster to whatever remained of the man underneath.

Until Sera.

When she'd looked at me tonight, when I'd confessed four centuries of dying slowly and she'd reached for my hands instead of recoiling in horror, I'd felt something crack open in my chest. Something I'd thought was lost forever.

But hope was perhaps the cruelest gift the witch could have given me, because it made the inevitable loss so much more devastating.

I closed my eyes, letting the weakness wash over me. Perhaps this was fitting. Perhaps after four centuries of violence and blood, of taking what I needed without thought for the cost, I deserved to die slowly and alone. Perhaps the witch had been right to curse me.

But even as the thought formed, I couldn't make myself believe it. Not when I remembered the way Sera had felt in my arms. Not when I could still taste her kiss on my lips, still feel the warmth of her skin against mine.

For a few precious hours, she'd made me feel human again.

37

The hotel lobby was beginning to stir with early morning activity as I crossed the marble floor toward the elevators. Business travelers checking out, people planning their day, the soft murmur of normal conversation in a dozen languages. I moved through it all like a ghost, hyperaware of how different I felt from everyone around me.

In the elevator, I caught my reflection in the polished steel doors. I looked exactly the same as I had yesterday—same brown hair, same brown eyes, same unremarkable human features. But I felt irrevocably changed, like I was shedding layers of who I used to be, revealing something entirely new underneath. The old Sera was dissolving, and I wasn't sure if I was ready to meet who was taking her place.

My hotel room felt smaller than I remembered. The bed where I'd tossed and turned for days, agonizing over my family's plans and my own conflicted feelings, seemed to belong to a different person entirely.

I moved toward the bathroom on autopilot, stripping off clothes that still carried the scent of candlewax and him. The hot water of the shower was a shock against my skin, and I found myself leaning against the tile wall as the events of the night crashed over me.

Four hundred years of dying slowly.

The image of Matthias collapsed on that stone platform, barely clinging to life, made my chest tight with remembered panic. The way his eyes had brightened when my blood brought him back from the brink. The desperate relief in his voice when he'd whispered that he couldn't survive losing me again.

You're my destined mate from the Sterling bloodline.

The words still felt surreal, like something from a novel rather than my actual life. But underneath the disbelief was a recognition so deep it frightened me. When he'd said it, when he'd told me the curse could only be broken by his true mate, something inside me had responded with absolute certainty.

Of course it's me.

I turned my face up to the spray, letting the hot water wash away the last traces of the sanctuary. But nothing could wash away the memory of his hands on my skin, the way he'd looked at me like I was salvation itself.

Forever means forever.

Stepping out of the shower, I dressed mechanically—jeans, sweater, boots—the same clothes I might have chosen any other morning. But my hands shook slightly as I pulled the sweater over my head, remembering the way Matthias had removed it with such care, his fingers threading through my hair.

My stomach rumbled, reminding me I hadn't eaten since yesterday morning, but when I started toward the hotel's breakfast buffet, I stopped short at the entrance. The dining room had its normal morning activity—tourists planning their sightseeing, travelers checking their phones, the comfortable murmur of ordinary conversation. I couldn't sit among them, couldn't pretend to be just another guest when my mind was spinning with impossible choices.

In less than forty-eight hours, the blood moon would rise. I could undergo a ritual that would bind me to Matthias forever and transform me into something new. Or I could walk away and watch him die while spending the rest of my life running from vampires who wanted to drain my blood for power.

The magnitude of it was overwhelming. How was I supposed to make a decision that would permanently change what I was? How could I choose between saving someone I cared about and remaining human?

But even as I tried to think through it logically, part of me kept returning to the way I'd felt in his arms. Complete. Like I'd finally found the missing piece of myself.

I needed to get out. Find somewhere neutral where I could actually process what Matthias had told me without the hotel's familiar comfort clouding my judgment. I went back to my room just long enough to grab my jacket and purse, checking that my room key was secure.

Back in the lobby, I barely noticed the other guests as my feet carried me through the automatic doors and onto Prague's cobblestone streets with a sense of purpose I hadn't felt in days.

The morning air was crisp against my face, sharp with the promise of autumn. Around me, the city hummed with life—shopkeepers opening their doors, commuters hurrying to work, foreigners emerging with cameras and guidebooks. Normal people living normal lives, completely unaware that their city was home to sacred magic and supernatural politics.

I walked without a destination, letting my feet choose the path. Away from the hotel district, through narrow streets that had witnessed centuries of secrets. Past Gothic churches and baroque palaces, under stone archways that had stood for decades.

Matthias was waiting for my decision. The thought sent a flutter through me—part anticipation, part terror.

A small cafe appeared at the end of a narrow side street, its windows glowing warmly against the morning chill. Inside, it was exactly what I needed—small, dimly lit, filled with the rich aroma of coffee and fresh pastries. A handful of early customers sat scattered at mismatched tables, absorbed in their newspapers or laptops, paying no attention to anyone else.

I ordered a large coffee and a croissant, which I probably wouldn't eat, and then claimed a corner table near the window. The view overlooked a cobblestone street lined with old buildings, their facades painted in soft pastels that caught the morning light. It was normal, peaceful. Nothing like the candlelit sanctuary where my entire world had been turned upside down just hours ago.

I wrapped my hands around the warm coffee cup, using the heat to steady my trembling fingers. The caffeine was exactly what I needed, something to cut through the exhaustion and help me think clearly about the most important decision of my life.

Around me, normal people lived normal lives. The woman at the next table was reading what looked like a romance novel, completely absorbed in someone else's love story. A businessman typed furiously on his laptop, probably handling some crisis that felt monumentally important to him but would be forgotten in a week.

None of them had to choose between remaining human and saving someone they... loved?

The word stopped me cold. Did I love Matthias? Or was I just caught up in the intensity of our connection, the electric pull that made every nerve ending come alive when he touched me?

I've spent my entire life feeling incomplete. That much was undeniably true. Even my most successful relationships felt like settling, like accepting something that was good enough instead of finding what I truly needed. But with Matthias, that void had disappeared entirely.

Was that love? Or was it just the supernatural bond he'd described, pulling me toward a choice that would benefit him more than me?

I stared out the window at Prague's shadowed streets, trying to imagine what my life would look like in either scenario. If I chose the transformation, I'd be bound to Matthias for centuries, sharing his world of darkness and danger. Enhanced abilities, longer life, but never fully human again.

But even as I tried to picture that future, I felt something tighten in my chest. There was no way back to my academic life, no path to the quiet, scholarly existence I had always imagined. The moment I met Matthias, the moment I learned about my family's supernatural legacy, that door had closed forever.

So the real question wasn't whether to remain human. It was whether to spend whatever time I had left running from the supernatural world, or to embrace it fully.

The transformation Matthias had described didn't sound like losing my humanity. It sounded like gaining something more. Enhanced senses, longer life, the ability to exist safely in a world I was already part of, whether I wanted to be or not. And I'd be with him. The man who looked at me like I was precious beyond measure, who'd waited four hundred years for someone like me, who'd given me the choice freely even though his life depended on my answer.

But was that enough to base such a monumental decision on? Was the feeling of completeness worth giving up my humanity for?

I broke off a piece of croissant, not really tasting it as I chewed. Outside the window, Prague continued its morning rhythm, beautiful and timeless and utterly oblivious to the supernatural drama playing out in its shadows.

The weight of my decision felt almost crushing. Matthias's life, eight centuries of existence, hung in the balance of my choice. No pressure at all.

But underneath the overwhelm, underneath the fear and uncertainty, a small voice in the back of my mind kept whispering the same thing over and over.

You know what you want. You've known since the moment he told you.

I pushed the thought away, not ready to examine it too closely. I needed more time, more coffee, more space to think through every angle before I committed to anything.

The cafe door chimed softly as another customer entered, but I didn't look up from my cup. I was too lost in my own thoughts, too caught up in weighing impossible choices, to pay attention to anything else.

Until I heard a familiar voice.

"Hello, Sera."

I looked up from my coffee cup. David was standing in the café doorway, his steel-gray eyes fixed on me. He looked worn down.

"David." I set down my cup with trembling fingers. "How did you—"

"I've been tracking you since you escaped the safehouse." He moved toward my table with slow steps, his hands visible, making no sudden movements. "May I sit?"

I gestured to the chair across from me, my mind racing. Where were Elena and the other hunters? Why was he alone? And why did he look more defeated than angry?

David settled into the chair with a heavy sigh, his weathered hands resting on the small table between us. Up close, I could see the exhaustion in the lines around his eyes, and guilt was written across his features. He reached into his jacket pocket and pulled out Helena's pendant, setting it gently on the table between us.

"This belongs to you."

I picked it up without a word, fastening the chain around my neck. The familiar weight of it settled against my throat, and I felt immediately more grounded.

"Thanks."

"You're not here to drag me back," I said.

"No." His voice was quiet, almost resigned. "I'm not."

"Then why—"

"Because there's something I need to tell you. Something I should have told you." David met my eyes, and I saw something I'd never seen there before. Fear.

"What kind of something?"

He was quiet for a long moment, staring down at his hands. When he finally spoke, his voice was barely above a whisper. "About our family. About why they want you specifically. About what you really are."

"I know what I am. I'm a Sterling. A descendant of vampire hunters."

"Yes." David looked up, his gray eyes holding mine with painful intensity. "But that's not all you are, Sera. That's not why your blood can do what it does."

The cafe around us seemed to fade into background noise. The woman with her romance novel, the businessman with his laptop, the gentle hum of normal conversation. All of it became distant and muted as David's words registered.

"What do you mean?"

"The Sterling bloodline isn't just a family of hunters," he said, each word seeming to cost him enormous effort. "We're something else entirely. Something I've spent your whole life trying to protect you from knowing."

My coffee cup sat forgotten between my hands, growing cold as I stared at the man who'd raised me. The man who'd been more father than uncle, who'd never lied to me about anything important. Until these past few weeks.

"Tell me," I whispered.

David closed his eyes briefly, as if gathering strength for what came next. When he opened them again, I saw decades of secrecy and guilt reflected there.

"We carry vampire blood, Sera. Have for generations."

The words took my breath away, and I felt dizzy. I grabbed the edge of the table to steady myself.

"What?"

"A Sterling ancestor, centuries ago, fell in love with a vampire." David paused, his voice steadying as if the hardest part was over. "She couldn't kill him, couldn't walk away from him. So she made a choice that changed our family forever."

I stared at him, unable to process what I was hearing. "She became a vampire?"

"Not exactly. She bound herself to him in a way that was new. Unprecedented. She remained mostly human, but she carried his blood in her veins. And when she had children, they carried it too."

Understanding flooded over me. Every question I'd ever had about myself, every instinct that had led me to supernatural folklore, every moment of feeling incomplete in the normal world. All of it suddenly made terrifying sense.

"That's why we can sense them," I said, my voice filled with shock. "Why our blood affects them."

"Why your blood can break curses," David confirmed. "Why you were drawn to supernatural studies without understanding why. Why you've always felt like something was missing."

I thought about Matthias, about the electric connection I'd felt the moment he touched me. Not manipulation or supernatural influence, but recognition. My blood calling to his, acknowledging what we both were.

"When you told me we were hunters, you left out the most important part. You told me half the truth and let me think that was everything," I said, anger starting to build beneath the shock.

"I was trying to protect you." David leaned forward, desperation creeping into his voice. "You were already struggling with learning about the hunting legacy. If you knew what else you were, if you understood that you were drawn to vampires because of what runs in your veins—"

"I might choose them over you," I finished. "That's what you were afraid of, wasn't it? That I'd embrace the vampire side of my heritage instead of the hunter side."

David's silence was answer enough. I sat back in my chair, my mind overwhelmed by the weight of this additional deception. It was bad enough learning that I came from a family of hunters. But to discover there was an even deeper secret, something that explained every moment of feeling incomplete in my own life—

"Even when you finally told me about the hunting," I said, surprised by how calm my voice sounded, "you couldn't tell me the whole truth."

"Sera—"

"No." I held up a hand, stopping him mid-sentence. "You don't get to 'Sera' me. Not after this."

"I thought if you could focus on the hunting legacy first, if you could accept that part of what we are, then maybe..." He trailed off, looking older than I'd ever seen him.

"Maybe I'd be so committed to the hunter side that the vampire blood wouldn't matter?" I shook my head. "David, do you have any idea what it's been like? Feeling incomplete my entire life, like some essential part of me was missing? And you had the answer all along."

David flinched as if I'd slapped him. "I was trying to protect you."

"You were trying to control me." The realization was crushing. "Just like the rest of them. Just like Elena with her plans to use me as bait, just like the hunters who see me as a weapon. None of you have ever seen me as a person capable of making my own choices."

"That's not—"

"It is." I leaned forward, holding his gaze. "But you know what? Thank you."

David blinked, clearly not expecting that response. "What?"

"Thank you for finally telling me the truth. Because now I understand everything." I stood up, leaving money on the table for my barely touched coffee and croissant. "I understand why Matthias and I connected the way we did. I understand why I've spent my whole life feeling like I was living at half power. And I understand exactly what I need to do."

"Sera, wait—"

But I was already walking toward the door, my mind clearer than it had been in hours. Maybe clearer than it had been in years.

38

I walked out of the cafe with David's words echoing in my mind like a prayer I couldn't stop repeating. *We carry vampire blood, Sera. Have for generations.*

The Prague streets blurred around me as I moved without conscious direction, my feet carrying me away from the cafe and the weight of David's guilt-ridden eyes. Everything made sense now. The way I'd always felt incomplete, like I was living at half power. My inexplicable draw to supernatural folklore. The electric connection I'd felt with Matthias from the very first moment. It wasn't manipulation or some vampire trick. It was recognition. My blood calling to his.

I stopped walking, my mind racing. Those mysterious Sterling family records Helena had shown me—the missing women, the symbols beside their names, all those gaps in the family tree where daughters simply vanished from history. What if they hadn't disappeared at all? What if they'd made the same choice as that first ancestor?

Helena had hinted at this, hadn't she? Those cryptic warnings about knowledge coming with a price, about different paths chosen.

The Strahov Monastery library. Helena would understand. After weeks of working together, uncovering those mysterious family records with all their gaps and symbols, she'd been the one to tell me I needed to ask my family for answers.

Well, now I have them.

Twenty minutes later, I found Helena in her usual spot, but when she looked up and saw my face, she immediately set aside her cataloging work.

"Sera," she said, her voice warm with concern. "You look like someone who's just had their world turned upside down. Again."

"David told me," I said, sinking into the chair across from her desk. "About what we really are. About the vampire blood in our lineage."

Helena's expression shifted from concern to something that looked almost like relief. "Finally. I was wondering how long your family would keep you in the dark about that particular detail."

"You knew?" I stared at her. "All this time, you knew about the vampire blood?"

"Sera, your family has been working with supernatural allies for generations. My grandmother didn't just help your great-grandfather hunt vampires. She helped him understand what he really was." Helena leaned forward. "The Sterling bloodline isn't purely human. It never has been."

"What do you mean?"

Helena glanced around the main library, then stood. "Come with me. There are records I didn't show you before. Personal accounts that I thought you weren't ready for."

She led me to the familiar hidden door, producing the ornate key I'd seen before. But instead of stopping at the secret room I'd already visited, she continued deeper into the hidden chambers.

"There's another room," she said quietly, leading me down a narrow stone corridor I hadn't seen before. "Records I keep separate from everything else. Even from what I showed you and David."

She stopped before a second door, this one even more heavily warded than the first. Mystical symbols carved into the stone frame seemed to pulse with their own light.

"These are the personal accounts," Helena said, her hand hesitating on this new lock. "Written by the Sterling women themselves. Their own words about the choices they made and what happened to them."

My breath caught. "You mean—"

"I mean journals, letters, testimonies." She turned the key, and I felt a rush of warm air carrying the scent of old parchment. "Written by Sterling women who chose vampires over their human lives. And lived to document what that choice really meant."

The room beyond was smaller than Helena's main archive, but somehow more intimate. A single table sat in the center, surrounded by glass cases containing what looked like personal effects—jewelry, clothing, painted miniatures. But it was the collection of journals on the table that drew my attention.

"How many?" I asked, my voice barely above a whisper.

"Forty-three," Helena said softly. "Spanning six centuries. Sterling women who fell in love with vampires and chose transformation over their human lives."

"And the symbols beside their names in the family tree?" I asked, remembering those strange markings I'd sketched in my notebook.

"Each symbol represents a different vampire house," Helena explained. "The women weren't just choosing trans-formation. They were joining the families of the vampires they'd fallen in love with. Some went to the old European houses, others to newer ones. The symbols were a way to track which bloodlines they were bound to."

I thought about those drawn marks, each one representing not a mysterious disappearance, but a woman finding her place in a new world.

I approached the table with shaky hands. The journals varied in size and age, but they all shared one thing. They had been preserved. Someone had treasured these stories enough to preserve them.

"My family has been guardians," Helena explained. "But we've also been friends. Confidantes. When Sterling women needed sanctuary while they decided what to do, when they needed someone to document their choices, they came to us."

I opened the nearest journal, dated 1678. The handwriting was elegant but urgent, as if the writer had been racing against time.

Tomorrow night, the blood moon rises. I have chosen to undergo the binding ritual with Vincent, despite the risks. If this record survives and other Sterling women find it, know this: the transformation is not a loss but a becoming. We do not sacrifice our humanity; we transcend it.

The signature at the bottom made my heart stop: *Evangeline Sterling.*

I looked up at Helena, my eyes wide. "Evangeline was my ancestor?"

"One of many Sterling women who chose love over fear," Helena confirmed gently. "And she documented everything about her transformation and what came after."

I flipped through more pages, finding entry after entry in Evangeline's hand. Descriptions of her transformation, the bond she shared with Vincent, and the supernatural abilities she gained. But most importantly, her happiness.

Six months have passed since the ritual. I am changed, yes, but not diminished. I am stronger, faster, and more alive than I ever was as merely human. And the bond with Vincent... it is beyond description. We are two souls sharing one existence, each making the other complete.

"She was happy," I said, surprised by the emotion in my voice.

"They all were," Helena said softly. "That's what I wanted you to understand. The missing women in your family tree. They weren't lost. They found exactly what they were looking for."

I picked up another journal, this one from 1823, then another from 1456. Different handwriting, different time periods, but the same story repeated over and over. Sterling women falling in love with vampires, choosing transformation, and documenting lives of fulfillment and joy.

"But why keep it secret?" I asked. "Why hide this from the family? If Sterling women were happy with vampires, why does my family hunt them?"

Helena's expression grew sad. "Because of one man's grief. In 1623, a Sterling woman named Catherine chose transformation to be with the vampire she loved. Her brother Edmund couldn't accept that she'd made the choice willingly."

She moved to one of the glass cases, pointing to a painted miniature of a young woman with familiar dark hair. "Edmund was convinced his sister had been seduced, manipulated, corrupted by supernatural influence. He couldn't believe she would choose a vampire over her human family unless she'd been enchanted."

"So he became a hunter," I said, understanding beginning to dawn.

"He became obsessed," Helena corrected. "He spent his life hunting the vampire who'd 'stolen' his sister, convinced he was saving her. When he couldn't find them, he decided to save future Sterling women from the same fate."

She opened another case, revealing old documents with official seals. "Edmund started the hunting tradition. He rewrote the family history, destroyed records of willing transformations, and taught his children that vampires were corruptors who preyed specifically on Sterling women."

I stared at the miniature of Catherine, seeing my own features reflected in her painted face. "And his descendants believed him."

"Four hundred years of believing vampires are pure evil, that any Sterling woman who chooses one must be under supernatural influence." Helena's voice was heavy with centuries of hidden truth. "Edmund's branch of the family convinced themselves they were protecting the bloodline, never realizing they were denying their own nature."

"David doesn't know," I said softly. "He genuinely believes he's protecting me."

"Your uncle is a good man living a lie his ancestors created." Helena closed the case gently. "But you have the chance to learn from the real history, not the version Edmund created."

I looked down at the journals spread before me, these personal testaments to love and transformation and choices freely made. "And the blood moon?"

"Is tomorrow," Helena said quietly. "I can feel the magic building. Which means—"

"Which means I have a choice to make." I closed the journal slowly. "And less than twenty-four hours to make it."

Helena's expression grew troubled. "I can sense both rituals building power. The enemy vampires are preparing for tomorrow night as well."

My stomach clenched. "Matthias told me only one ritual can succeed during a blood moon."

"Exactly. Which means tomorrow night becomes a race." Helena met my eyes. "If you choose the transformation, you and Matthias will have to complete the ritual before they can capture you for theirs."

"And if I don't choose it?"

"Then they take you anyway, and Matthias dies from his curse while they create their vampire king." Helena's voice was gentle but firm. "Tomorrow night, one way or another, everything changes."

I thought about David and Elena, about the plan to use me as bait. About my family's certainty that vampires were evil and transformation was damnation. Then I thought about Matthias, about the way he looked at me like I was precious beyond measure, about the connection I felt every time he touched me.

And I thought about these journals, these women who'd faced the same choice and found joy in their decision.

"I need to see him," I said, standing with sudden determination. "I need to tell Matthias what I've learned."

Helena smiled, the first truly warm smile I'd seen from her. "Then you'd better hurry. The sun is setting, and you'll want to reach him before anyone else realizes you're out."

I moved toward the door, then stopped. "Helena? Thank you. For keeping these stories. For showing me the truth."

Helena nodded.

I left the monastery with Evangeline's words echoing in my mind and my decision solidifying with every step. I knew exactly what I wanted.

I wanted what these women had found. I wanted to stop living at half power and become everything I was meant to be. I wanted the bond they described, the love that transcended mortal understanding.

I wanted Matthias.

39

The afternoon sun was already casting long golden light across Prague's cobblestone streets, deep shadows gathering between the buildings. I needed to get to him, to tell him I'd made my choice. But as I stepped onto the busy street, the protection pendant began to pulse against my chest, a gentle but insistent warning.

I wasn't alone.

The pendant grew warmer, its rhythm quickening. I forced myself to keep walking at a normal pace, resisting the urge to glance over my shoulder. The sensation of being watched crept along my skin, but I couldn't identify its source. Tourists and locals moved around me on the busy street, their chatter and laughter creating a false sense of security.

But I knew better now. Prague's shadows held predators, and I was exactly what they were hunting.

I turned down a tight side street, using the reflection in a shop window to scan behind me. There—a figure in dark clothing, staying just far enough back to blend with the crowd but close enough to keep me in sight. Male, tall, moving in the same way, I now know to associate with supernatural speed.

My heart pounded against my ribs, but something else stirred beneath the fear. The vampire blood David had told me about, the heritage I had spent my life not understanding. My senses felt sharper, more aware of danger. I could almost see the darkness radiating from my pursuer.

I needed to get to Matthias.

I ducked into a cramped passageway between two Gothic buildings, the sudden dimness making me blink. The alley was barely wide enough for two people, with stone walls rising on either side. Perfect for losing a tail, but if I got trapped...

I needed to find a way through to the next street over.

But as I moved deeper into the passage, I realized my mistake. The afternoon crowd was thinner here, and the stone walls muffled sound. When I glanced back, I saw not one but three figures following me now, moving quickly.

I broke into a run.

Behind me, I heard the sharp intake of breath that meant they'd dropped all pretense of stealth. Footsteps echoed off stone as they chased me, moving faster than any human could manage.

I burst out of the alley into a small square, gasping in relief at the open space and afternoon sunlight. A few elderly locals sat on benches, feeding pigeons. Normal people living normal lives, completely unaware of the supernatural hunt happening around them.

I veered left, heading for the streets that led toward the castle district. If I could reach the cathedral where Matthias spent his days, if I could get to consecrated ground—

A figure stepped out of an alley directly ahead of me.

I skidded to a stop, my enhanced reflexes barely keeping

me upright. The vampire was sharp-featured, devoid of warmth, with the kind of predatory stillness that made my skin crawl. His lips curved in a smile that revealed just a hint of fang.

"Miss Sterling," he said. "How lovely to finally meet you properly."

I spun around, looking for an escape route, but the other three had emerged from behind me. They moved with the coordination of a pack, cutting off each potential exit.

"We've been looking forward to this," the leader continued, taking a step closer. "You've led us quite a chase across the city."

My hand moved instinctively to the silver knife at my hip, and I saw his eyes track the movement with amusement.

"Oh, by all means," he said. "Though I should mention that Lord Casimir wants you alive and unmarked for tomorrow's ceremony. It would be unfortunate if you forced us to be rougher than necessary."

"I'm not going anywhere with you," I said, surprised by how steady my voice sounded.

"I'm afraid that's not your choice to make."

The vampire lunged.

My body moved before my mind caught up, the silver blade appearing in my hand as I twisted away from his reaching hand. But the first vampire reached me before the others, his hands extended toward my throat. The moment his fingers made contact with my skin, there was a brilliant flash of light and the sharp smell of burning flesh.

He screamed, jerking his hand back as if he'd been electrocuted. "What—"

The protection pendant was glowing beneath my sweater, its warmth pressing against my chest. The vampire stared at it in shock, his burned fingers already beginning to heal.

"No matter," the leader said, though he kept his distance now. "We just can't touch her directly."

But the pendant had bought me precious seconds. I grabbed a chunk of loose stone from the street, hurling it hard at the second attacker's head while spinning away. It caught him in the temple with a crack, sending him staggering backward.

The third one was too close. I drove the silver blade up under his ribs, angling toward his heart. The moment the silver pierced his chest, his eyes went wide with shock and pain. For a heartbeat, we stood frozen together, my blade buried in his body.

Then he crumbled to ash.

"Stay back," I warned, raising the knife.

"Or what?" The leader said. "You'll do what, exactly? You're one human girl against the three of us."

"Maybe," I said, tightening my grip on the silver blade. "But I'm not just any human girl."

I could feel it now, that vampire heritage that had been revealed. It sang in my blood, sharpening my reflexes, heightening my awareness. These creatures wanted to use me because of what I was, but that same heritage might be what saved me.

The leader's eyes narrowed. "Interesting. You can feel it, can't you? The power in your bloodline."

"I can feel enough to know you're making a mistake."

"The only mistake," he said, "would be making this harder than it needs to be."

The vampires circled warily now, clearly reassessing their approach. The pendant's glow was visible even through my sweater, pulsing with protective energy.

Then I heard the deep toll of church bells echoing across the city.

The vampires heard it too, their heads turning toward the sound with expressions of unease.

"The cathedral," the leader muttered.

Holy ground. Consecrated bells. Whatever power protected Matthias's sanctuary was calling across the city, and these creatures could feel it as clearly as I could.

An idea sparked.

"You want me alive," I said, backing slowly toward the street that led uphill to the castle. "That limits what you can do to me."

"It limits how much we can hurt you," the leader corrected. "It doesn't limit us from taking you."

"Try it."

I turned and ran, not away from the castle but directly toward it. The street was steep and narrow, lined with buildings that cast deep shadows. Behind me, I heard cursing in a language I didn't recognize as the vampires started to chase me.

But I had advantages they hadn't counted on. I knew these streets now, had walked them dozens of times on my way to and from the library. And more importantly, I was running toward help, not away from it.

The cathedral bells continued to toll, their sound growing stronger as I climbed toward the castle district. Each peal seemed to resonate in my bones, calling me home.

I could hear my pursuers falling behind. Not because they were slower, but because something about the sound of those bells was affecting them. Making them hesitate.

I reached the top of the hill, gasping but triumphant, the cathedral's spires visible ahead through the maze of castle buildings. Almost there. Almost safe.

A hand closed around my ankle.

I went down hard, my knees scraping against cobblestone as the vampire who'd grabbed me hauled me backward. He must have taken a different route, circled around while I was focused on the others behind me.

"Clever," he said, his grip like iron around my leg. "But not clever enough."

I twisted, bringing the silver knife down toward his wrist, but he caught my hand with his free one. His fingers tightened until I cried out, the knife clattering away across the stones.

"Now then," he said pleasantly. "Let's discuss this like civilized—"

A shadow fell across us.

The vampire looked up, and his expression shifted from triumph to pure terror.

"Release her."

Matthias's voice was soft, conversational, and absolutely lethal.

The vampire dropped my ankle like it had burned him, scrambling backward on the cobblestones. "Lord Matthias. We didn't know—that is, we weren't aware—"

"You weren't aware that you were hunting my mate?" Matthias stepped fully into view, and I felt the energy around us change. "On ground under my protection?"

Even as I sat there injured and breathless, I could see the power radiating from him. This wasn't the controlled vampire I'd grown to know. This was something deadly, with eight centuries of accumulated fury behind his green eyes.

"Lord Casimir's orders," the vampire stammered. "We were told to retrieve the Sterling woman before—"

"Before what?" Matthias took another step forward, and the vampire actually whimpered. "Before the blood moon? Before my ritual?"

Understanding flickered across the creature's face, followed immediately by desperation. "You can't. The girl belongs to our lord. She's meant for the greater ritual, the one that will—"

"The one that will fail," Matthias finished quietly. "Because she's already chosen."

He looked at me then, and I saw the question in his eyes. The hope he was trying so hard to hide.

I met his gaze steadily. "I have chosen."

The relief that flashed across his features was quickly replaced by protective fury as he turned back to my attacker.

"Run," Matthias said simply.

The vampire didn't need to be told twice. He scrambled to his feet and fled down the hillside, not even pausing to collect his companions who were standing at the top of the street.

Matthias watched them go with satisfaction, then turned to help me up from the cobblestones.

"Are you hurt?" His hands were gentle as they checked me for injuries, but I could feel the barely suppressed violence humming beneath his skin.

"Scraped knees," I said, accepting his steadying touch. "My pride is more damaged than anything else."

"You fought them off." His thumb brushed across a cut on my cheek I hadn't even realized was there. "Three of them, and you held your own until I arrived."

"It was four at first," I said. "But David told me about our heritage. I could feel it helping me."

Something shifted in Matthias's expression. "David told you?"

"Everything. About the vampire blood in the Sterling line, about why I've always felt incomplete." I met his eyes. "About why I was drawn to you from the very first moment."

"And?"

"And I went to Helena. She showed me journals, Matthias. Personal accounts from Sterling women who chose transformation." My voice grew stronger. "They were happy. All of them. They found exactly what they were looking for."

His hands framed my face, and I could see hope flickering with disbelief in his green eyes. "Sera—"

"I choose you," I said. "I choose this. Whatever it costs, whatever it changes, I choose you."

The kiss was inevitable, desperate with four hundred years of waiting finally reaching its end. I could taste the sweet relief mingling with a ravenous hunger, and there was something profound, deeper than mere desire, in the way his lips passionately claimed mine. The air around us seemed to shimmer with the intensity of the moment.

When we finally broke apart, his forehead rested against mine.

"The blood moon rises tomorrow night," he said quietly.

"I know."

"Once we begin the ritual, there's no going back. You'll be transformed, bound to me forever."

"I know."

"Your family—"

"Will have to understand." I touched his face, feeling the sharp line of his cheekbone under my palm. "Or they won't. But I'm done living my life based on other people's fears."

He pulled me closer, and I could feel the tremor in his hands.

"I need to get you somewhere safe," he said. "If Casimir's vampires are moving this boldly, the situation is more urgent than I thought."

I looked around the empty street, suddenly aware of how exposed we were. "Your cathedral?"

"Yes." He swept me up in his arms before I could protest, moving with supernatural speed toward the sanctuary where this had all begun.

40

The cathedral felt different when we arrived, charged with an energy I'd never felt before. Matthias led me deeper underground than I'd ever been, through passages carved from rock and lit by torches.

"The ritual chamber," he said as we stopped before a heavy stone door marked with symbols that made my skin tingle. "It's been prepared for this moment for over four hundred years."

He pressed his palm against the stone, and I felt power ripple through the air as locks disengaged. The door swung open silently, revealing a chamber that took my breath away.

The chamber was circular, its vaulted ceiling lost in shadow above. Silver symbols covered the black stone walls, gleaming in the light of countless candles that lined carved alcoves. The air was thick with the scent of wax.

A pool of dark water surrounded a raised platform at the center. The dais was carved from light stone that seemed to catch and hold the candlelight, with silver channels etched across its surface in spiraling patterns.

It was beautiful in a way that made my chest tight. Not

just a room but something sacred. Something that had been waiting.

"It's beautiful," I whispered.

The stone seemed to absorb my words, then give them back richer, deeper. Even my voice sounded different here.

"It's powerful," Matthias said. "This chamber has channeled supernatural energy for over a thousand years. Tomorrow night, it will channel the blood moon's power to break my curse and bind us together forever."

He moved to light more candles, and I watched the way the shadows danced across his sharp features. In this sacred space, he looked more otherworldly than ever—timeless, powerful, magnificent.

"What do we need to do?" I asked. "To prepare?"

"The space must be cleansed and blessed. Our bodies and souls must be prepared for the transformation." He turned to face me, and I saw something vulnerable flicker across his features. "Are you certain, Sera? Once we perform the cleansing rituals, you'll be bound to this choice. There will be no going back."

I moved toward him, closing the distance between us. "I've never been more certain of anything in my life."

He searched my face for any sign of doubt, then nodded slowly. "Then we begin."

The preparation was more intimate than I'd expected. Matthias guided me through rituals that were part spiritual cleansing, part physical preparation. We moved around the chamber together, lighting specific candles in a sacred pattern, speaking words in a language so old it seemed to resonate in my bones.

But it was the way he looked at me as we performed each ritual that made my pulse race. His eyes followed every movement, dark with barely restrained hunger. When our hands brushed as we reached for the same candle, electricity shot between us.

"The space is prepared," he said finally, his voice rougher than usual. "Now we must prepare ourselves."

"How?"

"Give me your hands," he said when the last candle was lit.

I held out my palms, trying to ignore the way my skin tingled in anticipation of his touch.

"Blessed water," he explained, dipping his fingers into a bowl. "It will cleanse away any lingering influence from the outside world."

I gasped when his fingers found the symbols on my palm. He traced each one slowly, deliberately, his cool touch sending heat up my arm.

"Hold still," he murmured when I shivered.

He moved to my forehead next, his touch feather-light but burning. Then my throat, where my pulse hammered visibly beneath the skin. His thumb lingered there for a moment longer than necessary.

"Matthias—"

"The ritual requires care," he said, but I could hear the strain in his voice. "Each symbol must be perfect."

When he reached the pulse points at my wrists, I couldn't suppress the small sound that escaped me. His fingers traced circles there, slow and thorough, and I felt heat pooling low in my belly.

"Your turn," he said, offering me the bowl. His green eyes were darker now, pupils dilated.

My hands trembled slightly as I dipped my fingers into the blessed water. "Tell me what to do."

"The same symbols. Here." He guided my hand to his palm, closing his eyes as I traced the pattern he'd shown me. "And here."

I moved to his forehead, having to rise on my toes to reach him. This close, I could smell his scent—leather and smoke that made me want to press closer.

"Sera." My name was a warning.

"I'm just following the ritual," I said innocently, though my fingers lingered longer than necessary at his temples.

When I reached his throat, I felt his pulse jump under my touch. The knowledge that I could affect him the same way he affected me sent a thrill through me.

"The wrists," he said, his voice strained.

I took his hands in mine, studying the elegant lines of his fingers, the strength in his wrists. As I traced the symbols there, he made a sound low in his throat that made my stomach clench with want.

"Is that it?" I asked, looking up at him through my lashes.

"No." His voice was rough now, all pretense of control slipping. "There's one more."

"Where?"

"Here." His fingers traced the hollow at the base of my throat, just above the neckline of my shirt. "The binding point. It's crucial for the ritual."

I swallowed hard, very aware of how his fingers felt against my skin. "Show me."

He dipped his fingers in the blessed water again, then stepped closer. So close I could feel the heat radiating from his body despite his supernatural coolness.

"This symbol is different," he said quietly, his fingers hovering just above my skin. "More complex. It may take longer."

"I can handle it."

The first touch made me arch against him involuntarily. He drew intricate patterns across my collarbone, down to the sensitive dip of my throat, each stroke deliberate and maddening.

"You have no idea how long I've wanted to touch you like this," he murmured, his thumb tracing the curve where my neck met my shoulder.

"Touch me how?"

Instead of answering, he leaned down and pressed his lips to the spot where he'd just drawn the symbol. The kiss was soft, but it sent fire racing through my veins.

"My turn," I said breathlessly.

He straightened, and I could see the pulse hammering in his throat. I dipped my fingers in the water, then reached up to trace the same symbol on his chest, just above the collar of his shirt.

But the fabric was in my way.

"I can't do it properly," I said, my fingers playing with the edge of his shirt. "The symbol needs to be on skin."

His hands covered mine, stilling them. "Sera."

"It's just for the ritual," I said, looking up at him with as much innocence as I could muster.

He studied my face for a long moment, then slowly released my hands. "Just for the ritual."

I nodded solemnly and began unbuttoning his shirt, taking my time with each button. His breathing grew heavier with each button, and by the time I pushed the fabric off his shoulders, his chest was rising and falling rapidly.

"Now," I said, dipping my fingers in the water again.

I traced each symbol slowly, deliberately. He didn't rush me, just watched my face with dark, hungry eyes as I explored the lean muscle and raised scars that mapped his torso.

"There," I said finally, my palms flat against his chest. "How was that?"

"Perfect," he said, his voice barely above a whisper.

We stood there for a moment, hands on each other, the

air between us crackling with tension. I could feel his heart beating under my palms, could see the way his control was fraying at the edges.

"Is the preparation finished?" I asked.

"Almost." His hands came up to cup my face, thumbs brushing across my cheekbones. "There's one final step."

"What?"

"This."

When he kissed me, it was like a dam breaking. All the restraint and ritual propriety vanished in a heartbeat. His mouth claimed mine with consuming hunger, and I could taste four hundred years of longing in the way he kissed me.

"I've imagined this," he said against my lips, his hands already pulling my sweater off. "In that chamber, surrounded by power, making you mine in every way possible."

The promise sent heat racing through me, pooling low in my belly. I could feel the overwhelming desire in the way he held me, his hands exploring my curves with a possessive urgency. Every caress sent shivers of pleasure coursing through my body, igniting every nerve ending.

His fingers trailed down my waist, skimming over my hips and back up again, teasing the edges of my skin. I gasped as his thumb brushed along the delicate line of my collarbone, the warmth of his touch making me arch towards him like a moth to a flame.

"Is this what you want?" he murmured, his lips grazing my ear, igniting a fire in my core. "To feel every inch of me against you?"

"Yes," I breathed, my voice trembling with need. "I want all of you."

He lifted me onto the stone platform, the cold surface making me gasp. But his hands were warm as they roamed over me, learning every curve, every sensitive spot that made me arch against him.

Then he captured my lips again, deepening the kiss as his hands slid lower, fingers dancing along the curve of my thigh. The sensation was electric, sending a wave of heat flooding through me as I instinctively wrapped my legs around his waist, pulling him closer, craving the intimate connection between us.

"You're driving me mad," he growled, his voice thick with desire as he ground against me, the heat of his body fueling my longing. "I can't hold back much longer."

"Then don't," I urged, my heart racing as his hands roamed up my sides, fingertips grazing the sensitive skin beneath my breasts. I could feel the tension building between us, a tangible force that threatened to break us both.

He captured one of my breasts in his hand, teasing my nipple with his thumb, sending shockwaves of pleasure coursing through me. "Tell me how much you want this," he commanded, his mouth trailing down my neck, his breath hot against my skin.

"I need you," I gasped, every word dripping with desperation. "I need to feel you—everything."

"Beg for it," he taunted, his eyes dark with hunger as he continued to tease, his fingers working their way lower, brushing dangerously close to where I craved him most.

"Please," I whimpered, desperate for his touch, for the sweet release that felt just within reach. "I want you, all of you. I want to belong to you."

His fangs brushed against my skin, teasing the pulse point at my neck, sending waves of desire crashing over me. He could sense my longing, the way my body responded to him, and the thrill of his proximity was almost unbearable.

"Beg me not to stop," he whispered against my neck.

"Don't stop," I gasped. "Please, don't ever stop."

When he bit down, the world exploded into sensation. The blood bond that had been building between us flared to life with overwhelming intensity. I could feel his hunger, his desperate need, his centuries of loneliness finally ending. And he could feel mine—the completion, the rightness, the absolute certainty that this was what I'd been searching for my entire life.

He drank deeply, and with each pull, I felt our connection strengthen. I could sense his thoughts, his emotions, the way my blood was healing something essential inside him that had been broken for so long.

When he finally pulled away, his eyes were bright with power and satisfaction. "Mine," he said, his voice rough with possession.

"Yours," I agreed, pulling his mouth back to mine.

His fingers slid down my arms, tracing the curves of my body, igniting a fire wherever his touch lingered. I writhed beneath him, my body begging for more, every caress sending me closer to the edge.

He leaned down, his mouth finding the sensitive skin beneath my ear, kissing a trail down to my collarbone while his hands explored my waist, his fingertips dancing teasingly close to the softness of my thighs. I could feel his breath against my skin, hot and tantalizing, as he took his time, savoring every inch of me.

"God, you're beautiful," he murmured, his voice thick with lust. "I could lose myself in you."

His hands moved lower, pressing against my thighs, urging me to spread my legs wider, to invite him in. My heart raced at the invitation, the blend of vulnerability and desire coursing through me like electricity.

"Please," I begged.

With a growl of consent, he surged forward, capturing

my mouth once more, the kiss consuming us with an intensity that ignited every fiber of my being. His body pressed against mine, the solid warmth of him enveloping me, making it impossible to think of anything but the need thrumming between us.

His hands found the waistband of my jeans, fingers curling around the fabric and pulling it off slowly, inch by tantalizing inch. My breath hitched as the cool air brushed against my thighs, contrasting with the heat radiating from his body. I could feel the weight of his gaze, hungry and possessive, drinking in every detail as he exposed the skin of my legs.

"Do you want me to touch you?" he asked, his voice low and gravelly, eyes locked onto mine, searching for permission. The tension hung thick in the air, and I could barely manage a nod, my heart racing as anticipation coiled tighter.

He wasted no time, his hands sliding up my thighs, fingers teasingly brushing closer to where I throbbed with need. I gasped as he explored, his touch igniting sparks of pleasure that made me arch against him, begging for more.

"Tell me how it feels," he commanded, his voice rough with the effort of restraint.

"It feels—so good," I managed to stammer, my body betraying me as I pushed against his hands. "I need more. Please."

He leaned down, capturing my lips in a scorching kiss, his tongue sweeping against mine as if trying to merge our very souls. His fingers finally found the edge of my lace panties, teasingly close, and my breath hitched in anticipation.

"God, you're perfect," he breathed, and in one swift motion, he slipped his fingers beneath the delicate fabric, and I gasped, the sensation of his touch sending a jolt through me.

His fingers found the sensitive spot, and I moaned softly against his mouth, the world around us fading into nothing but the rhythm of our bodies and the mounting pleasure that began to swell. Each stroke of his fingers was deliberate, drawing out the bliss, sending waves of heat pooling low in my belly.

"More," I gasped, my body writhing in response to his touch, desperate for release.

He pressed a finger deeper, curling it just right, and I felt myself tremble under the exquisite pressure. "You're so responsive," he murmured, his voice thick with desire. "I could do this forever."

The tension within me wound tighter, each stroke of his fingers igniting a fire that threatened to consume me. I was teetering on the edge, and I could feel him pulling me closer to it with each caress.

"Tell me what you want," he urged, his breath hot against my ear, sending shivers down my spine.

"I want to feel you inside me," I gasped, my voice quivering with need. "Please, I need to feel all of you."

He stilled for a moment, the urgency of my words hanging in the air like a sweet promise. Then, with an intensity that made my heart race, he withdrew his fingers, leaving me longing for that connection, that fullness.

"Soon," he promised, brushing his lips against my neck, his breath warm and tantalizing against my skin. "But first, I want to savor this moment, to break apart every piece of you."

With that, he lowered his mouth to my chest, trailing kisses down my body, his lips igniting a path of fire as he moved lower and lower. My skin felt electrified under his touch, each kiss bringing me closer to the edge of madness.

He took his time, teasing and exploring, his hands roaming over my body as if he were memorizing every curve, every soft contour. When he reached my panties, he looked up at me, his eyes dark with desire. "May I?"

"Yes," I breathed, giving him the permission he sought.

He slid the fabric aside, his mouth finding me with a fervent intensity. I gasped as his tongue flicked against me, the sensation overwhelming. He worked with intention, his mouth and fingers moving together in perfect harmony, drawing me closer to the brink.

"Just like that," I moaned, my back arching as pleasure coursed through me. "Don't stop."

He obliged, his focus unwavering as he lavished attention on me, each flick and stroke sending me spiraling higher. I could feel the tension coiling, tight and electric, threatening to snap.

"Please," I begged, the urgency in my voice matching the frantic rhythm of my heart. "I need release."

"Not yet," he murmured, a wicked grin playing at the corners of his mouth as he pulled away just enough to tease. "I want you to feel this—every part of it."

His hands gripped my thighs, holding me open to him as he returned to his worship with an intensity that left me gasping. The world around us faded, shrinking down to just the two of us and the electric connection we shared.

Each flick of his tongue ignited flames within me, sending waves of pleasure crashing over me. I could feel myself getting closer, that familiar tension tightening in my core, and I couldn't help but writhe against him, desperate for that release.

"Look at me," he commanded, lifting his gaze to meet mine, his eyes blazing with desire. "I want to see your pleasure, to feel every bit of it."

The intensity of his gaze sent a thrill through me, and I nodded, my breath coming in quick, ragged gasps as he drove me higher. The sensations were overwhelming, the world outside our bubble dimming into nothingness, leaving just his mouth, his hands, and the pleasure building within me.

"Just a little more," he coaxed, his voice low and sultry, as he increased his pace, his fingers working in tandem with his mouth to push me closer to the edge. "Let go for me, Sera. Let it all go."

With a cry, I felt the wave crash over me, every nerve ending lighting up in ecstasy as my body surrendered to the overwhelming pleasure. I was lost in a sea of sensation, spiraling into the depths of bliss as he continued to coax me through it, riding the waves of my climax with a deftness that left me breathless.

When I finally came down, panting and flushed, he pulled back, his eyes dark with a mix of satisfaction and hunger.

"Please," I whispered. "I want to be yours completely."

For a moment, I thought he would give in. His control wavered, his hands tightening on my hips as he ground against me. But then he pulled back, breathing hard.

"After the ritual," he said, his voice strained with the effort of restraint. "When the bond is complete and you're truly mine. When I can take you without any risk, without any chance of hurting you."

"You won't hurt me—"

"I might." His fingers traced my cheek with infinite tenderness. "The transformation magic is unpredictable. If we're physically joined when it happens, if something goes wrong..." He shook his head. "I won't risk you, not for my own desire."

I wanted to argue, but the way his hands trembled with

the effort of holding back told me how much this restraint was costing him.

"When you become mine forever, I'll claim every part of you. I'll make love to you until you forget your own name, until the only thing you remember is that you belong to me," he promised, pulling me close against his chest.

The promise sent heat racing through me, but I could also see the exhaustion in his eyes. The preparation, the blood sharing, the emotional intensity—it had drained us both.

"The blood moon rises in just a few hours," he said, glancing toward where moonlight filtered down through hidden shafts in the ceiling. "You should rest before then. The ritual will be demanding, and you'll need all your strength."

"What about you?"

"I'll be right next to you." He helped me gather our scattered clothes; his movements were efficient but tender. "Rest while you can."

We moved to the main cathedral and arranged ourselves in the cushioned alcove he'd prepared along one wall. Inside, the vast space enveloped us, with high ceilings supported by sturdy columns adorned with intricate carvings. The glow from stained glass windows painted the stone walls in muted colors, creating a serene ambiance. Flickering candlelight from the nearby altar added warmth to the cool air, and the faint scent of incense lingered around us.

The alcove wasn't quite a bed, but it was comfortable and intimate, perfect for holding each other through the remaining hours, wrapped in the quiet of the cathedral.

I curled against his side, my head on his chest, listening to the steady rhythm of his unnecessary heartbeat. His arms wrapped around me, protective and possessive.

"Are you nervous?" I asked quietly.

"Terrified," he admitted. "Four hundred years of hoping, and in just a few hours, it all comes to an end. Either I'll finally be free, or I'll die knowing I failed to protect you."

I tilted my head up to look at him. "What if it doesn't work?"

"Then at least we tried." His hand stroked through my hair. "At least we had this."

"That's not good enough." I settled back against his chest. "I didn't choose this just to lose you."

His arms tightened around me. "You won't lose me. Not after everything we've been through to get here."

We talked quietly for a while longer, sharing hopes, fears, and promises for the future we'd create together. But eventually, exhaustion took over. The emotional intensity of the day, along with the magical preparation and blood sharing, had completely drained me.

I drifted to sleep to the sound of his voice murmuring endearments in languages I didn't understand, his hands gently stroking through my hair with endless tenderness.

Hours passed in peaceful rest. Deep, dreamless sleep that felt safer and more satisfying than anything I'd ever experienced. In his arms, in this sacred space, I felt a deep sense of protection.

Until the alarm bells shattered the silence.

41

I jerked awake to the sound of bronze bells clanging urgently throughout the cathedral, their discordant noise cutting through the peaceful atmosphere like a scream in the silence. Matthias was already moving, supernatural reflexes bringing him to full alertness instantly.

"What—" I started.

"Attack," he said grimly, helping me to my feet. "They're here."

"Who's here?"

"Casimir's vampires. They're here." His hands were already reaching for weapons I hadn't noticed before— blades that gleamed with deadly intent. "They know they're almost out of time. They're making their move."

Terror gripped me, yet beneath it was something else. Determination. After everything we'd shared, everything we'd prepared for, I wasn't going to let anyone stop us now.

"What do we do?"

Matthias looked at me, his jaw tight. "We fight," he said. "And we complete the ritual tonight, while we still can. The blood moon will be rising soon."

The bells continued their urgent warning, echoing

through stone corridors. I could hear it now, the sound of footsteps above us, moving with speed. Shouts. The clash of weapons.

"How many?" I asked.

"Too many." Matthias pressed a blade into my hand. "But they have to come through that door to reach us. And this cathedral..." He gestured to the symbols and art surrounding us. "It's protected. They can't use their full power here."

A thunderous crash echoed from somewhere above, followed by a roar that made my blood run cold.

"Sera," Matthias said quietly, his eyes meeting mine. "Whatever happens, don't let them take you alive. Promise me."

Before I could answer, the temperature in the cathedral dropped sharply. The candles flickered as if an icy wind had passed through, and the symbols on the walls started to glow with a warning light.

The cathedral doors exploded inward with a crash that shook the walls.

I pressed myself against Matthias as enemy vampires poured through the breach, their eyes burning crimson in the blood moon's light streaming through the shattered rose window. The red glow turned everything into a scene from hell—shadows dancing, silver glinting, blood already beginning to stain the consecrated ground.

"Sera, go find somewhere to hide!" Matthias commanded, his sword appearing in his hand as he moved to intercept the first wave of attackers. "Stay hidden until—"

"No."

The word came out stronger than I'd ever spoken before. Something inside me had shifted the moment the blood moon's light touched my skin. A power I'd never felt, something deadly was awakening in my veins.

"I'm not hiding anymore."

I grabbed a fallen dagger from the floor and launched myself into the fray.

The moment I moved with purpose instead of fear, something extraordinary happened. My reflexes became lightning-fast, my vision sharper than any human's had a right to be. I could sense the vampires' movements before they made them, could hear heartbeats and breathing from across the cathedral, could smell the metallic tang of blood and the ozone scent of supernatural power.

My vampire heritage was manifesting.

A vampire lunged at Matthias from behind while he fought two others. Without thinking, I intercepted, driving the silver blade between the creature's ribs with inhuman accuracy. He dissolved to ash with a shriek, and Matthias spun to stare at me with wonder and terror.

"You're manifesting," he breathed. "The blood moon is awakening your true nature."

But even as my powers awakened, I could see him growing weaker. Each clash of blades, each supernatural movement, was draining him. The curse that had been slowly killing him for four centuries was accelerating, fed by the stress and our separation.

More vampires poured through the broken doors—Casimir's forces, their faces twisted with centuries of hatred. Behind them came David and Elena, silver weapons shining, their hunter training evident in every lethal movement.

"Matthias!" David's voice boomed across the cathedral. "Release her now!"

"She's choosing to be here," Matthias called back, never taking his eyes off the vampire circling him. "Ask her yourself."

But there was no time for conversation. Elena was already moving, her crossbow trained on Matthias while

David engaged the nearest enemy vampire. The cathedral became a three-way battlefield—hunters versus enemy vampires versus Matthias and me.

I watched Matthias stumble as he blocked a blow, his supernatural speed faltering for just a moment. The vampire he was fighting noticed and pressed his advantage, forcing Matthias back against a stone pillar.

That's when the terrible realization hit me.

If we didn't complete the ritual tonight, during the blood moon, he was going to die. The curse would claim him before the next lunar cycle, and I would lose him forever—not to my family's interference, but to the magic that had been slowly draining his life for four hundred years.

"Matthias!" I called out, ducking under a vampire's grasping claws and driving my blade up into his heart. "We do the ritual NOW. During the battle. I'm not losing you."

His eyes went wide with shock even as he decapitated his opponent. "Sera, no. It's too dangerous. The ritual makes us vulnerable, defenseless for nearly an hour. In the middle of this—"

"Then we'll be vulnerable together." I stepped closer to him, ignoring the chaos raging around us. The cathedral was filling with more enemies. I could hear them smashing through the side entrances, the sulfur scent of Casimir's older lieutenants filling the air.

Blood dripped from a cut on Matthias's forehead, and I could see the exhaustion pulling at his features. He was fighting a war on two fronts—against our enemies and against the curse eating him alive from within.

"Look at me," I demanded, grabbing his face between my hands despite the silver blade still clutched in my fingers. "LOOK at me. You're dying right now. The curse is killing you faster because of the stress, because we're apart. If we wait for a safer moment, there won't be one."

Around us, the battle raged. I heard Elena's crossbow fire, heard David shout orders to hunters I hadn't even realized were there. Enemy vampires were pouring in from every entrance now, and the air was thick with the scent of blood and burning silver.

"The ritual chamber," I said firmly. "We go there now, we complete this, and then we face whatever comes next as equals. As partners."

"Sera—"

"No." I kissed him hard, tasting blood and desperation. "I choose this. I choose you. I choose right now, in the middle of hell itself, because that's what matters. Not waiting for perfect moments, but creating them."

When I pulled back, his green eyes were blazing with something fierce and completely committed.

"Then we run," he said. "We run, and we don't stop until it's done."

42

He swept me up in his arms, and together we fought our way deeper underground, toward the chamber.

The stone steps spiraled down into darkness, each level taking us deeper beneath the cathedral's foundations. Matthias moved with speed, but I could feel his strength fading with every step. His breathing grew labored, and his skin grew colder despite the supernatural fire still burning in his eyes.

"Can you make it?" I gasped, adjusting my grip to support more of his weight as we descended the familiar stone steps.

"I have to." His voice was tight with pain. "We're almost back to the chamber."

Behind us, I could hear our pursuers—boots pounding against stone, the clash of weapons, and Elena's voice shouting orders to the other hunters. But there were other sounds as well, primeval and more terrifying. The unnatural snarls of Casimir's vampires grew louder with each passing second, closing in on us.

"They're gaining on us," I said.

Matthias stumbled, catching himself against the carved stone wall.

"Matthias—"

"I'm fine," he lied, pushing himself upright. "Just need to reach—"

A crossbow bolt whistled past my ear, embedding itself in the stone inches from my head. I spun to see Elena at the top of the spiral, already reloading.

"Move!" I shoved Matthias ahead of me, putting my body between him and the hunters above. More bolts flew, and I felt one graze my shoulder, leaving a line of fire across my skin.

But the blood that welled up glowed faintly silver in the blood moon's light filtering down from above.

Matthias saw it too. "Your transformation is beginning," he breathed.

"Good," I said fiercely. "Maybe it'll keep us alive long enough to finish this."

We reached the bottom of the stairs just as another wave of vampires burst from a side passage. These were different from the ones above—older, more powerful, with movements that were effortless and deadly—Casimir's inner circle.

"The chamber," Matthias pointed to an archway carved with symbols that seemed to writhe in the flickering torchlight. "We have to reach—"

One of the old vampires landed in front of us with swiftness, his smile revealing fangs like ivory daggers. "Matthias Cross," he purred. "Still running, after all these years."

"Damien." Matthias's voice was filled with hatred. "I should have known you'd crawl out of whatever hole you've been hiding in."

"Oh, I've been very busy." Damien's gaze slid to me, and I felt something hungry in his stare. "Thanks for preparing for tonight. The blood moon, the Sterling girl, the ritual that will make us gods."

That's when their plan became clear. They weren't just trying to stop our ritual. They had been counting on us preparing the sacred space for them. Every blessing we'd placed on the chamber, every protection circle we'd drawn, every drop of power we'd poured into sanctifying this place would amplify their ritual instead. They'd let us do all the work, then steal both the space and the blood moon's peak moment for themselves.

"That's why you've been driving us apart," I realized. "Weakening him, isolating me, making me desperate enough to become reckless and choose him."

"To run straight into our trap." Damien's laughter was like breaking glass. "Every choice you thought you were making freely was exactly what we wanted you to choose."

Rage flooded through me, hot and bright. They'd been manipulating not just me, but my feelings, my desperation, my need for Matthias. They'd turned my own heart into a weapon against us both.

"No," I said, my voice carrying a new power that made the stone walls tremble. "You're wrong about one thing."

Damien raised an eyebrow.

"I'm not your victim anymore."

The silver light in my blood blazed brighter, and suddenly I could move like them—faster than human, deadly as lightning. I drove my blade toward Damien's heart, but he twisted away at the last second, my silver leaving a burning line across his ribs.

"Impossible," he hissed. "You're not fully transformed yet—"

"She doesn't need to be." Matthias was suddenly beside me, his power flaring despite his weakening state. "She's a Sterling. Her bloodline carries power even untransformed."

Together, we fought our way through Damien and his allies, silver and steel flashing in the blood moon's light. My newfound speed let me duck under Damien's hands while Matthias's blade found the heart of another vampire, turning him to ash. I spun and drove my dagger into a female vampire's spine, her shriek echoing off the stone walls before she crumbled to dust.

But for every enemy we cut down, two more seemed to take their place. Matthias was moving slower now, his deflections coming a fraction of a second too late. A vampire's nails raked across his ribs, drawing lines of blood that glowed in the moonlight.

I could feel time running out—both for Matthias's strength and for the ritual window. The blood moon was reaching its fullness, and if we missed this chance, we'd never get another.

43

"The chamber!" I shouted over the sound of battle. "We have to reach the chamber!"

We burst back into the ritual chamber, and immediately, I could see how different it looked under the blood moon's power. The symbols carved into the black stone walls were now blazing with fire, and the channels cut into the floor around the central dais pulsed with light that seemed to have a heartbeat of its own.

The chamber, which had been mysterious before, was now alive with magic.

"This is dangerous." Matthias moved to the chamber's edge, placing his palm against a carved symbol. The massive stone doors began to swing shut behind us. "Once we begin, we can't stop. The ritual will take at least an hour, and we'll be completely vulnerable for most of it."

The sound of our pursuers grew louder. They'd reach the chamber any moment.

"Then we better start now." I pulled the small piece of parchment from my pocket, the one Helena had pressed into my hand weeks ago. "She said to burn this if I needed help."

Matthias looked at the paper, his eyes widening as he recognized the symbols written on it. "Sera, that's a summoning charm. You don't know what it will bring."

"I know Helena's been protecting this city from vampires longer than I've been alive." I moved to one of the torches burning in the wall sconces. "I trust her."

"But—"

The chamber doors shuddered under a massive impact. Our enemies had found us.

"No time for doubt," I said, and thrust the parchment into the flames.

The paper caught fire instantly, burning with purple flame that rose higher than any natural fire should. The smoke formed symbols in the air, and I felt a pulse of power shoot out from the chamber like a beacon.

Whatever was coming, it was coming fast.

Matthias had moved to the dais, his hands already working over the ritual implements laid out on the light stone. Ceremonial knives with silver blades, goblets carved from obsidian, and candles that burned with different colored flames.

"Sera," he said, his voice rough with pain and something deeper. "If this fails, if I die during the ceremony..."

"Then we die together," I said firmly, taking my place beside him on the dais. "But I choose this. I choose you. I choose us."

The blood moon reached its peak above us, and power flooded the chamber.

It was time.

The sacred words felt strange on my tongue, syllables in a language that predated any human civilization. But somehow, I knew them, as if they'd been sleeping in my blood for centuries, waiting for this moment.

"*Sanguis ad sanguinem, vita ad vitam, anima ad animam,*" I

whispered, my voice growing stronger with each phrase. "*Blood to blood, life to life, soul to soul.*"

The ritual dagger felt warm in my hand as I drew it across my palm. Silver blood welled up immediately, glowing like liquid starlight in the blood moon's radiance. Matthias did the same, his darker blood flowing to match mine.

"Together," he said, and we pressed our cut palms against each other.

The moment our blood mingled, power exploded through the chamber. The carved symbols on the walls glowed so bright I had to squint, and the air itself seemed to catch fire with the light. Every nerve in my body came alive with sensation. I could feel Matthias's heartbeat as if it were my own, could sense his thoughts at the edges of my mind.

The transformation was beginning.

My vision sharpened until I could see every detail of the battle raging around us with crystal clarity. My hearing expanded. I could distinguish individual heartbeats among our enemies, could hear whispered conversations three levels above us, could even detect the flutter of bat wings somewhere in the cathedral's highest towers.

But it was the connection to Matthias that stole my breath. I felt his centuries of loneliness like a physical ache, felt his desperate love for me burning through every fiber of his being, felt his terror that even now, even during the ritual itself, something would tear us apart.

"*Never,*" I whispered into his mind, our psychic link growing stronger by the second. "*Nothing will separate us. Not again.*"

The chamber responded to our joining. The stone dais beneath us began to glow, warm light rising from deep within the rock. The channels carved into the floor were filled with fire that flowed like liquid, creating intricate patterns that pulsed in rhythm with our shared heartbeat.

Matthias was growing stronger. I could feel it through our bond. The curse that had been slowly draining his life for four centuries was fighting back, but our combined power was winning. Color returned to his skin, and his green eyes blazed with renewed vitality.

"It's working," he breathed, wonder filling his voice. "Sera, it's actually working."

But then the chamber doors exploded inward with a crash that sent stone fragments flying across the sacred space.

44

E nemy vampires poured through the breach, followed immediately by David and Elena. The consecrated chamber became a battlefield, silver weapons clashing with supernatural speed and strength just feet from where we knelt on the ritual dais.

"Stop this!" David shouted, his crossbow trained on Matthias. "Sera, get away from him!"

But something had changed in me during those first moments of transformation. Where before I might have wavered, might have been torn between my family and my choice, now there was only clarity. Only certainty.

Only the absolute knowledge that anyone who tried to interrupt this ritual was my enemy.

I rose to my feet, still connected to Matthias by our joined hands, and felt power flow through me like nothing I'd ever experienced. When I spoke, my voice carried the authority of something far older and more dangerous than the human girl who had arrived in Prague just weeks ago.

"You will not touch him," I said, and the air around me shimmered with silver light. "You will not touch us. And you will not stop what we have chosen."

Elena raised her silver blade, her face twisted with disgust. "Look at what he's done to you. You're not even human anymore."

"No," I agreed, feeling fangs elongate slightly in my mouth, feeling my nails sharpen to points that could tear through steel. "I'm not. I'm something better."

The protective fury that rose in me was unlike anything I'd ever felt—a primal, territorial rage that was absolutely lethal. These people wanted to hurt Matthias, wanted to destroy the bond we were creating, wanted to drag me back to a life that had never truly fit.

They had made themselves my enemies.

And I was no longer helpless prey.

David lowered his crossbow slightly, his face filled with pain and betrayal. "Sera," he said, his voice breaking on my name. "You chose this. You chose him over us."

The accusation cut deep, but I didn't flinch. I couldn't. Not when Matthias and I were still connected by our joined hands, not when I could feel the ritual's power building between us, demanding completion.

"I chose myself," I said, the painful truth cutting through the chaos around us. "For the first time in my life, I chose what I wanted instead of what everyone else expected of me."

Elena's face darkened with rage. "What you wanted? He's been manipulating you from the beginning! Vampire compulsion, supernatural seduction—"

"Stop." The word came out with enough force to rattle the stone walls. "You want to know the truth about manipulation? You've been controlling my entire life. Deciding where I could go, who I could trust, and what I was allowed to feel. You made me afraid of my own shadow, kept me from knowing about my own heritage."

David stepped forward, his weapon now aimed directly

at Matthias's heart. "Your heritage is hunting creatures like him. It's in your blood, Sera. You're a Sterling."

"Yes, I am." I felt my transformation deepening, felt power flowing through me like molten lava. "And Sterling women have been making this choice for centuries."

Elena raised her blade and lunged toward the dais, clearly intending to strike at Matthias while he was vulnerable in the ritual circle. The silver blade whistled through the air, aimed directly at his exposed throat.

I moved without thinking.

My hand shot out and caught Elena's wrist with inhuman strength, stopping her blade inches from Matthias's neck. The silver burned my fingers, sending lines of fire up my arm, but I held on anyway.

"Elena, don't," I pleaded, even as supernatural power coursed through me. "Please. He's not your enemy."

"He's everyone's enemy," she spat, trying to wrench her arm free. "He's a vampire, Sera. A killer. A monster."

"So am I, apparently." I tightened my grip, and I heard her wrist bones creak under the pressure. "Are you going to try to kill me too?"

The shock in her eyes was answer enough. She hadn't fully understood what my transformation meant. That I was becoming something that could fight back, something that could protect what I loved.

"Let her go, Sera," David said quietly. "This isn't you."

"This is exactly me." I released Elena's wrist but didn't step back. "This is who I've always been, underneath all the fear you taught me to carry."

David's crossbow was trembling now, and I could see the conflict tearing him apart. He'd raised me, protected me, and loved me as a daughter. But he couldn't understand this choice.

"He'll change you," David said desperately. "Whatever

you think you feel for him, once the transformation is complete, you won't be the same person. The Sera I know will be gone."

Through our bond, I felt Matthias's anguish at those words. He'd been afraid of the same thing. That in saving his life, I would lose everything that made me who I was.

"Look at me," I said softly, meeting David's eyes. "Really look at me. Do I seem gone to you? Do I seem like someone else?"

For a moment, just a moment, his weapon wavered.

"I'm still me," I continued. "I'm just more. Stronger. Able to protect the people I care about instead of just hiding behind them."

"You're protecting a monster—"

"I'm protecting the man I—" I stopped myself, the words catching in my throat. Not because they weren't true, but because this wasn't how I wanted to say them for the first time. Not in anger, not as a weapon in an argument.

Through our bond, I felt Matthias's understanding, his acceptance. The words could wait for a gentler moment. The feeling was already there, flowing between us like electricity.

"I'm protecting someone who matters to me," I finished instead. "Someone who's shown me who I really am."

Elena had been silent during this exchange, but now she raised her blade again, her face set with grim determination. "Then you're both lost," she said. "And the only mercy I can give you is a quick death."

She moved with hunter's discipline, her silver blade aimed not at Matthias this time, but at me.

David screamed my name.

But I was no longer the helpless girl who needed protecting. I was something new, something powerful, something that would not be stopped.

I caught the blade bare-handed.

Pain raced up my arm as the metal bit into my palm, but I held on anyway, my supernatural strength matching Elena's momentum and stopping her strike cold. Blood—my blood, now glowing with silver light—dripped onto the consecrated stone of the ritual dais.

The moment it touched the altar platform, the entire chamber erupted with power.

The ritual had been waiting for this—for my blood, freely given in defense of my choice. The silver channels in the floor blazed with light so bright it turned night into day. The symbols on the walls pulsed with energy that made the air itself sing with magic.

And through it all, I felt Matthias's curse finally, completely, shatter.

45

The ritual chamber descended into even greater chaos as more enemy vampires poured in through every entrance, wave after wave of Casimir's army. They moved like shadows, their supernatural speed turning the sacred space into a blur of violence and flame.

Elena turned away from me so she could fight back-to-back with David, their hunter training evident in every savage strike and relentless movement. But they were greatly outnumbered, and I could see the desperation growing in their eyes as more enemies poured in.

On the ritual dais, Matthias and I were completely exposed. The ceremony couldn't be stopped now—too much power had been unleashed, the magic already set in motion. The carved channels in the floor pulsed with our combined life force, and the symbols on the walls blazed brighter with each passing second.

But we were defenseless, kneeling together as the transformation consumed us both.

A vampire broke through the hunter's defenses, his claws extended toward my throat. I couldn't move fast enough, couldn't break from the ritual circle without destroying everything—

The creature's head separated from his shoulders in a spray of ash.

"Touch her and die," snarled a voice I'd never heard before, cultured and deadly and carrying the weight of centuries.

Through the chamber's main entrance swept the most magnificent woman I'd ever seen. She was tall and regal, with midnight-black hair that flowed like silk and amber eyes that burned with power. Her skin seemed to glow with its own inner light, and when she smiled, her fangs were like pearls.

Behind her came a dozen vampires unlike any I'd seen— refined predators who moved with the precision of creatures that had perfected the hunt. Their eyes weren't the wild red of Casimir's forces, but the controlled amber of vampires who had learned to master their nature over centuries.

"Isadora Nightshade," Matthias breathed, recognition turning to shock.

The vampire queen's gaze swept the chamber, taking in the battle, the ritual in progress, and the silver light blazing from the walls. Her expression shifted to one of fierce protectiveness.

"No one," she said, her voice carrying enough power to make the stone walls tremble, "threatens the first bonding ritual in four centuries. Or my crown."

Her forces moved like death, cutting through Casimir's vampires. Where the enemy had been chaotic and brutal, Isadora's people were elegant and efficient, each strike calculated for maximum effect.

But they weren't the only ones responding to my desperate summons.

The air in the center of the chamber began to shimmer,

and suddenly Helena materialized in a swirl of purple smoke, her gray hair whipping around her face and her hands blazing with magical fire. Behind her came her coven. Six other witches, their faces grim with purpose and their magic crackling around them like lightning.

"Protect the circle!" Helena commanded, and immediately her witches spread out around the ritual dais, weaving shields of power between us and the battle raging beyond.

"Helena," I gasped, feeling the transformation deepening, feeling my very essence beginning to change. "You came."

"Did you think I wouldn't?" She raised her hands, and purple fire erupted from her palms, turning two attacking vampires to ash in seconds. "This ritual is the culmination of centuries of prophecy. I've been waiting my entire life to witness it."

The chamber had become a supernatural war. Casimir's old vampires fought with desperate fury, knowing their chance at godhood was slipping away. Isadora's forces moved with coordination, protecting the ritual from interference. Helena's witches wove shields and barriers, their magic creating pockets of safety in the chaos.

And through it all, the blood moon's power continued to pour into Matthias and me.

I could feel my transformation accelerating, feel every cell in my body changing, evolving, becoming something new. My senses expanded until I could perceive layers of reality I'd never imagined. The flow of magical energy through the chamber, the psychic connections between every creature present, the very heartbeat of the earth beneath Prague's weathered stones.

But most clearly of all, I felt Matthias's curse finally, completely gone.

Four hundred years of slow death vanished in an instant,

replaced by a surge of vitality so powerful it made him cry out in relief. His vampire nature, suppressed and weakened for centuries, roared back to full strength. When he opened his eyes, they blazed with green fire that could have lit the chamber on its own.

Our bond snapped into place with a force that sent shockwaves through every supernatural being in the room. I felt his thoughts merge with mine, felt his strength become my strength, felt his immortal life force intertwine with my own until we were no longer two separate beings but something new and unified and infinitely more powerful than either of us had been alone.

The blood moon reached its fullness, and power exploded outward from our joined forms like a supernova.

Every vampire in the chamber—enemy and ally alike—was thrown backward by the sheer force of our completed bond. The witches' shields flared and held, but I saw Helena herself stagger under the magical backlash. Even the stones of the chamber cracked under the pressure, silver light bleeding from the fissures like supernatural blood.

When the light faded and the echoes died away, an entirely new kind of silence filled the chamber.

Matthias and I knelt at the center of it all, transformed and bonded and radiating enough power to make every supernatural creature present take an involuntary step back. I could feel their awe, their fear, their recognition that something unprecedented had just been born.

Casimir's remaining forces began to retreat, their leader's dreams of a vampire king shattered by what we had become instead. Some of the hunters looked ready to flee as well, clearly unprepared for the reality of what a completed Sterling-vampire bond actually meant.

But it was Isadora who spoke first, her amber eyes bright with something that might have been approval.

"Well," she said, a smile playing at the corners of her mouth. "That was certainly dramatic."

I rose slowly from the ritual dais, marveling at how different everything felt. My body hummed with power I'd never imagined possible, and through my bond with Matthias, I could sense his amazement at his own restoration. The curse had been replaced by a strength that made the stones beneath our feet tremble.

But I was still me. Enhanced, transformed, more than I'd ever been before—but still essentially Sera Sterling.

"How do you feel?" Matthias asked, though through our telepathic connection, I could sense he already knew the answer.

"Alive," I replied. *"For the first time in my life, completely alive."*

The remaining enemy vampires had retreated to the chamber's edges, clearly recognizing that their mission had failed catastrophically. Where they'd come to capture a helpless human girl for their own ritual, they now faced something that could tear them apart with a thought.

Helena approached the dais, her witch's robes singed from battle, but her silver hair still shimmering in the supernatural light. "You chose well," she said, approval warm in her voice. "The balance has been restored."

"Balance?" David asked roughly. He was leaning heavily against a stone pillar, blood seeping from a gash across his chest, but his eyes never left my face.

The Sterling line has always been meant to bridge worlds," Helena explained, gesturing to the symbols still glowing on the chamber walls. "For too long, your family forgot that truth, chose only the path of hunting and killing. But Sera has remembered what her ancestors knew. That some bonds transcend the divisions between human and vampire."

Isadora stepped forward, her amber eyes studying Matthias and me with a knowing look. "Your transformation changes everything," she said directly to me. "You're no longer just a Sterling with vampire heritage. You're something entirely new. A bridge between worlds, as the witch says."

She turned to address the retreating enemy vampires. "Tell Casimir his dreams of godhood died tonight. Prague is under my protection, and this union"—she gestured to Matthias and me—"makes it stronger than he could ever imagine."

The last of Casimir's forces vanished into the shadows, clearly wanting no part of whatever Isadora might do to them. Smart choice.

"My queen," one of Isadora's lieutenants approached, bowing formally. "Your orders?"

"Establish a perimeter around the cathedral," she commanded. "I want to know if so much as a rat approaches this place without invitation." Her gaze shifted to Helena. "Witch, your people are welcome to coordinate with mine. This alliance serves all our interests."

Helena inclined her head gracefully. "My coven is honored to work with the Nightshade line."

I felt a strange pride watching these powerful supernatural beings form alliances around what Matthias and I had created. But my attention was drawn to David, who was staring at me with an expression I couldn't quite read.

"Uncle David," I said softly, stepping down from the dais. "You're hurt."

"I'm fine." But his voice was hollow, and I could see the shock etched across his face, grief just beneath it. "You saved Elena. When she attacked you, you could have killed her, but you saved her instead."

I glanced over at Elena, who was unconscious against

the far wall, breathing steadily but concussed from the magical backlash. "She's family," I said. "That doesn't change just because I've changed."

Something shifted in David's expression. "You're not what I expected."

"What did you expect?"

"A monster." His admission was barely a whisper. "I expected the ritual to take away everything that made you my niece and leave behind something that would hunt us for sport."

Through our bond, I sensed Matthias's old pain, how many had looked at him just like that, seen only the monster and never the man underneath.

"I'm still your niece," I said, reaching out to touch David's arm. "I'm just more capable of protecting the people I care about now."

He looked down at my hand, noting the subtle changes —skin that seemed to glow with inner light, nails that could extend to deadly points, strength that could crush stone if I chose to use it.

"The Council will never accept this," he said finally.

"Then the Council will have to adapt," Isadora said coolly. "Because this is the new reality in Prague. My forces, the witch coven, and the bonded pair. We represent a power structure that supersedes any human organization."

Helena nodded in agreement. "Your bond will change everything," she said to Matthias and me. "Use it wisely. Other supernatural powers will sense what happened here tonight, and they'll want to test your strength."

"Let them come," Matthias said, his arm sliding around my waist in a gesture that was both protective and possessive. "We're ready."

I leaned into his embrace, feeling the rightness of it down to my bones. Whatever challenges lay ahead, we would face them together—as equals, as partners, as something the supernatural world had never seen before.

"What happens now?" I asked.

Matthias's eyes met mine, and through our bond I felt the heat of his desire, the overwhelming need that had been building between us through weeks of tension and denial and interrupted moments.

"Now," Matthias said, his gaze never leaving mine, "I need you all to leave."

His voice was polite but carried an undercurrent of authority that made it clear this wasn't a request.

A smile played on Isadora's lips. "Of course," she said graciously. "We have much to discuss anyway—alliance terms, territory boundaries, protection protocols." She gestured to her forces and Helena's coven. "Come. Let's leave the bonded pair to celebrate their union."

The chamber fell silent as the last footsteps faded up the stone stairs. Helena had sealed the entrance with her magic, ensuring we wouldn't be disturbed. David had left without a word, supporting the still-unconscious Elena, but I'd seen something in his eyes that looked almost like acceptance.

We were finally, completely alone.

46

For a long moment, we just stared at each other across the ritual dais, the weight of everything we'd endured settling between us. All the stolen kisses that had been interrupted. All the moments of desperate need that had been torn away by duty or danger or family interference. All the times we'd come to the very edge of surrender only to be forced apart.

No more.

The blood moon's light streaming down from the hidden openings above painted Matthias in silver and shadow, highlighting the sharp planes of his face and the way his restored vitality made him seem to glow from within. Four centuries of slow death had been burned away, leaving behind something magnificent and powerful and utterly mine.

"Sera," he said, his voice carrying that tone of undeniable authority that made my knees weak.

"Finally," I whispered, and the word seemed to echo in the chamber.

Through our bond, I felt his own overwhelming relief. We had fought for this. Bled for this. Defied gods and family and fate itself for this single moment when nothing stood between us and what we both desperately needed.

"Come here," he commanded, his voice low and rough with desire.

I took a step forward, then another, drawn by the magnetic pull of his presence. The sound of my footsteps reverberated through the chamber, and I could see the way his eyes tracked every movement. The air seemed to thicken, and every inch of me hummed, my skin so sensitized it felt intoxicating.

When I was close enough to touch, he reached out and grasped the lapels of my jacket, pulling me against him with such force that I stumbled into his chest.

"You're magnificent," he breathes, and I flash a feral smile, baring my teeth.

"So are you," I reply

The kiss we share is anything but gentle; it's a collision of need. Teeth clash, tongues tangle, and the sharp snap of canines grazing lips sends shivers down my spine. My nails dug into his hair as he groaned into my mouth, hands gripping my hips with such intensity that I felt the imprint of each finger through the fabric of my clothes.

His hands glide up my ribs, warmth radiating through my shirt, thumbs circling my hardened nipples until I gasp against him. He doesn't hesitate—centuries of waiting have fueled his hunger, and now I'm his. His mouth trailed from mine, following the curve of my jaw, down my neck to where my pulse beats wildly beneath my skin. He bites down—not enough to break, but enough to send my knees trembling.

"Oh my god," I hiss, the word spilling from my lips dark and thrilling. I savor its taste. He chuckles against my neck, "You'll learn to embrace the hunger," he murmurs, and I feel the sharpness of his fangs, both a threat and an invitation.

I pressed my thigh between his legs, rewarded with a

low, primal growl. His hips ground against mine, and I could feel his arousal straining against the confines of his pants. My fingers moved to lift his shirt, revealing smooth skin etched with scars—some silver and thin, others thicker. I licked a path from his collarbone to his throat, and he shuddered, his eyes rolling back as I tasted the salt and smoke of his skin.

"You're not the only one who's hungry," I tease, shoving him backward until he stumbles, laughing, sprawling onto the altar at the center of the dais.

"So eager," he said with dark approval, but when I moved to straddle him, his hands caught my hips with bruising force. "But I decide the pace."

In a heartbeat, he flips us. One moment I was moving to climb on top, the next I'm flat on my back, his weight pinning me down, hands securing my wrists above my head. I arch against him, my hips searching, craving friction. He obliges, thrusting against me in a relentless rhythm that makes the world dissolve around us, leaving only the pressure, the heat, the insatiable ache. He bites my earlobe, his tongue flicking out to soothe the sting. "Is this what you want?" he asks, voice thick and low.

"Tell me what you want," he commanded.

"I want all of you," I reply, and a slow smile spreads on his face.

He releases my wrists, and his hands dive for my shirt, ripping it apart from collar to hem. The fabric gives way, and my breasts spill into the cool air, the chill teasing my nipples just before his warm mouth envelops one. He sucks, bites, and lavishes attention on the other, each flick of his tongue igniting fire beneath my skin. I tangle my fingers in his hair, holding him captive, demanding bruises and worship until I tremble beneath him.

He kisses a path down my stomach, tracing every scar,

every curve, every inch of me as if memorizing every detail. Kneeling between my thighs, he drags his fingers over the waistband of my jeans, glancing up at me through dark lashes. His expression was wicked and beautiful.

"I want to taste you," he murmurs, and the words alone nearly send me spiraling over the edge.

His grin sharpens, a predatory glint igniting in his eyes as he slides my jeans down, the rough denim scraping against my fevered skin before finally slipping away. The stone beneath me is cold and unyielding against my bare flesh, the contrast making me shiver as the cool chamber air kisses every exposed curve. With deliberate slowness that borders on cruelty, he spreads my trembling thighs wide, his calloused thumbs pressing into the tender flesh, leaving marks I'll discover tomorrow. He bends down, dark hair falling across his face until his breath fans over my slick, swollen core, the warmth of it igniting a wildfire that races up my spine and explodes behind my ribs. His lips press against the inside of my thigh, tantalizingly close to where I need him most, before his tongue drags in a long, languorous stroke up the entire length of my sex, flat and insistent against every sensitive nerve ending. A primal scream tears from my throat as I arch violently off the stone, my body a taut bow of desperation.

"Don't stop," I snarl, lifting my hips toward him, craving that pressure.

He holds me open with a firm, yet gentle grasp, his tongue delving into my depths with an urgency that feels both intoxicating and overwhelming. It swirls around my clit in a relentless, rhythmic pattern, generating waves of intense pleasure that ripple through my entire being. Each movement shatters my composure, leaving me breathless and trembling in a matter of moments.

I come hard, vision blurring to white as I claw at the

stone beneath me, leaving marks in my wake. Even as I writhe, begging and cursing him, he doesn't relent, wringing every aftershock from my body until I'm nothing but raw nerves and insatiable need.

Then, with a swift motion, he pulls back, his gaze dark and intense.

When I could finally draw a breath, I pushed up with shaking arms, determination blazing in my eyes despite my trembling limbs.

"My turn," I declared, my voice hoarse.

For a moment, he looked like he might refuse, his control unwavering. But then his expression shifted to something darker, more possessive. "Show me how much you want me," he commanded, leaning back on his hands.

I dropped to my knees before him, eager to worship him the way he'd just worshipped me. The heat of his cock brushes against my parted lips, the salt-sweet musk of him filling my senses as I take him in. I swirl my tongue around the swollen tip, savoring the way he twitches against my mouth, a strangled groan escaping his throat.

"That's it," he growled, his fingers tangling in my hair, guiding my movements with firm pressure. "Take me deeper."

I hollowed my cheeks and work my lips down his impressive length, feeling every ridge and vein pulse against my tongue, his fingers tangling in my hair as each thrust of his hips urges me deeper, faster. Just as I sense the tightening of his muscles, the quickening of his breath that signals he's nearing the edge, he grips my shoulders with bruising force, yanking me up and pushing me down onto the stone altar.

His weight pins me, the hard planes of his chest crushing against my breasts as he positions himself between my thighs, the blunt head of his cock pressing against my slick entrance—teasingly close yet maddeningly out of reach.

"Please," I whisper, unsure if I'm pleading for him to claim me or utterly obliterate me.

He positions his throbbing cock, pausing just long enough to lock eyes with me. "You're going to take all of me," he stated, not a question but a promise. "And you're going to remember this moment for eternity."

I nodded, breathless, completely under his spell.

He surged into me with one powerful, brutal stroke, filling me so completely I could barely breathe. My heels dug into his back, urging him deeper, a desperate craving for every inch of him to consume me entirely. He claims me with an unyielding intensity, each relentless thrust sending shimmering ripples of pleasure cascading through my body, intertwining with the bond that connects us, vibrating through the very air we share. The dais beneath us pulsates with a luminescent glow, silver light flaring brighter with each movement, casting a magical aura around us.

"You feel that?" he growled against my ear. "That's you becoming mine forever."

I meet his thrusts, a perfect match to his rhythm, driven by a desire to send him spiraling into madness just as he unravels me. My nails rake across his shoulders, down his back, leaving trails of possession, a yearning to mark him as mine. He grins down at me, his brow glistening with sweat, teeth bared in a savage smile, eyes wild and blazing with an untamed lust that mirrors my own.

He quickens his pace, driving into me with such force that the stone beneath us splinters, cracks, spiderwebbing outward from where my fists pound down in ecstasy. Each orgasm erupts like a dazzling explosion of light behind my eyelids, and I lose track of how many times he shatters and rebuilds me.

At last, he stills, buried deep within me, and I feel him tremble, a torrent of warmth flooding me as the bond between us snaps into place. We cling to each other, breathless and trembling, as the world around us reshapes itself into something entirely different.

For a long moment, the only sound is our hearts beating in perfect harmony, a rhythm echoing through the silence. I gazed up at him, tracing the glistening line of sweat along his jaw with my fingertips, a soft smile forming on my lips.

The blood moon was beginning to set, but its power continued to flow through us, a constant reminder of what we'd chosen and what we'd become.

"No regrets?" Matthias asked softly, his fingers tracing patterns on my skin that made me shiver with renewed desire.

"None," I said firmly, then smiled at him with newfound confidence. "Though I should probably warn you—now that I have supernatural stamina to match yours, you might have trouble keeping up."

His answering laugh was rich and warm and full of promise. "Is that a challenge?"

"It's a fact."

He rolled us over until I was beneath him again, his eyes blazing with renewed hunger. "Then I suppose we should test that theory."

47

I woke to light streaming through the stained glass windows of Matthias's private chambers, casting jeweled patterns across our intertwined bodies. The events of the night felt like a dream; the ritual, the battle, our explosive consummation, but the supernatural hum in my veins confirmed it was all real.

I was no longer human.

Matthias lay beside me, one arm curved protectively around my waist, watching me with an expression of wonder and concern. Even in sleep, I'd been aware of him through our bond. His heartbeat syncing with mine, his relief at the curse finally being broken, his amazement at what we'd become together.

"Good morning," he murmured, his voice a gravelly whisper. "How do you feel?"

I stretched, marveling at the fluid way my body moved, the strength I could feel coiled in muscles that looked the same but felt entirely different. "Different. Enhanced. Like me, but more."

"How do you feel about all of this?" His voice remained neutral, but I felt his anxiety through our bond.

"Complete," I said, settling back against him. "Like I've finally become who I was always meant to be."

"And the transformation? Any discomfort?"

I considered this, testing the new awareness humming through my body. "The opposite, actually. Everything feels sharper. More vivid than it's ever been."

I sat up, pulling the silk sheet with me, and gasped instantly at the sensation. Every fiber felt like pleasure against my transformed skin.

"That's normal," he said, amusement threading through his voice. "Your senses are about a hundred times more sensitive now. It takes some getting used to."

His fingers traced patterns on my bare shoulder that made me shiver with renewed desire. "But there's something else, isn't there? I can feel it through the bond. You want to understand more than just your new abilities."

He was right. Through the night, as we'd explored each other with all-consuming passion, I'd caught glimpses of his memories—flashes of centuries I couldn't quite grasp, fragments of pain and loneliness that made my heart ache for him.

"Show me," I said, meeting his eyes. "Show me everything. The curse, the centuries, why it had to be me specifically. I need to understand who you were to understand who we are now."

Matthias's expression grew serious. "Eight centuries of memories, Sera. Some of them are dark. Some will hurt you to experience."

"I chose you without knowing everything," I replied, reaching for his hand. "Now I want to know everything. I need to see what you've been carrying alone."

He studied my face for a long moment, then nodded slowly. "If that's what you want." He shifted, bringing his wrist to his mouth and biting down until dark blood welled up. "This will be intense. More than any blood-sharing we've done before."

I didn't hesitate. Leaning forward, I pressed my lips to the wound and drank.

The memories hit like a tidal wave.

———

1224

THERE'S cold mud beneath my knees. The metallic scent of blood thick in the air—too much blood, from too many bodies. My sword weighs heavy in my hand, silver blessed by priests who would condemn me if they knew what I'm about to do.

"You came alone." Her voice slides through the darkness like silk over steel.

I force myself to meet her glowing eyes. "They were my people to protect."

She steps over the corpses of the shadow creatures, her bare feet silent on the forest floor. No mortal woman should be able to kill what I could not even wound. "And now they're dead because you were too weak to save them."

The truth cuts deeper than any blade. "I know."

"Do you?" She tilted her head, studying me like a predator deciding whether I'm worth the hunt. "Or do you still believe mortal strength and mortal honor are enough?"

My grip tightens on my sword. "What would you have me believe?"

"That power without purpose is evil. But purpose without power..." She gestures to the village below, where smoke still rises from burned cottages. "Is just noble failure."

I think of little Anna, who brought me wildflowers every

morning. Of Henrik, who made me laugh with his terrible jokes. Of Marta, who baked bread that smelled like home. All dead now because I was too human to stop what hunted them.

"What are you offering?"

"Strength. Speed. The ability to actually protect rather than die trying." Her fangs caught the moonlight. "But you will never be human again. Never know mortal love, mortal death, mortal peace. You will be other. Always other."

I look down at my sword, at the blood on its blade. Human blood this time—my own, from wounds I cannot hope to heal. "Will I still be able to choose what is right?"

"That will always be your choice. Transformation changes your nature, not your soul."

I kneel, offering my throat to a creature that should terrify me. "Then make me what they need me to be."

Her bite is lightning and fire and rebirth. As darkness takes hold, I feel my mortal life burning away, replaced by something vast, terrible, and powerful.

When I wake three days later, I can hear heartbeats from the village below. I can smell fear and hope and the lingering scent of death. But I can also feel strength in my limbs that could move mountains.

Katerina teaches me to hunt animals instead of humans, to feed without killing, to use my new nature in service of my old purpose. On the night she leaves, she presses a silver cross into my palm. It burns, but I hold it anyway.

"Remember what you chose this for," she says. "The moment you start seeing them as prey instead of people you protect, you become the monster they fear."

I never saw her again. But I keep the cross for eight centuries, a reminder of the choice I made and why I made it.

———

I GASPED, pulling back as the memory faded. The experience had been so vivid I could still taste smoke and blood, could still feel the weight of that blessed silver cross burning into flesh.

"You became a vampire to save people," I whispered. "Just like I chose transformation to save you."

"The parallel isn't lost on me," Matthias said softly, his thumb brushing away a tear I hadn't realized had fallen. "Katerina offered me the same choice I offered you; become more than human to protect what you love."

"Eight hundred years," I breathed. "You've been protecting people for eight hundred years."

"Until the curse," he said, pain flickering across his features. "Ready to see how protecting people became my doom?"

I nodded, pressing my lips to his wrist again.

———

1624

THE SCREAMING REACHES me before I see the smoke. Children's voices rang out through the night air.

I find her in the grove where parents tell their little ones never to play. Withered trees twisted into unnatural shapes, their bark weeping red sap that steams in the cold air. At the center, an altar darkened by centuries of sacrifice.

Three children hang in iron cages above a fire that burns green and gold. Their eyes are wide with terror, their small hands reaching through the bars toward me.

"Please," the little girl whispers. "Please help us."

The witch notices me then. Rotting with age, her power made the air itself recoil. When she smiles, I see teeth filed to points, gums black with old blood.

"Matthias of Bohemia," she says, as if she's been expecting me. "Come to interrupt my work?"

"Let them go." I keep my voice steady despite the rage building in my chest. Four centuries of protecting these people, and this creature thinks she can harvest their children like crops.

"Or what?" She gestures, and the fire beneath the cages roars higher. The children scream.

I don't answer with words. I move.

Four hundred years of vampire speed and strength, focused into a single purpose. My blade takes her hand before she can complete the gesture that would drop the children into the flames.

She shrieks, a sound that makes the trees around us groan and crack. "You will pay for this interference, vampire! You and all who come after you!"

"Then I pay." I drive the holy blade deeper, aiming for her heart. "But they live."

Her laughter as she dies is worse than the children's screams. "Live? Oh yes, they will live. And you will watch centuries of them live while you slowly become nothing. Everything that makes your immortal existence bearable—your strength, your power, your ability to connect with others—I curse it to drain away drop by drop until you are a hollow shell wandering eternity alone."

The magic hits me, making me stumble back and feel it deep in my bones. But she's not done yet.

"Only your true mate from the Sterling bloodline can break it," she whispers with her final breath. "But the choice must be freely given, never taken by force. Love earned, not compelled."

As her body crumbles to ash, I free the children and carry them back to their families. They cling to me, calling me their savior, not knowing I have just doomed myself to centuries of slow death.

That night, I feel the first whisper of weakness in my limbs. The beginning of four hundred years of dying.

THE CENTURIES BLUR *together in slow decline. The world around me changes—medieval streets giving way to baroque architecture, gas lamps replacing torches, then electric lights replacing gas. Through it all, I weaken.*

Decade by decade, I feel pieces of myself vanish. My supernatural speed becomes sluggish. My strength, once capable of moving castle stones, barely suffices for normal vampire abilities. Worst of all, my capacity for connection dies piece by piece.

I try to form bonds with other vampires, but the curse makes me unable to trust, unable to open myself to friendship. I attempt to find companionship with humans, but the supernatural divide feels insurmountable. I become increasingly isolated, watching the world change while I slowly fade.

The Sterling women come and go over the centuries. I sense them when they arrive in Prague. Their blood calls to me like a beacon. But when I approach them, there is nothing. No recognition. No pull beyond their hereditary power. They look at me and see a stranger, sometimes a threat. Never a mate.

By 1900, I began to believe the witch's curse was simply elaborate torture. Perhaps there is no destined mate. Perhaps I will continue weakening until I am something less than vampire, less than human, wandering eternity as a hollow shell.

I JERKED AWAY from his wrist, my heart pounding. The centuries of loneliness I'd just experienced felt like a weight crushing my chest. The gradual loss of everything that made existence worthwhile, the endless parade of Sterling women who looked at him with fear or indifference instead of recognition.

"Four hundred years," I whispered, my voice breaking. "Four hundred years of slowly dying, thinking you'd never find me."

Matthias cupped my face in his hands, his green eyes intense. "But I did find you. The moment you walked into that library, I felt something I hadn't felt in centuries. Hope."

"All those other Sterling women..."

"Were not you." His thumb traced my cheekbone. "I thought I was going mad at first. The pull was so strong, so immediate. After centuries of nothing, to suddenly feel that connection..."

"Is that why you watched me for so long before approaching?"

"I had to be certain. I couldn't bear another disappointment." His voice dropped to barely a whisper. "But there was more to see, more you need to understand about what brought us to this moment."

I took a shaky breath, still processing the weight of his loneliness. "Show me."

———

Her Transformation

THE MOMENT *our blood mingles completely during the ritual, I feel the curse shatter like glass. Four hundred years of slow death vanish in an instant, replaced by power so intense it makes me cry out in relief.*

But it's what happens to Sera that takes my breath away.

I had expected her to diminish, to lose pieces of her humanity in exchange for supernatural abilities. Instead, I watch her expand. Every quality that made her uniquely Sera—her intelligence, her compassion, her fierce protective instincts—becomes magnified, enhanced, perfected.

She doesn't lose her humanity. She transcends it.

When she rises from the dais to face her family, power radiating from every line of her body, I realize the witch's prophecy was more complex than I understood. Sera wasn't just meant to break my curse. She was meant to become something new, something that could bridge the gap between worlds.

She is not less than human. She is more than human. And she is mine.

The moment she chooses to fight her own family to protect me, I understand that her transformation hasn't changed her moral core. If anything, it's strengthened it. She knows exactly who she is and what she stands for.

When we finally come together as equals in the ritual's aftermath, when I feel her new strength matching mine, when our bond completes fully, I realize that salvation was never just about breaking the curse.

It was about finding my other half. The person who makes me complete.

———

I PULLED BACK, tears of joy streaming down my face. "You see me as transcendent, not diminished. Even my transformation—you saw it as me becoming more myself, not less."

"Because that's exactly what happened," he said, pulling me closer. "You didn't lose your humanity, Sera. You perfected it."

I kissed him deeply, letting him feel my certainty through our bond.

"And it was worth every moment of suffering," he

replied, his voice thick with emotion. "Because you're here now. Because you chose me freely. Because we have forever."

As the sun rose over Prague, I finally understood the true meaning of our transformation. We hadn't just broken a curse or found love.

We had become something entirely new.

48

An hour later, I was discovering that supernatural transformation came with a steep learning curve.

"I barely touched it," I said, staring at the remains of what had been a crystal goblet. Now it was glittering powder scattered across the marble nightstand.

Matthias chuckled, wrapping his arms around me from behind as I stood naked beside the bed. "Vampire strength takes some adjustment. I spent my first month as an immortal accidentally destroying furniture."

"This is going to be a problem," I muttered, then froze as another sensation hit me. "Matthias, I can hear something."

"What do you hear?"

I tilted my head, concentrating. "Conversations. Multiple conversations. Helena is in the main hall arguing with someone about—" I paused, processing what my enhanced hearing was picking up. "About whether we're safe to leave alone? And there are hunters in the cathedral courtyard discussing whether to retreat or regroup."

His arms tightened around me. "Your hearing has enhanced beyond even normal vampire levels. Most of us need to concentrate to hear through stone walls."

"Is that unusual?"

"Everything about you is unusual," he said, pressing a kiss to my neck that made me shiver. "You're not just a vampire, remember. You're something new."

I turned in his arms, marveling at how easily I moved despite my new strength. "Show me. Help me understand what I can do."

He stepped back, his eyes glistening with a mix of pride and excitement. "Try to move faster than human speed. Just from here to the window."

I focused on the tall windows across the chamber and took a step—

The world blurred. One moment I was beside the bed, the next I was pressed against the glass, having moved so fast I'd created a small windstorm that sent papers flying.

"Holy shit," I breathed.

"Language," Matthias teased, but his voice was warm with approval. "Try coming back, but slower this time. Feel the movement instead of just willing it."

I concentrated, trying to control the supernatural speed thrumming through my muscles. This time, I managed something closer to a swift walk, reaching him in seconds instead of a blink.

"Better," he said, catching my hands before I could accidentally crush anything else. "Now try this. What do you sense in this room? Not just what you see or hear, but what you feel."

I closed my eyes, letting my new awareness expand. Immediately, the chamber came alive with information my human senses never could have detected.

"Your heartbeat," I said softly. "But also something else. Like warmth, but not temperature. It's coming from you, but it's different from body heat."

"Life force," he explained. "Vampires can sense the supernatural energy in other beings. What else?"

I stretched my senses further. "Helena is still in the main hall, and her warmth is different from yours. Warmer, but more complex. Like layers of power instead of one strong source."

"Witch magic," Matthias confirmed. "And the others?"

"The hunters feel..." I paused, trying to interpret what I was sensing. "Empty isn't right. But they don't have that supernatural glow. They're just human."

"Now reach beyond this building. Can you sense other supernatural beings in Prague?"

I pushed my awareness outward and immediately gasped. The city lit up in my mind like a constellation. There were points of supernatural light scattered throughout the streets.

"There are so many," I whispered. "Vampires, witches, and something else I don't recognize."

"Fae, probably. They prefer the old parts of the city." His hands moved to my shoulders, steadying me as the sensory input threatened to overwhelm. "You're detecting supernatural signatures across several miles, Sera. That's not normal vampire ability."

"What does it mean?"

"That you can sense and communicate with every type of supernatural being. No wonder the witch's bloodline was necessary to break my curse," he said, wonder in his voice.

I opened my eyes, meeting his gaze. "We should test more. I need to understand my limits."

"Careful," he warned, but he was smiling. "What do you want to try next?"

I grinned, feeling more confident by the moment. "Everything."

For the next hour, we eagerly tested my new abilities. I

could lift stone blocks that should have required three vampires. I could move through the chamber silently enough to sneak up on Matthias, which was no small feat. When I concentrated, I could hear specific conversations anywhere in the complex.

But it was the psychic abilities that truly amazed us both.

"Try reading my thoughts," Matthias suggested, sitting across from me on the chamber's faded sofa.

I reached out with my mind, following the warm mental connection that had been growing stronger since our bonding. Immediately, his surface thoughts flowed into my consciousness.

She's magnificent. More powerful than I dreamed possible. And she's completely mine.

"I can hear you," I said softly. "But it's not invasive. It's like you're sharing the thoughts willingly."

"Because I am. The mate bond creates a two-way connection, but it doesn't break down personal barriers unless both parties allow it." His mental voice joined his spoken words. *Can you hear this?*

Yes, I replied telepathically, amazed at how natural it felt. *It's like we're talking, but closer somehow.*

Much closer, he agreed, and I felt his love and desire wash through our connection like warm honey.

"There's something else," I said aloud, breaking the mental link to concentrate. "Helena, in the main hall. I can sense her emotions even from here, even though we don't have a bond. Fear, curiosity, and maybe approval?"

Matthias's eyebrows rose. "You're reading emotions from non-bonded supernatural beings?"

"Is that unusual, too?"

"Sera, what you're describing is empathic ability that usually takes decades to develop, if it develops at all." He moved closer, taking my hands in his. "Combined with your sensing range and physical abilities, you're not just a bridge between worlds. You're something unprecedented."

I felt a thrill of excitement mixed with apprehension. "What does that mean for us? For Prague's supernatural community?"

"It means," he said, his voice filled with awe and something like reverence, "that together, we're going to change everything."

As if summoned by his words, a soft knock came at the chamber door.

"Matthias? Sera?" Helena's voice carried through the thick wood. "I'm sorry to interrupt, but there are some people here who need to speak with you both. It's about what happened last night."

I looked down at my naked form, then at Matthias. "I suppose we should get dressed."

"Probably," he agreed, though his eyes were traveling over my body with obvious appreciation. "Though I'm finding it difficult to care about anything beyond this room right now."

I felt heat rise in my cheeks, along with a surge of desire that our bond immediately amplified and reflected back to me. For a moment, the knock at the door seemed unimportant compared to the way he was looking at me.

"Later," I promised, my voice husky with promise. "After we deal with whatever crisis is waiting for us."

"I'll hold you to that," he said, reluctantly moving toward the wardrobe where he kept spare clothes.

As I searched for something to wear among the elegant gowns he'd somehow acquired for me, I caught my reflection in the mirror and stopped.

I looked the same—dark brown hair, brown eyes, familiar features. But there was something different in my expression. A confidence that hadn't been there before. A sense of power and purpose that showed in the way I held myself.

I wasn't the uncertain academic who had arrived in Prague weeks ago, focused only on manuscripts and research. I was something new. Something that belonged in this world of shadows and supernatural politics.

Something that could stand as an equal beside an 800-year-old vampire lord and make him stronger rather than weaker.

"Ready?" Matthias asked, now dressed in dark pants and a white shirt that made his restored vitality obvious.

"Ready," I confirmed, slipping into a deep green dress that felt like liquid silk against my enhanced skin.

Together, we walked toward the door. Helena's voice was growing more insistent, and I could hear additional footsteps gathering in the main hall.

"Think they'll be surprised by how much I've changed?" I asked.

Matthias's smile was sharp and predatory. "I think they're about to discover that underestimating us was a mistake."

I felt an answering smile curve my lips.

49

The main hall of the cathedral had been transformed into an impromptu war council. Helena stood at the center, her silver hair catching the light from dozens of floating candles that hovered without any visible support. Around her, an unlikely assembly had gathered: David with his hunter's weapons still strapped to his body, Isadora with her amber eyes calculating and sharp, and several vampires I didn't recognize but whose power I could feel humming in the air.

They all turned when Matthias and I entered, and the immediate silence was deafening.

I felt their reactions wash over me through my new empathic abilities—shock, fear, awe, and from David, a grief so deep it made my chest tighten. Looking at me, he wasn't seeing his niece, who had grown stronger. He was seeing the human girl he'd raised disappearing forever.

"Sera," he said, his voice controlled. "How are you feeling?"

The question was loaded with meaning. Was I still myself? Was I under supernatural influence? Had the transformation broken my mind along with my humanity?

347

"I feel like me," I said. "Just more."

Elena moved from where she'd been lurking in the shadows, her hand resting on her silver blade. "You look different."

She was right. I could see my reflection in the polished surface of Helena's scrying bowl—same face, same features, but there was something indefinably changed. My eyes held depths they'd never shown before, and when I moved, it was with a grace that seemed almost feline.

"Different how?" I asked, genuinely curious.

"Dangerous," Elena said bluntly. "You look like you could kill someone without blinking."

Matthias tensed beside me, but I felt surprisingly calm. "I probably could," I agreed. "But I could probably save someone without hesitation too. The power doesn't change the choice."

"Doesn't it?" David stepped forward, his weathered face creased with pain. "The way you stopped Elena's blade last night, the strength you displayed, the way you threatened your own family. That wasn't human, Sera. That was something else."

"It was protective instinct," I corrected firmly. "Someone was trying to hurt Matthias during a sacred ritual. I defended him."

"You threw Elena across the chamber hard enough to crack stone."

I felt a flash of guilt at that. Through my enhanced senses, I could detect the lingering pain in Elena's ribs where she'd hit the wall. "I'm sorry about that. I was still learning to control my strength."

"Sorry?" Elena's laugh was bitter. "You nearly killed me. Your own family." She stepped closer, her face twisted with disgust. "Look at yourself, Sera. Look at what he's made you into."

"He didn't make me into anything," I replied firmly. "I chose this."

"You chose to become a monster." Elena's voice cracked with pain and betrayal. "The cousin I grew up with is gone, isn't she? Replaced by this thing that protects vampires over family."

The accusation hurt more than I expected. Elena and I had been close once, before family obligations and training took over her life. She was the one who taught me how to climb trees, sneak extra cookies from the kitchen, and braid my hair before important family events.

"Elena," I said softly, reaching toward her.

She jerked back as if my touch would contaminate her. "Don't. Just don't." Her hand moved to her weapons belt, and several vampires tensed in response. "I won't try to kill you again, Sera. But I can't... I can't accept this."

She turned to David, her expression resolute. "I'm leaving Prague. Tonight."

"Elena, wait—"

"This isn't over," she said, her gaze flicking between me and Matthias. "Maybe you've forgotten what vampires are capable of, but I haven't. Maybe you think love changes everything, but I know better."

She headed toward the cathedral entrance, then paused. "When this ends badly, and it will, don't come looking for me to save you."

The heavy doors slammed behind her, leaving an uncomfortable silence in her wake.

I felt other hunters shifting uneasily, some moving toward the exit as if Elena's departure had given them permission to retreat. But a few remained, laying their weapons on the stone floor in what looked like surrender.

"This is what I was afraid of," David said quietly. "You're

not thinking like Sera anymore. You're thinking like one of them."

"I'm thinking like someone who finally knows who she is," I replied. "David, I love you. You raised me, protected me, and gave me a life I'm grateful for. But you also lied to me about what I am, what our family really is."

"I was protecting you—"

"From what? From choice?" I stepped closer to him, letting him see that despite my transformation, my affection for him hadn't changed. "You taught me to value knowledge, to seek truth, to stand up for what I believe in. Did you think I would abandon those principles just because I learned about my heritage?"

"Your heritage is hunting creatures like him," David said, gesturing toward Matthias. "Protecting humanity from supernatural threats."

"Your heritage," Helena interjected smoothly, "is more complicated than the stories your branch of the family tells."

All eyes turned to the witch, who moved to stand beside a lectern that hadn't been there before. On it sat an open book, its pages yellowed with age.

"Sterling women have been choosing vampires over human lives for six centuries," Helena continued. "Sera is hardly the first to undergo a willing transformation. She's simply the first whose family forgot that such choices were ever made."

David went very still. "What are you talking about?"

"Edmund Sterling, your ancestor, rewrote the family history after his sister Catherine chose transformation in 1623." Helena turned a page in the worn book, revealing what looked like a family tree. "He couldn't accept that she made the choice willingly, so he started the hunting tradition to 'save' future Sterling women from the same fate."

"That's impossible," David said. "We have records going back centuries—"

"You have records Edmund wanted you to have," Helena corrected. "The real records are here, in my archives. Forty-three documented cases of Sterling women choosing vampire mates and living long, happy lives."

I felt David's world cracking apart through my empathic senses. Four centuries of family tradition, suddenly revealed as one man's inability to accept his sister's choice.

"Show me," David said hoarsely.

Helena pulled out a worn journal, its pages yellowed with age. "This belonged to your ancestor, Margaret Sterling."

She opened it to reveal pressed flowers between the pages, alongside sketches of couples and handwritten accounts of love stories.

"Your family's true heritage," Helena said gently. "Love freely chosen, bonds willingly made."

David stared at the portraits, his hunter's certainty crumbling. "All this time we've been fighting our own nature?"

"You've been fighting a lie," I said softly. "But that doesn't make you wrong for believing it. Edmund loved his sister and couldn't understand her choice. You love me and struggle to understand mine."

"I just..." David's voice broke slightly. "I don't want to lose you."

"You're not losing me." I moved to him, taking his hands in mine. "I'm still your niece. I still love you. I'm just more enhanced."

Through our bond, I felt Matthias's pride in how I was handling this revelation, not with anger at the deception, but with compassion for the pain that had created it.

"The difference," Isadora spoke for the first time, "is that

Sera has made her choice with full knowledge. She knows what she's gained and what she's sacrificed."

"And what have I sacrificed?" I asked, turning to face the vampire queen.

"Mortality. Simplicity. The ability to live in ignorance of what lurks in the shadows." Isadora's amber eyes seemed to see straight through me. "But you've gained something far more valuable."

"Which is?"

"Purpose. Power. And a partnership that will reshape the supernatural balance of power in Prague." She smiled, showing elegant fangs. "The question is what you intend to do with it."

I felt Matthias's hand settle on my lower back, warm and reassuring. Through our bond, I sensed his readiness to follow my lead on this. Whatever I decided about our role in Prague's supernatural community, he would support.

The enormity of it should have overwhelmed me. Instead, I felt something like excitement.

"What needs to be done?" I asked.

"What needs to be done," Isadora said, rising from where she'd been observing our family drama with patience, "is establishing what your transformation means for the rest of us."

She moved with the fluidity of someone who had centuries to perfect every movement, her amber eyes fixed on me with an intensity that made my new predator instincts prickle with wariness.

"Last night, you created something unique," she continued. "A successful Sterling-vampire mate bond, completed despite opposition from both our peoples. The supernatural community felt the power surge from your ritual across half of Europe."

"Felt it how?" I asked.

Helena approached; her expression serious. "The magical shockwave when your bond was completed was significant. Every supernatural being within a hundred miles experienced it. Most described it as lightning running through their veins."

"We got calls from covens in Vienna asking what had happened in Prague," Isadora added with dry amusement. "Some thought it was an attack. Others wondered if someone had torn a hole between worlds."

Through our bond, I felt Matthias's surprise. He'd been focused on me during the ritual's completion. He hadn't realized our joining had been felt so widely.

"So now everyone knows," I said slowly.

"Everyone knows that something powerful happened here," Helena corrected. "They don't all know what, yet. But word is spreading."

"Which brings us to the political problems," Isadora said, settling back into her chair. "For four hundred years, the supernatural community has operated under certain assumptions. Vampires and hunters are natural enemies. Sterling women are either prey or weapons, depending on your perspective. Individual vampires rule through fear and isolated power."

"And now?" Matthias asked, though his tone suggested he already knew the answer.

"Now we have a bonded Sterling-vampire pair whose combined power rivals that of the oldest supernatural creatures in Europe," Isadora said bluntly. "A pair that has already demonstrated the ability to bridge human and supernatural communities. Whether you intended it or not, you've positioned yourselves as major players in supernatural politics."

I felt a chill of apprehension. "We didn't ask for that."

"Power doesn't ask permission," Helena said gently. "It simply is. The question becomes what you do with it."

"Others are already making that decision for you," Isadora continued. "Casimir's remaining forces retreated from Prague last night, but they haven't surrendered. They're regrouping, likely seeking allies among the older vampire houses who won't appreciate the shift in power balance."

"What kind of allies?" Matthias asked, his voice taking on the edge I remembered from our first encounters.

"The kind who prefer the old ways. Who profit from the chaos between supernatural factions. Who see your successful bond as a threat to their influence." Isadora's smile was sharp. "Consortium vampires from Vienna have already sent messengers asking about my intentions toward Prague. They want to know if I plan to challenge your new authority."

"Do you?" I asked directly.

Isadora laughed. "My dear child, I didn't survive a thousand years by challenging unprecedented power when I could ally with it instead."

"You're offering an alliance?"

"I'm offering recognition," she corrected. "Prague has been neutral territory for decades, but it was weak neutral territory. A vampire lord slowly dying from a curse, witch covens keeping to themselves, hunters operating in the shadows. No real unity, no coordinated defense against external threats."

"And now?"

"Now Prague has a bonded pair whose combined abilities could repel any invasion, whose unique nature allows them to unite rather than divide supernatural factions." Isadora leaned forward, her eyes gleaming. "I'm not just offering an alliance. I'm offering to help you build something new. A supernatural haven where power is shared rather than hoarded."

Helena nodded approvingly. "The witch covens are prepared to support this new order. Sera's transformation makes her part of our magical community as well as the vampire hierarchy. We're willing to offer formal protection and alliance."

I looked around the cathedral hall, taking in the faces of supernatural beings who had been enemies just hours ago. Now they were talking about cooperation, about working together instead of maintaining centuries-old conflicts.

"What about the hunters who stayed?" I asked, gesturing toward the small group of David's people who hadn't followed Elena in retreat.

One of them, a middle-aged woman with silver-streaked hair, stepped forward. "Some of us have been questioning the old ways for a long time," she said. "If Sterling women have truly been choosing vampires for centuries, maybe it's time we considered whether our hunting tradition serves any real purpose."

"Blasphemy," David muttered, but his heart wasn't in the protest.

"Evolution," the woman corrected. "The world has changed, David. Maybe we need to change with it."

I felt the weight of their expectations settling on my shoulders. These supernatural beings, vampires, witches, and even some hunters, were looking to me and Matthias to provide leadership, to create something that had never existed before.

"What exactly are you asking us to do?" I said

"Rule together," Isadora said. "As equal partners. Create a new supernatural order in Prague that other cities could follow."

"I'm not qualified to rule anything," I protested. "I was an academic researcher just weeks ago."

"You're qualified now," Helena said firmly. "Your transformation didn't just give you physical abilities, Sera. It gave you the supernatural authority to command respect from all our kind. Combined with Matthias's centuries of experience and restored power..."

"We could actually create lasting peace," Matthias finished, understanding flooding his voice.

Through our bond, I felt his excitement at the possibility. For eight centuries, he'd protected individuals and small communities. But this... this was the chance to protect entire populations by preventing supernatural conflicts before they started.

"It won't be easy," Isadora warned. "There are vampire houses that profit from chaos, hunter families like Elena's branch that will never accept cooperation, supernatural creatures who prefer the old ways of fear and isolation."

"Let them come," I said, surprising myself with the certainty in my voice. "We'll be ready."

Matthias's pride in my words flowed through our bond like warm honey. When I looked at him, his eyes were blazing with the same determination I felt building in my chest.

"Then it's settled," Helena said, satisfaction clear in her tone. "Prague becomes the first supernatural haven. A place where our kinds can coexist openly instead of hiding in shadows."

"Under our joint leadership," Isadora added, making it clear this wasn't just about Matthias's traditional vampire authority anymore.

"Together," I said.

As the assembled supernatural beings began making

plans for this new order, I caught David watching me with an expression I couldn't quite read.

"What is it?" I asked softly.

"You look like your mother," he said finally. "When she was planning something that would change everything. Confident. Determined. A little dangerous."

"Is that a good thing?"

David was quiet for a long moment. Then, slowly, he unstrapped his silver weapons and placed them on the cathedral floor beside the other hunters' surrendered arms.

"I suppose we're about to find out."

50

The supernatural council had dispersed an hour ago, leaving detailed plans for Prague's transformation into the first openly integrated supernatural haven. Matthias and I now stood in the shadowed alcove of the cathedral's highest tower, watching the sun rise over the city that had become our responsibility.

From this height, Prague was spread below us. The gothic castle, the winding river, the maze of streets where humans lived alongside supernatural beings they didn't even know existed. Soon, that would change.

"Second thoughts?" Matthias asked, though our bond told him the answer before I spoke.

"None," I said, leaning into his warmth as dawn light painted the city gold and crimson. "Though I have to admit, when I came here to research medieval manuscripts, I didn't expect to end up running supernatural politics."

His laugh rumbled through his chest. "When I first sensed Sterling blood in Prague, I expected another failed attempt to break my curse. I certainly didn't expect to find my equal."

"Equal," I repeated, testing the word. Through my

enhanced senses, I could feel the truth of it. Where once Matthias had been weakened by his curse, now our bond made him stronger than he'd been in centuries. Where once I'd been vulnerable and human, now I possessed power that made older vampires step back in respect.

"The challenges ahead won't be simple," I said, thinking about Casimir's forces regrouping, about Elena's promise that this wasn't over, about vampire houses in Vienna and beyond who would see our new order as a threat.

"No," Matthias agreed. "But we'll face them together."

I turned to study his profile against the morning light. The curse was completely gone, and I could see it in the vitality that radiated from every line of his body, the confidence that had returned to his posture. But more than that, I could feel it through our bond. For the first time in four centuries, he was complete.

"What are you thinking?" he asked, catching me staring.

"That you look different. Not just healthier, happier." I reached up to trace the line of his jaw. "Eight hundred years of existence, and you're finally free to be who you were meant to be."

"We both are," he said, catching my hand and pressing it flat against his chest. "For the first time in my very long life, I'm not just surviving. I'm not just protecting others while remaining eternally alone. I have a true partner."

The word sent warmth spiraling through me. Partner. Not just lover, not just mate, but someone who could stand beside him as an equal in every way that mattered.

"The others expect us to transform Prague," I said. "To create something that's never existed before."

"Do you want to?"

I considered the question seriously. Leading supernatural politics hadn't been in my life plan, but then again, nothing about the past few weeks had been planned. I thought about Elena's disgust, about David's struggle to accept my choice, about the vampire houses that would see our bond as threatening their traditional power structures.

"Yes," I realized. "I want to prove that love doesn't make you weak. That choosing someone different doesn't mean betraying who you are. That bridge-building is stronger than wall-building."

Matthias turned to face me fully, his eyes blazing with pride and desire. "Then we build something different."

"As partners," I confirmed, and reached for him.

The kiss started soft, a gentle affirmation of our shared commitment. But the moment our lips met, the bond between us flared to life with an intensity that made the air around us shimmer. Matthias's hands tangled in my hair, pulling me closer as I pressed myself against the solid warmth of his body.

When his tongue swept against mine, I felt fangs that hadn't been there during my human life, and the sensation sent heat spiraling through me. I was no longer fragile, no longer at risk of being hurt by his supernatural strength. We were equals now in every way that mattered.

"Sera," he breathed against my mouth, and I felt his control wavering.

"I know," I whispered back. "I can feel it too."

When we broke apart, we were both breathing hard, the bond between us crackling with barely restrained desire and the promise of what we both wanted—time, privacy, and the freedom to explore what we'd become without danger or interruption.

"The city will still be there in a few hours," I said, my voice dropping to a husky whisper as I felt desire kindle between us again.

"Will it be?" Matthias asked, his hands moving to my

waist. "Because I've forgotten there's anything outside this place."

"Supernatural stamina," I reminded him with a wicked smile. "I believe we had a challenge to continue."

His answering grin was pure predator. "Then let me remind you exactly what eight hundred years of experience can accomplish."

He lifted me effortlessly, quickly carrying us back toward the tower's private chambers. Through the tall windows, Prague continued its morning routines, unaware that their new supernatural protectors had other priorities at the moment.

AN EXCERPT FROM BOOK TWO:
CLAIMED BY DARKNESS

Elena's Story

———

I'm not a Sterling. I never was.

The thought echoes through my mind as I crouch in the shadows of Prague's underground tunnels, silver stake warm in my palm. The air down here smells of damp stone and what might be old blood. Above me, the city hums with life. Tourists wandering cobblestone streets, locals heading home from late dinners, couples stealing kisses on the bridges. None of them know that beneath their feet, I'm tracking monsters through corridors carved centuries ago.

But then again, none of them are pretending to be something they aren't.

Cold seeps through my jacket where my shoulder presses against the rough wall. Water drips somewhere in the darkness, each drop echoing. The alcove I've wedged myself into is barely wide enough for my body, dim light from storm drains above casting shifting shadows on the walls.

The scent hits me first, that distinctive tang that means vampire. I press myself deeper into the alcove, counting footsteps as they approach. Three sets, moving with the predatory ease that only comes with centuries of practice. Not the clumsy fledglings I usually hunt. These are old vampires.

The thought triggers something inside me. For a split second, I'm eight years old again, hiding under my bed while monsters with voices like silk and dead eyes tear through my house. The screaming stops too quickly. Then footsteps, deliberate and unhurried, searching room by room.

"Where is the little one?" The voice was soft, almost gentle. *"We can smell her fear."*

I'd pressed my hands over my mouth to keep from sobbing, knowing even then that making a sound meant death. When the Sterlings found me days later, still hiding in that house with the bodies of everyone I'd ever loved, I'd made a promise with all the desperate determination an eight-year-old could muster: I would become strong enough to kill them all.

Every monster I'd staked since then had been practice. Preparation for the day I'd be worthy of hunting the ones who murdered my family.

But these creatures approaching through the tunnels moved with that same confidence, that same casual certainty that they're apex predators. The smart thing would be to retreat, call for backup, and wait for David or one of my adoptive siblings. The Sterling family has survived for generations by being careful, strategic, and working together.

But I've spent seventeen years trying to prove I belong among them, and tonight feels like my last chance. Casimir escaped Prague after Sera's transformation, and I tracked him to London only to watch him slip away again. Now he's back here, building a new network in the shadows of the city where it all began. The other hunters think we should wait, plan, and coordinate our response like we always do.

But I can't wait anymore. Not when I finally have solid intelligence on his people's movements. Not when this might be my only chance to prove I'm more than the traumatized child they took in.

Because they still see me as the broken eight-year-old they rescued, not the weapon I've forged myself into. And now, after Sera chose *him* over everything we stand for, I'm more desperate than ever to prove that at least one Sterling remembers what we're supposed to be.

The hunters are fracturing. David wants to "understand" Sera's transformation, speaking about vampires like they're individuals instead of monsters. Half the extended family thinks we should adapt to this "new reality" where hunters and vampires can coexist. The other half whispers that Sera was compromised from the beginning, that her vampire heritage made her weak.

I know which side I'm on. I have to be on the right side, because if I'm not, if everything I've built my identity around is wrong, then what am I?

"Real Sterlings don't need to prove anything," David said just last week, meaning to be kind. But I heard what he hadn't said: *Real Sterlings are born, not made.* And maybe he's right. Maybe that's why I'm the only one who still sees clearly, who still remembers that vampires destroyed my family and will destroy us all if we let our guard down.

The vampires are closer now, their voices carrying in the tunnel's acoustics. They were discussing safe houses and something about a gathering. Exactly the information the hunters need. Exactly the kind of breakthrough that would finally, finally prove I'm more than just a charity case with a tragic backstory.

I shift my weight, preparing to strike.

The stone beneath my boot chooses that moment to crumble.

Three pairs of eyes lock onto my position instantly. In the dim light filtering down from storm drains above, I see the lifeless faces turn toward me, and I know immediately I'm outmatched. One smiles, fangs shining in the weak light.

"Well," he says in accented English, his voice carrying the kind of authority that makes lesser vampires kneel. "What have we here?"

My training kicks in. But as I take in these creatures, the casual way they own the space around them, how the very air seems to thicken with supernatural dread, a single, crystal-clear thought cuts through my tactical analysis:

I'm going to die down here, and I'll never get to prove I was worthy of the Sterling name.

The vampires begin to circle me, and I raise my stake with hands that don't shake. If I'm going down, I'm taking at least one of them with me.

The first one moves faster than anything should be able to move. But I've been training for this my entire life. As he lunges, I drop low and sweep his legs, feeling the impact jar through my shin as I catch him mid-stride. He goes down hard, and I drive my stake upward with both hands, putting my full weight behind the blow. Silver slides between his ribs with a grinding sound, and the shock of contact travels up my arms.

He screams and crumbles to ash before he hits the ground.

"Impressive," one of them says, not sounding concerned at all. "But foolish."

The other two attack simultaneously from opposite sides. I roll behind a stone pillar, feeling claws whistle past my ear close enough to cut through strands of my hair. Stone chips explode where the vampire's hand hits the wall. My crossbow comes up in one smooth motion, and I squeeze the trigger. The bolt hits the second vampire in the center of his body with a thunk, piercing through cloth and flesh. Another scream echoes through the tunnels as he turns to ash.

For a heartbeat, I think I might actually survive this.

Then the last one moves.

He's nothing like the others. He's older, faster, stronger. When my stake comes up to meet him, his hand simply appears around my wrist, stopping the silver point inches from his chest. I put every ounce of strength I have behind the weapon, muscles straining, but it doesn't budge. He twists my wrist with ease, and I hear bones pop and grind. Pain shoots up my arm like fire, and the stake clatters to the stone floor.

"Now," he says conversationally, his grip tightening, "let's discuss what brings a Sterling hunting alone in my territory."

I try to knee him, but he catches my leg without even looking. Try to break free, but his other hand wraps around my throat, lifting me off the ground like I weigh nothing.

"Such fire," he muses, watching me struggle.

Dark spots dance at the edges of my vision. My lungs burn. Seventeen years of training, and I'm about to die like prey in a tunnel, having proved nothing except that I was never strong enough to belong.

I see something move in the shadows behind him, something that makes even this monster freeze.

"Dimitri." The voice that echoed through the tunnel

exuded absolute authority, making my captor's power seem trivial in comparison. "How disappointing to find you hunting in my territory without permission."

The vampire holding me, Dimitri, releases my throat so suddenly that I drop to my knees, gasping. He spins to face the newcomer, and for the first time since this fight began, I saw fear flicker across his features.

"Lord Alexander," Dimitri says, and there's actual submission in his voice. "I didn't realize you had returned to Prague."

"Clearly."

The vampire emerged from the shadows into the light seeping through the grating overhead, moving with the confidence of someone who owns not just this tunnel but the very air around him. Tall and lean, he had blonde hair and sharp, aristocratic features, his eyes a pale blue and burning with the kind of cold intelligence that suggested he was always three steps ahead of everyone else.

He's beautiful in the way a blade is—elegant, deadly, and sure to cut you if you're careless enough to touch. A monster wrapped in grace.

"The hunter is mine," Dimitri says, trying to salvage some authority. "Casimir has need of her."

"Does he?" Alexander's tone suggests mild interest, as if he were discussing something trivial. He takes another step closer, and Dimitri retreats. "How curious. I wasn't aware Casimir held any authority in this city."

"The old agreements—"

"Were with my predecessor." Alexander's smile holds no warmth. "I have different policies regarding uninvited guests."

One moment Dimitri is standing five feet away, the next Alexander has closed the distance and driven his hand through Dimitri's chest. There's no struggle, no dramatic fight. Just a swift and ruthless action.

Dimitri looks down at the hand protruding from his ribcage with surprise. "You... can't... the treaty..."

"Was dissolved the moment you entered my domain uninvited." Alexander pulled back his hand with casual indifference. Dimitri crumbled to ash without another word.

The tunnel fell silent except for my ragged breathing.

Alexander turned his gaze to me, and I realized that I'd gone from being prey to one predator to being observed by something infinitely more dangerous.

Rage floods through me—at my own helplessness, at needing to be saved, at the easy way he eliminated threats I couldn't handle. I'm on my feet before conscious thought kicks in, my backup knife sliding into my palm. If he thinks I'm some helpless victim who needs rescuing, he's about to learn otherwise.

I lunge at him with everything I have left, putting years of training behind the strike. The blade arcs toward his throat in a perfect killing blow.

He lets me get close, so close I can see the light ring around his blue irises, can feel the unnatural coldness radiating from his skin. For a split second, I think I might actually land the hit.

Then his hand just appears around my wrist, stopping the knife inches from his throat. His grip is unyielding but gentle, as if he's handling something delicate that could shatter with the slightest pressure.

We're close enough that I can see the faint amusement in his eyes, close enough that I can feel his breath on my face. It's cold, reminding me he's not human.

For a moment that stretches impossibly long, we're

frozen like that. My knife trembling in his grip, his eyes locked on mine with an intensity that makes my pulse race.

"Now that," he says, "was marginally better."

to be continued...

A LETTER FROM THE AUTHOR

You've just finished reading my first book.

I'm still processing that sentence. Six months ago, this story existed only as scattered fragments: scenes I'd scribble during breaks, character arguments that would jolt me awake at 3 AM, demanding to be written down before they vanished.

Those sleepless nights turned out to be perfect preparation for what came next. This book was written during a particularly difficult season in my life, when a childhood dream of writing finally demanded to be taken seriously. It's terrifying putting yourself out there like this. I'd wake up in the dark, make coffee (okay, fine, *lots* of coffee), and disappear into Prague's underground chambers while the real world stayed safely asleep. There's something about those quiet hours before dawn when you can believe impossible things. When vampires and hunters feel more real than your own reflection.

My husband learned to recognize the signs: finding me at my desk during odd hours with a slightly unhinged look, trying to get my characters to cooperate. He'd quietly give me a hug and tell me he believed in me. Without him, I probably would have forgotten that humans need things like meals and sunlight.

But somehow, in those early mornings and caffeine-fueled late nights, something dark and beautiful emerged. A love story that demanded blood and sacrifice, characters who refused to stay safely on the page, a world where the line between desire and danger became impossibly thin.

Writing about vampires changes how you see shadows. It makes you notice how darkness can be both terrifying and seductive, how the most beautiful things often exist in the spaces between safety and surrender.

Thank you for following Sera into those underground chambers. For trusting a first-time author with your time. For reading a story that clawed its way out of the darkest months, fueled by stubborn determination and questionable amounts of caffeine.

This is just the beginning. Elena's story is next, and trust me, she's going to make Sera's journey look easy.

I hope you'll follow me back into the dark.

Nora Nightingale

www.ingramcontent.com/pod-product-compliance
Lightning Source LLC
Chambersburg PA
CBHW030227120726
47903CB00005B/1396